T.M. SMITH

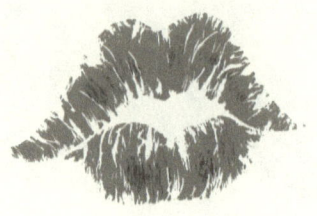

EVERNIGHT PUBLISHING ®

www.evernightpublishing.com

Copyright© 2023

T.M. Smith

Editor: Jessica Ruth

Cover Artist: Jay Aheer

ISBN: 978-0-3695-0824-9

T.M. SMITH

DEDICATION

My thanks to Evernight Publishing. Stacey Adderley provides authors with a place to show off. As if that isn't enough, while she is juggling books and staff assignments, she patiently answers this author's annoying questions. Thank you to Jessica Ruth, a terrific editor, who does not "kill" all my "darlings." Sorry, Stephen King. Just the worst ones. And how about Jay Aheer? Fantastic cover. Thanks.

As always, I appreciate my critique group of many years. Kendra and Sallie are my lifejackets in a sea of first drafts.

T.M. SMITH

Terms and Places for the Blood Coven Series

Aerilon
The ylve region of Scath.

Aeternals
A species made up of various breeds who pre-date *Homo sapiens* on Earth. Their creator is the Genitrix Gahya, an immortal who resides in The Vast. After centuries, they grew more cruel and violent, feeding from humans, threatening the continued existence of mankind.

The Alliance Security Agency
A human agency where employees have a distant Aeternal ancestor in their family trees. Once travel between the realms of Scath and Earth became possible, these descendants created an organization to assist Aeternals. Their organization provides Aeternals with access to trade on Earth and assistance in policing Aeternals who enter Earth illegally. They operate a successful cover business, hiring out as bodyguards, private security, and soldiers of fortune. The internal structure includes the Legal Division, Human Resources, Information Services Division, Security Division, and Finance. A board of directors oversees the company.

Amanita Muscaria
A drug used by berserkers before battle. It whips them into a frenzy.

Amori
The incubus and succubus region of Scath.

Angor
A dimension of dark storms and unpredictable weather where immortals are tortured and punished. It is also the final destination of unworthy Aeternals after they die.

Arisen Dawn
A rebel group led by Cerberus. Their beliefs include purity of the breeds and the domination of mankind.

The Assembly
The local government elected by mages.

The Awakening
A ceremony marking an Aeternal's attainment of full power, usually in their early to mid-twenties. The event is different for each breed.

BCA Variant Test
A test developed by Eliphias, Alarik's science lead, to determine if the subject is a Blood Coven descendant.

Blood Coven
Led by the Cambion from Wales, these powerful mages created the realms of Darque, Earth, and Scath in AD 452 where only one world had been before. Aeternals went to Scath, mystical creatures to Darque, and humans remained on Earth. It was the only way the two sentient species would survive.

Bludclan
Vampires are identified by their Bludclan, a social/family group.

Blud Den

A place which specializes in feeding all Aeternal breeds, not just vampires. An Aeternal feeds on the host's blood, soul, fear, energy for magic, lifeforce, orgasm, power, or arousal. O blud dens are more specialized. Here a host takes a drug (most notably opium). The feeding from the host provides a high but is not as addictive as taking the drug itself.

Bludfrenzy
When a vampire is controlled by the need for blood. It becomes the sole reason for living, an addiction.

Bludhaven
The vampire region of Scath.

The Bludhunt
A violent ceremony marking the mating of two vampires.

Breeds
Amazons, berserkers, demons (seven tribes within their breed), djinn, incubi and succubi, mages (or witches and warlocks), satyrs and nymphs, vampires, and ylves. Though each breed has distinct gifts, or powers, all are stronger than *Homo sapiens* and possess better sight, hearing, and smell. Like humans, breeds eat food, but they must supplement it with other nourishment—blood, soul, lifeforce, flesh, fear, arousal, orgasm, or energy for magic.

Camp Follower
An Aeternal who makes himself or herself available as food or sex for Jarek's Firebrands.

The Cede
The Aeternals' funeral ceremony.

The Coalition
The alliance of Firebrands, loyal Scath citizens, loyal members of Scath's government, and humans to defeat Cerberus.

Covenkirk
The seat of Scath's government, the mage region, and the location of the Eastern Stronghold.

The Cubes
Run by gaffers, holding cells for Scath prisoners awaiting trial or interrogation.

Custodes Templii
Formed on Earth by the Cambion before he died. Through the centuries, the group keeps track of Blood Coven descendants, the offspring of the mages who stayed on Earth after the Karmic Schism.

Darque
The realm of mystical creatures, home to harpies, questing beasts, Kalli, Spriggans, Yeti, gagans, polar rats, hellhounds, and more.

D-chip
Digital Implant Communication Chronometer. It is an amazing device embedded into the wrist of each Firebrand warrior and wired to their brains. Its functions are many–telepathic communicator, shadowflasher, GPS locator, emergency portal creator as long as the Firebrand is out-of-doors, a more efficient version of a portal jumper to allow travel through established gateways, temporary cell for captured offenders, and more.

Dionysia
Local government of nymphs and satyrs.

Directorate of Seven
The local ruling body of demons. Each member represents a tribe—animus, avarice, carnal, envy, hedon, pride, sloth. They are chosen by combat.

Elysian Isle
The nymph and satyr region of Scath.

The Encampment
The Amazon, berserker, and djinn region and location of the Southern Stronghold on Scath.

Evermore
A dimension of serenity where worthy Aeternals go when they meet true death.

Freron
A term used by Firebrands to denote another brother- or sister-in-arms.

Gaffers
Like police, the managers of the day-to-day minor crimes on Scath.

Genesis Rite
An ancient ritual where demons fought in combat. The winner spent the night with the ceremony's guest of honor.

Gold Dust
An addictive drug, making users fanatic followers of Arisen Dawn.

Humans First
A paramilitary unit organized by Dante to gather intel on and expose Aeternals.

Isolationists
A group originally organized by Simonis, an ylve, to protest Scath's involvement in affairs outside the realm. He was shoved out as the group became more radical, espousing breed purity and displaying a rising nationalism set on conquering humans. It became the foundation for Cerberus's Arisen Dawn.

Karmic Schism
The splitting of the world into three realms. In AD 452, the Blood Coven cast spells to create Scath and send Aeternals there. At that time, they also created the realm of Darque for magical creatures and Earth for humans.

Knife's Edge
The demon region of Scath.

Lawgivers
Elected drafters of the laws for Scath. A member is chosen from each breed.

Outcast Keep
An area on Darque where Aeternal prisoners are kept.

Ministry of Compliance
Governmental office which regulates travel. Boden is the current director.

Ministry of Coin
Governmental office which regulates finance and drafts

the realm's budget.

Ministry of Culture
Governmental office which regulates education, schools
of magic, and Awakening ceremonies.

Ministry of Death
Governmental office which operates prisons, the Cubes,
and Outcast Keep on Darque, controls day-to-day crime
and gaffers, and regulates the use of explosive weapons.

Ministry of Labor
Governmental office which regulates worker welfare.

Ministry of Prosperity
Governmental office which regulates trade with wildings
and humans.

Ministry of the Shield
The only governmental ministry which reports to the
Temple of Justice rather than the Lawgivers. The Scion
Firebrands are under its auspices. Cadmon is both high
commander of the Scion Firebrands and director of this
ministry.

Ministry of Well Being
The governmental office responsible for medical
facilities, research, science, technology, and history.
Alarik is the current director.

Ministry of Wildings and Realm
The governmental office which regulates the wildings
and both realms' natural resources, parks, and
environments.

Mitakon
A bi-annual Olympics. Winter events are in North Shelters and summer events in the Encampment region.

Monarchy
The king and queen who lead the incubi and succubi.

North Shelters
The shifter region and location of the Northern Stronghold on Scath.

The Path
The words of the warrior Ohngel as recorded by the Cambion from Wales and contained in five-volumes. These books relate tales of the salvation, the betrayal, the creation, the fall and rise, and the destiny of Aeternals.

Pitchblende
A substance which weakens djinn.

Portals
Gateways to and from the realms, created by the Blood Coven at the time of the Karmic Schism but not accessible by all. In the beginning only powerful and approved mages could cast spells for travel. Later, GPS technology allowed for portal jumpers to be distributed to authorized Aeternals.

The Prophecy of Karma
A scroll found by the fire-winged assassin Ohngel, the mentor/guide to the Cambion from Wales, in a cave in the Vakataka Kingdom. The first stanza, though it presaged a dark future for mankind at the hands of Aeternals, it predicted a coven would save them by separating humans and Aeternals. The second stanza

noted the rise of Hades's hound who would lead an army to enslave humans. The last stanza hints at the role of destiny in the prophecy.

The Rage
When a demon loses control of the beast. Usually, they must be put down.

The River Am
A river which defies explanation and natural laws. The witch Indigo, as the Guardian of Time, reads the river. The middle course is the present. Possible futures flow upstream. The lower course, or downstream, shows the just-past to the long-past. No one but Indigo knows the river's location.

Scath
The realm where Aeternals have lived since the Karmic Schism.

Schools of Magic
There are seven schools of magic–Elemental, Conveyance, Forging, Influence, Investigation, Manipulation, Protection. Each mage's powers fall primarily into one category where they are trained in those gifts at the Thaumaturgy Institute. Extremely powerful witches or warlocks may excel in more than one school of magic.

Scion Firebrands
The elite warriors of Scath who follow in the footsteps of an ancestor. Founded soon after the Karmic Schism, they protect Scath and Darque from the most violent Aeternals or creatures. As a side-gig, they also protect humans from the threat of Aeternals who escape to Earth.

When Aeternals are called to join, the initiation begins with the Phoenix brand which burns itself onto the candidates' upper left arms. They experience intense pain until they reach a decision. Join or reject the offer.

The Settling
The demon mating ceremony.

Shadowflash
Old, powerful vampires can trace from shadow to shadow as long as the spot is within sight. It makes travel faster. D-chips give Firebrands this ability also.

Strange But True
The Seattle paranormal tabloid owned by George James, Braelyn's father.

Strigodierna Ceremony
A vampire spiritual ceremony. It is led by the Cruor and his fifty Carnemia.

Supreme Pack Alpha
Chosen through combat to lead the shifters.

Temple of Justice
The body of elected justices who try offenders on Scath. A member is elected from each breed.

Thaumaturgy Institute
Where witches and warlocks are trained in the different schools of magic.

Tribes
The sub-breeds of demons. The inspiration for Christianity's Seven Deadly Sins--animus, avarice,

carnal, envy, hedon, pride, and sloth.

Triumvirate of the Wise
Chosen every fifty years to govern ylves. A chancellor, an imperial secretary, and a grand commandant.

Vampire Conclave
The local rulers of vampires, led by the bludcrown.

The Vast
A dimension of clear skies and pleasant weather where immortals, such as Gahya, Gabriel, and the OneCreator reside.

Walkabout
The requirement for influential Aeternals to live on Earth for periods of time to keep current with human activity.

War Council
The governing body for Amazons, berserkers, and djinn, chosen by combat to govern locally.

Watchers
The mages who keep an eye on and maintain the portals and the whorl for Alarik's ministry.

The Whorl
What separates the three realms from each other. Travelers to another realm access it from a portal, travel through it, and reach a portal in the other realm.

Winged Assassins of the OneCreator
Aka The Feard. They or Michael are the only beings who can bring true death to an immortal. Ohngel, the Cambion's mentor and guide, is the fire-winged assassin

of the OneCreator.

LIST OF CHARACTERS IN *THE DEMON'S FIRE*

Abrahm   Murdered Kole's parents, an ancestor of Skyler Maxwell, demon

Aedon   Kole's father, Firebrand, animus demon

Aestes   Leads an attack on Skyler, satyr

Aisen   Silas's half-brother, operated stockades for Cerberus, vampire

Alarik   Director of the Ministry of Well Being, Rein's father, Indigo's half-brother, warlock-incubus

Alden Maxwell   Skyler Maxwell's father, once the CLO of the Alliance

Allias   Alarik's employee in Echo's department who finds evidence of *Custodes Templii*

Anjeli   Chay suspects she may become his soulmate, ylve

Anna   Skyler Maxwell's administrative assistant at the Alliance

Aras   High Justice of the Temple of Justice, eagle shifter

Azamat A contender in the Genesis Rite,
pride demon

Bade A Firebrand recruit, vampire

Boden Director of the Ministry of
Compliance, demon

Bounty Kole's executive assistant, vampire

Braelyn James Rein's mate, writer for Strange But
True

Brak A carnal demon, Firebrand

Cal Morris The assistant legal officer at the
Alliance

Caleth Grand Commandant of the
Triumvirate of the Wise, Laegon's soulmate, ylve

Cadmon High Commander of Scion
Firebrands and director of the Ministry of the Shield,
ylve

Castia The love of Alarik's life, mother of
Rein and Elisabeta, vampire

Celene Bailey Held captive by Cerberus, heiress,
daredevil, adrenalin junkie

Cerberus The hound of Hades whom
prophecy foretells will destroy the portals and enslave
mankind

THE DEMON'S FIRE

Chay   Full name Chayton, Firebrand,
ylve

Cleatra   A scryer who works for Alarik,
witch

D Monz   A demon rapper

Dante   Upper-class Englishman who
conspires with Cerberus

Darius   Jarek's second, Firebrand, djinn

Dax   Full name Daxton, Firebrand,
vampire

Dermott   Victor of the Genesis Rite, envy
demon

Dolph   Temple of Justice, warlock

Draven   Temple of Justice, vampire

Echo   Chief historian at the Ministry of
Well Being, a pride demon

Eliphias   Chief scientist at the Ministry of
Well Being, a warlock

Elisabeta   Rein's sister, Alarik's daughter,
vampire-witch-succubus mix

Emily Caldwell Wife of Abrahm, Skyler Maxwell's
ancestor

Eron   Temple of Justice, female demon

Faeth   Lobo's mate, ylve

Fera   Supreme Lawgiver, shifter

Gahya   The Genetrix, creator of Aeternals, an immortal in The Vast

Galena   Firebrand, Amazon

George James   Braelyn's father, owner of Strange But True, Alliance board of directors

Gilda   Temple of Justice, Amazon

Golarg   Berserker who knocks on Spear's door

Hestia   Kole's mother, Firebrand, animus demon

Horach   Kole's uncle, Directorate of Seven, animus demon

Indigo   Guardian of Time, Alarik's half-sister, Rein's aunt, witch

Jace de Vries   Held captive by Cerberus, worked as vintner in New Paltz, NY

Jarek   Firebrand commander of the Southern Stronghold, djinn

Jedson Maxwell   Skyler Maxwell's grandfather, descendant of Abrahm

Jezzi   Proper name is Jez, Firebrand, panther shifter

Juno   The guide for Kole and Skyler to the Greeting Chamber, ylve

Kat   Full name is Katrina, Firebrand, witch

Kole   Firebrand commander of the Eastern Stronghold, animus demon

Laegon   Chancellor, Triumvirate of the Wise, ylve

Lauri   Receptionist at the Alliance

Lizette Lee   Radio talk show psychologist at WMR radio production studio in New York, Spear's sex slave

Lobo   Wolf shifter, mate of Faeth, Firebrand

Logan   Firebrand computer expert, incubus

Loredana   Skyler and Kole's guide into the Strigodierna Shrine, vampire

Lort   Cerberus's general, vampire

Margo Hunter　　　Sculptor from Cleveland, OH

Miller Nash　　　Head of *Custodes Templii,* Blood Coven descendant, ex British intelligence

Mowart　　　With Dermott's band on Darque, demon

Nace　　　Full name Nacon, commander of the Northern Stronghold, Firebrand, jaguar shifter

Nelo　　　The Cruror of the Strigodierna Ceremony

Nico Abello　　　Lead agent with the Alliance until he becomes a Firebrand

Niviane　　　One of the original Blood Coven, witch

Ohngel　　　The fire-winged assassin of the OneCreator and mentor to the Cambion, an immortal

OneCreator　　　Ruler of Vast and the Evermore

Oskar　　　Indigo's conjured pet, a gryphon

Ram　　　Firebrand, satyr

Ranca　　　Kole's guardian after the death of his parents, Firebrand, animus demon

Raymond Maxwell　　Descendant of Abrahm, Skyler's ancestor

THE DEMON'S FIRE

Rein Vampire-warlock-incubus mix, Firebrand, Braelyn's mate

Roshan Temple of Justice, djinn

Sabine Celestial nymph, Firebrand

Samuel Maxwell Descendant of Abrahm, Skyler's ancestor

Sarah Jenkins Also called Siri, head of the information services division at the Alliance

Seraphine The daughter of Niviane and the Cambion

Sig Firebrand recruit, demon

Silas Operated stockades for Cerberus, disgraced Firebrand, vampire

Simonis Founder of the Isolationists, ylve

Skyler Maxwell Chief legal officer of the Alliance

Sparse Spriggan chief

Spear Keeps Lizette Lee as a sex slave, berserker

Thannor Imperial Secretary, Triumvirate of the Wise, ylve

The Cambion The warlock who gathered the Blood Coven and created three realms of Earth, Scath, and Darque from one world in AD 452

Thorn Firebrand, wolf shifter

Tyr Firebrand, warlock

Ulfur Worked for Silas to bring humans
to Scath, shifter

Uwrick His blocking spell isolated Kole
and Skyler on Darque, warlock

Winston Callahan At one time, Skyler's fiancé

Wynnfrith A respected Firebrand killed by a
harpy

Zora Alarik's executive assistant,
succubus

THE DEMON'S FIRE

The Blood Coven Series, 2

T.M. Smith

Copyright © 2023

Prologue

If left unbroken, the chains of the past will shackle the present.
—Ohngel

Wales, One Month after the Karmic Schism of AD 452

The wind howled, whipping through the branches of the trees. As frenetic leaves danced, dust devils stirred the forest detritus. In a dark hooded cloak, the witch Niviane trudged forward, stumbling, forcing a bent arm in front of her face to block volatile debris. She leaned into the gale, one foot pushing stiffly ahead, the other leg struggling to catch up. Her progress was slow, laborious, determined.

And emboldened by fear.

At the door of a run-down cabin, she knocked. As

she glanced over her shoulder, the moon caught her eyes, aglow with a fierce intensity. Realizing she might not be heard above the storm, she pounded harder. When an aproned female answered, the frightened traveler drew a bundle from beneath her cloak and thrust it into awaiting arms.

"Take her!" Niviane shouted above the turbulent wind, rushing past her sister to gaze out a window. "He may have tracked me."

The aproned female looked down at the swathed child who was unaware of the role she would play in the Aeternals' history. "The Cambion is a little crazed, is he?"

Though still unnerved, Niviane turned from the outside view, eyeing her babe and the blazing fire beside which sat two comfortable chairs. She removed her cloak before she collapsed into one of them, exhausted from her arduous journey.

She rocked back and forth, exhaling a labored breath. "I shared his lofty mission when we began the quest. The Prophecy of Karma could not come to pass. It is true. Aeternals have grown savage. Left among mankind, we would eventually extinguish their species as predicted. That is why two other mages and I lived among the uncivilized Celtic Gauls for a hundred years to study their ancient elemental invocations. When we returned, we joined others of our coven who had also traveled afar to gather mystical knowledge. In the cavern, we commingled our blood and cast our spells. With the Cambion's final offering, the Karmic Schism was complete. From one world, we created the three realms of Earth, Scath, and Darque."

Niviane stared into the fire. "To signify our success, a bright-feathered Phoenix, a good omen, carried off the prophecy grasped in its talons. But the

Cambion had one more request. Nay, command. He ordered our Blood Coven to scatter across Earth with our offspring, to hide among the humans, to be forever ostracized. We were forbidden to travel to Scath with other Aeternals. If there, he claimed powerful mages could use us to unravel what we had done. They could dismantle the portals, dissolve the Whorl, and re-unite the realms. Once again, endangering mankind."

She rubbed a palm across her forehead, twisting toward her sister. "I will not isolate my daughter from our mage breed. I will not chain her gifts. Beloved sibling, take my child to Scath with you."

At the sound of her mother's voice, the babe cooed.

"Is the Cambion aware he is the sire?" The aproned female looked down at the bundle in her arms.

"No. He has neither touched me nor been close during my bearing season. When I have seen him, I have hidden my belly beneath layers of clothes or heavy cloaks." Niviane shifted to perch on the edge of her chair. "I trust you to do as I bid."

"Your faith is warranted."

Niviane rose to approach the infant cradled by her sister. She stroked the child's cheek, innocence staring into her mother's violet eyes. "Farewell, my Seraphine. May your life be full. May your spells be potent."

The sister encircled Niviane's neck with her free arm, whispering a goodbye along with a blessing. "I will raise her well among our breed, speaking your name around the fire, telling of your sacrifice. All will understand your power runs through her veins."

The Blood Coven witch gripped her sister's forearm, her eyes sparking with fear. "Never. No Aeternal can know I am her mother nor the Cambion her father. Promise me this."

"I so promise. Nobody shall know the child's parentage." She patted her sister's hand. "Relax, my dear."

Niviane nodded while she retrieved her cloak, once more cocooning herself in it, preparing to brave the storm. "I must hasten while you must ready for the journey to Scath. Tarry no longer."

As she flung open the door, a gust of wind roared into the cottage, causing the fire to tremble. The Blood Coven witch cast a glance over her shoulder before she turned her back on her daughter forever.

From the shadows outside a window of the hovel, Ohngel, the fire-winged assassin of the OneCreator, observed the exchange. His hearing acute, he had listened. The Cambion, the warlock he had selected to lead the Blood Coven in its task, had been lonely. In that state, the powerful mage had fornicated with Niviane. Now, she betrayed him, humankind, and her own.

The winds being no problem for Ohngel's gigantic fiery wings, he masked himself to follow aloft while the witch struggled in the storm. He dropped to the forest floor as she clutched her cloak, trudging along a cumbersome, overgrown path, stumbling forward without the support of her breed or coven.

His feathers pulled tight into his back, Ohngel cast his gaze upward, wondering at the heavy clouds in the sky, the sense of foreboding in the gathering storm. Whatever Niviane's betrayal presaged, he feared it would alter his plans and the destiny of mankind.

Chapter One

Chicago, IL, Present Day

One moment Skyler Maxwell was standing on the platform at Chicago's Fullerton Station, mentally reviewing her day's schedule while she waited for the commuter train.

The next, she wasn't.

Her feet lost contact with the deck. Her body stretched into a graceless dive. A rush of air cooled her face. She saw the ground rise as she fell toward it.

With the roar of an approaching train sounding in the distance, a prolonged, piercing scream rang in her ears. Later, she realized it had escaped from her own lips.

Then she heard nothing until she awoke in an ambulance heading for the ER.

A man bent over her, adjusting a blood pressure cuff on her upper arm, putting the stethoscope bell against her skin. When he inflated the band, it grew tighter. Still tighter. He released the air with a *swoosh*.

His lids flipped up, brown eyes studying her. "You're awake. Good. Just don't move around too much. You hit your head pretty hard."

He turned to write something in a book. Probably her blood pressure.

Skyler inspected the blurry ambulance. The gurney jiggled with each bump in the road, making her aware they were traveling. How did she get here? She blinked a few times, wiggling her fingers. Lifting her arms was more difficult. Unable to rise, she took deep calming breaths to fight the panic bubbling inside her.

She cleared her throat and swallowed, her words slow, ragged. "What happened?"

"You had a nasty fall. From reports, some guy

jumped down to drag you back onto the platform. If he hadn't, you'd be gooier than the peanut sitting on the railroad track."

"What?" she asked, her eyes slitting.

"You know, peanut butter." He smiled at his joke.

Skyler was not amused. "I kind of remember falling, though I recall nothing afterward." She touched the bandage on her forehead. "Ow!" Her arm flopped to her side. After a moment, she patted the surrounding area on the gurney. "Where's my cellphone?"

"You can call people later. And don't touch your head too much. You were bleeding a lot. We did a fast patch." He shifted when the siren stopped blaring. "We're here. Sit tight. We'll get you out."

After two guys lifted her stretcher from the ambulance, they wheeled her into the ER. Her memory was still fuzzy. They transferred her from the cart to a bed, followed by a flurry of activity. Someone shined a light into her eyes. The same person took her blood pressure again. A needle pricked her arm. The emergency medical team said goodbye as they wished her luck. The nurse instructed her to remain quiet while she waited for a doctor.

Then, the only sounds she heard came from outside the room. Soft-soled shoes padding up and down corridors. Beds wheeling to and fro. Voices shouting orders. Chit-chatting. Messages blaring over an all-call.

A woman wearing glasses, a stethoscope, a white coat, and clogs entered. "Okay, let's see what's wrong." She scanned a chart. "What's your name?"

"Skyler Maxwell."

She waved a penlight in Skyler's eyes, telling her to follow the light.

Pushing away the hand, Skyler said, "Find my cellphone. I must call my office."

"Plenty of time for that later. We'll assess the severity of your injury first. Tell me what happened."

"I was waiting for the red line L at Fullerton Station when I fell onto the track."

Skyler did not say someone pushed her. Though commuters rubbed shoulders, jostling each other in the crowd, she remembered two hands on her back before a shove off the edge. "The EMT said a man pulled me out of danger. If not for him, I would be dead. Now, I insist you hand me my purse." Skyler eyed the name badge. "Dr. Longmer. And my cellphone. My office will want to know why I'm late."

"Have you been ill or dizzy lately? Anything that might make you fall?" The doctor persevered.

"No." Skyler struggled to sit. She glanced around for her leather bag before the room tilted.

"Not so easy to get up, is it?" Dr. Longmer watched, finally grabbing an arm to assist her.

Skyler twisted away from the woman, returning her head to the pillow.

"Your pupils are okay, but I still want a CAT scan. If all checks out, we'll release you. The nurse will re-bandage the gash on your forehead. You should visit your regular physician to see if a medical issue caused you to fall. In the meantime, you can take acetaminophen, rest, and avoid strenuous activities. Let's get you to radiology."

"I don't need a CAT scan. What I need is to sit still for a few moments before I call my office."

Unfazed, the doctor breezed out, sending in the nurse to help Skyler out of her clothes and into a gown. Before she could voice another objection, the nurse stepped aside for an orderly who arrived to wheel her down the hall where a lab tech administered the scan.

With that out of the way, he returned Skyler to

the room. She drummed her fingers on the mattress as the nurse wasted valuable time talking with someone in the corridor before sauntering inside to check wounds, slap on some medication, and re-bandage her forehead.

"Keep an antibiotic cream along with a dressing on this for a few days. It's gonna swell, and you've got a pretty big gash there. Watch for an infection. You have minor cuts and abrasions elsewhere. Nothing serious. You were lucky. Apply the salve to the scrapes, too. Now, stay put until we hear about your scans."

The nurse scurried off to another room, leaving Skyler alone to think about the accident, giving her time to steady her nerves.

Why would someone push me off the platform? Is a psycho who likes to shove commuters into trains on the loose? Or was I the target? No! Why would I be a target?

Dismissing the ridiculous notion, Skyler pushed onto her elbows. No dizziness. But a whopper of a headache was using her temples for drums. After stretching to reach her purse on the chair beside the bed, she rifled around for her cellphone. *Found it. And it's intact. Amazing.* She punched in the number for her office.

"Alliance Security Agency. Your protection is our mission. Anna for Chief Legal Officer Maxwell," said a lyrical voice.

"It's me. I've had an accident." Skyler removed a compact from her handbag, her fingers trembling slightly as she balanced the phone between her ear and shoulder.

"An accident? Oh my God. What kind? Are you okay? What happened? We wondered why you were late. It's not like you. So, I called. Left two messages. We were getting…"

That girl can go on.

Her tone brusque, Skyler interrupted Anna. "I'll explain when I get to the office." Then she remembered her goal to be more amiable. "The short of it is, I fell off the L platform. I need the company car to pick me up at Rush University's ER. I'm okay. No one should worry. Just a scrape."

"I'll send Allen at once. What do you want him to bring?"

Anna, at only five foot two, compensated for her height by wearing four-inch stilettos. With permed, short blonde hair, cherubic cheeks, and an animated smile which brightened her eyes, she looked too young to be the administrative assistant for the Alliance's CLO. But she had the goods. A quick wit, spectacular memory, sixth sense when it came to her boss's needs, and the ability to keep pace with Skyler's grueling hours. Added benefit? She wasn't too irritating.

Skyler's initial act as the newly appointed chief legal officer had been to hire Anna from the clerical pool. The first brilliant decision in what promised to be a distinguished career.

"Yes, have Allen bring me a change of clothes. The works. Suit, shirt, stockings, underwear, shoes. Include my makeup bag. My coat will have to do. I must look a mess. Later, send someone to pick up antibiotic cream along with bandages from the pharmacy."

"I'm all over it. Hang tight. He'll be there in a few. I'm sure glad you're okay."

"I am. Just get Allen here soon."

During the conversation, the nurse stood in the doorway, tapping a foot, signaling her patient to disconnect from the phone. Skyler raised an index finger. Once she put down her cell, she reproached the woman. "Can't you give me a second? I have important business to attend to."

"So do I. You're not my only sicky, cupcake. The scan looks good. But watch yourself for a few days. Your shoes are in the bag over there with your suit, blouse, and coat. Everything's a little scruffy. I hope someone is picking you up."

"Of course someone is. Now, crank up the bed."

The frowning nurse pressed a button. "Anything else, your majesty? If not, I'll be with the peasants."

Skyler swung her legs over the edge of the mattress, tucking the gown and sheet around her. Still holding the sterling silver compact mirror, she adjusted her hair, sticking errant white-blonde strands back into their proper place. An unattractive bandage covered most of her forehead.

Ugh.

She swiped a cleansing cloth over her face to remove dirt and waited for Allen's arrival. After a while, Skyler spotted a man wandering the corridor and looking at room numbers.

It sounded as if he found the unpleasant nurse. "Are you here for the lady who fell off the L platform?"

"Yes," he said.

"Over there. And good luck. I don't envy you your job."

"It pays well." He shrugged.

Despite the open door, he knocked before entering. "Chief Maxwell, I hope everything is okay." Allen handed her a carryall with fresh clothes, shoes, and a makeup bag.

Skyler's impatient foot bobbed. Not acknowledging his greeting, she grabbed her things. "What took you so long?"

"Traffic, but I thought I made good time." He glanced at his watch. "I'll wait out here." Allen closed the door.

Skyler changed, sailed through the doorway, brushed by the chauffeur while handing off the bag of damaged goods, and hustled toward the emergency room exit. "Let's get to the office. I'm in a hurry."

"Yes, ma'am. If you think that's a good idea," said Allen, rushing to keep pace with Skyler.

She threw a scathing look over her shoulder.

"Goodbye to you, too," the nurse called from the reception desk. "And thanks."

On the drive to her office, Skyler took out the comb to re-do her hair, smoothing it, perfecting the classic, professional knot she wore low on her head. Satisfied, she rested against the gray leather seat, alone with her thoughts.

What if my life had ended today? Has it been enough?

I have accomplished everything my father wanted for me. I graduated from Harvard law, top of the class. Fresh out of school, the Alliance hired me as one of its legal assistants. When my father died earlier this year, they promoted me to succeed him. I work twelve to fifteen hours a day securing agreements for Scath, eschewing fun and friends for the job.

When a well-respected surgeon, who happened to play cards and tennis at our exclusive club, asked me on a date, Father had approved, saying he was excellent son-in-law material. Our engagement had warranted a prominent headline, both careers on a fast track. Winston. A man like Alden Maxwell.

I am a model of reason. Dispassionate. All I have achieved should be enough. Why do I feel something is missing? My father would have said I was ungrateful, spoiled, willful. Perhaps. But...

The minute Allen pulled to the curb of a three-story structure near the historic Wrigley Building on

Michigan Avenue, Skyler opened the door, shooing unwanted thoughts from her mind. When she stood, pain rocketed through her head. Wincing, she charged toward the awninged entry, her heels a staccato beat on the sidewalk.

This is all I've got. Yes. It's enough.

Assistant Legal Officer Cal Morris and Anna were waiting in the outer area along with Laurie, the receptionist.

Anna rushed to Skyler but stopped short of hugging her. Dropping her arms to the side, she seemed at a loss for what to do next. Her hand flew to her mouth. "Oh, your head. Are you sure you should be here?"

"Don't fuss, Anna. We need to get back to work. I have a lot to do before I leave at the end of the week. I must finish the trade agreement for the S/I core processors manufactured on Scath. Some details are still missing for the distributers. Also, the new Farm-to-Table Grocers company wants to buy organic produce from Aerilon. I'll set that up. Cal, what about the demon rapper? What's his name? D Monz?" Skyler didn't take a breath as she hurried through the reception area toward her office in the rear.

Cal, with Anna and Laurie, scurried forward to catch Skyler. "I arranged contracts for a squad of our agents to provide security for D Monz. We'll have a visible but legitimate presence at the concerts where we expect quite a few Aeternals from Scath to show. The demon rapper has his followers."

The assistant legal officer was average. Medium build. Medium height. Washed-out blond hair. Dull blue eyes. Acceptable grades in law school at Southern Illinois University. On the Alliance's board of directors, Cal's father had arranged a spot in the organization for his son. But Cal did stand out in two ways. He had a closetful of Brioni and Zegna suits he wore with flair. And he had a great sales pitch. His fast-talking, friendly manner, interrupted by snorted laughs, made him a favorite among demanding clients looking to hire security or a private army.

Skyler waved the three nervous hens out of her office as she opened the file on the S/I core processors to fine-tune the contracts. She lost herself in her work.

Knock. Knock. Knock.

She recognized Anna's annoying raps on her door. Slamming down her pen, she rolled her tired shoulders and snapped the folder shut. "I asked for time to work."

Her admin assistant darted in, a hand pressed to her chest. "Sorry to interrupt, but Laurie just came back from lunch at the new deli across the street. The one we've all been wanting to try."

Skyler glanced at her watch while patting her classic do, making certain not a hair was out of place.

"Right," said Anna. "Get on with it. You need to see what Laurie opened."

The receptionist was sitting in her ergonomic chair where she spent most of her days greeting visitors, answering phones, checking company e-mail, or completing assigned tasks. Bobbing her head toward the computer, she said, "Get a load of this."

Skyler frowned as she gripped the back of Laurie's chair, leaning forward. Anna and Cal, who had joined them, also peered over the receptionist's shoulder to read the e-mail from an unknown contact, TheBigReveal.

The message was brief. "Hey, Alliance. Nothing can make you bleed like an outed secret. You'll need a big man-daid to cover this wound. Do we have your attention? Not yet? Just wait until you tune in to our website and blog. They're out of this world. We'll send the password when we're good and ready. How ya doing, Skyler?"

"This is fucking bad." Laurie's hand flew to her mouth. "Sorry, but this seems like the perfect time to cuss."

"Hmm. It's not good," said Skyler.

Cal jammed his hands into his front pockets. "It's cryptic. They talk about a secret, but they don't say what it is. Maybe they're baiting us. Maybe it's a hoax."

Secrets. Yes, the Alliance has secrets.

After the Karmic Schism when the world had been divided into three realms by powerful mages, some Aeternals had stayed behind with their human mates or offspring. They bred. In time, their descendants contacted Scath with offers to assist. The Alliance began.

Centuries later, the organization stepped partially into the sunlight by creating a public face, a lucrative side-business which supplied investigators, bodyguards, protection, and private armies to human contractors. As such, the Alliance was well-respected, not only in Chicago but worldwide. Cal arranged contracts for the Security Division's agents assigned to these tasks. For sizable fees.

But their real business remained hidden in the shadows. It was so secret that any MI6 agent would have sold the World War II enigma machine to expose it. Their special agents monitored Aeternals with legitimate financial interests on Earth. They also assisted in the capture of breeds who crossed illegally.

As CLO, Skyler oversaw the entire Legal Division of the Alliance but focused her own efforts on inter-realm trade agreements, making Scath businesses pass for human enterprises, and serving as liaison between her offices and the board of directors.

Because Earth clients had no idea they were trading with entities from another realm, Skyler made the fairytale real. She provided each Scath company with a registered name, address, staffed storefront, websites, business licenses, patents if appropriate, or whatever else they needed to run a legitimate organization.

So, yes. The Alliance has secrets.

"I don't like their use of the phrase 'out-of-this-world.'" Anna tapped a nervous foot.

Cal straightened, smoothing the lapels of his navy-blue suit. "Could be accidental. It's a common expression. Skyler, do you think they know about your accident today?"

She shrugged.

"It could be a joke. The newer agents are always pranking each other," said Anna. The other three gave her disbelieving stares. "Okay, unlikely. And none of the guys would prank you, boss."

"I agree. It's not a practical joke, but Cal could be right." Skyler was unsure how much she should explain about her accident this morning. *Surely, the e-mail and her incident were unrelated.* For now, she would let the office believe she had stumbled from the platform. "Anna, get Sarah to monitor TheBigReveal's communications. See if she can trace the sender. Wait for the password. We need to know if this is a hoax or the real thing."

"What about telling the board?" asked Cal.

"Not yet. We will if they pose an actual threat. If this is it, we'll ignore them. Contact the other divisions, though. Find out if they received a similar message."

Chapter Two

Scath, Present Day

Disbelief short-circuited Kole's brain. For a sec. Then his massive body exploded from the chair like lava from a volcano. Pressing his palms hard against his desktop, he leaned toward High Commander Cadmon, his mouth curled into a menacing snarl. "Hell no!" Flames shot from his fingertips. "I'm a soldier, not a fucking social director. Besides, I don't much like Earthers."

Seated in front of Kole's desk, Cadmon steepled his fingers as if waiting for a misbehaving child to calm down. "No one else is available. Commander Jarek is tracking the human sex slaves from Cerberus's operation. Commander Nace in North Shelters is ass-deep chasing a pack of drug-dealing shifters. You're it. You will not only escort Chief Maxwell to Scath, but you will also be a tour guide."

He and Cadmon were not alone in the office. Bounty, Kole's secretary, or as she reminded him, his executive assistant, sat with her long legs crossed, her eyes ping-ponging between the two males. The blonde, big-breasted, narrow-hipped vampire out-drank, out-cussed, and out-arm wrestled Kole's legendary Firebrands who kept peace in this violent realm. A few secretly admitted they feared her. But she happened to be one helluva secretary.

Executive assistant.

Bounty had followed Cadmon into the office, obviously appointing herself as Kole's babysitter to make sure he didn't fry his boss. That meant she had advanced intel as to the meeting's subject. Or he had to add psychic to her list of skills. *No.* She had a direct line to

Cadmon's secretary. *Damn. Executive assistant.* After living nearly four hundred years, he had difficulty keeping current on the lingo.

Kole, using his mountainous wall of pure muscle to intimidate, looked down on Cadmon, the cucumber-cool ylve. He inhaled, expanding his chest beyond its normal size. By nature, animus demons were hot-tempered. Lucky Kole got an extra dose of pissed-off at birth. Sane Aeternals feared him. Everyone but his boss. The guy had balls of steel. Fireproof nuts.

The high commander's lids lowered while he tugged on a sleeve of his uniform.

Instead of punching something or setting it ablaze, Kole glanced at Bounty. She cocked her head, arched a brow, and scowled.

Message received. Enough said.

"I'll assign Chay. He's perfect, amiable, easy on the eyes. Young. Pleasant." Kole resumed sitting behind his desk, his jaw clenched tight, his teeth on the verge of cracking.

"No. That will not do. I have planned a series of events for this newly appointed CLO's visit—meetings with dignitaries from the Aeternal societies, galas, ceremonies, the works. Someone high-profile will be the escort. You're my choice. You will not slough this job off on an inexperienced warrior."

Kole shot up again, angry flames sparking on the tips of his fingers.

Cadmon rose to confront his warrior's fiery gaze with the threatening-but-calm demeanor only an ylve radiated. "You said it. You are a soldier. Soldiers follow orders. As your commander, I am giving you a direct order."

Though large for his breed, Cadmon was a cruiserweight beside Kole, but he wore authority like an old comfortable jacket. For centuries, he had been a skilled fighter. He also had created the longbow. Rumor was, he gave the yew-staffed weapon to William the Conqueror, who armed his men with similar bows before the Battle of Hastings, bringing about a decisive victory in 1066 against the forces of the Anglo-Saxon King Harold.

The Scion Firebrands lost a great warrior when Cadmon became high commander. To do their job, to protect the realm from the most violent Aeternals among them, they needed boots on the ground. Still, he was the perfect choice to lead them since he was as politically astute as he was handy with a longbow.

"Coffee anyone?" asked Bounty, not usually the let-me-serve-you type.

Both males said, "No," their eyeballs locked in a showdown.

"You're right," she said, "too much caffeine. A shot of whiskey?"

Kole turned his angry glare toward her.

Grrrr.

"No need to get snarly," she said.

Reason filtered through his haze of anger. He was a soldier. Cadmon was his commander. The animus demon ground his teeth, considered his predicament, and called back the heated energy coursing throughout his body, igniting his fingertips.

He didn't have to be happy-happy with the assignment or kind to the all-mighty Earther. He only had to do his duty.

Duty first. Always.

Kole smothered his fury. "Yes, sir."

"How is the search for Cerberus going?" The ylve resumed sitting, crossing his legs, flicking off an imaginary bit of lint as he changed the subject.

Bounty relaxed in her chair, probably relieved she didn't have to sweep Cadmon's ashes into the trash.

Kole focused on the question instead of the boot-licking task ahead. No use setting off another round of finger flares. "Nothing yet. I am meeting later today with Director Alarik at his Ministry of Well Being to see if his scryers have uncovered anything about Cerberus. When we ID the bastard, I'd enjoy frying him with 500,000 volts of electricity."

The ylve let a rare malevolent smile curve his lips. When it faded, he said, "It's thanks to you we have the intel we have."

Kole shrugged off the praise. His quick action had been the direct result of itchy skin. His Firebrands had shut down a lucrative human sex slave trade. Each captive had unwillingly given a blood sample to their kidnappers. *Itch.* So, Kole had healers test all the victims before returning them to Earth.

Surprise, the prisoners were not random Earthers. They shared similar DNA markers, unrecognizable to their human medical experts, just another puzzle in their complicated genome. But each captive was the descendant of a witch or warlock. *Scratch. Scratch.*

Before Rein lobbed off his head, the vamp who ran the operation dropped the name of his boss. The big kahuna, Cerberus, had employed lackies to hack medical records, seeking Earthers with the specific markers identifying them as mages. Silas and Aisen kidnapped them. Why? *Scratch. Scratch.*

The hound of Hades, Cerberus, stars in the Prophecy of Karma. He hunts for the lost descendants of the Blood Coven so he can jumpstart the same old end-of-the-world shit. Conclusion? Silas and Aisen re-tested their captives to see if they were from a Blood Coven line. *Itch cured.*

Now, they had to find this Cerberus before he caused more trouble.

"Yeah. Sometimes I'm not as dumb as I look."

"Do you think your Firebrands shut down the hunt when you dismantled the operation?" Cadmon jacked an ankle onto his opposite knee.

Kole scrubbed a fist across his jaw. "Can we take that chance?"

"No. That's why we need the Ministry of Well Being. Alarik's researchers will use the same process used by Cerberus. Meanwhile, they'll look for a faster means. We must locate these human descendants of mages before he does."

"A lot's riding on the good guys getting to them first."

Nodding, Cadmon rose, his uniform crisp with a razor-sharp crease in his pant legs.

"Cerberus may already have Earthers with Blood Coven ancestry in his possession," said Kole. "Perhaps he stashed them somewhere other than the stockades we raided."

The ylve high commander nodded. "It's possible. When Alarik's people uncover more humans with mage DNA, his healers must test them. I am assigning your Firebrands to accompany them to Earth. If they notify you any are descendants, bring them to safety on Scath."

Bounty rushed to open the door, shooting Kole an okay sign.

Cadmon clasped Kole's arm, fist to elbow. "Remember, I am depending on you to make a good impression on the Alliance CLO. Don't let me down. Call for the itinerary of your tour. I leave this in your hands, *freron*."

Kole swallowed a growl and snapped his shoulders back to indicate assent.

Once the door closed, the animus demon commander paced from wall to wall, the Who's Moon the Loon pounding out a drum solo on his temples. Walking one length of the office, he ranted against the political side of his job, refused to kiss human ass, and resented this assignment. Striding back, he reminded himself he didn't have to like the task. He just had to do his duty.

But heat continued to build in his extremities, the pain in his head increasing with each surge. When it reached the level of an exploding fragmentation grenade, Kole halted his back-and-forth, a spark flaring from an index finger. Pointing it toward the wall, the one Bounty had rigged with fireproofing, he used it like the nozzle of a flamethrower, charring the plasterboard and burning a hole in it.

Kole exhaled, his lips warping into a contented smile.

There. Better.

Demons, especially animus demons, were aggressive, some would say feral. When they lost control of their powers, the rage took them. Kole would never visit that point-of-no-return. To maintain balance, he released his fire, a safety valve whenever he felt the need. He felt the need often.

After his headache dulled, he opened the door to bellow into the outer room. "Get Rein here now. He's working with two recruits. Tell him if he knows what's good for him, he'll double-time it to my office faster than a Kalli coming out of his tunnel in mating season."

For once, Bounty had no smartass comeback.

****

Rein leaned against the gym's concrete wall with his brawny arms folded across his chest while two new Firebrands, bare from the waist up and sweating, sparred.

Kole liked to call him his second in command. The title, even though fake, made him bristle. And when Rein bristled, Aeternals quivered.

An incubus *freron* recently transferred to the Southern Stronghold because Commander Jarek was short a warrior. The vamp Bade, currently dodging an assault on the mat, replaced him.

Lobo, a wolf shifter and hell of a fighter, returned to North Shelters because of a family emergency. Sig, who was lobbing weak fireballs at Bade's head, was an animus demon like Kole. He replaced the wolf.

Rein fingered the scar through his brow, a gift from his battle with a questing beast during his Awakening.

Was I this bad when I first reported for duty? Hell no!

A vampire-warlock-incubus, Rein was a powerhouse of gifts, skills, abilities. He shouldn't be. Mixes tended to be weak versions of one of their breeds. Not him. He came out of his Awakening a triple threat. But he fought a constant battle against the bludfrenzy. Right now, these two inept recruits tested his limits.

Shaking his head, Rein barked an order. "I'm going to say this once again. If you forget, I'll beat the shit out of you. You are here to use your fists, your feet, your heads."

The demon newbie had been shooting streams of fire at his opponent. The vamp was a Jack-in-the-box, disappearing or reappearing at will, flitting around the flaming projectiles, popping up everywhere. Meanwhile, Rein was fighting a giant headache.

"Looks like you two are fresh from your Awakening, all wobbly-legged and lame-brained. I'm going to prove a point. You ladies will try very hard to stop me. Got it?" He pushed off from the wall.

The new Firebrands' heads nodded in understanding.

Short on words but long on pain, Rein strode toward the demon first, the young warrior ramping up his gift, readying a fiery orb, balancing between spread legs in a fighting stance.

With a flick of his wrist and only a single digit raised, Rein cast a spell. The recruit flew across the room into a rock-solid wall, burning ball still in his palm.

Splat. One down.

Scraped and bruised, the demon shook his head as if to clear it before he staggered to his feet.

"Come on, suckhead." Rein motioned with a hand, urging the other newbie to step forward.

Despite swallowing a gulp, the young vampire approached.

Kudos to his balls. Even if he is about to lose them.

"Now, be sure to get your vamp speed on. Are you ready?"

The recruit popped in front of Rein. Before he could blink, the mentor-trainer face-slammed him into the mat without touching him. Of course, the spell chilled the room.

Rein offered him a hand. "Bloody nose. Maybe a few cracked ribs. Suck it up, kid. What's the lesson, recruits?"

"Don't fuck with you?" said Bade.

"Truth. But there's another. Someone always has a more badass gift than you. That's why you learn to fight *mano a mano*. Weapons, footwork, fast hands might save your sorry dicks someday. You can perfect your sissy breed skills with the specialists. In this room, you use your head. Your muscles. Your fists. Your weapons."

Only a select few became Scion Firebrands. And

all were descendants of previous warriors. When called to join, the Phoenix tattoo appeared. Like a hot branding iron, it burned itself onto your arm. Unbearable agony and the stench of seared flesh lasted until a choice was made. Wannabe heroes joined, the mark becoming permanent. Dickheads rejected the offer, the brand disappearing.

Rein signed on to be a hero. In doing so, he redeemed himself despite his daily battle to control the bludfrenzy. In addition, like all Firebrands, he was BFS, as his partner Chay described the warriors. Bigger. Faster. Stronger. Perks of the job.

The recruits returned to wrestle each other on the mat, not using their breed's gifts. They were sloppy. While Rein wondered if the Phoenix had gotten his wires crossed this time, his D-chip sounded in his mind. He tapped his wrist, taking a message from Bounty.

Happy to leave, he shot instructions at Bade and Sig before he stormed into Kole's reception area. Bounty waited at her desk.

"Get in there." She didn't glance away from her hand-held mirror. "Free advice. Agree to anything he says today." She rubbed a finger across her lower lip, smoothing her deep red lipstick.

"Bad, huh?"

"Worse."

Kole's fiery skills made him not only a formidable enemy but also the perfect Scion Firebrand commander. Who better to control the uncontrollable? His prowess in battle awed his warriors while his breed powers inspired loyalty touched with a healthy dose of fear.

Rapping on the door once before entering, Rein eyed a scorched hole in the wall, Kole still lobbing fireballs at it. "Nice look. You called?"

"I have a fucking assignment which will take me Earthside to shuttle some fat-ass human over here, showing him around. So, you're in charge while I'm tied up for a few days."

"Me? Why me? I'm not temp material." Rein's fangs pushed from his gums. He retracted the bitches, not wanting his commander to fry his ass.

Kole shot back a fierce stare, his gold irises sparking with flames. "I didn't know you'd have to approve my decision." He examined his fingers, probably waiting for them to shoot fire again. "Name someone better."

Rein rolled his eyes. Left. Right.

"Yeah. I thought so. You're it. Congrats."

The reluctant Firebrand warrior resigned himself to fate, heeding Bounty's advice. "Fill me in. What's going on other than the gagan-Yeti problem on Darque?"

"There is that. The Yetis are pissed those ugly gray bastards are destroying forests again. We could be looking at another Darque-wide war. As if the realm isn't dangerous enough. On the lighter side, Crazy Igmon keeps trying to crash the portals. Why he wants to go to Earth is beyond me, but he does. Lock him in the Cubes until he settles down."

Igmon, a sloth demon lost to the rage, craved the human realm every so often. Behind bars for a few days, he'd recover until the next time. Most raging demons were violent, dangerous, having to be eliminated or imprisoned at Outcast Keep on Darque. Not Igmon. He had this single, unexplainable, harmless obsession.

"The most important task is to stay in close contact with your father. Cadmon assigned us to lend an assist if Director Alarik finds Earthers with mage DNA markers. Since his healers will need a blood specimen, we're the muscle who'll accompany them. If they find a

Blood Coven relative, bring them in, willing or not, before Cerberus or his merry band of pricks get to them."

Rein slapped a hand on Kole's shoulder. "Have fun, Comm."

The commander snorted. "Yeah. Party time. Just me, a few blades, and a flyweight Alliance CLO. Humans are crazy. I don't understand them. No offense intended toward Braelyn."

"None taken." Sure, Rein's mate was human, but Silas, working for Cerberus, had kidnapped her because she had a drop of ancient mage running in her veins. He didn't get to keep her long enough to find out she was a Blood Coven descendant. Only Rein's family, along with Brae's father, knew the secret. And they'd locked the intel down tight.

Chapter Three

It was the same each time he transported through the Whorl to Earth. Kole closed his eyes to the bright flashes of light, fighting the urge to upchuck, rubbing fingertips across his pants to control the sparks. A soft pop sounded when his feet reconnected with solid ground. He scanned the arrival room at the Alliance building in Chicago before he walked into the corridor, jiggling the doorknob to make sure it latched behind him.

Can't have strangers accessing the portal.

Striding along the hall, Kole patted his chest to check the double-edge daggers. His hip once for the SIG.

The Ministry of Death forbade bang-bangs on Scath, saying it was dishonorable to employ manufactured firepower when all breeds had their own innate abilities. *Drivel!* The truth? Scath breeds were dangerous enough without adding explosive firepower into the mix. Before they had banned firearms and shit, enormous body counts racked up daily. To keep everyone honest, an entire department of witches and warlocks maintained a spell to prevent weapons such as these from working. Kole could take a gun to Earth, though.

Satisfied, he strode into the legal office. With a one-eighty, he surveyed the room. Facing a curved, waist-high reception counter where a petite brunette sat, Kole stomped to her on steel-toed shitkickers.

When he cleared his throat, the receptionist glanced up from a computer screen. "Oh, hi. Sorry. I didn't hear you." She spoke with a smooth, bluesy cadence, an elbow resting on the desk, her chin cradled in her hand, her brown eyes flirtatious.

He brandished a slow, sizzling smile, the one he reserved for attractive females. As he angled his head toward her, he leaned close, his voice gravelly but warm. "Commander Kole. Here to escort Chief Legal Officer Maxwell to Scath."

See. He could play nice.

"I'm Laurie. I'll let the boss know you've arrived." The brunette stood but didn't move. Rather, she let out a breathy sigh, her admiring gaze traveling from his boots to his hair.

Kole hooked a thumb in the strap of his leather chest holster.

"Oh." Her lashes fluttered. "Yes. Now don't go anywhere." She stepped backward, maintaining eye contact.

"Wouldn't dream of it, sweetheart."

She pivoted, walking away from her desk, provocative hips swaying.

Kole chuckled, enjoying the view. The trip was looking better.

Toward the back, the receptionist knocked before entering an office, leaving the door ajar. "Excuse me, but your escort from Scath has arrived. Boy, is he…"

Kole pushed through behind her. In a booming voice, he announced, "I'm here to collect Chief Maxwell."

Towering over the receptionist, he masked his surprise. A female sat at an L-shaped executive desk. Cadmon hadn't told him his job was to entertain a female. A beautiful one. Marble-carved high cheekbones, a regal nose, pale flawless skin, a haughty chin. Frosty white-blonde hair pulled into a low, business-like knot.

Kole imagined her locks unpinned, falling across her shoulders in gentle waves, bouncing when she laughed at something he whispered in her ear. With her face tilted toward him, her cheeks flushed, her red lips parted, she begged for a kiss. And more. The female was an enticing vision.

Then she spoke.

The fantasy dissolved with her wintery tone, made chillier by her icy blue eyes and thick lashes below deep-arched brows.

"Excuse me, but I have not invited you into my office." She rose, hands on hips, meeting Kole's gaze over an upturned nose.

The temperature dropped a few degrees.

The Firebrand inspected the female's curves, slender waist, shapely breasts, all unsuccessfully camouflaged beneath an expensive but practical gray skirt and jacket. She was tall for a human. He judged five-eleven.

Tapping Laurie's shoulder, Kole dipped his head to smile at her, nodding, before he moved the receptionist aside to barge forward.

"Commander Kole. Invited inside or not, I'm your escort to Scath." He pushed out a calloused palm, more at ease grasping a long blade or dagger.

She stared. Finally, she clasped it, her grip professional, firm. *Frost bite.* Kole reasoned she was sizing him up. He came out sub-standard either because he was not human or because he was a scary demon.

When he clutched her fingers longer than proper, she struggled to wiggle free. Once he released her, she wiped a quivering damp palm on her skirt.

Scary demon it is. Good. That will settle who's in charge.

"Skyler Maxwell, Alliance chief legal officer."

Kole pointed to a brass sign on her desk. "Yep. Says so right here. Are you ready?"

She returned to her seat, folding her arms around her ribs, drawing his eyes to her breasts. "You can't simply walk in, Commander, and order me to jump up and leave. Since I did not expect you until a bit later, I have tasks to complete yet. Please wait in the reception area." The icy blonde tossed him a dismissive wave while she resumed looking down at paperwork.

Kole stood still for a heartbeat, heat traveling to his extremities. Then he planted his fingertips on the surface of her desk, angled forward, and brought his face near Skyler's. The scent from her perfume made him lightheaded as he spoke barely above a growled whisper. "I'll wait for now, Chief. But I have limits. You don't want to cross them."

Skyler's chin popped up, her lashes framing squinted eyes. Her tone was so chilly, he thought his balls might freeze. "I care nothing about your limits. I won't be hurried, Commander. Now, unless you intend to carry me out of my office, kicking and screaming, you will wait in the reception area."

Lips pressed tight, the muscles in Kole's jaw twitched. He drew in a slow breath, catching another whiff of her heady perfume. When he shook off her alluring scent, sparks shot from his fingers, landing on a few papers. Balling his hands into fists, he shoved them to the sides of his body.

Beautiful, but bossy.

Play nice, he reminded himself, having no idea why he was acting like an asshole. Her cool demeanor brought out the worst in him.

Kole's eyes flared. "Okay. I'll be right over there." He motioned at a chair against the wall, sauntering toward it. "Hurry, though. If you make me wait too long, I'll choose the option to carry you off kicking and screaming. Sounds fun."

With his back to the female, he chuckled at the sound of her hand slapping out the small desk fires.

Kole might have a good time yet. He looked forward to sparring with the CLO, breaking through her frigid exterior, ruffling her enough to ignite a response despite the ice cubes in her veins.

He tossed his leather jacket onto a chair. Stretching out in another, he tilted it to lean against the wall on two legs. He spread his thighs apart, laced his fingers behind his neck, and closed his eyes. His mouth twisted into the crooked grin he reserved for females he wanted naked in his bed or bent over a couch with their perky ass in the air.

****

Skyler raised her chin, stabbing a glare into Kole's back, her lips parted in shock. Most people lacked the temerity to challenge her. She balled up the charred document on her desk, tossing it into the trash can.

How dare he.

She steadied her breathing while she focused on another task. But she couldn't concentrate with the testosterone-laden barbarian sitting a few feet from her. After rereading the same paragraph five times, she peeked at the brute.

The man sprawled in the chair was one hundred percent danger, a tank on two boots. At what she guessed was six-foot-eight and thick-necked, he could be a nearly 300-pound blocking powerhouse, an offensive tackle for the Chicago Bears. *Correct.* Her love for the hometown team, a few beers, and a televised game on a Sunday was a guilty secret.

Likely, the man was arrogant enough to think women fell at his feet when he flaunted his crooked smile.

In the overhead light, his buzzed hair looked like

fiery bits of straw glinting in the sun. A stubborn jaw along with the shadow of a beard set off a battle-worn, strong face. Muscles stretched his painted-on T-shirt. As his left bicep flexed, what she could see of his colorful Phoenix brand appeared to ruffle its feathers.

Weapons crowded into a harness strapped across his chest. Taut thighs strained the fabric of his jeans, and his spread legs clearly showed his... *What would Anna and Laurie call it? Yes, his package. Impressive!* In fact, the commander was so impressive, she struggled to breathe.

The man was attractive in a brutish way. *Handsome if you liked rough, violent men.* She did not. *But if she did... No! Definitely not!*

Resting her chin on a fist, her work forgotten, Skyler unabashedly stared until Kole's fire-flecked gold eyes shot open. She thought flames sparked from his irises, but they died out in a flash.

An illusion?

"Why, Chief, if you keep looking at me that way, we're gonna try out the top of your desk." With a deep chuckle, he slammed his chair forward, bringing all four legs onto the floor, his elbows on his knees. The crooked smile returned to his face, taunting her.

Heat crept from Skyler's neck to her cheeks, where she felt it erupt in bright crimson. "I have no idea what you're talking about."

"Yes. You do." He spread his thighs farther apart.

Though the headache from the incident on the L had left her days ago, the commander was giving her a new one. Her office phone rang.

Rescued.

When she motioned for Kole to leave, he shook his head.

Blinking, Skyler *hmphed* while she lifted the

receiver. "Maxwell." She stared at the trade contract on her desk. "Winston. Just a moment." She covered the receiver with her hand. "This is a private call. Do you mind leaving?"

"Yes. I do."

Skyler pursed her lips.

Brutish. Rude.

"I only have a few minutes to talk, Winston." She flipped a page. "Certainly, I look forward to the trip." Trapping the phone between her shoulder and ear, she jotted a note in the margin. "You need not remind me to be safe and, yes, I am taking a coat. ... What? Meet you for dinner?" She turned another page. She thought she had been clear with Winston about their relationship. Apparently, she needed to use stronger words. "I suppose. It will have to be Saturday evening when I return. And since I will be playing catch-up after touring Scath, I must be home early. How about the Grill House? ... Okay. Manfredo's at seven. ... Eight o'clock then. Goodbye."

On heels meant to show off her well-toned legs, Skyler rose from her chair to advance on Kole. "That was ... my fiancé." The white lie might be effective in keeping the brute at a distance. "I would have appreciated privacy."

"Yeah? Sounded like a business deal. I have ice cubes in my freezer warmer than your chit-chat. If you were my intended mate, you'd be getting more than a phone call before you left."

As Skyler frowned, rubbing the crease between her brows, the barbarian's gaze traveled over her body.

Caught, he shrugged.

She whipped around, marched to her desk, and reopened a folder, making him wait while she phoned a client or two, gave directions to her employees, and resisted the temptation to look at the brute.

Kole had resumed his vigil, seated, leaning against the wall while Skyler's heart fluttered in her chest.

Crash.

The commander toppled his chair. His head jerked toward the door as he sprinted for Skyler, launched himself across the desktop, scattered papers, and tumbled her backward onto the floor.

****

Kole rolled off Skyler, shoving her under the desk.

"What the hell?" She wrapped her arms around her knees, cramped in the small space.

"Lock your lips, Chief, so I can listen."

"To what?"

He clasped a hand over her mouth. There it was. Gunshots, yelling, doors slamming, running feet.

Kole shot upright, a finger pointed at Skyler. "Stay here until I come for you. Right here." He unholstered his gun, handing it off to her. "Do you know how to use this?"

"Yes, but…"

"No buts. If a stranger comes through the door, you shoot. Got it?"

"Got it, but I should go out there." She scooted from under the desk.

Kole pushed her back, banging her head on the underneath side of a drawer. "You're going to keep your pretty ass parked here until I come for you. Are we clear?"

She glared. "Crystal."

He doubted she'd follow his orders.

"What are you going to do?" She peeked from her cover.

"Won't know until I get there."

Kole drew a double-edge dagger, opened the door, charged through, and fell into a crouch. Four Alliance agents stood in the outer office, guns drawn, facing the hall.

"What's happening?" He pushed upright.

"Unsure, Commander. Heard shots. Came running. Abello directed us in here to protect the chief along with her people," said the shortest of the four men.

A blond with a crew cut pointed toward the door. "The other guys are holed up in the hallway. Somebody's taking potshots at them. Butch is down."

The youngest agent, who was probably still carded in a bar, blinked and turned to his buddy. "Fuck, you say. Butch?"

"How's everybody in here?" Kole scanned the office.

"We're all good," shouted Laurie behind an overturned table with another female. "I don't know where Cal is."

Kole spotted other employees hidden by furniture.

"Some people are safe, locked away in their offices." Laurie's voice wavered.

Kole fixed on the young agent who was nearest the exit. "Shut this door behind me."

"It's crazy out there, Commander. Are you sure you want to go?"

"Crazy's my kind of place. Love it." He grabbed the knob, turned it, and raced through with bullets flying over his head. A guy in the hallway duck-walked toward him with a shield.

"Heard you were here, Commander. I'm Agent Nico Abello."

With ammo pinging the guy's top-notch shield,

Kole asked, "What's going on?"

"I stopped three guys who were heading into the CLO's office. They said they were phone repairmen. They were wearing uniforms, had badges, a work order even. Then I see they're a little fidgety. So I hold them while I call Laurie. They drew, and I raced for cover, calling for backup. The trespassers took position on that end of the corridor. They got one of us."

Kole saw a body in the hallway, closer to the assailants. "Butch?"

"Yep. He's dead. No use risking anyone to go after him now."

"Sounds like over three men down there."

"More joined them. We had them on cameras before they shot them out. The corridor divides at the end. The attackers control two access points. I got more agents coming, but these guys will be hard to get without casualties."

"Are they humans?"

"No outward signs of being anything else, but I got no way to tell."

"Best if I head toward the excitement. I can't stop anybody from here." Kole smiled.

Finally, some action. Other than the icy blonde's challenge.

Abello grasped his shoulder. "I don't want to fire too many bullets. Don't know who else we might hit. People are in these offices. We can lay down flash bangs or smoke grenades to hide you."

"Nix the flash bangs. My head and ears will ache for a month. Sensitive. A demon thing." Kole tugged on a lobe. "But I'd appreciate a cloud cover."

Abello signaled his men to create a smoke screen. The grenades clinked on the floor, rolling, releasing a hissing gray haze which spread throughout the corridor.

No fire, Kole reminded his animus demon beast.

Since he didn't know who was around, he couldn't expose the existence of Aeternals. He bounded out of a crouch, zigzagging through the hall into flying bullets, hiding in a cloud of smoke. Dodging left and right, he charged forward.

When a bullet tore into his upper arm, his shoulder jerked. He rolled, ignoring the sharp bite of pain as his injury made contact with the floor. Rising, Kole took off again until another slug to his thigh dropped him to one knee. He pushed up on his good leg and continued to race into the line of fire.

A shadowy figure emerged through the fog. Like a runner sliding into home, Kole stretched out and skidded boots first. Coming in low, he grabbed the shooter's ankle, yanking him onto the ground. But the guy wasn't a human. *Nope.* Vamp. Fortunately, a skinny short one. Grappling with his opponent but staying away from his pearly whites, Kole wrapped an arm around the asshole's neck. He rose, lifting the guy, using him as a shield to go after another invader.

When bullets chewed up the bloodsucker Kole held in the crook of his elbow, he tossed the body at the second shooter, an incubus, sending him into a backward stumble. Recovering his balance, the armed attacker pointed a gun at Kole. Kole's eyes narrowed, and he squeezed his brows together as his hand shot out lightning fast. He grabbed the barrel. Using all his demon strength, he rotated it toward the guy.

"Pull the trigger." A thin smile on his lips, Kole urged his opponent to fire, the business end pressed into the invader's chest.

The incubus shook his head, but Kole shrugged, pulling it for him.

Abello along with another agent raced by, going

along the left corridor. Kole yelled a warning. "Not human."

Just then, a body slammed into Kole, taking him to the wall. The barrel of a gun tapped the commander's temple. "Greetings from Arisen Dawn, mutherfucker."

With the weapon snatched from the last assailant still in his left hand, Kole jammed it against the satyr's stomach and pressed the trigger.

Fastest finger wins.

Shaking off the pain and considering the strange words, he bolted toward another shooter who was trying to make a break for it.

Kole tackled him, but before he could plunge his blade into a sure spot, the jugular, a hallway door opened. A gray-haired woman peeked out. Her eyes widened when she spied the massive blood-and guts-covered Firebrand with his knee rammed onto a captive's chest. Before she could scream, Kole signaled her to go back into the office. She did. Once the door closed, he sank the knife into the asshole's flesh.

No remorse.

He wiped his blade on his pants, limping toward Skyler's offices, trailing blood. Abello and his agents were taking care of the trash. Kole reminded them of one of the sure ways to make certain a dead Aeternal stayed dead. Behead the bastards.

When Kole walked through the doorway, his gaze tagged Skyler Maxwell, fists to hips, standing alongside Laurie. His heart skipped a beat. Growling, he threw his hand out, motioning for the CLO to follow him into her office. She shadowed him, eyes lowered, tracking his blood as it dripped onto the carpet.

He slammed the door, stood splay-legged, and tried to contain the flames surfacing on his fingertips. "What the hell were you doing coming out from under the desk? Which part of 'stay there until I come get you' was hard to follow?"

"I was trying to calm everyone. It's my job." Her voice was a whisper as beads of blood dripped from Kole onto the carpet, holding her spellbound.

"Is it your job to get dead?"

"Of course not." She lifted her chin, face taut, eyes bright blue.

Kole ground his teeth. The female had no business putting herself in danger. The attackers could have broken in and shot her. Flames sparked from his fingers again. He shook out his hands to contain them.

"You, however, are injured." Skyler's tone was soft as she inched closer to him. "We need to get you to a hospital."

"Not happening. I'll heal fine unless the slugs are iron." Kole flipped his knife so he was holding the blade. He handed it hilt first to Skyler.

Her gaze pinged from the knife to Kole. Back again. Hesitating, she took it into her hand. "What am I supposed to do with this?"

"Take out the bullets."

"You must be joking." Her already light skin paled.

Kole's forehead crinkled. "I'm not. They must come out before the holes seal."

Skyler looked around for someone else.

"You're the only one here." He lifted his T-shirt sleeve, revealing the wound bloodying his Phoenix brand's feathers.

"There's a room of capable people out there."

Tired of arguing, Kole pointed at the bullet hole. "You're not afraid of me, are you? I promise I won't bite if you hurt me. I know you wanted to earlier."

Skyler humphed. Swallowing, she cradled his

upper arm in her palm. After she guided him to a chair, she motioned for him to sit.

His muscle twitched in response to her touch. It was not because of pain. Her hand was soft, warm. He liked it. Seated, Kole spread his knees wide, creating an opening for her during the makeshift surgery.

When she stepped between his thighs, Kole pinned her sky-blue eyes. He fought the urge to take her into his arms, run his hands along her spine, cup her ass while he drew her tight against his growing erection. Sure, it was an inopportune time for a hard-on, but he was a demon. His body responded to the excitement of battle and a gorgeous woman between his legs.

Trembling, Skyler touched the tip of the knife to his wound but jerked it back. "I can't."

Clutching her hand on the hilt, Kole guided the blade deep. He looked at her. "See. No pain. Now dig."

Skyler ground her teeth together, searching for the slug. Using the tip of the knife along with her fingers, she pried it out. "Ugh."

"Don't faint on me, Chief."

She pulled her brows tight. "I don't faint."

With the bullet pinched between a thumb and digit, Skyler waved it around, looking for a place to drop it.

"Here." Kole snagged it, jamming it into a pocket. "Now the other."

Skyler inhaled, her gorgeous breasts almost popping a button on her blouse when Kole ripped his pant leg from hem to thigh, exposing a nasty injury.

She swayed. Kole thought she might truly faint. "I see you're disappointed I ruined my best pants. Don't deny it. I caught you eyeing my ass in them. Nice fit, huh? Don't worry, though. I'll get more." He gave her his lopsided grin.

A weak smile crept onto Skyler's lips. "Not funny. As much as I may have wanted to hurt you earlier, this is not what I had planned."

While she dug for the bullet, Kole asked, "What did you have planned?"

Her laughter was a beautiful sound, warm, soothing. "Never mind. The mood has left me."

Sirens sounded in the distance.

"We're out of here." With the second slug out, Kole heaved to his feet, grabbing Skyler's hand.

"I can't go now. I must talk with the board."

"No time. You're coming to Scath. You aren't safe here."

"I can't..."

Ignoring her protests, Kole hauled Skyler into the outer office, her shoes flying across the floor. Struggling to keep pace in her heels, she clutched his hand in both of hers, resisting as he thundered toward the corridor.

"Stop. Dammit. I'm not ready."

"Wait. Wait," yelled a female. "Your bags." She pointed to the corner where Skyler's luggage was stacked. "Hi, Commander. I'm Anna, Skyler's administrative assistant."

"Nice to meet you." Kole detoured, seizing the bags in one fist. Anna gathered a file and portal jumper from her desk, shoving them at a moving Skyler. "Here. You wanted to take these with you."

As Skyler flew out the door with a determined Kole, the employees looked at each other. Speeding toward the portal access, he heard them giggle.

Chapter Four

When they landed on Scath, Skyler broke from Kole's grip. Her gaze swept up his large frame. His jaw was clamped tight, the muscles in it twitching. Obviously, he hadn't enjoyed the ride.

To distract herself from his nearness, she patted her hair and smoothed her skirt. Just because the invaders had shot him twice and Alliance workers proclaimed him a hero, he was no less of a barbarian.

How embarrassing to be whisked away in front of her employees.

Before Kole could take her elbow to lead her toward his office, she stepped away to avoid further contact.

He showed off his sexy grin.

No. Not sexy. Annoying.

"Okay then. This way. I'll check in at the stronghold, take care of a few things, review our itinerary before we start from here. But I suggest you rest after the excitement."

"Resting is not on my agenda. Anna sent High Commander Cadmon's office my plans. We will stick to them. Though I will need a few moments to call the board about today's episode."

Skyler debated telling Kole about the L incident, which could be related to the attack on the Alliance. But surely not. Then there was the strange e-mail. Also unrelated. She'd discuss the issue with her bosses first. Together, they could decide how to proceed.

Regardless of her wishes, the barbarian commander latched onto her elbow. "I have ideas about the tour."

"I am uninterested in hearing them. Stick to the itinerary. It's what I want." The Alliance board of directors urged new division heads tour Scath as part of their training. She used her father's old journals as a guide for her visit.

"Yes, Chief Maxwell. We'll damn well follow your plan. You need to change clothes, though." With that said, Kole dropped her arm to stride with determination toward an office.

Skyler, wearing Christian Louboutin black pumps, struggled to keep up, the *tap-tap-tap* of her heels mixing with the *thud-thud* of Kole's boots on the stone floor.

Charging through the door, he let Skyler enter on her own behind him.

"What's wrong with my clothes?" She glanced down at her gray three-quarter sleeve St. John knit suit with a pencil skirt. There was no damage to the expensive ensemble, despite Kole cramming her under a desk. She just needed to freshen her makeup.

The commander stopped, his gaze crawling up the length of her body. "They're okay for a stuffy board room or maybe tea at the Peninsula in Hong Kong. A little formal for a tour of Scath."

She gathered enough ice in her voice to freeze water. "My suit is quality, but I doubt you'd recognize stylish fashion. Given the kind of man you are." Struggling with her portal jumper, she finally shoved it into her purse.

"I'm not a man. But what kind would I be if I were one?"

"Brutish, unkind, uncaring, violent. You get the picture."

"I do." He winked. "And right on."

The nerve.

"We're here, Bounty." Kole slammed Skyler's bags onto the floor.

A tall woman floated from her desk chair, sauntering toward them, unconcerned with the commander's blustering voice and probably having listened to their entire conversation. "I know you're here. I heard everything, including your stomping through the corridor." She tapped a bright red nail on her chin, studying Kole's torn clothing and injuries. "Earth doesn't agree with you." She sniffed the air. "Demon blood. Yours. And bullet holes. There must be a story there. If only I cared."

The woman approached Skyler, holding out a hand. "So nice to meet you, Chief Legal Officer Maxwell. I'm Commander Kole's executive assistant, Bounty."

Skyler studied the woman's shapely legs, trim hips, more than ample breasts, smokey eyes, pouty mouth, and blonde hair. Instead of grasping her palm, Skyler bobbed her chin in a slight nod. "Nice to meet you, too. Could I have a cup of coffee, please?"

A smirk grew into a wide smile on Kole's face as his gaze pinged from Skyler to a narrow-eyed Bounty.

His assistant asked in a syrupy voice, "Sugar? Cream?"

"Black will be fine. Your office, Commander? I don't want to spend a lot of time here. We have a busy schedule."

Bounty arched an eyebrow at Kole.

"In here." He led the way, heading straight to his desk where he flung himself into a massive chair. "Where's Rein?" he shouted into the outer office.

"He's covering for you in a meeting Director Alarik called. Said he hoped it didn't take too long."

Bounty sashayed into Kole's office with a cup of coffee. She offered it to Skyler. "Vampires have sharp hearing. Nonetheless, the commander insists on yelling at me as if I am deaf."

"You forgot mine." Kole grinned at his assistant.

"No, I didn't. It's in the pot. Where you left it and where it's likely to stay until you get off your misogynistic ass to pour it." Bounty returned a charming smile.

Skyler ignored the exchange, sipping her coffee. *Ah. The jolt of caffeine is perfect.*

Bounty's head twisted toward the outer office, her brows scrunched together. "There's a fight in the gym."

"I'll be back." Kole flew out of his chair, quick for such a big, solid man.

Skyler tapped her watch, a hint he should hurry.

Kole frowned, muttering under his breath while he rushed from the room.

****

In his Alliance office, Cal leaned back in his chair, feet propped on the edge of his desk, ear to the phone, while he arranged the final details of the agreement for a security gig. "We'll have plenty of protection there as per your contract. Our principal agents near the stage will be working in conjunction with the police. Our operatives will station themselves backstage as well. Don't forget, D Monz has personal bodyguards assigned to him also. In addition, we'll have plants among the crowd, keeping a finger on the pulse of the audience. Uniformed security will wander the aisles to handle miscreants." He looked up. "Just a moment." Cal palmed the speaker when Laurie stood in his doorway.

"Alarik, Scath's director of the Ministry of Well

Being, is on the phone."

"For me or Skyler?"

"You."

Cal jacked his feet off the desk. "I gotta go. I'll get back to ya."

Nodding, he signaled for Laurie to put the call through. The bigwigs from Scath never called him. They talked to the board or the CLO.

"What can I do for you, Director Alarik?" Cal held the phone between his cheek and shoulder while he logged info into his computer, noting the date, the caller, the contents.

He stopped typing, shooting straighter in his chair. "The board referred you to me?"

Things are looking sunnier.

"I'll check the legalities and draw up medical releases for all Alliance employees."

Cal resumed typing into his computer. "I don't foresee problems. Everyone at the Alliance understands their unique ancestry. Some know who is in their family tree. The breed and so on. Many don't. So let me be sure I've got this straight. Each employee needs at least one blood test. Maybe two."

Already, he was running through a mental list of human resource department contacts at each Alliance facility. He'd need a list of all employees. Medical releases. Logs for the tests. "You want to meet with me, Director? I'd be happy to get together anytime at your convenience. Do you prefer coming to my office at the Alliance or meeting at the ministry?"

Opening his calendar, Cal said, "Yes. I am available tomorrow at three. I'm sure I can have some information for you by that time. The rest later."

Cal resumed logging Alarik's call. "Think nothing of it, Director. Happy to help."

A smile spread across his face as he lowered the phone, ending the unexpected conversation. This could be a big deal. An Aeternal was reaching out for his assistance. Cal could perform a valuable service for an important person. No telling where it would lead. Influential contacts were an asset.

****

Kole watched from the rear of the training center, his arms folded over his chest, a frown on his face. Two of his younger Firebrands, Tyr and Brak, usually friends, were going at it.

Tyr, the light glinting off his dumbass piercings, cast a spell which tossed Brak smack into the wall.

Splat.

Sliding to the mat, the carnal demon jumped upright, dropping his massive frame into a fighting crouch, eyes locked on his opponent. "Unfair, warlock."

"*Freron*, if you know what's good for you, you'll keep your demon in check, or I'll do it for you."

Sabine, a celestial nymph with her sun-streaked blonde hair twisted into two braids hanging down her back, nudged Ram with a playful elbow as they watched. "My money's on the warlock."

"You're on," the satyr Firebrand responded.

Brak's demon flickered but shut down again when he bolted toward Tyr, locking his arms around the warlock's waist, taking him to the ground. They grappled, rolled. Brak on top, pummeling Tyr's face. The mage shot to his feet, tossing fists which glanced off Brak's chin.

Ram and Sabine, off to the side, laughed, shouting taunts at both fighters. When the nymph Firebrand spied Kole, she punched Ram. "Busted."

She rushed to Brak, jumping up to hook an arm around his thick neck, pulling him away from Tyr. Ram, a satyr whose ego along with his playboy rep knew no bounds, stiffened his spine. He had the smarts to get between the combatants, pushing the warlock backward.

Ram stared at the ground, trying to stifle a laugh. "We told you idiots to knock it off."

Glaring at the satyr and Sabine, Kole stormed onto the mat, all eyes on him, his blood, bullet holes, and flapping pants leg. "I expected more from you two."

The fighters shrugged while Sabine choked on a giggle, still holding Brak.

When Ram moved away, Tyr charged the carnal demon, sucker punching him. The satyr Firebrand grabbed the warlock's arms, flinging him aside. "Are you crazy, dude?"

Kole reached Tyr in three long strides, drew back a meaty fist, and slammed his knuckles into the warrior's jaw. The young warlock skidded across the mat. Blinking, he rose, dazed, rubbing his chin. "Damn, Comm, that hurt."

"What the fuck is this all about? You first." He pointed at Tyr.

The warlock's eyes narrowed, fixed on his *freron*. "I've got nothing to say."

Kole growled. He swung toward the demon. "Your turn, punk. And I better not hear 'nothing' again."

"I may have said something about Rein's sister, Elisabeta, being at the Blood Shed, drawing a crowd. My bad."

"And you got pissed? She isn't yours anymore. Get over the female."

Still rubbing his jaw, Tyr nodded.

Kole planted fists to his hips. "I've got the icy B from hell in my office waiting to go on a tour led by yours truly. Now, I've got two otherwise normal males acting like assholes. Shake."

Hanging his head, Brak stuck out a palm.

The warlock Firebrand stared a few moments before clasping it. "Sorry, man. I'm stupid."

Brak laughed, a roar as big as his size. "I can't argue with ya."

Kole approached them both, gripping behind each of their necks until they winced. "There, now. That's more like it. Brothers in arms. *Frerons*." Then he slammed their heads together. Hard.

Brak rubbed his noggin. "Hey, Comm. What gives?"

"We made nice." Tyr shot him a wide-eyed glare.

"You did, but I feel better when I drive home a point. You are both A-holes." When he moved toward Sabine and Ram, they backed away. "And you two morons. Since when do you allow your brothers to fight?"

Sabine looked at Ram to answer. He shrugged. "We were bored. Besides, sometimes dudes need to let off a little steam."

Hmph. Kole grunted when the four Firebrands left the gym arm in arm, laughing. This was his life. Watching his warriors exchange blows. Escorting a frigid, uptight but gorgeous female around Scath, making nice when what he wanted was to test her out in bed. Would she melt in his arms? Or would she freeze his dick? He scrubbed a palm across his jaw. His demon was up for a shot of hot sex. It was how his breed fed. And he was long overdue.

Fun shit.

****

The housekeeper stood in the doorway. "Yur lordship, the phone in the room I am forbidden to enter has been ringing off the hook. Better come answer it. I don't think the bloke is going to stop."

Dante frowned, slapping his hands together to remove the soil from his gardening gloves. It was a sunny day in the English countryside. Since he did not want to waste the pleasant afternoon, he planted bulbs. Digging through dirt, he satisfied a need for creating beauty. Life. His daughter had preferred daffodils, perhaps because her hair had been as yellow as the flower she loved. The estate's garden contained a multitude of these. Tall. Short. Bright. Pale. Deep gold. Then there were gladiolas. Irises. Tulips, his favorite, in patches based on color. But everywhere daffodils. He hoped she was smiling down on them.

Brushing the dirt from his trouser knees, he gazed upon the day's work. Pleased, he walked toward the ancient house, one owned by his family for many generations. With just him in residence, it was too big. It should go the way most large estates had. No. That day would come after his death. Now, his daughter's memories and her spirit roamed the halls of this home where she had spent most of her time when she was young. So, he would stay. If for no other reason than to give her unseen form a familiar spot to haunt.

The dutiful housekeeper left the area once he opened the door to the private study. The phone rang again. He knew who was calling. Dante picked up the receiver. "Yes?"

When a check of his pants found them clean enough, he took a seat in his well-used high-back chair, knowing the conversation would not be quick. He listened.

He ran a finger over the side table. No dust. "Sometimes these things take longer than we would like. Your men will succeed next time." Dante twisted his neck toward the window, staring out over the garden he had been planting. He crossed a knee over his leg. "You are persistent, Cerberus. An excellent quality."

The Englishman poured two fingers of scotch into a tumbler. With the drink in his free hand, his gaze returned to the garden. "On a more positive note, my hacker has been quite successful using the backdoor into patient files in doctors' offices, labs, and hospitals. He's finding more and more candidates with special markers."

Dante set the half-empty glass on the table. He rose. "I thought the results might please you."

Putting a log on the fire, he stared at his daughter's picture on the mantel. Whenever he saw her photo, his heart broke, just as it had the day she died. Dante clutched the frame, rubbing a thumb across her cheek, once so rosy, once so beautiful, once so alive. She had been his princess. After her mother had died, he had raised her, sat on tiny chairs to drink tea from empty cups, arranged for her to buy her first bra, and escorted her to the father-daughter dance at school. The poshest ladies' educational institution in all of England. Then an imposter entered, stealing her love and eventually her life. The deceptive creature would pay along with the entire realm where he hid.

The Englishman was doing what he had to do. Nonetheless, he tired of intrigue, forking over money to fund one enterprise or another, and meeting with Cerberus, the Aeternal who served his own distorted purposes. Dante's partner contended his aim was to open portals, a move to benefit both of their business interests. But the country gentleman did not trust his co-conspirator.

To do his part, Cerberus claimed to need descendants of the Blood Coven who had created the realms fifteen hundred years ago. When Scion Firebrand Rein killed Silas, the means to find these offspring ended. But Dante's new hacker was a genius. As he uncovered those with trace DNA marking them as mage descendants, Dante turned the contact information over to Cerberus. He had done so with a recent file.

Dante returned the picture to the mantel. No sacrifice was too great to avenge his daughter's murder. He paced to the floor-to-ceiling window, once more admiring his gardens. "I'll contact you with more names soon. In the meantime, good luck."

He placed the receiver onto the hook, his lips pressed tight but his eyes betraying no feelings. After all, he was without emotion. It had left him the day a killer murdered his daughter.

****

Celene Bailey's morning started as usual. She and Jace tidied the kitchen before beginning their exercise routine. Then, Jace fixed their breakfast, washing the dishes afterward.

Boring.

"Shall we start the next volume of *The Path*?" Jace stared at the bookcase, fingering the ancient book's spine. "Come on. What else do we have to do?"

"Abso-fucking-lutely nothing. You read." The stories were entertaining, a jumble of tales, mixing the history of Aeternals with a healthy dose of fiction.

With Celene on one end of the couch, Jace took the other, curling her bare feet beneath her while she leaned into the cushions. "I found the next volume of *The Path: Words of the Warrior Ohngel*. Like the first book, the Cambion transcribed it after the Karmic Schism when the Blood Coven created the three realms." She opened to the front and began to read.

Weary from a lengthy truth-seeking journey, I, the Cambion from Wales, rested beside a late evening fire after finishing a meager repast. A nightchat flew from the trees, singing. The warbler-like bird trilled, chirped, and whistled, its raspy notes a message from Ohngel, the fire-winged assassin of the OneCreator, the male I would deem prophet and friend in the coming years.

Oft thereafter, Ohngel or the prophet-warrior's emissary, the nightchat, emerged from the thickets to tell a tale of hope, courage, caution, or enlightenment for the Aeternals placed upon this world by the Genitrix Gahya.

Fatigued from the arduous tasks required to gather the coven and perform the schism, I idled outside the cavern in Wales that was my home, gazing upon stars as they winked in the sky. The nightchat, flaunting its bright yellow feathers, ignored my weariness, settling on the ground to relate events unknown. Here in Volume II: The Betrayal, I documented a dire warning.

Near the time of the Karmic Schism, Ohngel, the warrior-prophet and winged assassin of the OneCreator, delivered a dictum, dooming me and the Blood Coven to isolation from our kind. After the event, we and our offspring were to remain on Earth, scattered and hidden, ostracized from our breed. He assured me the measure was necessary.

Though disheartened by the pronouncement, I remained true, submerging my personal needs beneath the desire to save the many. With my coven, I created three realms from one world: Earth for humans, Scath for my Aeternals, and Darque for dangerous magical creatures. Afterward, we went our own way, isolated from our kind on Scath and cut off from one another.

Jace closed the book. "You're not paying any attention, roomie."

"You're right. I need action."

Jace nodded, dropping the volume onto the table beside her.

Celene sprang off the couch, doubled up her fists, and stormed toward the locked door. She and Jace de

Vries had waited, talked over the pros, the cons, steeled their resolve to devise a plan. It was time to take the first step.

After all, she was a daredevil, an adrenaline junkie who had base jumped Angel Falls in Venezuela, run with the bulls in Pamplona, and skied Delirium Dive in Banff. She didn't have the patience to sit around forever, listening to some dusty old stories.

Though her latest endeavor hadn't ended well, the jump had been successful. It was when she touched ground that everything turned to shit. In the landing zone at the bottom of Angel Falls, Celene had been zapped with a stun gun and kidnapped, awakening in a dingy, cold cell, guarded by aliens or something. It was a nightmare, from which she still had not recovered. Now she was here. Imprisoned.

Jace's experience had been even more horrific. According to her, a monster had abducted her from New Paltz, NY, where she worked in a winery, having studied viticulture and enology at Cornell. The asswipe kept her locked in a stinky, damp cellar. Though she escaped from the first hellhole, she was re-captured. That's when she learned vampires were real. A crazy one was sucking on her neck.

Both women landed here where they each had a bedroom and adjoining private bath, a shared sitting area with a TV, a kitchen, and dining room. Wherever here was. The surroundings may have been better than their original cells, but they were still prisoners, held captive by creatures Celene once pooh-poohed. They had books. A lot of DVDs. They created their own exercise routines, cooked, made tubs of buttered popcorn to go with the films, and talked endlessly. Each day dragged on, though, until she could no longer bear the boring pattern of her life.

Jace, equally disheartened, had come up with the plan.

Celene pounded on the door with both fists. "Hey out there. Dickhead, get in here now." She took her shoe off, using it to bang louder. "I'm not stopping."

She heard a loud, deep snarl from the other side. "Get back."

"No." She continued making a racket.

"I'm coming in. Back the hell up."

A six-foot-six massive creature slammed through the opened door, stomping across the floor. "What?" He grabbed Celene's elbow, flinging her onto the couch.

She rubbed where she was sure to bruise. "We demand to see someone who can give us answers. Where are we? Why are we here?"

The guard laughed, a gruff sound erupting from his mouth. "Not fucking happening."

"Well then, we're going to be in for a fun time, asswipe."

Chapter Five

During Kole's absence, Skyler studied his office. She assumed the well-worn massive wooden table in the adjoining room was where he strategized with his Firebrands. On its visual journey, her gaze swung to the weapons mounted on the wall behind his desk.

A barbarian would proudly display gruesome killing implements. The blood of his victims probably still dirtied the blades. How many people had this brute killed? Too many to count.

She gestured toward the weapons. "Those. Do they belong to Commander Kole?"

"No." Bounty ambled to the wall. "They belonged to his *frerons*." She pointed at one weapon. "The incubus commander before Kole owned this scythe." She touched another. "The trident was a favorite of an Amazon queen, a warrior who fought by Kole's side for a century until a bludfrenzied vamp ripped off her head."

"And those?" Skyler stepped alongside her, pointing at a pair of strange blades. The grip was in the center, the weapon meant to be held like a baton. A gold band with writing on it encircled the shiny metaled hilt, or handle, in the middle. Off each side was a slightly curved double-edge blade. They were graceful, beautiful, and most likely deadly, but she admired them as works of art.

"Those are haladies, dangerous tools in the right hands. This one was in the hands of Kole's father. The hilt is inscribed with his name, Aedon. The weapon next to it belonged to his mother, Hestia. They used the same style blades, fighting side-by-side for centuries. Together in life. Together in death."

Skyler returned to the chair, crossing her legs, smoothing her skirt. She tried to reconcile the gruff, fearless soldier Kole with a boy, laughing, playing games, being tucked in at night by his parents. She couldn't.

A growl came from the doorway. The demon leaned an immense shoulder against the frame. Spotting him, Bounty pointed to a white-handled, curved blade. "The Scion Firebrand Wynny owned this one. The Phoenix called her to serve at the same time Kole was a rookie. Right, Commander?" She paused. Then, with a hand pressed to her lips, she chuckled. "The warriors still talk about your first meeting with her. Rumor says you told her most witches were petty wand waggers?"

Kole nodded. "I did. In my defense, I was young and stupid. Wynny's fingers flew out in front of her innocent, freckled face. She wiggled them around, giving me an angelic grin before she cast a spell. An ugly rash covered my chest, oozing shit for a week. Couldn't even wear a shirt. Put me in my place, but it gave me a whole new respect for mages. Afterward, she and I were close *frerons*."

Bounty pivoted toward Skyler, her smile fading. "Commander Kole takes each weapon down on the anniversary of the fallen warrior's death, polishes, hones it, keeps it in fighting shape."

"Cut the shit. Enough." Kole grumbled, striding to his desk, cutting off any personal discussion. "This doesn't interest Chief Maxwell."

Passing near Skyler when she exited, Bounty leaned close, cracking her lips to show the points of her fangs. "That's the kind of male he is." She turned on her heel, strutting out, closing the door with a bang.

Okay. Bounty had overheard their earlier conversation.

Kole growled. "It's unhealthy to get on her bad side. Sure, she badmouths me, doesn't listen, sasses, cusses, orders me around. But she's feral when it comes to protecting her Firebrands. Including me."

"I'll keep it in mind." Skyler eyed Kole, trying to see the man behind the wide shoulders, muscular build, fire-gold irises ringed with black, and masculine, brutish face.

When the commander caught her, she snapped her eyes away, appearing to study the room.

While Kole read and reread the same pieces of paper, frown lines formed creases above his nose. "Bounty, get in here. Is this what you were given?"

"Yep. Straight from the high comm's office. He said it came from her admin assistant." The vampire had an ear-to-ear grin, wiggling an irritating thumb in Skyler's direction.

"This is what you want to see?" Kole pinned Skyler with a disbelieving stare. "The ylven Inimicus Ceremony? The demon Genesis Rite?"

Bounty put a hand on the back of Kole's chair. She asked Skyler, "Any changes?"

"Absolutely not. My father's journals are my guide. This was his agenda when he first visited Scath as a new CLO. I want to retrace his steps. No alterations. Am I clear? How hard can it be to follow directions?"

Skyler held out an upright palm before the commander opened his mouth again. "Matter settled."

Kole exchanged a glance with his vampire assistant. "Make the arrangements, Bounty."

"Already made, Commander." She did a little dance step when she left the office.

Strange.

Kole pushed out of his chair to open a drawer, removing a fresh pair of black cargo pants along with a matching tee. He unfastened his sheath, loaded with knives, and stripped off his bloodied, torn shirt.

Skyler watched as he bared rippling, rock-hard abs and a muscle-padded chest with its inky runes dipping into his waistband. Her attention flipped to his Phoenix brand. Its head rested at the top of his enormous upper arm, its wings wrapped around a thick bicep, its talons reaching his elbow. It was the fierce symbol of a Firebrand warrior. She swallowed, her mouth dry.

At a sink, Kole dampened a cloth and washed off blood. While she was mesmerized, he began to unzip his pants. "No peeking now. I'll blush."

Skyler bounded out of her seat, giving her back to him.

Rude. Crass. Barbarian.

But she was glad she had turned away from Kole. With the sound of his pants brushing down his legs, Skyler palmed her cheek. Her face was warm.

I would have peeked.

"You can look now. If you want to change to something more sensible, I promise to keep my eyes closed."

"Not another word about my clothes." Skyler smoothed her stylish, expensive skirt. It was her armor, a symbol of her success.

Bounty interrupted, slipping through the door, escorting a man inside. "The healer's here to stick it to the chief."

"Getting a blood sample isn't necessary since I know my heritage. My Aeternal ancestry is only several centuries old. I have no mage DNA."

"There are no exceptions, Chief Maxwell," explained the healer, withdrawing a syringe along with a vial from his case.

"Very well." She removed her jacket, tossing it onto a chair, her foot tapping while he extracted blood.

****

Alarik, the director of the Ministry of Well Being, sat at the head of a large mahogany table in his conference room.

When he stood, clearing his throat, his sister Indigo winked at him. She twirled a strand of thick black hair around her finger while she blew chewing gum bubbles. It was her way. He accepted it.

After he smiled at her, he brushed her off to maintain an air of authority with the group he had called together. He glanced at somber faces, each reflecting the burdensome knowledge he had shared with them. "We have a job to do that requires stealth. Therefore, I have concocted a cover story. Here it is. Scholars at the Ministry of Well Being are writing a new history of Scath. It will document the genealogy of both Aeternals and any related humans. This is the fiction we will present to others. Of course, our real task is to find human descendants of the Blood Coven."

His son, the Firebrand Rein, slouched in his chair, arms folded over his chest, surreptitiously checking out the time on his D-chip.

Echo, a pride demon who was chief historian at the ministry, stroked a finger across her chin. "If the name Cerberus gets out there, rumor and fear will spread."

"Hence, the cover story is important. It hides our tracks." Alarik laced his fingers together, his elbows resting on the table.

The pride demon tapped an entry into her electronic pad.

Alarik pointed toward an incubus. "Logan is a

technical expert. Please explain what you've done?"

The Firebrands' resident geek shuffled in his chair, obviously more at home with a computer than with speaking to a group. "Sure. After hours at a keyboard, I found backdoors into all the major medical software used for patient recordkeeping. Let's just say, one male's necessary actions due to exigent circumstances is another dude's hack into not-so-secure files. Anyway, I have an automated search running for specific data. When I locate witch or warlock DNA markers in an Earther's test results, I will pass the shit ... um ... stuff on."

Logan looked relieved when the chief healer took over. "Our job is to root out the patients Logan has identified. Once we do, we notify Kole at the Eastern Stronghold of a scheduled visit. You'll be handling this for the time-being, Rein?"

When Alarik's son nodded, the healer continued. "It is a three-step process. Using technology, Logan will find those humans with mage ancestry. Accompanied by the Firebrands, my people will obtain a blood sample from the candidates he identifies. Finally, scientists at our ministry, using the BCA Variant Test, will analyze the sample and determine if the human is a descendant of the Blood Coven."

The chief healer angled his head toward the table as he consulted his notes. "In our perusal of medical records from Logan, only this morning we identified a female with ancient mage DNA who lives in Cleveland, Ohio. Her name is Margo Hunter. We need a blood sample."

"Done." Rein tapped on an electronic pad. "Galena and Chay will reach out to you. If it turns out she's a descendant, we'll be bringing her to our stronghold for safety. We're also focused on the hunt for Cerberus." He glanced at his mate. "Brae has put an interesting plan into action."

Alarik and others turned their attention to her as she spiked fingers through her short auburn hair. "Sure thing. I write for my father's tabloid in Seattle. Some might question whether it's really journalism, but it serves a purpose." She waved her hand in the air, dismissively. "Anyway, the paper's called *Strange but True*. Most of the stories we print are from crackpots, but sometimes an article flushes out an Aeternal who has illegally crossed to Earth to commit a crime. That's why my father runs the rag. When we uncover valuable intel, we turn it over to Alliance agents to handle. I had an idea, similar to one police use to trap violators with too many traffic tickets. We ran a contest to draw out people who believe they are witches or warlocks or descended from them. We offered big cash prizes. Alliance volunteers are screening thousands of phone calls. Mostly crazies have flooded the lines, but I'm still hopeful we'll get lucky."

When the meeting attendees began to whisper among themselves, Alarik raised his hand for quiet. "Thank you, dear. Your idea is brilliant. Moving on, my chief scientist, Eliphias."

The warlock nodded. "My people perfected the method noted by our esteemed healer. We call it the BCA Variant Test. Simply put, it detects humans with Blood Coven ancestry. The hang-up is the initial search of Earth medical records for those with ancient mage DNA. The process is slow and hit-or-miss. We need a faster one. Once we have a potential candidate, we can gather a specimen from them to analyze with the BCA Variant Test."

Alarik tapped his pen on the table. "It is a laborious method. We think Cerberus uses the same process. Which means he has talent, money, and a network at his fingertips. Anyway, Eliphias just hinted at why you are here. We need fresh ideas on how to detect coven descendants faster."

Echo lifted her hand, rising, patting down her black robe when Alarik acknowledged her. "Ever since you contacted me, I've been thinking about how my historians can assist. My people will pore through archaic documents on site, researching relevant lineage. Though we house many ancient books which may prove valuable, we must handle them with care. Some, if spelled, could destroy themselves when we try to open them. We would appreciate the aid of a witch or warlock powerful enough to detect and remove spells. I had someone on staff. Unfortunately, she is no longer with us. Does anyone here have a suggestion?"

Her gaze pinged around the room while she continued. "Though many books are in our own library, some Aeternals have private copies of their family histories. We shall put out a call for these documents, using the cover story, of course." She nodded toward Alarik. "My researchers will also tap Earth resources, both online and in libraries. Salt Lake City, where the Church of Latter-Day Saints keeps a variety of genealogy records, is a visit on my list. We shall follow any thread."

"Thank you." When Echo sat in her chair, Alarik rested his elbow on the table, chin on fist. "Along with their other duties, healers are preparing to test Alliance employees and any other known Aeternal descendants on Earth."

Eliphias rose to address Echo. "I would like to recommend Sauro. He's a mage expert at detecting or removing spells from old texts." After she entered a note on her device, he turned his attention to the entire group. "My department is working on a way to identify human descendants more quickly than the laborious method of combing through medical records to review blood sample results. We have been unable to find such a process yet, but we are at it twenty-four hours a day."

"What have you considered?" Alarik tried not to let the disappointing news show on his face.

"Powerful spellcasters in my department deliberated over a summoning which might draw descendants to us. They tell me no. Impossible. We tossed around using an object, like a plant or talisman, something the human offspring might react to. Though the concept has possibilities, the logistics of distribution are staggering." Eliphias waved his hand through the air. "We'll keep at it." He fell into his chair.

Indigo let out a loud shiver. "Ooh! Try Karmas Root. You can use it to summon mages, but it has nasty side effects. Chills, fever, an ugly-ass rash which lasts for days. Kind of a nice high." She paused when mouths gaped open. "Oh, I never tried it myself, though I did give it to a frenemy." Her hand stifled a snorting laugh. "Of course, if you use it, you'll need to watch the hospitals for any signs of Karmasitis. I coined the term myself." Her lips drew into a smile.

Eliphias scribbled notes with his electronic pencil. "We'll look into it, but it does not sound promising."

Indigo shrugged, wrapped a dark curl around her finger, and popped her bubblegum.

Jarek, the Eastern Stronghold djinn commander, pushed back his chair, cocking an ankle onto his knee, the war braids at his temples dangling onto his shoulders. "The vampire Silas, working for Cerberus, kidnapped mage descendants like Rein's mate, Braelyn, selling them as sex slaves to Aeternals once he determined they didn't have the correct Blood Coven ancestry. My stronghold is tasked with rounding up these humans. If they are still on Scath, we find them, wipe them, and send them home. Afterward, we, along with Alliance agents, keep an eye on them so they don't get snatched again. The healers also give us the names of those who don't pan out as descendants. We keep an eye on them, too, since we don't want some new Cerberus flunky nabbing them and auctioning them off to the highest bidder."

Nace, the shifter commander of the Northern Stronghold, stroked his close-trimmed, straw-colored beard, his golden eyes as feral as a jaguar's. "While Jarek and Kole's strongholds handle their new assignments, my Firebrands are taking over the day-to-day tasks, including quashing the rampant drug trade."

Alarik fixed his gaze on his quirky sister. "Do you have anything to share? Of course, you all know Indigo communicates with the River Am."

When everyone nodded in her direction, she blew an enormous bubble on cue. *Pop.* Smoothing her long skirt, flipping a strand of curly black hair onto her back, the surprisingly powerful witch stood. Five times she cleared her throat before she tilted up her chin. "The river," her gaze flitted from eye to eye, "sucks. I saw Cerberus in the Chance Rapids. I couldn't see his face because he had his back to me, his black robe billowing, as puffed up as his ego. Another male stood beside him. A human. Didn't get a bead on him either. I've got bupkis." When she flopped into her chair, her jaws moved up and down with each chew of her gum.

"Thank you, dear. Let's move forward with our plans. Questions?" Alarik looked at the attendees, their heads shaking. "Time is our enemy. We must assume we are in a race with Cerberus. My thanks to all."

Once participants left, Indigo skipped over to her nephew Rein, tucking her arm through the crook of his elbow. "Don't worry about me, Boyo. I'm tough. And when the tough get going, we … um … get out of here. Ta. Ta." Releasing him, she strutted out the door.

Braelyn and Rein cast concerned looks at Alarik.

"I know. The river weighs on her mind. I fear what she will do if she misses something important in its waters. She acts carefree, but she's not. My sister has always carried heavy responsibilities on her shoulders. First me. Then our realm. Anyway, you two go on."

Braelyn sighed when Alarik placed a reassuring hand on the small of her back. "I feel like a useless cog. I hope my idea pays off. For now, I'm off to my stint at phone duty."

Rein grabbed her around the waist. "You aren't useless. You're smart and sexy."

She arched her brows. "You know what that kind of talk will get you?"

"I'm counting on it."

"Ah, youth." Alarik shooed them out the door.

Chapter Six

Excited to be starting the tour, Skyler followed Kole through a portal. They exited near a lake where four swans, as mysterious as their mirrored reflections, glided across the water. She drew a slow, deep breath, catching the intoxicating scent of winter flowering honeysuckle crowding the banks.

Moving to the edge of the rise where they landed, she admired the view. Mist wound in and out of craggy hills which bordered the lush valley below, giving the area a hushed peacefulness. Below, forests, cleared farmlands, and clusters of rambling houses appeared and disappeared in the winding ribbons of fog. In meadows, sheep and cattle grazed.

A female as graceful as the swans walked toward them on a steep, meandering path which led uphill to an alabaster building, so bright it glistened in the sun. With each step she took, her diaphanous white dress fluttered, her lithe body exposed beneath see-through layers of fabric.

Covenkirk, like Chicago, was cold, but in this hemisphere of Scath, the weather was warmer. Skyler draped her St. John's coat over her arm.

Reaching them, the figure offered her hand. "Hello, I'm Juno. You are Chief Maxwell?" The woman's voice was an angelic whisper, serene like the environment.

"Yes." Clasping the ylve's soft palm, Skyler felt loud, large, and clumsy beside the woman.

"Welcome to Aerilon." She gestured at the surroundings, her arm extended. "You are in the Therion region, specifically, the western foothills of the Lost Souls Range which divides our territories from Knife's Edge."

With a more mischievous smile, Juno turned her attention to Kole, flipping her long, blonde hair over a shoulder. "Commander." She grasped his hand for some time. Too long. "I am happy to see you again. It's been a while."

"Juno. Always a pleasure."

Kole's eyes softened, small crinkles forming at the edges when he shot a ridiculously sexy grin at the guide.

"Please, follow me to the Greeting Chamber." Juno glanced at Skyler's shoes, but her expression remained unchanged, warm, welcoming, benign.

"What is the Greeting Chamber?" asked Skyler.

Juno signaled Kole to walk ahead while she clasped Skyler's elbow, wrapping her hands around it with unexpected familiarity. "It is where the Triumvirate of the Wise will meet you. The Inimicus Ceremony on your agenda is an ancient ylven tradition. We use it to greet friends or foes. In the past, we have welcomed notable enemies to peace talks, including the demons after their breed's two-hundred-year war. Those insurrectionists walked into the same chambers where you will stand today. They relinquished their arms to the Triumvirate of the Wise, restoring tranquility to the realm once again. The ceremony has also been used to welcome dignitaries such as you. Your father attended. A formidable man, I recall. Today, you will meet our current Chancellor of the Wise, Laegon."

"I look forward to meeting him as well as Imperial Secretary Thannor and Grand Commandant Caleth."

She squeezed Skyler's elbow. "I am pleased you

acquainted yourself with our Triumvirate. They are the honored ylves who will serve as our governing body for fifty years. Afterward, the distinction passes to the next three elected by our breed."

Since it was a long walk from the portal to the top of the bluff, the trail steep, winding, Skyler accepted Juno's arm. She frowned at Kole when he glanced back at her, his brows arched in an I-told-you-so expression.

Each time Skyler stumbled, Juno tightened her grip but continued chatting about ylves along with their customs. Reaching their destination, Skyler sighed, appreciating the guide's assistance. No twisted ankles. No wear-and-tear on her designer shoes.

At the foot of the steps leading to the temple, a group of twenty-five people waited in silence, somber in their black robes. Some had tape over their mouths, and some wore blindfolds. Others clasped hands over their ears.

"What are they doing, Juno?" Skyler asked.

"Protesting."

Kole frowned, moving aside to let Skyler and the guide climb the marble steps.

Skyler allowed Juno to latch onto her elbow again, preventing her from tumbling. "Thank you. Protesting what?"

"Your tour, the relationship between Aeternals and humans, cross-mating between breeds, progress. You name it. They call themselves Isolationists. Today, they are peaceful, but they are not always so nowadays."

They proceeded toward the white structure. Up close, it was impressive, open to the air on four sides. They passed through a single row of colonnades, forming a sort-of marble curtain around the edge of the temple. Skyler angled her head to study several friezes which decorated the facade. One showed an ylve, his long spear taming a bull. Another portrayed a woman drawing an arrow to her bow to kill a centaur-looking creature. Still another depicted nude male and female figures wrapped in an embrace.

When Juno led Skyler and Kole into the interior between the fluted columns capped with fern leaves, more than a hundred ylves awaited them, bowing to the visitors. Most wore diaphanous white robes like Juno, exposing their naked, supple, graceful figures. Three, wearing pale purple, strode forward. Skyler observed nipples, penises, the works, all visible beneath the fluttering gossamer clothing.

Tipping her chin higher, Skyler handled surprise with her usual cool demeanor.

As if he read her mind, Kole grinned, leaning over to whisper in her ear. "Transparency is part of the Inimicus Ceremony. The ylves show they bear no ill will toward you. Despite the breed's calm exterior, they are warlike, known for trickery, having something up their sleeves, so to speak. Their see-through robes make it evident they carry no weapons."

Skyler's chest expanded with a deep, deep breath. She released it slowly. "I can see they aren't armed." Her brows lifted, her expression icing over while she prepared to greet the ylve dignitaries.

Kole cleared his throat. "Just saying. This is what you requested."

She hissed in his ear, her business-like smile never wavering. "I know I did."

Laegon approached, introducing himself. Waist-length black hair and a bedroom smile. His midnight eyes, topped with dark brows, could have given him a brooding look, but full lips made him more sensual than moody. Skyler tried not to stare at the trim, muscular body of the man beneath the transparent purple robe. She failed.

He pointed at the two ylves beside him. "This is Imperial Secretary Thannor. And this is Grand Commandant Caleth, my soulmate."

With his shoulder-length curly brown hair, a close-trimmed beard, and sparkling green eyes, the handsome Thannor captured Skyler's hand. When he raised it to his mouth, his kiss tickled like a feather. After he released her, she offered him a brief nod. Again, she tried to direct her gaze everywhere except at his groin. It wasn't easy since his penis tented his see-through robe.

Caleth was regal, an athletic body, slim hips, long legs, prominent cheekbones, a straight nose, bowed lips, and cat-shaped amber eyes. When she smiled at Skyler, her entire face glowed with an inner light. She twirled until her gown swirled around her bare feet. "As you see, we hide no artifice." Her laughter rang out, high-pitched, musical, confident. To Skyler, Caleth was an unlikely grand commandant in charge of an ylven army.

Thannor placed a palm low on Skyler's back to lead her toward the awaiting ylves in the chamber hall. While his hand caressed her, his thigh slid against her hip. Trying to hide her blush when he guided her forward, Skyler glanced over her shoulder to see Kole smirk. Twisting her head around to greet the assembled business and agricultural leaders, she stiffened her spine, lifted her chin. She avoided the touch of the imperial secretary's thigh, but there was no tactful way to escape his wandering fingers.

The ylve leaned toward her, so close his breath warmed her ear. "May I say, I never expected such a lovely chief legal officer. Now that I know, I might visit Alliance headquarters myself." He straightened, giving Skyler some relief. "Tell me, you share the same last name of the previous CLO who attended this ceremony.

Are you related?"

Skyler's lips tilted into the smile she reserved for public occasions. "Yes. He was my father."

"Ah. You are more pleasing." His voice louder, Thannor announced, "We are honored to be your first stop on Scath. The farmers, vintners, and ranchers you have assisted with trade contracts are here to greet you. They hope to continue profiting from business deals you arrange." He introduced her to each ylve while Kole chatted with Laegon and Caleth.

****

Three Alliance employees were manning the phones in the call center when Braelyn entered. She waved, unslung her purse, and arranged her jacket on the back of a chair at an empty station. She sipped a Frozen Monkey Mocha with multiple shots of espresso from her favorite Seattle coffee shop, setting it on the counter.

Calls had been coming in at regular intervals since her father had published her article about a contest for those who could prove they were witches or warlocks or descended from them. Huge cash prizes went to those with undeniable proof, stating the data was for an upcoming story. She hoped the ruse netted results.

A short-haired, dark-skinned Alliance agent disconnected from her caller, laughing. "The woman is bat shit crazy. She offered to take me flying on her broomstick. I'm tempted to take her up on the deal to see what she comes up with."

A redheaded agent leaned back in his chair. "I can outdo you one. A man yesterday told me he was trained at the Magic Academy in Ohio. I asked where it was. He said in Dayton. You know what happened when I Googled it?"

He waited for heads to shake. "There really is one. Anyway, he got his degree in physical education.

Quidditch is his sport. As the team's Seeker, he told me he's an expert on his Nimbus 2000 broomstick. I called the Chicago Alliance office to see what they knew about the place since they're nearby. They laughed me off the phone. Apparently, they are aware of the guy and the school for crackpots."

Between listening to workers one-up each other with bizarre phone chats, Braelyn answered nine calls in an hour. As she hung up from number ten, she spotted the redheaded agent waving, frantic for her attention. She hustled over to listen in on the conversation, her ear near the speaker.

"Have you heard of Masoud?" The male caller had a deep, steady voice with an English accent.

"Who?" The agent followed up the caller's question with one of his own.

"A warlock."

"Who are you?" Braelyn interrupted, her lips near the mouthpiece.

"I'm not saying unless this offer is legitimate. Let's not muck around. I'll be off the phone in two minutes, by the way. I've started counting."

Braelyn shooed the agent out of his chair. "Let me give you my cell number. Then you give me yours. Call me back on my phone when your time's up."

"I may call you back, but you're not getting my number, luv. I don't know you well enough to dance so close."

She gave the caller her contact info. "Fair enough. Why so paranoid?"

"Somebody's after me. They tried to slip a bag over my head and shove me into a van, but I got away."

Braelyn shivered, sitting straighter in the chair, recalling when Silas had kidnapped her. This information alone made her believe the caller. "What do you know about Masoud?"

"My family is English royalty. We're uppity shites who've kept genealogy records dating back centuries. Nearly a thousand years ago, an ancestor claimed to be a warlock offspring of Masoud. Time's up. Goodbye."

"Wait. Wait. I was kidnapped and locked in a cell. Probably the same bastards are after you. Stay safe."

The caller paused. "I'll call."

Braelyn bit her lower lip, the Alliance agents gathered around her. "He hung up, but he might be legit."

A few minutes later, her cell phone rang. The screen read anonymous. "Braelyn here."

"It's the crazy warlock."

"Why did you respond to the newspaper article?"

"I need the money to stay on the run, luv. Can't use my usual resources since I think they are being used to track me."

"If you are a warlock descendant, I will get $50,000 to you, but I need verification. Have you had blood tests run recently?"

"That's a strange question."

"Go with me on this. Have you?"

He paused for so long Braelyn thought maybe she had lost him. "Six months ago, I was in an auto accident."

"Is that about the time they started chasing you?"

"Spot on, luv."

"I need your name and the hospital."

"Tit for tat. I want intel on you. How do I know you're not out to bag me?"

"I know the people who came after you are dangerous because, as I said, they succeeded in kidnapping me. I was held in a cell until my ... um ... husband rescued me. I don't want that to happen to you.

Not only are you in danger because you are a human descendant of a mage, but your ancestor was Blood Coven. They want you super bad. They won't give up. I can protect you. I'm Braelyn James. My father owns *Strange but True*."

There was silence. "Miller Nash. The hospital is Surgeon's General in Knoxville. I'll be in touch."

"Wait. When?" Her caller had disconnected, though.

****

Kole leaned a shoulder against the wall, confabbing with Laegon and Caleth while tracking Skyler's movement through the crowd.

"Lovely. You must enjoy taking the new CLO around Scath. It does not seem to be an unpleasant task." The ylve leader winked at his soulmate.

"I should say not." Caleth stroked Laegon's shoulder.

"It's not as pleasant as you might think. She isn't always easy to get along with." Kole watched Skyler chit-chat with small groups. He wanted to yank Thannor's arm from its socket. If his fingers dipped any closer to her ass, he might do it.

"Still, she is easy on the eyes." Laegon threw an arm around Caleth, pulling her close to his body. "A mate is a wonderful asset. Someone to warm your bed every night so you don't have to go looking."

"That's my worth to you—keeping your bed toasty?" Caleth humphed.

"Of course. It doesn't hurt you are the legendary ylven warrior commandant who saved my life on more than one occasion."

"Such flattery. Be careful or your feet will be cold tonight, my soulmate and chancellor." Caleth wrapped her arms around Laegon's waist, squeezing.

"Besides, I don't recall you having to look for company. The females seemed to find you."

"See," said Laegon, "a mate is wonderful. She strokes my ego along with other places."

Kole studied the two ylves, part of him envying their bond. "I'm not mate material, but if I were, the female with Thannor would be my last choice." As he said this, Skyler peeked over her shoulder, a small smile curling her lips, her blue eyes brightening. When she caught herself, her icy expression returned.

Shaking off the moment, Kole changed the subject to something he was more comfortable with. "Tell me about the Isolationists outside your temple. Are they becoming a problem?"

Laegon deferred to his commandant. "They are less often law-abiding than in the past. We are told they are divided. A small faction wants to maintain peaceful protest. The larger faction believes the non-violent actions no longer work. They favor changing tactics."

"How so?"

"They want to up the hostility. We hear the pacifist ylve Simon, who started the group, has lost control of it. Other breeds are joining, spouting purist lingo."

Caleth adjusted the folds of her transparent robe. "They kidnapped an ylve from North Shelters. Faeth. Her mate used to be one of yours, I believe. Lobo. For de-programming, they claim."

Kole tugged on the blade harness across his chest. "I heard. Didn't realize she was Lobo's. Bigoted ugliness is on the rise again even though laws preventing interbreed mating no longer exist."

"Yes." Laegon brushed a palm along Caleth's hip.

"Commander Jarek is negotiating with the

Isolationists," said Caleth.

Kole tightened his brows. Another problem to add to a mounting number of shit-shows.

Laegon and his mate dropped the topic. A smiling Caleth slipped her hand through the crook of Kole's arm to lead him toward the open bar. "It's time to sample our local wine."

"Just what I've been waiting to hear."

After nearly three hours of meeting ylves, making small talk, and drinking ylven wine, Kole approached the group gathered around Skyler. Apologizing, he led her aside.

"We're due at the Scion Firebrand stronghold in North Shelters before nightfall. It's time to leave." Since she'd snapped at him the last time, Kole hesitated before he charged ahead. "Tomorrow would be a good time to consider a clothing change and a different ceremony in Knife's Edge."

Skyler glared at him, her arms folded. "You spend an inordinate amount of time, Commander, worrying about where I want to go and how I dress. These are not your decisions. My clothing choices are always professional. As far as the ceremony in the demon region tomorrow, it remains my choice."

"Right, then. On to North Shelters where we'll spend the night. Your bag with inappropriate clothing is already there." Kole knew he was being petty, but *oh well*. He stomped ahead, letting Skyler say her farewells before she maneuvered alone down the path to the portal. Whenever he heard her mutter or stumble on the rocks, laughter rumbled from his chest.

Yeah. Petty. But rewarding.

By the time they trekked to the bottom, traveled through the portal, and had a meet with Nace, commander of the Northern Stronghold, Skyler nearly face-planted in her late-night dinner before tottering off to her quarters.

In his own room, Kole tapped his wrist to call Bounty. *She still insists on the demon Genesis Rite in Knife's Edge. I've tried to talk her out of it, but she won't even let me explain why. Hand goes up. Frown comes on. So, fuck it. Besides, if things get out of control, I'll deal. Tell them it's a go.*

Do you think the chief knows what it is?

Kole flopped onto the bed, stretching out his legs. *Damned if I know. I can't remember the last time a human visitor participated in the demon rite. Apparently, her father did. Which is why she's hellbent to keep it on her list.*

I would love to be in the audience. Damn. It would be so worth it. I don't suppose you'd take pictures.

Kole grunted, disconnecting. "Yeah. I can hardly wait," he muttered.

Chapter Seven

From her accommodations in the Northern Stronghold the next day, Skyler took a break after the early morning tour to join a video conference.

Technology expert Sarah Jenkins, Siri to her friends, led the session from a TelePresence room at the Alliance, complete with monitors, cameras, and speakers. State of the art. Cal, Anna, and Laurie sat on the same side of the table facing the camera and monitor while taking notes or doodling on their own tablets.

With her laptop in front of her, Sarah cleared her throat. "TheBigReveal sent a password—MonsterMash. So let's look at their e-lingo. Right now, they're protected, but heads up. If they remove the security, the whole world gets an eyeful."

She paused while everyone absorbed that tidbit. "On to the homepage. It's down-and-dirty but just wrong. The blinking arrow pointing to the image gives me a headache. By the way, do we know the two guys in the grainy photo outside our building?"

Skyler leaned against the headboard. "Yes. On the left is Alarik, the director of the Ministry of Well Being. He's with the vampire lawgiver, Viktor. They met with the board in Chicago a while ago."

"WikiLeaks would be proud. Let's see what we can see. The design and colors are outdated. And, OMG, the negative space is a time capsule transporting me back to the late 80s. The sidebar is pretty standard. When I click on *About*, we get their mission statement. To unwrap the truth—one secret at a time."

The tech expert rolled her eyes. "When I open

Contributors, we see M&M listed. The Managing Maniac."

Sarah rubbed the nape of her neck. "Below that name is DotNet. She's in charge of planning all upcoming events, having been a kickass wedding planner. The third contributor is Slash, a guy fresh from a stay at a local psych ward where nobody believed his stories about Aeternals. They also say he's willing to commit acts of atrocity to get their point across. Sounds to me as if he should still be riding the tractor at the funny farm."

The tech paused to take a sip of coffee. "They could be intentionally making us think they're noobs. Let's move on." She pointed out the top of the website. "Can I have a blogroll, please?" When nobody responded, Sarah shrugged. "Okay, then. When I click on *Blogs*, we find two. They could use some dancing baloney."

The room exchanged puzzled looks while Cal turned to Anna. "What?"

Sarah muttered, "Technotards." More loudly, she said, "You know. Artwork? The first blog is a lesson on the Blood Coven's creation of the realms. It could be from the pages of *The History of Scath* if the deadly dull tome had some spice. Peruse, guys."

In AD 452, thirteen powerful witches and warlocks, aka the Blood Coven, created three realms where before only Earth had existed. Homo sapiens, the heroes of our story, stayed here. Aeternals holed up on Scath. Darque was the prison for the awful, bad, scary creatures who look nothing like us—harpies, sand leeches, gagans, questing beasts, hellhounds, Spriggans, Yeti. You get the picture.

Who are Aeternals, you ask? They are who you might see on a Bella Lugosi or Lon Cheney movie set—

vampires, shapeshifters, mages, incubi and succubi, demons, nymphs, satyrs, Amazons. But they're real, and they look human when they keep their fangs in their mouths, their claws trimmed, and their powers corked in a djinn bottle.

Aeternals disappeared from Earth. Kinda. Some stayed behind, passing for human, living among us, breeding, creating generations of mixed offspring. Oh, and eating. Who's their favorite snack? We are. Better than chips and salsa.

And guess what? Even today, some sneak from their realm to ours to impregnate us or feed. You are skeptical? I would be, too. But I will offer proof in future blogs.

"Amateurs." Cal tugged on the knot in his tie. "They sound like baked college kids."

Skyler heard a tapping noise. Everyone around the table glanced toward Anna. She smiled sheepishly. "My foot has a case of the jitters. Sorry."

Sarah waited until the attention swung to her again. "The other blog goes into detail about our operation. It tells how there was no contact between the realms for centuries until a mage's spell made it possible for communication and travel. Later, after an Aeternal created GPS technology for travel through portals, hook ups between Earth and Scath became easier."

Laurie rubbed a finger across her lower lip. "Holy you-know-what. Everyone thinks the US Department of Defense invented GPS. Truth is, we leaked the knowledge, letting them take the credit."

Descendants of the semen-spreading, Earth-bound Aeternals eventually hooked up with Scath to form the Alliance, an organization designed to protect secrets. Oops. Gender bias alert. It could have been descendants of egg-incubating monsters.

"They also elaborate on the Alliance's cover, our private security operation." Skyler crossed one ankle over the other, adjusting her laptop while she maintained a quiet, expressionless voice, not at all how she was feeling.

"Look." Cal squirmed in his chair, staring at his screen. "They talk about the bludfrenzied vampire who escaped from Scath and killed the grandmother in San Francisco. There's another paragraph on the gang of young incubi who terrorized a college dormitory in upstate New York. How do they know this shit? Sorry, ladies. And the demon who stalked the movie star. Clean-up was a bitch after the incident. Sorry, again."

Sarah drummed two pencils on the table. Laurie cleared her throat to speak but then shook her head. Anna lifted coffee to her lips but decided to cradle it in her hands instead. Cal leaned into his chair, fingers laced behind his neck. Skyler knitted her brows together, gazing out the window at a pine-treed forest in North Shelters.

After reading silently for a few seconds, Sarah spoke. "They posted the origination history lesson about four weeks ago. The blog on the Alliance was two weeks afterward. Next, they promise to 'unbeast' demons."

She sipped her coffee, setting her cup back on the table quietly. "*Events* is interesting. Here, they claim their first planned activity was to kill Chief Legal Officer Skyler Maxwell. Since it didn't come off, Slash is looking forward to another go at her."

All four sets of brows in the room arched.

Answers my question. TheBigReveal and my accident are connected.

Skyler lifted her chin as she searched for the right words. It was time to confess. "I didn't slip or get dizzy and fall as I suggested. Someone pushed me the other day."

Everyone's mouth fell open while Skyler stuck to business. "If we're finished, I have a call to make. There's no doubt any longer. They do know our secrets. Contact me if they communicate again. Needless to say, Sarah, we must find out who this group is."

Skyler signed off and phoned the board president, sharing information on the murder attempt at the L station along with everything they knew of TheBigReveal.

Not too long after she disconnected, Cal called. "When you return, Skyler, I'm arranging for a security detail to stay on you."

"I agree. According to the board prez, Lead Agent Nico Abello, who recently relocated from Seattle, will handle the investigation. It's fortunate I'll be on Scath for the rest of the week. We all need to be careful, though, Cal. When you meet with this new guy, suggest bodyguards for other employees, not only me. Tell him to warn the Alliance offices in other cities as well. Give him everything." Skyler paused. "If this group goes public, the fallout will be disastrous. Especially if they present believable proof. But I don't understand. Why not unmask us now? Why show their hand first? And what could they gain from my death? What about the Aeternals who raided our office? Are they part of this mess?"

****

Kole breathed in the air, his lids half-masted, a smile tugging at his lips. The desert at late afternoon during early summer was hot, hostile, and covered with sparse ground-hugging plants struggling to survive. Here in the demon region of Lucifer's Forge in Knife's Edge, the wide red valley gave way to flat-topped hills which spread across the horizon.

When he glanced at his traveling companion, Skyler teetered backward, her heels sinking into the sand while a hand shielded her eyes from the merciless sun. The only sound was the wind spinning up dust devils in the distance.

"Follow me." Kole refused to offer an elbow for support as he tromped toward the Tribal Coliseum ahead of them. She wore ridiculous shoes. Let her deal with them. He was enough of a gentleman to tote her small piece of luggage and his even smaller duffle.

"Why don't we ever transport closer to where we're going?" Trudging forward, Skyler squinted in the bright light.

"To protect important facilities from invasion, gateways are set a distance away unless they can be secured." He glanced over his shoulder. *Yep*. She was struggling. He stifled a laugh.

Skyler pulled at the neck of her blouse while Kole eyed the dip between her breasts where moisture seeped through the fabric. She stared at him, seeming not to notice his leer. "Doesn't this bother you? You're fresh. Even dry."

"No. Used to it. I grew up thirty miles from here." He stopped to stare at the jutting rocks, switching both bags to one hand, the other cupped above his brows. "Sometimes, I miss the desert."

Skyler shrugged. "Well, it's damn hot."

"Come on." Kole strode toward a gigantic red adobe structure which blended into its environment, the front visible but the rest disappearing into a surrounding sandstone cliff.

While Skyler labored to walk in the soil, Kole smirked. "Good walking shoes."

"Can't you drop this subject?"

But when she stumbled, Kole, feeling sorry for

the stubborn female, grabbed an arm to steady her. Though she hadn't shared, something was weighing on her after the call to her office. He wasn't one to pry.

Skyler spit out a begrudging thanks, not shrugging off his effort.

"During the ceremony, my word is law. If I tell you the sky is green, you agree. Understood?"

"Are you joking?" Skyler sighed, righting herself after a backward tilt.

"Not if you value your life."

Reaching a twelve-foot-tall wooden door, they waited until it creaked open, revealing a huge shirtless demon. When the male spotted Kole, he glared through slitted eyes, his craggy face dominated by a bulbous boxer's nose which had been broken too many times. Or not often enough. Perspective.

Though shorter than Kole, the demon was broader. Runes as dark as the surrounding rocks decorated his arms, chest, torso. Kole knew that beneath his loose black pants, tied with a gold sash, more ancestral markings covered his legs.

"Uncle." Kole's greeting was brittle. "This is Chief Legal Officer Maxwell."

Skyler cast a surprised look at Kole, unaware of his relationship to Horach.

"Indeed. Welcome." He bowed, an unaccustomed smile twisting his lips, a hand reaching out for Skyler. "I am Horach of the Directorate of Seven."

"I am pleased to meet you." With a grace Kole admired, Skyler walked through the entrance to the coliseum, brushing dust from her skirt, her shoulders squared, her chin tilted high.

In the enormous entry, she inhaled the crisp air, a cool draft ruffling tendrils of her usually tame platinum-blonde hair. Kole thought he might like to see her even more disheveled.

Special to demons—a place of government, a ceremonial hall, and an events center—the coliseum must have awed Skyler. Her lips parted as she eyed the thirty-foot-high domed ceiling with stained glass, shimmering patterns of light bouncing on the walls.

When Kole dropped her luggage and his duffle on the floor, the thuds stole her attention. She turned her icy glare his way. Nothing new.

Skyler's heels clicked on large tiles of polished red stone as Horach guided them through three rooms adjoining the arena. He explained how each space honored a tribe's colors. She paused in the first hall, the walls decorated with green mosaics depicting a lush forest. The second room was as red as the surrounding rocks of Lucifer's Forge. The third was blue, the mosaic walls decked out like oceans, rivers, and lakes of the region.

In a rotunda the size of a pro basketball arena, varying shades of white tiles sheathed the walls and floor. A triple row of polished stone seats lined the immense space, each section a different color.

Horach led them toward six males and females, each wearing a cloth belt in their tribe's color—carnal, hedon, envy, pride, avarice, and sloth. "These are the other members of the Directorate."

They greeted Skyler with a dip of the head. Some nodded at Kole. Others ignored him. She cast an inquisitive look his way.

Kole, always prepared for the unexpected, sized up the males. Like him, they were muscular, a few herculean, making him seem small at six-foot-eight. The females were athletic and tall but no challenge.

Horach guided Skyler to a throne next to his. Dropping into his gold seat of honor, he directed Kole to the other side of the room.

"With all due respect, I remain with Chief Maxwell at all times." Kole moved to stand beside Skyler's chair. He didn't wait for his uncle's approval because he didn't give a shit whether he got it or not.

Before she challenged his decision, he lifted his brows in warning. She pressed her lips together. Tight.

Good girl.

"As you wish." Horach's disapproval was evident when uncontrolled sparks bounced on his fingertips. Like Kole, he was an animus demon who called fire.

Once Skyler settled into place, the remaining members of the Directorate did the same. A boring discussion of business interests—breweries, distilleries, wineries—followed. Skyler listened, asking questions at times. She chitchatted about a few contracts she could set up to support the rising construction industry in Knife's Edge, pleasing the leaders who were eager to bring more wealth into the region.

When the give-and-take ended, hundreds of demons poured through the doorways lining the great rotunda, the pounding of their boots deafening. Before Skyler could flinch, Kole rested a hand on her shoulder, letting his palm heat, sending reassurances through her. Her muscles relaxed so quickly, he doubted Horach or the others noticed her moment of nerves.

With the crowd settled along the edge of the chamber in sections by tribe, Horach rose, his bold stance as full of false pride as he was. "Today we welcome the Alliance's Chief Legal Officer Maxwell. She honors us with the request for the Genesis Rite. *Neka ceremon pocetak.*" He bent toward Skyler to whisper. "Let the ceremony begin." Horach raised his arm and chopped it downward.

Twenty bare-chested males entered the hall, boots

laced to their knees, pelts tied to their waists by colorful sashes indicating their tribes. Each strode in front of Skyler, banging his weapon on a shield or the floor while dipping a chin to honor her. With the greeting out of the way, they faced off in pairs.

Skyler turned a wide-eyed look toward Kole, understanding creeping into her baby blues but not showing in her expression.

Her courage under fire surprised Kole. Nothing seemed to rattle her. *On the outside.* But he was beginning to recognize the subtle signs of her caged emotions.

The battle began. An evenly matched pair, their shields raised, faced off in front of Skyler. The combatant wearing a red sash lunged, his short blade thrust forward. Though the male with an orange sash brushed the weapon aside with his shield, he was too late. His opponent had slashed his upper arm.

Injured, the hedon demon wearing his tribe's orange lost momentary control. His beast flickered, its larger body encasing him like a mirage, claws extending from fingers and fangs piercing gums. Then suddenly, he returned to normal. Skyler rubbed her eyelids.

Horach shouted to the combatants. "Warriors. We have a guest."

Kole leaned close to Skyler's ear. "He doesn't want the fighters to scare you. Our beasts can be … imposing to a human."

Skyler nodded, her cool gaze returning to the violence on the floor of the rotunda. Inhaling a deep breath, she maintained a passive expression.

Kole judged she wasn't about to show disbelief. As he had suspected, Skyler knew fuck-all about the Genesis Rite. She'd find out soon enough. He patted the blades in his holster, hoping he wouldn't need them.

Being the better fighter, the red-sashed carnal demon played with his opponent. He crouched low to slice his combatant's leg. Ducking left, he poked the tip of his knife into his opponent's chest. With a grim smile on his lips, he drove the blade deep.

Clutching his wound, the injured contestant howled, falling to the ground.

With a thumbs-up from Kole's uncle, the victor wiped his weapon on his pelt, casting his battle-heated eyes around until he found another victim.

Horach twisted in his throne toward Skyler. "Once was the day we fought to the death. Do not worry, though. Now, a healer will mend the fallen warrior."

Kole was certain his uncle would love to see bloodied dead bodies dragged from the hall rather than this newer, kinder approach.

"Hmm." Skyler nodded while she stared at the fighter writhing on the white tile floor. Deafening cheers, along with scattered boos, rolled through the audience like waves, the sounds bouncing off the walls, echoing throughout the chamber, ramping up the potential danger.

Another two adversaries faced off near Skyler, her gaze tracking their motions. A yellow-sashed avarice demon swung a flail in a circle above his head.

The other contestant gripped a battle axe, his shield high to block attacks. But when the deadly spiked balls on a chain whipped toward him, the blow to his shield sent him to his knees.

Before he could rise, the avarice demon kicked him to the floor, a foot on the fallen male's neck. Horach cast a thumb up, gesturing the end to their battle. The defeated warrior slunk from the rotunda while the superior fighter sought another opponent.

Kole eyed the two largest fighters in the arena, each topping his own six-foot-eight height. He recognized Dermott with the axe, warding off his opponent's blows with a metal shield. Runes covered nearly his entire body, a roadmap of his ancestry, while scars showed he was a seasoned warrior.

His opponent wielded a long blade in one hand, a shorter dagger in the other. No shield. Like all the breed, he bore heritage markings. A healed wound running from his forehead to his chin suggested he had seen battle.

"Ah." Horach touched his palm to Skyler's arm. "Dermott in the green sash is from the envy tribe. Azamat, who wears purple, is a pride demon. They are our best fighters, formidable soldiers during the Insurrection."

When he mentioned the war, he glared at Kole, who gave as good as he got, never blinking, never glancing away, showing no shame. It was the traitorous uncle who should hang his head.

The big mutherfuckers circled each other, ignoring the din arising from the crowd. Sweat rolled down their bodies as each waited for the other to make a move, to make a mistake.

Dermott crouched on massive legs, preparing to strike. Kole figured this male to win the tournament. Though he had a slight height and muscle advantage, it was his eyes that spoke of victory. They were cold, deadly, merciless.

Azamat charged, his long blade slicing into Dermott's flesh, but his short blade was deflected by the shield. He stepped back, bringing his weapons into position again.

Dermott snarled, swinging his axe overhead, chopping downward. When his opponent ducked to the side, his weapon missed by inches.

They danced around each other once more. Azamat lunged, thrusting his knife forward.

When he fell short of his target, Kole knew it was the mistake Dermott waited for. Taking advantage of Azamat being off balance, he swung his axe, burying it blade deep in the pride demon's chest, barely missing his heart.

Azamat pawed at the slippery handle, struggling to pull it out while blood flowed from the wound, puddling on the white floor. His legs folded.

Dermott fisted his weapon handle, ripping it from the male's flesh, resting a foot on his downed opponent until Horach thumb-upped him. He sought another combatant.

The defeated Azamat jerked, his breath a series of gurgles, his chest barely heaving.

When blood sullied much of the tiled floor, only one fighter remained—Dermott. He strode forward, stepping over the bodies of his fallen comrades.

Though most of the audience cheered his triumph, others booed, dissatisfied with the outcome. Skyler's shoulders stiffened, her back straight.

Kole sniffed the air, redolent with a coppery scent. The violence aroused the spectators, their demon beasts flickering, eager to be set free, to revel in the savagery, to dip their hands in blood. Even he had to inhale-exhale to cage his monster.

Skyler twisted around to glance at Kole, who waited for a crack to appear in her armor. It didn't. With the battle ceremony at an end, he squeezed her shoulder, trying to warn her to stay calm. She knit her eyebrows together while she searched his eyes. He shook his head, almost imperceptibly. She faced forward again, white-knuckling the arms of her chair.

Dermott took a slow, swaggering stroll around the arena to the cheers and catcalls from the crowd. He waved his axe high in the air, blood dripping down his arm while he absorbed the glory of his victory. When he approached the pride demon section, he paused, daring a challenge from one of Azamat's tribe. None came, though they hurled boos and insults. He lumbered on to stand in front of his fellow envy demons. They rushed from their seats to hoist him onto their shoulders, marching him once more through the rotunda.

Kole rubbed the back of his neck, clenching his jaw so tight, he felt bones shift. He spread his legs apart, his biceps flinching as he prepared for trouble.

Horach tapped Skyler's arm, smiling with obvious pleasure at the bloody event. "Forgive our display of bravado, Chief Maxwell. It has been so long since we practiced this ritual. You have given us a glimpse into our heritage. We are heady with it." A hearty laugh arose from his barrel chest.

The envy demons set Dermott on his feet when they reached Skyler. He passed off his shield, pounding a fist against his blood-splattered chest. "My services are yours, Chief Maxwell." He glanced around, bouncing his axe in the air, getting new cheers from the crowd.

Horach unfolded from his stone-carved seat, his hand held high. "A worthy victor awaits you. We have readied the Genesis Chamber with a hot bath, luxury oils, food, and drink. Dermott will feed you there. He is yours until daybreak or until he satisfies your hunger."

When he addressed Kole, his voice was cold. "You may collect Chief Maxwell in the morning. We have prepared quarters for you in another wing."

Chapter Eight

Celene was on a tirade, having summoned the guard again today. As usual, he stared at her with dead eyes.

"Suit yourself, asshat. We're implementing our plan. Let this be your notice. The humans are on strike." To make her point, she stomped to the refrigerator, flung open the door, and started tossing food onto the floor. A tub of butter. A bowl of leftovers.

Jace, who had been leaning against the wall, observing, hurried to the cabinets where she launched plates, saucers, and canned goods.

A slow smile traveled across the guard's face. "I'll force feed you myself, bitches."

"Good luck with that. I bet you can't cram enough into us to keep us healthy. I'm also guessing your boss won't be happy. Someone seems to want us alive." Celene poured milk onto the floor, where it spread out in a slippery sheet of white.

Jace whipped her strawberry-blonde hair around, grabbed a plate, and lobbed it at the guard's head, forcing him to duck. She smiled when he growled.

The asshat crossed the room, snatching Celene by the back of her neck. He forced her to her knees, soaking her pants in milk. "Now lick up this shit."

"Make me, dickhead." She winced when he squeezed hard, but she made no attempt to kowtow to his order.

He pushed her face into the spilled liquid.

Jace attacked from behind with a forceful kick between his legs.

He dropped his grip on Celene, doubling over. "Bitch." As he stumbled toward her roommate, another guard entered the room.

He stared at the mess. "Stop, Bayd. We aren't authorized to harm them. What caused all this?"

Bayd held his crotch while he glared at Jace. "They want to meet Lort."

"We have to contact the general with their request. Let him decide."

Celene grinned as the guard continued to rub his injured joystick. "I bet that's the most action your dick's had in a long while."

Bayd snarled, the other guy bodychecking him. "Soon, bitches, my time with you will come."

When the asshats left, the two women looked at the disaster in the kitchen and then at each other. Celene started giggling. She couldn't stop. Her hand flew to her mouth, but sounds kept pouring out.

Jace, infected with her roommate's laughter, slumped to the floor, tears rolling down her cheek, her palm clasped to her belly. "We don't know why we're here, where we are, or who's keeping us. They could kill us today, tomorrow, or twenty years from now. I'm going to starve myself while I sit right here." She stretched out her legs and leaned against the wall.

Celene laughed harder, sinking alongside her fellow prisoner. When their giggling fit ended, she turned serious. "Let's hope our hunger strike brings the big boss for a visit. Maybe he'll have some answers."

"Not knowing is the worst."

"In the meantime, if we get an opportunity to overpower them or escape, we do it. Before we collapse."

Jace snorted. "Like that's going to happen. Look at our jailers. Each guy's bigger than the other. We know they aren't human. Hah! There's a phrase I never thought I'd use. The doors are locked. They hear everything we say, and our attempts to escape so far have failed."

Celene took Jace's hand. "I sure wish we had started this hunger strike thing after dinner. I'm starved."

"Me, too. But it beats doing nothing."

"Get *The Path* down. It'll cheer us up."

Jace pushed off the floor and snatched the story about Aeternals from the bookshelf. She lounged on the sofa while Celene, on her feet now, paced the room.

"Here we go." Jace flipped through the pages until she found the right spot.

Home to gods, goddesses, and the OneCreator, the Vast is a buffer between Angor and the Evermore. Though it is a place of eternal sunlight and warmth, it is not without problems.

To manage those problems, the OneCreator had his winged assassins, the Feard. They chased down unredeemed, unrepentant immortals who had defied the laws. They locked the perpetrators forever in Angor or delivered true death. Only they, Michael, or the big man himself could smite everlasting beings, ending their existence for all time.

Ohngel, one of the OneCreator's Feard, hovered above his current assignment.

He watched as Basil zigzagged across the skies, his flying erratic, his feathers mottled with the blood of his victims. The boss himself had summoned Ohngel, handing him a containment order, a pleasing assignment because capture required more skill than a straight out kill. It promised a prolonged battle and his prey's ensuing, infinite pain.

Ohngel almost felt pity for the guy. Not enough to give him a break because, after all, justice unserved was chaos. Besides, today Ohngel had a need to punish. Rage blasted in flames off his wings. It wanted an outlet. Basil, who had nothing to do with the problem facing Ohngel, would be the outlet. Lucky him.

The fire-winged assassin's complication was the betrayer in the Blood Coven. The Cambion, as ordered, had instructed his witches and warlocks to remain on Earth with their offspring. Niviane had not complied. New stratagems were required to offset her perfidy.

But now, Ohngel had his pressing assignment. Though unrelated to the cause of his rage, the chase and capture might assuage his anger.

He flew with effortless grace to follow Basil, who had become entangled in an ageless tale. He loved Elise, but she had broken faith with him, heaping her favors upon another. In his fury, the cuckolded lover had cut a bloody path through the Vast, taking down those who got in his way. Assholes and innocents. The young and the mature. Males and females. Though his victims would not die, they would require much time to heal, and their pain would be excruciating. So, the containment order went out, accepted by the nearest of the Feard, Ohngel.

Spotting the OneCreator's warrior, Basil paused in flight, his wings marking time until, in a second of frightful clarity, he took off—trying to put distance between himself and certain seizure.

"Idiot," muttered Ohngel, his feathers of red, gold, blue, and crimson blazing outward from his spine. Now was the moment he relished, when his fiery, razored wings whipped forward, jetting him toward his prey and battle.

Basil, turning to defend himself, his options for escape nil, lashed out. His wings were also weapons, overlapping knives which he wielded with some skill. But he lacked precision. He lacked the killer instinct. His broad downward strokes left his underbelly open to attack.

Ohngel took advantage. Holstering his dagger, he used his blazing feathers as laser swords, lunging, thrusting, slicing, whipping one out and then the other. His motions were so quick they blurred. With a forward drive, he stabbed into his opponent's abdomen with the tips of his hot blades.

His eyes wide with horror, Basil glanced at his bloody injury, crying out from the pain.

Before his opponent recovered, Ohngel lobbed off his left arm. It was only sporting to leave him an uninjured limb with a blade in hand.

Basil took off in a burst of speed, blood spurting from the open wound below his shoulder.

"Why do they always think they can outfly me?" Ohngel tucked his head to follow, leaving a fiery trail across the sky. When he caught up, he maneuvered a forward overhead roll to block Basil's path.

Basil pulled up hard. His brows squeezed tight together and his eyes glassed over when he saw Ohngel's wings curl forward, the searing blue tips ready to strike once more. He realized he would not escape. But he refused to surrender. He fought until his blade arm grew weary and his knifed feathers drooped.

Ohngel, on the other hand, had almost limitless stamina. With ease, he avoided the cutting edges of his tired opponent's wings, countering the attacks with slice after shallow slice, humiliating and further exhausting his opponent. Growing bored with the pursuit, Ohngel lobbed off Basil's left wing.

Rolling head over heels despite a frantic beating of his uninjured wing, Basil plunged toward the earth, his flight ugly, barely adequate to keep him aloft.

Ohngel rushed to follow his prey. "Surrender now. If I sever the other, you will suffer pain unlike any *other when your wingless body meets the ground."*

"Fuck off, assassin."

"I intend to. After I take you to Angor." With Basil's flight like a wounded, wobbling bird, Ohngel caught up and cut off his opponent's other wing. Whipping out a net from a pouch at his hip, he ensnared his prey. "You'll hate me in the morning, but trust me, this makes you easier to carry."

Ohngel streaked across the sky with his bound package, slowing only when he approached Angor. After depositing Basil in a facility where he would receive a modicum of care for his wounds before an eternity of pain, Ohngel flew home.

Though an oddity, the winged hunters of the OneCreator chose to live in Angor among those they had imprisoned rather than with their own kind in the Vast. Here in these territories, they thrived in the unpredictable environment. One moment sun, soft breezes. The next stormy skies and intermittent light, a place cold, icy, stark, and often as cruel as those it contained. But it was always honest, always just.

Once in the familiarity of his abode with a cup of mead in hand, Ohngel lounged on pillows, music playing to muffle the tormented cries from the tortured in Angor.

He crossed an ankle over the other as he devised new strategies. Ones to negate Niviane's betrayal.

When Jace closed the book, Celene was snuggled into the couch, her feet propped on the coffee table, milk still soaking her knees. "Very uncheerful. You want to flip for who cleans the kitchen?"

****

Skyler inched to the edge of the carved chair. She was missing something. "Thank you, Horach, but I can feed myself." Her gaze shot back and forth between the commander and his uncle. When her attention settled on

Kole, his hands moved to the hilt of a knife in the sheath across his chest.

"You choose to feed yourself when such a worthy victor will provide the service? I don't understand?" Apparently, her behavior was puzzling, if Horach's tugged down brows were an indication.

Skyler twisted toward the commander, her lips barely moving, her voice for his ears only. "What's going on?"

Kole leaned close, maintaining a grim expression, shaking his head to signal he would speak.

"Chief Legal Officer Maxwell appreciates Dermott's offer. Though she was thrilled to watch the Genesis Rite, her role was ceremonial. Since I am her guide for three days, I feed her. Earthling females generally accept only one male at a time. Since I'm her escort, I'm convenient."

"Bullshit." Dermott pushed against Horach's back.

Kole's uncle pivoted around, shoving chest to chest against the angry envy demon.

When Dermott continued to power forward, Kole snarled, his voice threatening, gravelly. "This female will not be yours tonight."

Over Horach's shoulder, Dermott raised his bloody axe in challenge. "I have rights as victor."

Kole withdrew a blade, moving to block Skyler from view with his massive body. He spread his thighs, distributing his weight equally. "Come any closer, demon, I'll cut off your balls and stuff them up your ass."

Skyler rose from her chair, tilting far to the side to see around the commander. Whatever the problem, and she was developing a guess, the argument was accelerating, about to go explosive.

The large crowd who stayed to watch shouted in

support of Dermott.

"Quiet!" Horach yelled out the command as he squared off in front of the envy demon. "Don't be an idiot. My nephew will kill you. The female will settle the matter."

Skyler rested a palm on Kole's shoulder, peeking around him.

Dermott inhaled, puffing out his chest but lowering the axe. "Of course. It is her choice. The traitor or me."

Kole sheathed his blade, turned, and offered Skyler his hand. When she placed her pale, trembling fingers in his palm, he drew her close to his body. She raised her chin to stare into his fire-gold eyes.

Kole bent toward her, his lips drawing nearer. When his mouth brushed hers, rather than push him away, she opened to him. Kole's lips pressed hard against hers, his tongue thrusting inside, his exploration wild, hungry.

Skyler gasped, shocked by either the kiss or her response. Her knees weakened, her hands resting on Kole's warm chest for support. Short bursts of electricity flowed into her, eliciting soft moans as he pulled her tighter against him, his arousal a hard prod at her belly.

When he withdrew, he met her gaze with confusion. He cleared his throat. "Choose, Chief Maxwell. Dermott or me?"

Skyler touched fingers to her lips before she shook her head to clear it. "You." Though still not understanding why she had to pick, she had an inkling. And she didn't like it.

"Done. She's mine for the night." Kole's voice was gruff, thick.

Horach's lips turned down, his words belying his expression. "I understand. I was unaware human females preferred only one male at a time. Forgive my ignorance, Chief Maxwell. The matter is settled. Is it not, Dermott?"

He nodded but didn't look happy.

"The chamber is ready for both of you." Horach introduced a guide who would take them to the room. He dismissed the crowd, some booing in disapproval of Skyler's rejection of the Genesis Rite victor.

In silence, she followed Kole, still dealing with the purpose of the ceremony. And the commander's brief but passionate kiss. She tugged on his elbow, whispering. "Am I correct in assuming Dermott offered to be my lover?"

Kole's brows drew tight. "Lover? No. All-night fuck? Yes."

"Now Horach thinks you and I are...?" Skyler gripped his arm, her fingers digging into flesh.

"Yep."

"We are sharing a room?"

"Yep."

"Unacceptable." The guide glanced over his shoulder when her voice grew above a whisper.

Kole stopped. "You've changed your mind? You want Dermott instead?"

"That is not what I mean. I don't want either of you that way."

He touched his lips to her ear. "Him or me, sweetheart? You picked me. Now let's hold off on this convo until we get to the room."

Skyler nodded. The guide ushered them into a spartan chamber where food and drink had been laid out on a round table. He backed out, closing the door.

"Why didn't you tell me about the ceremony?" Skyler hissed.

"I tried."

"Not hard enough."

Kole shrugged his massive shoulders. "Most likely."

Skyler pointed at a gigantic bed. "Mine. You can sleep in the bathroom."

"I'm bigger. I can sleep wherever I want." Kole whipped off his harness, weapons and all, tossing it on a bedside table.

Skyler sighed, flopping onto the couch, kicking off her heels. "This is the ceremony my father attended? I thought… I thought… I don't understand."

"Figured as much. The Genesis Rite is about creating life. The victor feeds the guest. You know what feeding is to a demon, right?"

"Yes. No. Not really." Skyler slumped further into the cushions.

"For an Alliance bigwig, you are unenlightened. Do you know anything about Aeternals?"

She stiffened at the insult, even though it was deserved. "I handle contracts and deals. I meet with representatives from Scath who come to my office in business suits. I admit I have not studied my clients' culture. What does 'feeding' mean?"

"It means fucking. All night if you're starved. Sex not only controls our aggression or stabilizes our moods, but it's also our food. At least, orgasm is. Without it, we'd be six feet under. Hence, feeding. Dermott's offer was an honor."

"How often do you need sex? No. Don't answer. I was unaware of the purpose of the Genesis Rite. I'll explain everything to Horach."

Kole shoved her back onto the couch. "No, you won't. He'll wonder why you're ignorant of demon rites. He'll question your competence along with your lack of a healthy sexual appetite."

She didn't lack a healthy sexual appetite. The

irritating demon in front of her was living proof. "But my father … He…"

"Fucked a demon?"

"Yes. Must you be so crass and brutish?" She smoothed a hand across her hair.

"How else can I describe it? What would you say?"

"Um … made love, I guess."

Kole laughed, a deep, unreserved sound rolling from his chest while he dropped onto the bed. "Oh, sweetheart. I doubt Daddy romanced the victor after she, or he, battled other demons to win the right to feed the guy for a night. Trust me. He accepted the offer, but love had nothing to do with it."

"Whatever." Skyler waved off any further discussion of her father, the Genesis Rite victor, or which gender he had bedded. "Now what do we do?"

"We bathe, eat, drink, sleep and in the morning we leave."

"There will be no sex. Do you understand?"

"Believe me when I tell you I like my females less icy." Flames sparked from Kole's fingertips.

"Watch the bed. You'll set it on fire. You didn't seem to mind when you kissed me."

"It was part of the act. But I think you enjoyed it." His lips curled into a lopsided, sexy grin.

She felt her cheeks warm. "I was acting, too."

"Hmm. We should both be on stage."

Skyler rose from the couch, slipping off her suit jacket, folding it, laying it on the arm. "I'm showering and changing. Stay out here."

"Yes, Chief Maxwell. I'll be diddling my dick, wondering what I did to deserve you."

She glared at Kole while she picked up her small overnighter. As an afterthought, she clicked the lock in the bathroom, imagining the commander on the other side of the door, smirking.

Infuriating, crass man. But really good kisser.

She tapped her lips. *Forget it.* When Skyler dragged her fingers through the water in the tub, she oohed. *Perfect.* On the side were several bottles. She uncorked one. *Hmm. Lilac.* The whiff aroused her, her breasts heavy, her heart thumping against her ribs. She poured it into the bath.

A single kiss from Kole and I'm a horny schoolgirl.

Skyler soaked longer than planned. Once out, she brushed her teeth and let down her hair, brushing it until it was glossy. Slipping into a black silk negligee, she stared in the mirror. Since the gown was more see-through than she wanted, she carried a towel in front of her to hide the outlines of her body.

Kole sprawled on the bed, fingers laced behind his neck. When Skyler entered the room, he sniffed the air and dropped his legs over the side of the mattress.

She hoped her eyes smoldered as hot as her body, beckoning the commander to take her in his arms.

In one long stride, he reached her, yanking her to him and tucking her tight against his erection. He brought his face close until his lips met hers. He traced the fullness of her mouth with his tongue. This time, his kiss was demanding, even angry. With a jab, he was inside, delving, exploring, tangling with her, sucking.

Skyler offered no resistance, opening to receive him. Moaning, she let the towel slip from her fingers as she rubbed against the bulge in Kole's pants.

While he continued to devour her, his hand drew up the fabric of her gown. Reaching her bare flesh, he stroked and kneaded. Cradling her buttocks in his palm, he lifted her until her core met his erection. His hips surged forward.

Groaning with pleasure, Skyler wrapped her legs around the demon, her frantic hands gripping his shoulders, sliding down his arms. His skin was hot, his muscles rippling beneath her touch. She couldn't get enough of him.

Suddenly, he pulled away, letting the hem of her gown fall as he slid her to her feet. "Damn, female. Are you crazy? You used one of the oils."

"What? I put some in my bath water."

"They're an aphrodisiac."

"Hell." Skyler's head was fuzzy while she concentrated on his words, trying to understand.

Without the towel in front of her, Kole eyed the body beneath her thin garment. His chest bounced in and out, his breath ragged. He stepped further away. "Exactly."

"Why didn't you warn me?"

"I didn't think you were having a spa day in there. Don't you know anything about us or our habits?"

"No. I don't. Haven't I proved that?" She advanced toward Kole.

His hand shot out. "Stay away from me."

She stilled, retreated, closed her lids tight. *Oil?* At least there was a reason Kole stirred intense feelings in her. She eased her hands over her gown as if she would straighten out her emotions, too.

Kole rushed to turn the thermostat fan to the "on" position before he threw open a window, despite the heat outside. "Stop touching yourself. It excites me." He gulped in fresh air. "Damn. Get rid of the smell."

Skyler paced the room, rubbing a hand across her forehead. "This is awful. I'll bathe again." She darted into the bathroom.

When she came out, he was still taking deep

breaths of desert air.

"Is this better?" She had soaked again and changed into pajamas.

Kole faced her, sniffing. "Better, but we'll leave this open."

Skyler glanced at the table set with covered dishes and bottles of wine. "I'm going to eat. Anything I should avoid?"

"How can you think about food?"

"I eat when I'm nervous."

"No. It's just food." Kole stormed into the bathroom, not shutting the door. He stripped his shirt over his head before he stepped out of his pants.

Skyler paused, a silver *cloche* in her hand, to stare at his muscular thighs, tight buttocks, tapered waist, broad shoulders. He was magnificent, beautifully proportioned, a gladiator.

Not my type at all.

He turned.

When he did, Skyler's gaze dropped to his groin where his thick, long cock jutted out. Was he always erect? Heat shot through her as she remembered his hard length rubbing against her. When she grew wet between her legs, it took all her strength not to throw herself at his feet. Or his penis.

Hell. The oil is still affecting me.

Silhouetted against the light, Kole tilted his head to the side, locking onto her in defiance, his eyes lit with fire. When he touched his fingertips together, sparks jumped from digit to digit.

Embarrassed, Skyler spun around. Kole slammed the door, chuckling.

Damn demon. Sexy, barbaric, hot demon.

Chapter Nine

Chowing down while he guzzled wine, Kole sat on the floor across from Skyler.

She broke the silence. "I felt tension between you and your uncle. In fact, quite a few demons seemed angry at your presence. Why?"

"It's a long story."

"We have all night."

Kole considered not sharing the painful history with Skyler, but what the hell. "The Demon Insurrection was a war between my breed and Scath's government. A few, my parents among them, remained loyal Firebrands. Because they believed the rebels were wrong, they fought against their own, bringing them to justice. An unforgiving lot, many demons blame me because I'm their son. You know, the old sins-of-the-father crap."

"When was this war?"

"About four hundred years ago."

"It's a long time to hold a grudge." Skyler took a bite of chicken, washing it down with a sip of wine, her slender, pale throat bobbling with each swallow.

Kole wanted to kiss it, figuring the oil was still messing with his mind. And dick. He reminded himself she was off limits for many reasons. A fiancé. Human. CLO of the Alliance. A stick up her frigid ass. Unlikable. "My breed has long memories and does not forgive."

"What caused the war?" Skyler eyed a piece of apple pie.

"Demons wanted to form an independent country, unfettered by Scath's laws. They saw themselves as freedom fighters. My parents saw them as traitors. It was your Civil War. Only longer. Bloodier."

Skyler rested her fork across her plate and dabbed her mouth with a napkin. She rose from the floor, yawning, stretching, generally avoiding Kole. "I'm exhausted. I think I'll head off to bed. We'll put all of this behind us and move forward. As if none of it happened. Agreed?"

Icy words froze on her lips. *Sad.* For a moment earlier, Kole had felt their warmth. Likely because of the oil. Of course, her response to his kiss in the arena had been unexpected. *No.* The female was cold, haughty, off the menu.

"Sure." He had to feed tonight. His fist wouldn't do the job. A self-applied hand was satisfying for a bit. Eventually, a male demon needed more than an orgasm. He needed to shoot swimmers. That happened for Kole only with a female. Could be different for others which was okay by him. If he didn't satisfy his hunger soon, he feared he'd toss Skyler onto the bed, part her thighs, and fill her with his seed. He'd regret it. But the deed would be done.

With the corner of the coverlet in her hand, she spun toward Kole, her shoulders steeled. "I will listen more closely to your warnings in the future. I am sorry I prepared for this trip so poorly."

Kole read her eyes. Apologies were difficult for her. "I'm going for a run."

Yep. I need relief before I do something stupid. If the beast takes over, he thinks with the wrong head.

He stomped from the room, rushing from the Tribal Coliseum into the desert where he lifted his gaze toward the stars. Comfortable to be home, he smiled, breathing the night air. His chest expanded as he inhaled the scents of his childhood, some sweet, some bitter like his memories. Then, sadness crossed his face as a cloud passed in front of the moon.

Kole jogged a good five miles before he came to a familiar house. When he knocked on the door, a companion he had once bedded opened it. Her waist-length black hair was slung over her shoulder, resting on one breast, and her dark eyes sparkled when she recognized him.

No blue-eyed blondes here. No icy females. No humans.

"I need to feed." He was matter-of-fact.

"I'm glad you chose me." While she took Kole's hand to lead him into the bedroom, her musical voice stroked his ache and his conscience.

He stayed most of the night, returning to his and Skyler's shared chamber just before the sun creeped over the horizon.

****

The next morning, Skyler was pleased Kole kept his word. No mention of the Genesis Rite, her ignorance of Scath's culture, or the kisses. They dressed, ate a late breakfast, and took a portal to the Scion Firebrand Southern Stronghold.

Waiting for them was a savage-looking, square-jawed man with long dark hair, a braid hanging at each temple. Slabs of muscle showed beneath his open, sleeveless leather vest while soft flowing black pants were tucked into his scuffed boots. Pale glyphs covered his skin, only slightly darker than the desert sand hue of his complexion. His colorful Phoenix brand stood out on his arm. Unknowingly, Skyler leaned into the safety of Kole's body.

Spotting the commander, the fearsome warrior's eyes morphed from a squint to crinkled amusement. "*Freron.*" He and Kole greeted each other, fist clasped to elbow. "I have not seen you since we shared drinks after

I saved your ass."

"We had already wiped out the berserkers. You showed for the glory and photo op." Kole laughed as he pressed a hand to Skyler's shoulder. "May I introduce Chief Legal Officer Maxwell? Chief, this is Jarek, commander of this stronghold and one tough sonofabitch."

Jarek bowed, his build like Kole's. Tall, muscular. It was a toss-up for who looked more brutal. "It is my pleasure to meet you. The berserkers in my region say their lumber industry is booming because of you. The Amazons are buying health clubs across Earth at your recommendation. They all sing your praises. I thought the Phoenicians were clever making trade agreements. It would seem their blood runs through your veins. Come greet my warriors."

Jarek placed a war-hardened palm on Skyler's lower back to guide her from the stronghold's portal toward the center field of what appeared to be a tented encampment surrounded by high walls.

"Thank you, Commander." As they walked, Skyler glanced from Kole to Jarek, feeling small between the two gigantic males.

A line of rag-tag men and women gathered in the sun, weapons and shields at the ready. When Jarek approached, they drew straighter. Some donned animal pelts and fur boots. Some wrapped desert scarves around their faces, and others were bare headed with long hair worn loose, pulled back, or braided. They seemed war-tested, their bodies littered with scars or tattoos, making them look like murderers, thugs, savages. Their feral eyes sent a chill to Skyler's heart.

"My Firebrands are not as slick as Kole's or Nace's," explained Jarek, "but they are no less honorable. Just less stylish." Despite being grim, a few in the line stifled laughter. He pointed at a male. "This is my right hand, Darius, a warrior to have at your six. Step forward."

A man with coarse features dipped his chin at Skyler. He was made fiercer by a snake tat which disguised a scar winding from his left brow to his jawbone and down his neck.

Jarek slapped his shoulder. "A berserker nearly cut off his head a century ago. He was way too pretty then. Now, the rest of us stand a chance with the females."

Darius's lips curled into a grin, in no way diminishing his feral visage. "Still, my bed is never empty."

Skyler strolled with Jarek along the line of men and women, greeting each while Kole followed. Once she had chatted with the Firebrands, asking polite questions, Jarek escorted his visitors to a centrally located tent. Surprisingly, not a cloth structure, she discovered. It was solid metal made to resemble fabric.

Inside, the huge yurt-like abode was welcoming, its polished wood floor raised and decorated with colorful scattered Persian rugs.

While Kole and Skyler shared a large brown sofa, sinking into its thick leather cushions, Jarek extracted a bottle from a liquor cabinet. He poured a whitish fluid into three tumblers, adding water to each before he offered the drinks to his guests. "It is arak, a Levantine spirit I treasure. A little like anise." He raised his glass. "Salamati." He tossed down the contents.

Skyler and Kole followed suit.

When she coughed, tears welling in her eyes, Kole patted her back. "Good. Huh?"

"It's quite strong. Thank you, Commander Jarek, but I'm a lightweight when it comes to alcohol."

"I am pleased to say I handle it well. Do you have questions for me, Chief Maxwell?" He sprawled in a fabric-covered chair, a long leg thrown over the arm.

"Skyler, please. And yes. The djinn fascinate me. I love ancient history. If I had not followed in my father's footsteps to become a lawyer, I would be a stuffy college professor, wearing a plaid wool suit, glasses, and comfortable shoes."

Kole snorted.

She scooted to the edge of the sofa. "Is it true the Ten Thousand Immortals of Persia's past were djinn warriors?"

"Yes. Herodotus called us by the catchy name, but we have fought under many monikers."

Skyler waved off the offer of a second drink while Kole accepted. "Were you with Darius I?"

He chuckled, his braids slapping against his jaw. "You are familiar with your djinn history."

When Kole snorted again, Skyler squinted at him. "Their breed is interesting."

"Unlike demons," he mumbled.

Jarek continued as if he hadn't caught the exchange. "No. I'm somewhat younger. My first adventure was with Abbas I of Persia in 1605. I was seventeen. Though before my Awakening, I was big, fast, and good with a sword despite my youth." Something like sadness clouded his eyes. He pointed to the skin above his heart. "I earned this glyph. Djinn get tats for wars they fight."

From what she could see, Jarek must be a prolific warrior.

"Yes. And there is no shortage of armed conflict in any realm. But now, I'm a Firebrand, a drinker, a lover, a commander."

"I hope this question isn't inappropriate. I've

been told I am ignorant of Aeternal culture. What skills do djinn possess?"

He smiled, pouring another glass of arak for Kole and himself. With the bottle still gripped in his fist, Jarek waved his free hand, disappearing in a smoky cloud which swirled around him. When it dissipated, he materialized. "A trick of my breed. Handy when fighting. Or spying."

"Fascinating." A stunned Skyler held a palm over her glass. "No more. Thanks. May I use your phone, Commander? I promised to contact my office." Cell service between realms was iffy at best.

"Of course. This way." Jarek led Skyler to another room.

Her gaze traveled around his sumptuous library, warmed by brightly colored rugs, gigantic maps on the walls, and a well-used, polished desk. "You must be a history buff yourself, Commander."

"I confess. I'm enthralled with ancient events." He left, pointing toward the phone.

Skyler approached a floor-to-ceiling case filled with antique leather-bound books, drawing a finger across the spines, lingering on familiar titles. She pulled out a faded copy of *The Histories* by Herodotus, returned it, and continued to tap the back strips of various volumes until she came to *Meditations* by Marcus Aurelius. Beautifully wrapped in an aging red binding, the book was as elegant as the philosopher-emperor's words. She drew her nose closer, inhaling, enjoying the smell of aged knowledge. Skyler turned from Jarek's exquisite library with a sigh.

Her gaze caught a chair, the seat sagging from frequent use. Beside it was a table where a collection of poems by Rumi lay. The tattered cover had been opened many times.

She walked to the desk to pick up the phone. A less-than-chipper Anna filled Skyler in on the status of pending agreements, office business, and the investigation into TheBigReveal before she closed with, "Cal needs to tell you something. Hold on while I transfer you."

"How's it going, Skyler?" her assistant asked, clearing his throat.

"Good." She paused. "Scath is different from what I expected."

"I have bad news."

****

Returning to Jarek's desk after a full-day tour of the regions near the Southern Stronghold, Skyler logged onto her laptop. She opened the *Chicago Tribune,* scanning it for the news Cal had relayed to her this morning.

Sarah Jenkins was dead, murdered in her home late last night, seemingly a random robbery gone wrong. When the police arrived early to interview people at the Alliance, her office had assisted them, appearing most cooperative. After all, the organization knew how to handle outsiders. It had developed ways over the years to protect itself from snooping eyes. The officers would have seen only what it wanted them to see.

Skyler found the article.

Sarah Jenkins, head of the Information Services Division at the Alliance Security Agency, was shot in her home last night. Unable to recover from the critical wounds, she died later at Chicago General.

According to sources in the Chicago PD, an intruder broke into Jenkins's house. At the present time, the suspected motive is robbery. Though the home was ransacked, police have not determined yet whether any items are missing.

An official with the Alliance stated Jenkins was an excellent employee with a bright future. Joining the firm only five years ago, she advanced quickly to lead the technology division. Nothing, they said, about her tasks would indicate she was in any danger.

Services are being arranged by Carter Funeral Home.

Once she had read the *Trib's* story, Skyler closed her computer, sitting still with her hands in her lap.

****

Several hours before dawn, Kole woke Skyler and led her from the Southern Stronghold through a portal to the vampire region of Bludhaven. Fire shot from his fingers, a torch to light their way along a path toward the grand stairway to the Strigodierna Shrine.

"A handy skill." Skyler cast wide eyes at Kole.

"I have many."

"I'm sure. Is there anything I need to be aware of in the ceremony? I don't wish to be surprised."

"Nope."

"Will there be fighting?"

"Nope."

"Sex?"

"No. But thanks."

Her brow furrowed. "You know what I mean."

"No sex, unless you find a strapping young male vampire you want to bed." Kole tipped one side of his mouth into a grin. Feeling a bit snarly this morning, he wanted to ruffle Skyler's perfect do.

"I have no intention of having sex with a male vampire."

Her icy blue eyes nearly froze his nads. "If you aren't attracted to males, we'll look for a hot female vamp."

"No. I don't want any vampire."

"I see. Bloodsuckers don't do it for you. Only demons?" Kole pressed on, trying to knock her off her emotional balance beam. Skyler had frost in her veins. Unless angered. He liked her warm.

"What? Don't be ridiculous. I am not having sex with a demon, either."

"You could fool me. Yesterday, males battled each other for the chance to feed you. Later, you drowned yourself in erotic oil to lure me into your bed. I'd say you have a thing for my breed." Kole eyed her, fire dancing in his eyes.

At the foot of the stairs to the shrine, Skyler's hands flew to her hips. "I didn't understand the purpose of the Genesis Rite. I admit I made a mistake. And about our kiss…"

"Kisses."

"…last kiss, you said it was the effect of the oil I used. Accidentally! I didn't know about erotic oils. There. I say again, I am woefully ignorant of Scath's customs. I'm a fast learner, though, and I'm trying. You agreed to be a gentleman and not bring up the matter again."

"Hmm. Doesn't sound like me." Her hackles were up, the ice melting.

"Stop trying to irritate me. You understand what I mean. Is there anything, Commander, I will be unable or unwilling to fulfill at the Strigodierna Ceremony?"

"Like being fu … uh … fed by a demon?"

A weighty sigh escaped Skyler's lips. "Exactly."

Kole shrugged. "Doubt it. The spiritual gig honors Gahya. Can you handle drinking blood?" Kole offered an elbow, which she grabbed onto as they climbed the steps to the black marble shrine adorned with pinnacles, flying buttresses, and pointed arches.

"Just a sip. Yes." Skyler's chin jutted out, the

cool mask slipping over her face.

Kole bristled when she got all chilly. Only one thing to do. He re-stirred her emotional pot. "No hurling. It wouldn't look good for your rep as a stone-cold lawyer." He taunted her with a grin. "If you do upchuck, don't hit my boots. These are my favorite pair."

"I said I can handle it. Let it alone."

Yay. Mask off again.

"Okay, Chief. Blood it is." They climbed in silence.

Skyler paused for a moment, staring ahead at the remaining steps. "Who is Gahya?"

"The immortal who created Aeternals. She's known as the Genitrix. Vamps are very spiritual, most still believing she watches over us. The rest of us pretty much know she's missing in action. Gahya's an underling of the OneCreator."

"Who?"

"The big boss of Angor, the Vast, and the Evermore."

"What are those places?"

"When honorable Aeternals croak, they go to the Evermore. The not-so-good end up in Angor. The OneCreator and his immortals, including Gahya, call the Vast home."

Skyler released his elbow when they reached the tall arched doors. They would wait here for their escort. Kole glanced at his D-chip. Early.

She hem-hawed. "You didn't return to the room the other night at the Tribal Coliseum."

"Miss me?"

Poke. Poke.

"Don't be ridiculous. I'm making conversation."

"After you paraded around smelling of come-get-me, I needed sustenance."

"I didn't parade. Why are you trying to provoke me?"

"Because it's fun. Besides, you send mixed messages. You were ogling my bare ass through the bathroom door, weren't you?"

Crimson crept from Skyler's neck to her cheeks. "I… I… You didn't shut the door. It was an accident." She patted her face as if to wipe off the blush.

"Did you have to stare so long? Accidentally, I mean."

"I … never mind."

When he laughed, Skyler's eyes iced over. "You are a fine specimen. Of course I looked. It meant nothing." She tilted her I'm-better-than-you chin higher in the air.

"Specimen, huh. Fine, huh." Kole nodded. "I get that from a lot of females. Which part of my specimen had you drooling?"

Skyler pursed her lips, glaring. But before she could open her mouth to snap shit, a female swept through the two-story high doors.

She threw back the hood of her red cloak, revealing bright green eyes and blonde hair in a coiled braid circling the top of her head. "Chief Legal Officer Maxwell. I am Loredana, your escort and translator for the ceremony. It is my pleasure to welcome you."

Over her arm was another cloak of the same color, which she offered to Skyler.

"Thank you. It's lovely to meet you." Skyler slipped the robe over her prim, proper business suit.

The color looked good on her, though Kole doubted she owned any clothes in it. Too daring. Too sexy. He pictured her in crimson barely-there panties and bra. Just to torture himself, he clad her legs in thigh-high stockings, held in place by a red garter belt.

Yeah. Definitely her color.

Loredana produced a black-hooded robe for Kole, holding it for him to shrug into. "Welcome, Commander." Her warm fingers brushed his shoulders.

When the corners of her mouth curled, her lips parted to reveal small fangs she had once buried in Kole's flesh. It was a pleasant memory. Between it and the vision of Skyler in sexy lingerie, his pants were getting snug.

She escorted them through the heavy doors of the Strigodierna Shrine and along the polished marble floor of the nave. Above, stone arches vaulted across the ceiling. Red- and black-robed participants filled the pews.

"Are you familiar with all the women guides?" whispered Skyler to Kole.

"I seem to be, don't I?"

Loredana led them to an empty row near the back.

Everyone Jack-in-the-boxed to their feet when a deep-toned bell chimed, signaling the beginning of the ceremony. The Cruor, the big honcho, drove a showy procession from the nave down the aisle toward the main altar. His bearing was soldier-proud, a cowl shadowing his face as he glided forward. He bowed his head, his hands clasped in front of him, obscured by the sleeves of his robe. On his tail were fifty adoring female vampires in traditional red cloaks.

Chapter Ten

The procession mesmerized Skyler, from the somber, tall man in front to the magnificent, statuesque women trailing him.

"He is Nelo, our Cruor, the sacred practitioner in the Strigodierna Shrine. Behind him are his priestesses, the Carnemia." Loredana leaned close to whisper.

When the Cruor arrived at the altar, he raised his arms high, the Carnemia dropping to their knees, ten to a row. Their robes created a sea of red in the dimly lit shrine where candles flickered on the walls.

Turning toward the congregation, Nelo began to chant. Every tight muscle in Skyler's body relaxed, his voice rich with a velvety texture, calming like gentle blue waves and as smooth as decadent chocolate. When they rose, the Carnemia's song rang out, joining him.

Between Loredana's explanations of the rite, Skyler's thoughts wandered to Sarah. She had a girlish face but a sharp, analytical mind. She had graduated from Chicago's Circle Campus and was the youngest division manager in Alliance history. If life were fair, she would have grown older, married, had children, and left her mark on the organization. Life was so rarely fair, though.

Her thoughts jerked back to the Strigodierna Ceremony when the Cruor thrust his hands skyward, falling to his knees to thank Gahya, the Genitrix. When he rose, he ascended the steps to the altar and pivoted toward the congregation, eyes closed, his deep breaths pushing his black cloak in and out.

Loredana whispered, "He's using telepathy to contact Gahya."

When his lids drifted open, he seemed dispirited. Loredana explained it had been centuries since a Cruor had connected with their Genitrix. Nonetheless, they persisted.

The Carnemia raised their hands toward the overhead arches before falling prostrate upon the black stone floor. In unison, they surged to their feet, one approaching the altar to select a chalice. With the Cruor, she proceeded from priestess to priestess. His fangs extended, he bit into the wrist of each woman, collecting blood, each offering dripping into the gold bowl. When he was finished, they divided the contents into several chalices. Once again, their voices echoed throughout the shrine.

The priestesses stopped singing while the Cruor spoke to the crowd. "*Y emi vite. Potane.*"

Loredana, her voice breathy, her eyes adoring, translated. "I am life. Drink."

Drifting down the center aisle, their red cloaks skimming the ground, the Carnemia passed the chalices along the rows, beginning in the front.

Skyler steeled her shoulders for the blood-drinking. Maybe she'd just let her lips touch the fluid.

Kole leaned toward her. "No more than a sip. The stuff is strong."

Skyler tracked the progress of the chalice in her section. From the corner of her eye, she observed the Cruor. The flickering candles on the walls created strips of light or shade throughout the shrine, and he shadowflashed from dark spot to dark spot until he appeared at the end of her row, his gaze fixed on her. He stretched out an arm in front of Loredana, an unspoken bid for Skyler to grasp it. Once she did, he pulled her from her seat.

Clasping her hand, the holy man removed his

cowl, revealing a young, smooth face with a comforting smile. The Cruor cocked his head to the side, scrutinizing Skyler.

She shivered when his remarkably old eyes probed deep, settling in what she thought might be her soul, brushing dirt from buried emotions. Once he unearthed them, a healing light from his gaze bathed her in warmth.

Appearing satisfied with what he saw, he pushed back the sleeve of his robe, bared his fangs, and bit into his own wrist. "Drink from me. I am truth, freedom, life. As my essence has passed through the OneCreator on its journey to me, may it strengthen you for what lay ahead." He stretched the self-inflicted wound toward Skyler's lips.

Bright red blood bubbled to the surface. After a moment's hesitation, she accepted his offer to drink.

The Cruor's intoxicating blood flowed down her throat like a languid river, coursing to every part of her. Her lids grew heavy. When the fluid exploded into her heart, her eyes rolled back in her head, her body seizing. She felt as though the organ might rupture, flood, overflow. When her knees wobbled, threatening to send her to the floor, the Cruor tapped her cheek, his touch kind but persistent. She forced herself to stop drinking.

Skyler removed her mouth from his wrist, swiping fingers across her lips. Nelo dropped his sleeve, giving her a slight nod. Tugging the cowl into place, he returned to the altar.

"What was that about?" She collapsed into her seat, her body filled with contradictions, weak but invigorated, relaxed but strengthened, sleepy but energized. It was as though her emotional burdens had lifted, every cell plumped, more alive. Skyler latched onto Kole's hand for support.

The lines above the bridge of the commander's nose furrowed. "Damned if I know. Loredana?"

Their escort seemed stunned, her eyes wide, pinned on Skyler. "I don't know. I've never seen him offer blood from his wrist. It's quite an honor. Perhaps he had a vision. He sometimes does when he taps into a mind."

Skyler's skin prickled. The other Strigodierna participants had turned in their seats to stare. They whispered among themselves, their hands covering their mouths.

****

After she rested from the pre-dawn vampire ceremony, still weak though at peace, Skyler rose, ate a late lunch in her room at Casa Purgatorio, and logged onto her laptop.

She re-fluffed the pillows on the bed, leaning against them, her computer resting on her thighs, her ankles crossed. The accommodations at the luxury hotel in Covenkirk, the seat of government for Scath, were posh. The Aeternals housed visiting dignitaries in the old country house with its three buildings laid out in a horseshoe around a courtyard, garden, and natural lake. Skyler's suite on the first level overlooked the water, which she now surveyed while she absorbed the information she had read.

The problems of the world once again came crashing down. Anna had e-mailed, telling her to check out TheBigReveal.

The bloggers had carried through on their promise to post about demons. Skyler's gaze returned to the screen. Tapping a finger on her lower lip, she re-read, muttering, "Damn. Damn. Damn."

Let's begin with a history lesson—in the early 1400s, a little-known work, The Lanterne of Light, *classified demons according to the Seven Deadly Sins. But they got the whole thing backassward. Demons gave rise to the Seven Deadly Sins. Not the other way around. You see, pride, carnal, hedon, greed, sloth, animus, and envy are names for their breed's tribes.*

Let's clear up another myth. These guys and gals, we'll call them the Sins, were never angels. So, they are not fallen angels as Christianity would have us swallow. LOL.

All demons have a few things in common. First, they are Superman, or Superwoman, strong. Second, they have two forms—one human-like and the other a beast. Their beasts can arise willy-nilly during emotionally charged sitches, such as battle or S-E-X. Of course, they can also force their creature to surface.

The orange-sashed fighter during the Genesis Rite grew claws and fangs. Azamat's bull form had flickered, too.

To survive, the Sins feed off sex just as vampires drink blood (we'll feature them in a later blog). Demons need nooky. A hand job works for a while. Not for long. They require lots of bootie bumping.

Demons celebrate their Awakening, or attainment of their powers, between ages twenty and twenty-six. Your cousin Bernie's Bar Mitzvah has nothing on this ritual. Then there's their mating ceremony. Rumor has it, the Settling is really harsh. Talk about the Bride Goes Wild. Afterward, they are monogamous for life. No divorce lawyers or alimony for them, my loyal blogophiles.

It is not uncommon for demons to lose their shit, aka the rampage. If they don't leash the beast, their own kind usually kill them or isolate them on Darque.

Let's take a gander at each tribe. Animus demons are the strongest, biggest, meanest mutherfuckers. They manipulate fire and electrical energy. The most powerful call the hottest, deadliest burn—hellfire. While they can use their power to heal, the side effects can be wonky. Having sex with one will curl your hair, light-socket style, since they blast electrical impulses to make their partners orgasm repeatedly.

An image of Kole barreled into Skyler's mind as she stared out at the placid lake. Her thoughts were anything but serene as she envisioned him propped above her, his brawny arms flexed, his hips doing pushups, and his fire-gold eyes ablaze, fixed on her. Controlling her skittering heart, she focused on the here and now.

A hedon demon pops dangerous claws, along with long, sharp canines. They are your basic flesh-and-bone shredding machines, enjoying a good hot serving of cannibalism if they rampage. Since they're drawn to blood, able to sniff it from far away, they are skilled trackers. Sloth demons are like a shot of morphine. One jab and you're snoozing. A scratch from envy demons is emotionally paralyzing, flooding your mind with a fierce need or want. They've been known to make scratchees slit their own throats. carnal demons smell desire, zap willpower, and bring on a serious case of do-me-baby-oh-yeah-that-feels-good. They can also cause shifters (another soon-to-be blog) to change to their animal form. Avarice demons are frenzied speedsters, seeming jacked on PCP. Pride demons are Star Wars lightsabers, sizzling your eyeballs with the blinding, searing beams of their arrogant self-regard.

Sighing, Skyler clicked on *Upcoming Events.*

The latest event went off without a hitch. What did Shakespeare say? Oh, yes, "Let's kill all the techies." Or was it "lawyers?" Oops! Our mistake.

Losing track of time, Skyler stared at the lake. Sarah's murder was not part of a random robbery. They took credit for it as they had for the attempt on her own life. She dug her cell out of her purse to call her office. Anna picked up immediately.

"It's me. Any more about the bloggers or Sarah's murder?"

"No on both counts. TheBigReveal has been silent since the demon exposé. Agent Abello is investigating Siri's murder and your ... um ... accident. Of course, Chicago PD specifically warned against doing such a thing. So, it's all on the hush-hush. Everyone here is pretty sad. Oh, and the funeral is two days from now. We're closing for the afternoon. Everybody from here is going. Laurie volunteered to arrange it since Siri's parents live out west. I think they appreciated the help. When they arrive tomorrow, Allen will pick them up at the airport to transport them to their hotel. I told him they were a priority while in Chicago. What else? Yes. We are filling the funeral home with flowers. It should look nice, all at the company's expense. Since her parents wanted cremation, Laurie arranged for it. I think that's it."

Skyler waited for Anna to take a breath. Her tendency to go into detail without coming up for air was strangely calming right now.

"Have we tightened security?"

"Yes. Since Siri's murder and your incident are not random crimes, guards are on the Legal Division and Information Services employees 24-7. Other divisions have been warned to use caution, to report anything suspicious. If someone feels the need for protection, security will be assigned. Our agents, of course, are on heightened alert. We are stretched thin but getting by. How is it on your end?"

"We are proceeding through the itinerary quite nicely, thank you. Tonight is the ball. Tomorrow more travel around Scath. Then I'm home Saturday. I plan to make it for the funeral."

"That reminds me. I don't know how I overlooked it, but I found another stop on your father's tour. An entry from his journal must have gotten stuck between some pages. I missed it. Sorry. Anyway, he also did a quick trip to Darque. Can you squeeze it in?"

Skyler opened her laptop to access her calendar. "I can add it, but it'll mean another day here. I won't have the entire weekend to catch up on what I missed, and I won't make the funeral. Will you arrange something special from me to honor Sarah?"

"All over it, Chief. I'll donate to her favorite charity in your name. She loved animals. So we're all giving to Paws and Claws Adoptions."

"Perfect. Also, call High Commander Cadmon's office with the change to my schedule. Phone Winston, probably at the hospital. Let him know I need to postpone dinner Saturday night." She scrolled through her appointments. "Push back the signing of the sales agreement on the new health club chain. I won't be ready for it on Monday. It can wait a day. Call Farm to Table Grocers to inform them my proposal will be on time though later in the afternoon. I don't want them to think I'm blowing them off."

Skyler typed a few reminders into her notes.

Anna said, "Speaking of Winston, when Sarah was taken into Chicago General, he was the on-duty surgeon. He phoned to tell us how sorry he was and to let us know she didn't suffer. She never regained consciousness, her wounds so severe."

"I'm still puzzled, Anna. If TheBigReveal's looking to expose Scath or the Alliance, why not just do it? Why not open the site to the public? Do you think they plan to ask for money?"

Anna's sigh was loud. "I don't know. I guess

we'll find out soon. Anyway, enjoy the rest of your trip."

"I'm not here to enjoy myself. It's business."

"Sure, but it can't be all biz. Your escort's a stare-worthy hunk of gorgeous. And after what I read in the blog about those guys... Well, I repeat, enjoy."

"I assure you, I am not interested in the commander." When she disconnected, an unbidden vision of Kole's naked hard body poised above her invaded her mind again. Skyler rubbed the goosebumps on her arms, rattling her head to clear the spicy illusion of the damn animus demon.

****

Dante entertained Cerberus in his home beside the fireplace, sipping eighteen-year-old Macallan, one of the best single malt scotches in the world.

Cerberus sniffed the aroma of the fine liquor. "With Silas's operation destroyed, our search for living descendants of the Blood Coven could have come to a standstill. I am appreciative of your contacts." He poised the tumbler near his lips.

"Yes. My hacker is going through medical records quickly." Dante rolled the golden liquid around his glass in sheets, his legs crossed, the creases in his pants crisp. "He's costly, but efficient and discreet. He already identified the Alliance employee."

Cerberus leaned forward to clink his tumbler against Dante's. "Whatever it takes. The end is more important than the means. Our hunt must continue."

"Rightly so." Dante slanted his lips into a pleased aristocratic grin. "How are our prisoners holding up? You are certain they fit your needs?"

"When Silas located humans with ancient mage DNA markers, he brought them to Scath. Out of all the subjects, only two, a Celene Bailey and a Jace de Vries, tested positive for Blood Coven lineage. They are under constant guard in rather nice accommodations where nobody can find them. In the meantime, we hunt for more. The process is slow. I have hundreds of years to wait, my friend, but you ... ah ... not so many."

"True. Though I am a patient man, I want to see this through before I die. Do the prisoners exhibit any powers, even slight ones?"

"None we have detected."

Dante plunked his glass on the table, angling his body toward the fire, a chill settling in his bones. "This must work."

"The prophecy foretells of my success. Aeternals will once again walk Earth beside our human allies. And you, old friend, will have kept your promise to your daughter."

"Though she fell in love with a man from Scath, he died before they could mate. She made me vow on her own early deathbed to help bring your realm to light. To exist side by side, to learn from each other, to be a united people, different but the same, had been their shared dream. I have taken up the mantle of her cause, lucky to have found you. Of course, it will not hurt to profit from the venture."

Dante's stated goal was a lie intended to win Cerberus's trust.

The Aeternal sipped his drink. "The portals will fall, re-uniting the realms. We will tread upon Earth again with your species. Since Gahya created us long before you, we will be your protectors, the bearers of peace and prosperity to a world made whole. Of course, as you say, it does not hurt if we grow richer."

"The fire and your words warm me." Dante turned his face away from his guest to hide a sneer. "With your age has come wisdom."

"A wisdom I am happy to share." Cerberus rose,

setting his empty glass on the side table. "I will be attending a ball in honor of Skyler Maxwell."

Dante escorted the Aeternal to the door. "Strange coincidence since she is the Alliance mage descendant you must test for any Blood Coven ancestry."

"Yes. Interesting. I have arranged for her kidnapping while she is on Scath."

Dante stood in the entry, a hand curled around the door's edge, watching Cerberus descend the steps, climb into his auto, and drive toward the nearest portal. He rubbed his chin, muttering, shutting the door harder than necessary. "Friend, indeed."

****

Kole waited in Casa Purgatorio's courtyard. The female was late. Dressed in the formal Scion Firebrand uniform, the upper right sleeve bearing an image of the fiery Phoenix, he paced beside the lake.

When Skyler cleared her throat, Kole pivoted, his breath hitching.

After a few silent moments, she waved a hand along a black gown, the color a stark contrast to her pale skin. "Organza. A halter top. Donna Karan."

Creases lined Kole's forehead. "You're wearing another female's clothes?"

Melodic laughter, which he hadn't heard before, spilled from her lips. "No. She's the designer."

"Turn around." A circling finger accompanied Kole's command.

Skyler obliged by doing a slow rotation on her heel.

"There's no back," he said.

"It's fashionable."

"I like the … uh," he gestured, "long skirt. And your hair…" He touched his head. "Up. With pieces falling out."

"Oh, is it a mess?"

"No, I mean it looks soft. Natural."

She had pulled her white-blonde hair into some twisty thing at her neck, from which feathery wisps had escaped, making her seem less frigid, less stick-up-the-ass. A simple diamond hung between her breasts with matching drop earrings shimmering in the courtyard lights.

Kole's heart thrummed against his ribs. This Skyler was stunning. But shivering. "Here. Give me your coat."

"I'm sorry I was late. It was important for me to look appropriate for this event."

Kole assisted her into a long black coat he thought looked a little thin for the weather. He swallowed a hard rock in his throat. "Don't worry. It was worth the wait."

Skyler raised her eyebrows. "Almost a compliment, Commander?"

When he offered his arm, she glanced down at it and, smiling, tucked her hand in the crook of his elbow. Sparks flew from Kole's fingers. "Sorry. animus demon hazard."

From her lodgings, they jumped to Covenkirk's Aldkeep, a historical building which had once been a government house where lawgivers and the Temple of Justice met. With their offices in a newer facility, Aldkeep was reserved for large, formal events, such as tonight's.

Skyler's hand quivered on Kole's arm. When he placed his palm over hers to warm it, to calm her, she released a long breath of air.

Kole's gaze crawled over her body. "You have nothing to worry about. You look perfect."

"What is the world coming to, Commander? Two

compliments in one night." Despite her flippant tone, her smile told him she was pleased.

"Stick with me. I'm bound to be an asshole eventually."

Chapter Eleven

Entering the foyer, Skyler pulled Kole to a halt. She stared wide-eyed through an arched entryway to the ballroom. She rose onto her toes to whisper in his ear. "It's what my father described in his journal." She gave up her coat to a male at the door.

"What did he say?"

"He said an Aeternal ball was a step back in time to an era when royalty danced until dawn while orchestras played Viennese waltzes. It's breathtaking."

Skyler peered into the ballroom where women in floor-length dresses of every hue whirled around in the arms of tuxedoed men who guided them with gloved hands on their backs.

"Do you waltz, Commander?"

"Only under pressure. My guardian Ranca tried to teach me. I often skipped the lessons to play soldier, attacking a straw man outside."

Skyler gave him a quick smile before returning to admire the dancers.

"Some of what your father wrote is correct. The shindig in your honor is outdated. Perhaps when you live as long as we do, it's difficult to part with the past. You try to hold on tighter to keep memories from slipping away. But never forget a savage is always a savage. Even when he's wearing a tuxedo."

"Don't ruin this for me, Kole. Remember, I love history." She patted his arm, still scanning the room.

"Especially djinn history. I'm a bit jealous of your interest in the breed."

"I do have my favorites."

One brow shot up. "Dare I ask?"

"Demons are complicated."

"Hmm. Back to your fear, Chief. I have no intention of spoiling your evening. I want tonight to be special."

Surprise. He sounds sincere.

Her blues locked onto his fire-gold eyes when he tucked her hand into the crook of his elbow to lead her into the dining hall. In his dress uniform, he seemed different, no longer a brute.

Inside, gazes turned toward Skyler, who tipped her chin a little higher, her public persona sliding into place.

A woman in a lovely red strapless gown, her trim but muscular arms on display, hastened to them. "Chief Legal Officer Maxwell."

Kole bent to whisper, "Supreme Lawgiver Fera, a shifter."

Fera snagged Skyler's other arm, dismissing Kole. "Thank you, Commander. Chief Maxwell will sit with us. I believe your table is over there with Commanders Nace and Jarek."

Skyler's gaze flipped to Kole. She fought to keep from showing him her weakness. She had never been comfortable in social situations. The larger they were, the more off-balance she felt. After all, the attendees might see beneath her cool exterior. Might see her imperfections.

She inhaled, releasing him to accompany Fera across the floor. Strange. Kole, the huge, brutish warrior, lent her his strength without crippling her, almost as if he saw beneath her mask but didn't care. Glancing over her shoulder at the commander, she sighed. He nodded, his lopsided, knowing grin slow to curl his lips as the shifter escorted Skyler to a table in the front shared by lawgivers, justices, and directors of ministries.

****

Kole strode to his table, joining the other two Scion Firebrand commanders.

Jarek sprawled in a too-small chair, tugging at the collar of his formal uniform. "This is a nightmare."

Nace rested his chin on his fist, propped on an elbow. He looked as uncomfortable as Jarek.

Kole pulled out a seat. "I can think of a lot of places I'd rather be."

"Yeah," said Nace, "like in Angor being tortured, unarmed in the middle of a herd of questing beasts, or in the crapper."

The jaguar shifter's eyes were an unsettling amber, his beast prowling close to the surface. Kole couldn't blame him. They were out of place here.

Jarek winked at Nace. "So, while I'm assisting the ylves with some radical Isolationists, who are a pain in the ass, Kole here is hand-in-hand with a gorgeous Alliance bigwig. Doesn't seem fair."

Kole sought Skyler in the crowd. She was gorgeous. "What makes you think my job is not a pain in the ass also?"

"Is it?" asked Nace.

"Sometimes."

Talk stopped when waiters set endless platters of chicken, beef, and lamb on their table. Some meat was cooked. Some floated in blood. Nace snatched the latter. Shifters enjoyed their flesh with the heart still beating. Plates heaped with vegetables, bread, fruit, and cheese came next.

Screw the veggies. Protein powers fire.

Once appetites were satisfied, the commanders chose to stand. Years of experience made them uneasy sitting in the middle of any room where they were vulnerable to attack from all sides. They leaned against the wall, tugging at too tight jackets, dying to take off stiff shirts, and wishing the time would pass faster.

"We saw some Isolationists protesting outside the ylves' Greeting Chamber. What's their story?" asked Kole. He'd already gathered info from Caleth and company, but more never hurt.

Jarek folded his arms over his chest. "The more peaceful are demanding a permit to cross to Earth so they can picket Alliance headquarters. Hell no. But I am stuck at the table, negotiating with the idiotic bastards. The more violent among them are absent from the face-to-face. They want to bomb the human realm. My answer to them is fuck no. Simonis, the founder of the Isolationists, is silent. The group is radicalizing. I feel it in my djinn bones."

"I heard they've been hassling mix-breed mates."

"True. In my region and in North Shelters."

With Braelyn tucked under his arm, Rein paced up to the three commanders, as uncomfortable as his *frerons*.

"Minister Alarik's your father. Couldn't you escape this charade?" asked Nace.

"No. Besides, we were double whammied. Braelyn's dad is George James. The human over there." Rein pointed to a dignitary table near the front. "He's on the Alliance's board of directors. Here to support Chief Maxwell."

"This is fun, though." Braelyn squeezed Rein's arm, sounding almost bouncy.

Four grunts met her comment.

Her gaze pinged from one dour face to another. "It's exciting to dress up sometimes. You guys would fare much better if you stopped acting as if you'd rather kill something." She snapped her fingers. "I know. We need drinks. Rein, be a dear."

Kole coughed into his hand while Nace and Jarek stifled grins. The vampire mix blinked, his lips squeezed together. Trying not to look whipped, he stomped off to get booze, bringing back five specially blended Blue Legend Reserve whiskeys distilled in Wildwynd by satyrs.

Rein passed glasses around, giving Braelyn a stern warning as he handed off to her. "You remember when you had this the other night?"

"I do. Bottom's up." With that, his human mate chugged her drink. Not to be outdone, Rein, Kole, Jarek, and Nace downed their whiskeys, eyeing Braelyn with what bordered on admiration for her unteared eyes.

"My turn." Kole lumbered off for another round. Alcohol had only a minimal effect on Aeternals. A plus. Except the satyrs' special blend. He wasn't sure how Braelyn could handle it.

She waved off the second drink when Kole returned, instead heading off to find Sabine, the celestial nymph Firebrand. When Braelyn had come across Rein in a Seattle alley last summer, she had seen him pin a Kalli to the wall. Unable to wipe her memory, the normally in-control warrior got a bad case of idiot, kidnapping her and bringing her to Scath. It was Sabine who had befriended her by teaching her to throw spikes and knives. The nymph had become a friend, a trainer, and an adviser.

Supreme Lawgiver Fera dragged Skyler toward the Scion Firebrands. She was traveling from group to group with her trophy. Before they could begin any meaningless chit-chat, an exuberant witch, decked out in wild-colored silk pants, a fringed scarf, long shirt, and sandals, slapped Skyler on the back. Minister Alarik, her brother, looked on, nodding to his son, Rein.

Before Skyler tumbled face first, Indigo clasped her arm. "I'm right. You've met me, dear." The witch winked.

"I don't think so." Skyler's eyes narrowed.

"Of course you have. The strip joint in Philly? No. Not there. Do you have a regular corner in Hollywood?"

"I beg your pardon?"

"Why? What did you do?" Indigo's eyebrows arched while she snatched hold of Skyler's hands. "No. No. Shit. I didn't want to talk river biz here."

Greeting Skyler, Alarik filled her in. "My sister is the only Aeternal who visits the River Am. She gathers knowledge there, some of which is meaningless."

"What's the River Am?" asked Skyler.

"The present, past, and future. An evil, wet snake sent to vex me. Futures are the worst. Maybe that one. No, look. Maybe that one." Indigo threw her arms into the air, her shitload of bracelets jangling. "How am I supposed to know which one will become the present? A whole bunch of maybes. Get my drift?"

Indigo tapped her own head with her fist. *Tap, tap, tap.* Alarik grabbed her hand.

"Thanks, bro. Say, what did the Cruor think of you? He sees possibilities, too, but he seems wrapped tight."

Before Skyler could answer, Indigo spun around. "Hold it, buddy." Mid-twirl, she snagged a glass off a passing tray. "When you see me, always offer a drink. Otherwise, I might have to give you a permanent case of the crabs."

His expression dry, the waiter said, "I'd rather you didn't."

"Oh, I'm only messin' with ya." Indigo smiled, winking at him while she took a huge gulp. "There.

Much better. Where were we? Oh, yes. I was talking about... Boyo." She pushed through the group to her nephew.

"Auntie." Rein wrapped her in a warm embrace. "You're going to cause a stir, aren't you?"

"Only if I can, Boyo." She grabbed another drink from a passing tray. "This female needs to rethink her choices." She jerked her head in Skyler's direction.

Skyler's eyes widened. "What choices?"

"Why all of them, dear, but you aren't gonna listen to a word I say. Nobody ever does."

Spotting Kole, Indigo sidled up to him, dropping her empty glass on the floor where it shattered. "Hiya, handsome." She arched a brow at Skyler before she rose onto her toes to give him a peck on the cheek. "Gotta dance. Ta ta." Indigo twirled toward the ballroom, a new drink in hand.

Skyler looked at Kole, who shrugged. "She's a powerful witch with a big heart and great intel from the River Am. She's also Director Alarik's sister and Rein's aunt, as you likely guessed."

Interrupting, the Temple of Justice warlock, Dolph, approached the group. He bowed slightly. "May I have this dance, Chief Maxwell?"

When she accepted, he whisked her toward the ballroom, a hand low on her back.

Kole tamped down the heat threatening to blast from his fingers. He barely noticed Fera moving away to chat with another group. He lost track of the conversation. When Skyler disappeared among the crowd, his focus returned.

Braelyn pulled up alongside Rein, her fingers trailing from one of his shoulders to the other, which in every female's vocab meant she wanted something.

The vampire-mix warrior popped fangs as his lips

spread into a smile, his large hand covering his mate's.

While they made goo-goo eyes at each other, Kole excused himself. He wandered into the ballroom. Of all the dancers in the room, his gaze sought Skyler. Justice Dolph, his arm wrapped around her waist, swept the chief along the floor while her dress swayed in rhythm with the music. Kole's jaw clenched as Dolph's other hand pawed her bare back. The warlock leaned close to her ear, his nearness betraying more than admiration. The mutherfucker was hitting on her, just like a common wand waggler.

Skyler smiled at the justice, but Kole recognized the expression. It was artificial, put on with her makeup.

When a waiter walked by with a tray of drinks, Kole grabbed a whiskey in each fist, draining them with a toss. Trying to get somewhat drunk seemed a good idea. He stared at Skyler in the male's arms.

Let her dance with the idiot. If she's set on bothering me with another male, she can have at it.

A hand tapped him on the shoulder before he could escape the ballroom. He blinked twice before recognizing the young Firebrand Chay. With his long, dark hair pulled into a braid, he looked less like a warrior and more like an innocent ylve. Until his wild, playful smile turned up the corners of his lips. Kole had paired him with Rein because one talked too much and the other hardly at all.

"Comm, this is Anjeli, my guest this evening."

Kole nodded at a demure strawberry-haired ylve who cast shy eyes away when Chay introduced her. In a soft, whispery voice, she said, "Nice to meet you, Commander."

"My mother hooked us up." Chay's attention strayed to a passing succubus who flashed a willing smile. The ylve cleared his throat.

Just then a female ylve with raven hair passed, a hand linked to the crook of a friend's elbow. When she saw the young Firebrand, she giggled, whispering something to her companion. Chay winked but looked back at Kole, folding his arm over Anjeli's shoulders. "Her father owns a ranch in the Rainse region of Aerilon."

When a passing guest called Chay's date away, he walked with Kole toward Nace and Jarek, confessing, "I think Anjeli might become my mate."

"Splendid." Kole smirked. He slapped Chay on the shoulder, rejoining the other Firebrands while his young warrior hustled off. "A match made in heaven."

"Who's the woman, er … female, with Chay?" Braelyn squeezed Kole's arm.

"I don't remember."

Rein's mate sighed. "I need to join a different group. You guys are no fun."

Kole, Jarek, and Nace exchanged puzzled frowns, settling on Rein for an explanation of Braelyn's behavior.

"It's a human thing. She likes to know what everyone is doing, who they are with, and so on. Gossip."

"Why?" asked Jarek.

Braelyn slapped her forehead, spinning on a heel, hustling away.

"Did I insult her?" The djinn commander of the Southern Stronghold shook his head, his braids tapping his shoulders.

"I doubt it. That's her frustrated look. I get it a lot. It's best to ignore it." Rein's gaze fixed on the sway of Braelyn's hips as she stomped off.

Kole glanced up to see Skyler enter the dining area. When she stumbled and grabbed onto Dolph to steady herself, he groaned. "Fuck. I'm on duty again.

Excuse me."

He powered across the room. "Justice, I need to speak with Chief Maxwell about our schedule." His fingers biting into Skyler's arm, he ushered her away from the warlock.

"Ow. You are hurting me." Though Skyler tugged, Kole held on.

He sniffed the air. "How much have you had to drink?"

"Two's my limit. Always. I know exactly how many whiskeys I can hold." She pursed her lips. "But I've had no more than three." When she reached toward the tray of drinks behind her, Kole captured her hand before she could snag a glass.

"This is Blue Legend. It's a Special Reserve made on Scath for Aeternals. You're drunk."

"Oops. Big mistake, Commander." She finger-poked Kole's chest. "Nice. Hard. Oops." Skyler blew a wisp of fallen hair out of her eyes.

"You're smashed. We're leaving."

With a hand to each side of Kole's face, she pulled him down to whisper. "I can't. I'm the guest of honor." Skyler spun around, but before she took a step, Kole nearly jerked her off her feet.

"Come on, Chief."

"I am not drunk. My father would disapprove."

"Congratulations. You broke your daddy's heart."

Skyler giggled. "You're funny. My daddy's heart. He didn't have one."

"Just nod and smile when we leave. Nobody will notice."

Skyler yanked them both to an abrupt stop, wobbling on her high heels. She ran her hands along the sides of her gown. "How could anyone not notice me dressed in this?"

"Let's go."

"No. I'm not moving unless you answer a question. Am I noticeable?"

"You are definitely noticeable, but this might be a good time to fly under the radar."

She put both palms on Kole's temples, tugging him to her level again. "I have a confession. When I'm nervous, I eat and drink too much."

"I'm aware."

Once out the door, Kole lifted Skyler into his arms and tapped his D-chip to create a portal outside Aldkeep. Firebrands could generate their own gateways when they were in the open air, but they didn't do it often because it drained their devices. This was an emergency. He transported them both to her quarters at Casa Purgatorio.

"Wow. That made me dizzy." She swayed when Kole set her on her feet.

"Sure. The portal's making you dizzy." Kole put a hand on each of Skyler's shoulders to guide her toward the room.

When she fumbled with the keys, he snatched them to open her door. He paused, allowing Skyler to pass.

"I think I may need more help." She wiggled a finger at him.

Eyeing her suspiciously, Kole followed into her suite. Once he closed the door, she pointed at her back. "Please unfasten my dress. It's rather hard to get to." Skyler cast glittering blue eyes over a bare shoulder while she brushed aside a wisp of unruly hair.

For the first time in his life, Kole's hands shook as he slipped the hook from its clasp. Skyler spun to face him. Holding onto the front of what she had called a halter dress, she inched her hand away, the top falling to reveal her firm, rounded, lush breasts.

Damn. No bra.

Kole's chest heaved with short, rapid breaths when she slithered toward him, her gait unsteady. She stopped and began to unbutton his jacket.

His gaze remained on Skyler's breasts. He imagined rolling a nipple between his thumb and index finger, making it a tight bud before he sucked it into his mouth, his bite gentle. In his vision, she arched her back, moaning, pushing against his lips, begging him to take more.

Skyler finished unbuttoning his jacket, slipped it off his shoulders, dropped it on the floor, and started on Kole's shirt. One button. Another.

He let her, his gaze still absorbing her tantalizing breasts with tawny nipples. She drew his shirt down his arms, her palms stroking his biceps.

Kole's heavy lids half-masted as he inhaled, savoring her sweet-spicy perfume. She closed the tiny distance between them to rub the tips of her nipples against his chest. His arousal strained the zipper of his pants. While his demon struggled to surface, he resisted tearing off her clothes, throwing her onto the bed, slamming into her.

Despite the hard-on from hell, Kole shocked himself.

He gripped Skyler's bare shoulders, gentling her away. He resettled his shirt and then lifted the front of her dress. Once it was in place, he slapped her hand on it. Wrapping his arms around her, he pulled her in tight, touching his lips to her ear, whispering, "As much as I want to taste you and bury my cock deep enough to make you scream, I'm going to walk out. Damn fool that I am."

"Oh, Kole." Skyler covered her mouth while she

ran for the bathroom. He heard her gag and heave.

"This female is nothing but trouble." Kole pushed through the doorway. At the edge of the toilet, Skyler half sat, half sprawled on the floor.

Kole looked around for night clothes. Finding them, he stood over her. When she stopped upchucking, he lifted her onto wobbly feet, took off her dress and shoes, and slipped a flimsy nightgown over her head. Skyler shoved at his hands, fleeing to the toilet again, falling beside it to retch.

Kole plopped alongside her, cradled her forehead in his palm, and rubbed her back with his other hand as she continued to barf up her guts. When she stilled, he wet a washcloth to wipe her face, sweeping her hair from her cheeks.

"I'm so sick. Sorry. Sorry."

"It's okay, Frisca. Sleep's the best thing for you." He lifted her into his arms, her weight a feather.

"Tell me you forgive me, Kole. I'm so sorry."

"Nothing to forgive. When you're nervous, you eat and drink too much."

"You're right. How did you know?" Her words were slurred.

"Lucky guess." He carried her to the bed, tossed back the linens, and lay Skyler down, drawing a sheet over her. On the edge of the mattress, he stroked her hair until she closed her eyes. He did not leave her side until he heard soft snuffling sounds.

When Kole shut the door, jacket in hand, she mumbled, "Sorry … sorry … sorry."

Chapter Twelve

Skyler slammed through her courtyard door, storming toward Kole, her index finger waving in the air. "I don't want to hear one word about last night. I do not do well in large social settings. Not! One! Word! Am I clear?" She had decided in her morning shower to approach last night's embarrassing situation with a full-on frontal assault.

"Crystal. Besides, a gentleman never tells." Kole's grin spread across his face, rendering Skyler nearly speechless.

She recovered. "Hah! You're no gentleman."

"You're right. But I walked away like fucking King Arthur in shining armor."

"I warn you. Not one more word. I was drunk. I had no idea the whiskey at the reception was more potent than what I usually drink. I always have two libations to be sociable. My reasoning is never affected."

"You were very sociable. If you had been any more sociable, my pants would have been around my ankles. I would have been pounding into you, and you would have been shouting my name." A rumble of laughter erupted from Kole.

Scowling, Skyler charged, hammering his chest with both hands. Again and again. "I said, 'Not one word.' I wasn't myself."

Kole snorted, swallowing a full-on guffaw. "Whoever you were, I liked her." He kept a tight hold on her fists.

"I'm glad you enjoyed her, because you won't see her again. Let me go."

"Too bad. I could grow on that version of you." His lopsided grin emphasized the double meaning as he released her.

Skyler shook her head. "Disgusting! You are validating my belief. You are a brutish barbarian."

"You brought up the subject. I was going to pretend it never happened. Being the gentleman I am not. Your tits are nice, though. Big. Succulent."

Skyler's mouth opened. "Oh ... oh. Just shut up. I beg of you."

She shot forward, not knowing if she was headed in the right direction. She needed to act. "By the way, I've added Darque to our itinerary for tomorrow. I made Cadmon aware." She flung the news at Kole.

He rushed to catch her, grabbing an arm, squeezing hard enough to bruise. "Whoa. Just a minute. Darque? No. It's dangerous. Too many chances for you to get hurt."

"Are you incapable of protecting me, Commander?" Skyler pried off Kole's fingers. He didn't resist.

"Hell, no. I'm saying shit happens." Kole tapped his D-chip.

Since the device allowed thought-to-thought communication, she couldn't tell who he called or eavesdrop on the conversation. She suspected it was Cadmon.

Kole punched his wrist to disconnect. "Fucking brainless human females who know squat about squat."

Instead of taking offense at his less than flattering rant, Skyler grinned. Like a cat with a mouse by the tail, a live, squirming one. After all, a win was a win. "Well, Commander? Are we going?" The Alliance board required a visit to Scath. Since her father's journal also included Darque, she was determined to add it to the tour.

She stood her ground as Kole barreled up to her, his eyes glowing red, fire bouncing off his fingertips. "You'll get your way. I'll take you because I'm your best bet to make it out alive and because I follow orders. Though why I should give a rat's ass, I don't know."

In deafening silence, they began and ended their tour of the nymphs' and satyrs' Elysian Isle, followed by a brief trip to Amori, the incubi and succubi region. When Kole dropped her off in Covenkirk early evening, he was still angry, his jaw set, his teeth grinding together. "I'll pick you up at eight. Be on time. Pants. Long. Shirt. Sleeves to your wrists. Shoes you can walk in without falling on your stubborn ass. Make those boots. Sunscreen. Gloves. A hat. A warm jacket. A backpack."

"And what if I dress the way I choose?" Skyler fisted her hips.

The nerve of the man.

Kole advanced on Skyler until she had no choice except to back into the wall, his body radiating electric energy. Sparks prickled her skin when he touched her cheek. He leaned into her, resting a forearm against the brick above her. A knee pushed between her legs, imprisoning her. His lips were near enough she felt the warmth of his breath. She closed her eyes, his gravelly whisper scorching her flesh. He was beyond angry, but the thick jut of his arousal prodded her belly. "I'll carry you inside, rip off your clothes, and dress you myself. Only this time you won't be too drunk to remember."

Skyler opened her mouth to speak. Kole held up a hand. "Try me. Please, try me."

She lifted her chin, an icy, determined look settling in her eyes. "I get it." Her eyebrows knitted into a frown. Skyler squirmed, attempting to dislodge herself from Kole's imprisonment.

"Chief, I don't give a damn whether you get it or not." His fingers tangled in her hair.

"I could call Cadmon to have him replace you as my escort." Skyler twisted to the side, struggling to escape contact.

"I think somewhere in those frozen veins you have the good sense not to do that."

"Have it your way, Commander."

He released her and stepped away. "Hand me your portal jumper."

Skyler passed it to Kole. "What are you doing?"

"Syncing it to my D-chip so your frosty ass doesn't get separated from mine on Darque."

After a few strained moments of Kole punching information into her jumper, he stomped off, leaving Skyler still against the wall but free to open her own door, walk into her suite alone, and try to shake off her reaction to his fiery touch.

****

"I'm picturing a big grilled steak and a giant baked potato with the works." Jace stared into the kitchen they hadn't used except to store bottles of water in the fridge.

Celene stretched out on the couch, her neck propped on the arm. "Does your baked potato have bacon bits on it? Because I really like them on top of the sour cream."

"Most definitely." Jace shook the vision from her head. "We need a distraction." She snatched *The Path* off the coffee table. "I have just the thing." Snuggling into the over-stuffed chair, she opened the book.

After the successful schism, Ohngel came to me with news. I had unknowingly been complicit in a betrayal to our cause.

In my loneliness and need, I, the Cambion from

Wales, had sought succor in the arms of Niviane. She had returned from her century-long journey in Gaul, more beautiful, her hair a deeper black, her curves softer, her smile more radiant, her body a welcoming heat and salve for my solitude. In my presence, she took advantage of every opportunity to brush against me, to ask questions, to listen to my answers with rapt attention, to ply me with sultry gestures. A glance. A laugh. A sway of her hips. A touch. Both lonely, I think, we agreed to find solace in each other.

Despite no desire on our parts to join as mates, we fornicated. Often. With her moans a soothing melody, her passions a medicinal balm, I thrust inside her. Flesh to flesh, I delivered my seed into her embracing body.

But after the schism, Ohngel revealed that Niviane, my sultry, welcoming bed partner, had borne my child and given the girl to her sister. Against the edict to remain on Earth, she had sent our daughter to live among our own breed on Scath.

With the knowledge of my role in the betrayal, I questioned my value. Had Ohngel chosen the wrong warlock for his tasks? Despondent over my guilt, I asked my guide, my mentor, what the betrayal presaged.

Sadness shadowed Ohngel's eyes. "What has been done by the coven can be undone by its descendants."

"Can I not bring the child back to Earth?" I asked.

"No. Events must play out as they happen."

My guilt ate at me. "Is there nothing I can do?"

My mentor Ohngel, who was never without a plan, said, "Yes. There is something you may do."

"A mystery." Jace closed the book, her lids too heavy, the words blurred.

Celene wiggled her bare feet. "Yep, but I still

want a steak and baked potato with the works."

****

Skyler lifted one foot, then another, sinking into the squishy bog of a swamp on Darque, thankful for her rugged gear. With sweat trickling between her breasts, she eyed her boots, already steeped in green slime.

Kole, in khaki tactical pants and a snug dry tee sinfully molding to his massive pecs and arms, looked fresh, like an ad in *Soldier of Fortune*. Jungle edition. He shoved his aviator sunglasses into place and slapped his knapsack onto a shoulder. While his gaze darted everywhere at once, his hand patted his chest harness, loaded with three short daggers. A battle axe hung from a loop on his belt while a long blade was sheathed at his hip. From his close-cropped haircut to his bulky muscles and weapons, he was ready for guerrilla warfare.

Other than the clothing he had insisted she wear, Skyler was not. She swiped a hand across her watery eyes, the fetid odor doing a number on them. "What's that smell?" She pinched her nose.

"Rotting vegetation, algae, decaying corpses." Kole scanned their surroundings. "Careful where you step. The swamp is alive with crawling things. Always look up, too. You can never tell what might wiggle from a tree. If that's not enough, be on the lookout for flying wildings." He sent her an I-told-you-so grin. "This place is more dangerous than shopping on Chicago's Mag Mile."

"Obviously, you've never been to opening day of a sale at Bloomingdale's." Despite her snapped response, Skyler heeded Kole's warning, her eyes darting everywhere at once, checking for slimy, crawling, tree-hugging, airborne critters. "Why did we start here? It's smelly and…" Skyler stopped talking to swat an insect on her hand. "…buggy."

"Noir Swamp was the first destination on your list, home to primordial slime, dead flesh, foul odors. Enjoy."

Skyler nodded, flicking a bug off her cheek. "I suppose there's a certain beauty to it." She brushed back damp strands of hair sticking to her neck as they escaped her usually chic do. With a slap to her arm, Skyler smashed what appeared to be a mosquito the size of an Oreo cookie. "I am well dressed for the occasion, though. Thanks to you. I'm thinking of recommending you as a fashion consultant for the rich and adventurous."

"Was that a joke, Chief? I think it was. Be careful, we're almost getting along."

"Almost." Skyler trudged around a willow-like tree whose limbs dipped into the water. She slogged through reeds which sprouted from the motionless, lazy wetland. In the stagnant water, flowers floated alongside fallen branches and rotting debris. Mysterious splashes, gurgles, and glug-glugs reached Skyler's ears.

She plodded, ankle deep in the dark muck. With the trees forming a thick canopy which blocked the sun, she avoided the shapes darting about in the murky swamp, their shadows creating a macabre dance.

When they stepped onto a somewhat solid patch of ground, Kole pointed.

Skyler followed his gesture. Some distance away, a four-foot tall, green frog-faced wilding leaned against a tree, standing on two squat hind legs. Its protruding eyes stared at her while it nodded its large, bulbous head in greeting. Its lipless mouth twisted into a grin. Without thinking, she grabbed Kole's arm.

He nodded back at the creature. "Loveland Frog. They aren't dangerous. Kiss him. Maybe he'll turn into a prince."

"I don't need a prince." She released Kole,

realizing she was clinging to him.

"So true. You have me."

Skyler stifled a laugh. "You are definitely not prince material."

Kole slapped a hand over his heart. "I'm hurt. How about your fiancé?"

"My fiancé? Um. Sure. Of course he's fit for the job."

Kole drew his long blade. "This way. We'll walk to drier ground."

Skyler followed the commander, who hacked through thick brush. Something slithered onto her boot. "Kole."

He didn't answer. She raised her voice. "Commander! Something's on my foot."

He pivoted, propped his sunglasses on his head, and grimaced. "Don't move. Amphista. Nasty critter."

Skyler stood as still as the swamp water, her breath caught in her throat. But the two-headed snake slithered around her ankle, preparing to climb her leg. "No way." She kicked out a boot, muffling a scream. A certain amount of dignity was necessary. The creature landed hard. Hissing, it faced Skyler, both mouths open, each with a forked tongue flicking outward. It glided toward her. All four eyes zeroed in on her.

"Do you want the honors, or should I fight for your honor, m'lady?"

Skyler lifted her chin, glaring down her nose at Kole.

In what seemed like a single motion, he scooped Skyler up in one arm and, with the hand of the other, touched the wilding on its closest head. It sizzled, turned black, died. Its charred remains floated atop the swamp water until a creature from beneath gobbled it up.

Kole slid Skyler onto her feet.

Shuddering, she swiped at her pant leg to brush off all imagined remnants of the amphista. "I dislike snakes! Even those with a single head." Skyler inched forward, again behind Kole, looking everywhere while he cleared the trail.

"You weren't in much danger. They prefer to snack on rotting corpses."

Skyler stifled an *ugh*.

Picking up his dropped blade from the murky waters, Kole resumed his hack through the dense undergrowth, clearing a wider path. "Oh, and don't bother to thank me. I know you were about to do that, Chief. Tell me, why would you come to a such a dangerous realm just to follow in your father's footsteps? Did you admire him so much?" He paused mid-swing, twisted around, and cocked his chin to one side. "No. You don't. It's a competition. You need to prove to yourself you're equal to or better than him. Hell of a way to establish your worth."

Skyler answered Kole with a frosty glare, upset when he read her too well. "You have an unhealthy interest in my motives."

They slogged on for half an hour before Kole stopped. When he turned to Skyler, his sexy, playful one-sided smile revealed amusement, but his fire-gold eyes blazed hotter than the swamp.

She glanced down at her shirt. Soaked with sweat, it clung to her breasts as if she were a contestant in a wet T-shirt contest. Arching her brows, she pulled the damp fabric away from her skin.

Kole shrugged, giving her his back along with a chuckle while he resumed slashing through obstacles.

"If you're tired, I'll take a turn," Skyler offered.

"I can keep going all day and night. I'm told I have amazing stamina."

"Your double entendres do not go unnoticed, Commander."

On harder ground with the swamp behind them, Skyler breathed in the fragrant aroma of colorful flowers. Ferns of varied hues surrounded them—greens, reds, yellows, blues. Drizzling rain wept from leaves while purple vines wrapped their arms around the lush trees. She angled her neck to look overhead. Small furry animals swooshed through branches. Flamboyant, musical neon-colored birds with long, golden beaks nested high in the limbs.

Before Skyler stretched out a hand to touch an exotic orchid, Kole grabbed her elbow. He pointed toward a tree. A spider the size of a two-year-old crawled down its trunk. Its lisping sounds were not a friendly greeting.

"A rainforest tanasi. Time to jump." Kole urged her to the gateway.

Snakes were scary. Giant spiders were worse. Skyler punched her handheld portal jumper synced with Kole's D-chip.

****

Kole shielded his eyes from the bright light when he and Skyler stepped out of the gateway onto the crest of a dune. Below them, cacti, sparse vegetation, and wildings competed with the sun in a dry, hot climate. In the distance, dust-devils sent tumbleweeds rolling, kicking up sand. A waterless creek bed wandered between wind-ravaged crimson sandstone hills.

Skyler leaned against Kole, probably unaware of the contact. He felt it like a blast of heat. "It's so quiet here. Beautiful though desolate."

"It reminds me of home."

"Lucifer's Forge in Knife's Edge?"

"The same." He bent toward Skyler, noticing her

blouse was now dry. *Damn shame.* He had enjoyed seeing it stick to her breasts. Of course, he'd already had a better view of them the night of the ball.

She licked her lips as if they were parched.

"Thirsty?" he asked.

"Yes."

Kole retrieved a bottle from her backpack side pocket. He opened it. "Here. Drink. It's important to stay hydrated in this region."

"Thanks."

A movement caught Kole's eye. He threw an arm out and shoved Skyler behind him, knocking the water out of her hand. "A sand leech is burrowing through the canyon toward us."

She peeked around him. "Where?"

"See the mound coming this way. They haven't been spotted here for a while. If it surfaces, do not look into its eyes. Its gaze will draw you into its mouth. Move when I do."

He inched them backward in the direction of the portal, always monitoring the leech's progress. It was a big muther. At least twenty to thirty feet long. Before they reached the gateway, the fucker cut them off at the base of the dune, rearing its grinning bloated head, trying to lock onto Kole's eyes. With its mouth wide, exposing a double row of teeth, it prepped to unleash a stream of fire. Kole was faster. He gathered a blazing ball in his palm and heaved it at the creature. With a piercing scream, the deadly beast dug underground with its giant claws. It was attempting to flank them.

Skyler pulled alongside Kole, watching the leech.

"Stay the hell behind me." He pivoted again to face the monster. It drew its worm-like body out of the sand, its claw-tipped tentacles stretching forward. Without looking into its eyes, Kole launched a stream of fire at its head. The critter swung to the right to evade the assault. Before he could create another blast, the wilding exhaled a flame. Kole threw himself on top of Skyler, taking them both to the sandy ground. His forearm sizzled from a hit.

Leaping to his feet, Kole responded with his own strike. Because he could use only his peripheral vision, he missed the critical mark again. The wilding ducked underground to maneuver behind them.

Kole yanked Skyler upright. "Move!" Roughly, he flung her at his six once more. She wasn't fast enough.

When the beast stretched ten feet out of the sand, four sharp-clawed tentacles straining forward, it nearly snagged Skyler. *Damn female.* He didn't have time to fight the wilding and worry about her. Kole fixed his eyes on the beast's neck but aimed higher. He launched a prolonged, direct blast of flames. It let out a high-pitched shriek. Kole clasped hands over his ears until silence returned. The leech was dead, its head ablaze, the smell of burning flesh heavy in the air.

Kole spun toward Skyler, fire sparking from his eyes and fingers, his inner beast pissed as hell, struggling to be free. "When I push you behind me, female, you fucking better stay behind me. When I tell you to turn, you fucking better turn."

Skyler brushed sand from her pants, apparently unafraid of his demon temper. "I did stay behind you. I did turn when you told me to. Don't take your pissy mood out on me."

"Then get faster."

"I can't..." Skyler glanced up at Kole, fixing on his singed arm. "My God. You're hurt." She inhaled, nostrils quivering.

Kole eyed the wound. "It's nothing. Just a little

sand leech burn. It'll heal. Let's boogie the hell out of here. They hunt in pairs."

Chapter Thirteen

Skyler shoved the sand leech incident to the back of her mind, a herd of fascinating questing beasts grazing on the plains below her. "There must be hundreds of them."

"Looks like. Because their horns are silver, they can do a lot of damage to shifters or bloodsuckers. Don't confuse them with Earth cattle. They're bigger, nastier, and meat eaters. They'd rather graze on you than the grass."

After a few minutes, they returned to the nearby portal. The next stop was a thick pine forest where shafts of light barely touched the needled ground. Skyler shrugged off her backpack to remove a jacket. "It's much cooler here."

"Sand Leech Dunes, the Questing Beast Plains, and Noir Swamp are in the Southern Hemisphere of Darque. We're in the Northern Hemisphere now. Different season. Different ecosystem."

Kole no longer seemed pissed at her. Of course he never had a reason to be in the first place. She had handled the sand leech event quite well. The commander? It was likely someday books would be written about his heroic deeds. He was a man she grudgingly began to admire.

"When we get to the Yeti camp, let me do the talking. They are allies but also easily insulted. So not a word."

Skyler shrugged into the sleeves of the jacket and tugged up the zipper. "I'm quite tactful, not a complete twit." He was being an ass again. Maybe she had been too early to applaud the man.

"So far, your understanding of our various cultures is nil. Do I need to remind you of the Genesis Rite?"

Skyler squeezed her lips tight. "Will you ever let me live the incident down?"

"Someday. Today is not the day. Do not thank a Yeti."

"Why not?"

"It insults them. Implies you think them incapable of a kind act. Also, do not say their names."

"Why?"

"It's like stealing their souls. And do not ask questions. Questions are rude. Pretty much anything offends the Yeti. They're a touchy lot. Speaking of. Do not touch them. Do not eat their food, but use tact when you refuse."

"What's wrong with their food?"

"Let's just say it's undercooked. So, I'll talk while you smile and nod."

He's still a snarly, self-righteous barbarian. No matter how many sand leeches he fries.

Her gaze crawled from Kole's boots to his fire-gold eyes framed by dark, long lashes.

But he is a breathtaking, towering wall of muscle.

"Where is the village?" she asked, clearing her head of the arrogant but virile commander.

"We're at its edge. Start smiling and nodding, Chief."

****

Margo Hunter stared through the peephole at three breathtaking people in the hallway. "Hell. I can't afford so many. I only asked for one. I'll choose and send the other two on their way," she muttered to herself while she opened the door, swooping a hand through the air.

"Come right in."

- With her lips pursed, she angled her head, studying the hunky man in low-slung jeans topped off with a tight black tee. A tattoo peeked beneath his left sleeve, only talons and feathers showing.

- *Some kind of bird.*

- She judged the guy was about six-foot-three, lean but muscular, a swimmer's build with broad shoulders and a narrow waist. "Well, turn around for me." Margo eyed his confusion.

"What?" Hot Guy's brows drew tight.

When she motioned a spin with her finger, he got the drift, doing a slow rotation.

Margo sidled alongside him. She closed her eyes when she combed her fingers through the strands of dark hair flowing down his back, held somewhat in place by a band of red cloth tied Apache-style around his head. Her palms glided downward, stopping just before his taut buns.

While she circled to the front of the dude, her gaze took in every inch of his delicious body. He grinned the whole time, a spellbinding cocky grin, kinda cheerful-like. But he oozed contradictions. Sexy though dangerous, his gray eyes the color of a gathering storm. Open though guarded. A youthful face, harshened by the rough stubble lining his jaw. She fondled his chest. "Flawless. Ripped. I could do a lot with you."

He flashed his smile again. "Have at me, Red."

With her hands on her hips, she continued to ogle the subject. "Very nice."

When the tall, black-haired woman cleared her throat, Margo twisted toward her. The visitor wore skin-tight cargo pants tucked into thick-soled boots. Her jacket fell open enough to reveal a cropped knit shirt hugging sizable breasts. Margo would kill for the shiny straight hair. Of course, she would wear it longer than shoulder length and get rid of the multiple braids. The gal was a lean, leggy gym rat with a dream body and tan. Basically, a threat to all other women.

The third visitor dressed in a patterned blue shirt with matching pants—an attractive version of scrubs—but the shapelessness of the clothes made her body type hard to visualize. Still, her short-cut hair surrounded a soft, round, cherubic face.

Suddenly, Margo's brows furrowed. "Say, how did you get up here? I live in a security-protected building. The guy didn't phone telling me I had guests. Was the guard at the desk asleep again? I'll have his lazy ass fired." Her fists darted to her hips once more. Her head cocked to the side as her long red hair bounced with angry energy.

"No. No." Hot Guy, soon to be her next subject, twisted his lips into a roguish curl when he sauntered toward Margo. "The human was awake, doing his duty."

Strange.

Hot Guy took her right hand and placed it on his pec, covering it with his own.

Hard. Nice.

Margo drew back. Her palm was on fire. She turned to Long-and-Leggy and Scrubs Gal. "You're both lovely, too. Don't get me wrong, but I'm really feeling the guy. I can only afford one of you. So, bye-bye." With a grip on each woman's shoulder, she shoved them toward the door.

Her visitors exchanged glances. Hot Guy spoke for them. "Whoa, Red. We're from the Cleveland Clinic where you had a series of blood samples taken to determine your risk of coronary artery disease." He patted his chest. "Chay. This is Galena and ... um ...

Healer."

"Yeah. It runs in my family. I don't get it. You're not models sent by my agency?"

All three shook their heads.

Margo chuckled. "You must think I'm crazy. I'm a sculptor and was expecting a model for a project I'm starting. So, what's this clinic thing?" She gave them a skeptical squint.

"There was a problem in the lab, corrupted specimens. We need to take another sample." Long-and-Leggy moved a step closer.

"And you've come to my home to do it?"

Hot Guy nodded, his eyes smoldering with seduction.

I'd love to get him into my studio. The body. The muscular-skeletal structure. The bronze skin. The aquiline nose. The genitalia. Crap. Where did that come from?

Margo's hands snapped back to her hips. "Doubtful. I can't even get a doctor to return a call, but the clinic sends three lab assistants to retake blood. Give me a break. I'm no idiot." Her hair was once again bouncing with energy, her head bobbing from side-to-side in disbelief.

Margo gripped the door edge, prepared to push them out. The one Chay had called Galena planted a hand on the frame and spun toward her.

"Oh, holy schism." Galena grabbed both of Margo's shoulders, setting her aside. With ease. "Your charm is not working, Chay. You can't pretty your way into her apartment. Healer, do your stuff."

Margo's temper trumped what should have been fear. "You are no lab tech. Neither is he. They don't wear combat boots or skintight cargos. Now get the hell out of my condo."

Scrubs Gal flicked a wrist. "Please admit us."

"Nice spell." Galena tossed an errant braid behind her ear.

Margo paused, rubbing her arms, a sudden chill giving her goosebumps. "Sure." She stepped away from the door, inviting her guests into her apartment. "What did you say you were here for again?"

Throwing an arm around her waist, Chay drew her toward a chair in the kitchen. "Have a chair, Red."

Margo's feet imitated the robot shuffle. But before she was fully seated, she sprang up. "Hey, I asked you to leave. Get out now."

Scrubs Gal's eyes owled open. "The spell should have lasted longer. I must do a stronger one." She moved close to Margo, muttering soft words. "We're here to help you. We're friends."

While she flopped into the chair, Margo's quizzical brows pulled down as the familiar chill made her shiver.

Galena smirked. "She doesn't look completely spelled to me. Let's hurry. Healer, I think you must be a defective witch."

"I'm the best at my job, Amazon." Scrubs Gal opened a black case, taking out a wicked syringe. She stepped over to Margo, grabbing her left arm, putting it outstretched on the table. Tying a band above her elbow, she asked Margo to tighten her fist. She did, but jumped up again and ripped the band loose, tossing it onto the floor.

She shook out the cobwebs. "Whoa, right there. Leave. Now." Margo sprinted to a drawer where she whipped out a large butcher knife, waving it at the three of them. "I'll cut you. I will."

Galena removed her jacket as if she was planning to stay. "Well, this is a monumental disaster. At least, they won't be sending us on a blood-getting mission again."

****

Skyler latched onto Kole's elbow when the Yetis streamed from their hiding places in the thickets, waving large clubs and surrounding them. A gigantic man stepped forward, his skin weathered, hair matted, his waist-long braided beard tied off with a narrow strip of leather.

Kole raised a hand in greeting.

The giant lowered his club. "Commander of the Firebrands of the Scions. Welcome."

"Woodsman, I greet you. Take us to the elder of the Yeti."

"Come." He motioned for them to follow him into the pines where the camp was well hidden.

Sitting in a clearing on a large throne of tree branches was a man bigger than the others but older, if wrinkles were any indication. His skin was leathery brown from what Skyler could see of it under a white-streaked beard hanging past his waist. Twigs and moss tangled in his long, matching hair.

What surrounded him had her sidling slightly behind Kole. Near the giant was a semicircle of poles, each with a grotesque desiccated head impaled on it. "What are those?" whispered Skyler.

"Gagans."

Kole had explained to her earlier how the Yeti appointed themselves managers, police, and the moral compass of Darque. Since they were Firebrand allies, they had a free pass through Scath as their reward. On occasion, they portaled through the Aeternals' realm and onto Earth, where they amused themselves by giving rise to Sasquatch or Big Foot tales.

But apparently, they were fierce with their

enemies, lobbing off their heads and impaling them on stakes for everyone to see.

"Greetings, Commander of the Firebrands of the Scions." The elder curled gnarled fingers around the arms of the throne.

"Greetings, elder of the Yeti. I come with a guest." Kole motioned for her to move beside him. "She is the Alliance's chief legal officer, a human, a friend. She also greets you."

Skyler took this as her cue to nod and smile, her expression dimwitted but gracious.

"Greetings to you likewise." When the elder grinned, he exposed gaps between his front teeth.

Once again Skyler smiled and nodded.

Kole clasped his hands behind him, appearing at ease. "We ask to tour the village of the Yeti of the Woods."

As if on cue, a young man exited a nearby hut.

He was a smaller, younger version of the throned chief. His hair, though darker, was not as long. Like the elder's, it was knotted with twigs, moss, and leaves. His teeth were yellowed, his shorter beard black, his bare chest tanned, and he wore an animal pelt strapped to his hips. Fur boots laced to his knees. Like other males in the camp, tattoos decorated his arms and legs. "It is my honor to take you around our village."

"My firstborn," explained the elder.

Skyler felt Kole's hand at her back, steering her as they followed their guide along the well-trodden, winding, narrow path. Lining it were large huts, some standing alone, some linked to others, creating small communities within the larger community.

"A single home houses one family, but multiple abodes may adjoin a main house if the woodsman cares for close relatives or has other mates with children."

The guide pointed out a domed hut which was constructed of branches bound with reeds and weatherproofed with mud. Through an open doorway, Skyler observed a woman sitting on a bench at a massive wood table. A cooking pot hung on an iron arm over a fireplace behind her. At her feet, a child played on the floor. While sewing pieces of leather together, the busy mother nodded at the guests.

When they resumed their tour, Skyler tripped on a protruding root on the path. Instinctively, she grabbed onto their guide's shoulder. Villagers sharing the winding road gasped while the young man drew away, his eyes wide.

Skyler froze. She had made a mistake. "I'm so sorry. Truly sorry…" She clasped a hand over her mouth.

Kole pressed a finger to his lips.

Skyler ignored the sign to shush. "I didn't mean to touch you. Have I offended you?"

Again, neighbors and passers-by gasped.

"Now what did I do?" She blew out a breath. Of course, the young man did not like to be touched. She had followed up the first *faux pas* with a question.

Kole seized her elbow, whispering, "Zipper your lips."

His long legs eating up the ground, his arms swinging, the guide sprinted back along the path toward the elder and the large crowd gathering around him.

Kole dragged a mortified Skyler to the throne. "The female touched your firstborn, a move intended to steady herself. In no way did she mean to indicate a desire to mate with him. Though I am sure he is most worthy."

Skyler flicked her eyes to Kole as he pleaded her case before the elder. He cleared his throat. "I am her mate. It was a foolish human error on her part. She begs understanding from the firstborn." He bent toward Skyler. "Take off your scarf." Then he continued talking to the elder. "She offers him a gift in exchange."

When Kole jerked his chin several times in the direction of the young man, she seized on the clue. Skyler unknotted the scarf binding her hair in a ponytail. She pushed it toward their guide.

Rather than accept the gift, he shook his head vigorously. "I demand the offer of mating in its place."

Kole looped a heavy arm over her shoulders. "Not an option since this foolish human is mated to me."

Skyler let a cool expression wash over her face, accepting Kole's ridicule. Anything to get out of this mess.

He waved his hand the length of her body. "As you can see, she is skinny. Not much to look at."

Skyler's gaze swept from Kole to their guide.

"She offered herself as my mate. I accept." The firstborn appealed to his father.

Kole dropped his arm from Skyler's shoulders to step into the young man's space. The Yeti was taller than him by four or five inches but not as muscular. "The offer was not hers to make. It was mine. I will not share the female." Demon fire sparked on his fingertips as the Yeti widened his stance in preparation for Kole's attack.

The elder rose, his voice a bellow which surely could be heard at the edge of the village. "Halt. We will talk. My firstborn, advisors, and I will discuss the matter. Only deficiencies in her nature would make her unfit."

Kole glanced at Skyler, his lips inching into a devious grin. "This female is riddled with deficiencies."

With a meaty hand on each of Skyler's hips, Kole thrust her forward, her back to his chest. "She is narrow hipped, too scrawny to bear a male of much worth. And these. Well."

Skyler swatted at him when he actually squeezed each breast as though testing melons at a grocery store.

He grabbed her hands, turning them palm up. "Look. These are small and without callouses." He fisted Skyler's bicep. "Her muscles are underdeveloped, making her unable to carry buckets of water from the river to the village. You can tell she is unaccustomed to hard work. She lacks kitchen skills. If I want an edible meal, I must prepare it myself. All in all, she's useless."

The young man blurted, "I want her only for my bed."

Skyler pinched her lips tight when Kole continued.

"Alas, her faults there are many. When I bed her, she has trouble making me erect because she lies still, unresponsive to my more than ample charms. Better to dip my wick in a tree hole than in this female."

Over her shoulder, Skyler shot an if-looks-could-kill stare at Kole. Though he was trying to get them out of the trouble she had created, he was having far too much fun concocting her shortcomings.

When the elder entered a hut, followed by his son and advisors, Kole obviously read Skyler's frown. "If I had praised you, you'd be keeping the kid's feet and other appendages warm tonight. I can take him, but once I do, his tribesmen will attack. I can't beat them all." He gave her his lopsided grin, his eyes sparking with amusement.

"I'm sorry, Kole."

"May I say, Chief, I am getting tired of claiming to be your fuckbuddy. It's becoming a dangerous occupation. First the Genesis Rite. Now the Yeti camp. Maybe you could get your fiancé to travel with you. He can fight for your honor. You seem to require a full-time hero. I don't think I'm fit for the task."

"I'm in no mood for jokes, Commander."

"Who says I'm joking?"

The elder returned to the throne, his son and advisors flanking him. "The firstborn will accept the gift instead of the mating."

Skyler clamped a hand over her lip, stifling a loud exhale. She walked up to the young man and, pinching the scarf between her thumb and a forefinger, offered it to him, avoiding any chance of physical contact. He took his time accepting it, his lips a wide unhappy slash, his dark eyes brooding.

"Ah," sighed the elder, "we are friends again. Let us eat."

Kole tsked. "I do wish we could. The sand leech steaks, the harpy wings, and the pine root salad make my tastebuds water, but we must decline because we fed before our arrival. Had I known you would offer food, we would have waited."

The elder waved an understanding hand.

Before they left, Kole approached the throned leader, leaning in to speak in his ear. When Kole finished, the elder threw back his head and roared with laughter.

Skyler shot a narrow-eyed glare at an unrepentant Kole. He shrugged. Any admiration she had developed for the commander disappeared.

Pfft.

****

Chay bolted to Margo to disarm her, grabbing her around the waist, lifting her, her legs scissoring, her feet contacting his shins. Over and over. He held on tight despite her kicks and high-pitched screams.

"Hey, Red. Stop." He shifted her weight so she was slung along his hip. Kinda horizontal-like.

"Let me go." She pounded her fists, hitting

Chay's groin.

"Okay." He set her bare soles back onto the floor but constrained her, his arms wrapped around her, crushing her breasts. "Be gentle, Red. My balls are precious. There. Better. Isn't it?"

"Let me go, you pervert." Margo continued her useless struggle.

Chay put her in the chair. He dropped to his knees in front of her where he plastered her arms at her side. His eyes slid up her body. Down her body. Freckles dotted her creamy light skin. She wasn't tall, but she had curves in all the places he liked. Her red hair was wild, as if she'd just crawled out of bed after a night of sex. He suspected she was untamed like her mane, a lot of energy packed into a small package.

The healer returned to Margo, syringe in hand, shouting above the screams for help. "I have to touch her. It's the only way I can cast a more powerful spell. This human is resistant."

While Chay held a squiggling, yelling Margo, the healer rested a palm on her shoulder. "You will calm so I may take a blood sample. It's for your own good."

Margo shivered, slumping forward into Chay's arms, her cheek rubbing against his chest. She moaned.

Her sexy sounds were doing a number on his libido. He pictured a bed. Both of them naked. *Wait.* He was serious about Anjeli. How could he want to tango with Red?

The healer drew blood, securing the sample in the case. "I don't like her reaction to my first spells. They should have worked on a human. I had to give her a pretty heavy dose this last time. I hope she's all right."

"What could go wrong?" Chay heard the distress in his own voice.

"A million things. After we leave, she could

decide to take a bath, fall asleep, and drown. She could trip going down the steps. She could have a heart attack from being spelled three times. She could accidentally slice herself with the butcher knife she wanted to use on us..."

"I get it." Chay stroked the comatose Margo's back. "Okay. I'll stay behind for a while. You two hot-foot the sample to our lab."

"Aren't you sweet." Galena sent a smirk in Chay's direction. "This isn't a pleasure cruise we're on here."

"I know. I'm all business, dudette."

"Yeah, funny business. And stop with the dudette shit. Call me Galena or don't call me anything. Listen, she better be just fine when you leave. No hickeys, no bruised lips, no trouble walking in the morning. You get my meaning, stud?"

"I get it. Besides, I'm as good as mated to Anjeli."

"You don't act as good as mated." Galena strode out the door in front of the healer.

Chay picked up Margo, enjoying the feel of her curly hair tickling his chin. He deposited her on the couch, fluffing pillows under her head. Then he settled on the other end, content to sit with her legs in his lap until she came out of the spell-induced stupor.

Chapter Fourteen

Kole portaled from the Yeti's forest camp to a northern tundra.

"What did you say to the elder?" Skyler slipped gloves on and tugged down a knit hat until it covered her ears.

He shook his head. "Guy talk."

"It was about me." She snugged the collar of her coat against her neck.

"Jump to conclusions much?"

"Go on. Have your little jokes at my expense. I deserve some ridicule. But you loved fabricating a long list of my faults. By the way, no one has ever complained about my skills in the bedroom."

Kole bared a grin. "Care to demonstrate them?"

"Certainly not with you."

He enjoyed her snapped response, but when her shoulders slumped, guilt spreading across her face, he decided to confess.

"I may have exaggerated the dangers at the village. Though I would have had to pound the elder's son into the ground if the kid hadn't taken the gift in lieu of mating, the rest of the Yeti would've accepted the outcome. No need to battle them all."

Skyler's haughty chin did a toaster pop-up. "Why did you let me believe...?"

"You're an easy mark, fast to rile. When you're pissed, you come alive." Kole didn't say her crackling blue eyes stirred parts of him best not aroused.

"You were intentionally cruel."

"Probably. But you have a knack for inserting

your foot in your mouth. And once it's there, instead of spitting it out, you try to swallow it."

"Just say it. Say, 'I told you so.'" Skyler fisted her gloved hands.

"I'm not an I-told-you-so kind of guy."

She relaxed, her arms drifting to her side. "I admit I should have listened to you and Bounty. I should have acquainted myself with the various cultures on Scath and Darque before I ever came on this tour. I was wrong about the Genesis Rite. I miscalculated how much I could drink at the ball. I made an error at the Yeti village. I have shortcomings. I know it, Kole, but I will get better. I learn from my mistakes. Are you bad at anything?"

"Sure. Small talk, keeping my temper in check, kissing ass, and drinking coffee from tiny cups."

Her lids shuttered her eyes.

Damn. She is beautiful. And way out of my class.

Skyler's shoulders slumped. He could handle her icy arrogance—in fact, he enjoyed pricking it until she sizzled—but her defeat? Not so much. He sauntered over to her, toe-to-toe, and gentled her chin up with his thumb. "I've been rough on you. Your shortcomings are … strangely attractive. Few humans could meet the challenges on Darque. You got through Noir Swamp alive, tangled with an amphista, and dodged a sand leech."

She straightened her spine. "I certainly did."

"You could learn to take advice better, though."

Her big blues fixed on him. "I'm working on it." She tugged her hat down, sliding her frosty expression into place. "Where are we now?"

When Skyler shivered, Kole wrapped an arm around her shoulders, tucking her into his body for warmth, liking how she fit against him, head under his chin. He gestured toward an open, treeless plain where sparse vegetation and frost spread across the surface. Small-leafed shrubs dotted the rolling hills in the distance. "This is a tundra."

"Look. What are they?" A restored Skyler pointed at a pack of fourteen white wolves who emerged from a canyon. They jumped, leaped, and pranced around, their necks arched, their noses lifted, their howls echoing across the permafrost terrain.

"Loup Garou. They're shifters, proud, lethal beasts incapable of controlling their change or hunger for flesh. That's why they live here instead of North Shelters on Scath."

Kole glanced down at Skyler. His mouth gravitated toward her lips. He straightened at the last moment. Sheltered under his arm, she seemed soft, willing, in need of protection. In the crisp air of the tundra, her eyes sparkled like the sky. Her cheeks pinkened from the cold. Her up-tilted face was an invitation to a welcome kiss.

Nope. Not going there. Besides, I don't poach another guy's female.

The earlier kisses had been necessary or mistakes.

"Let's go." Kole shook off the momentary urge and portaled them to the Frozen Northlands, where they watched gigantic white polar rats roam across ice floes. Since the frigid winds coming off the water were strong, they rapidly jumped to the Painted Rock Forest to keep Kole's balls from icing over. They exited in a burned-out section of the woods, the trees bare, their trunks blackened, the ground littered with ash.

"What happened here?" asked Skyler.

"Gagans happened. The hissing, dragon-headed beasts are mean sonsabitches. A couple of their hunting parties from the Great Prairie to the south set these sacred oulder trees on fire just to piss off the Yeti. It was probably their heads on display in the village."

The next stop was a rise looking over Narobi Flats. Kole scanned for hellhounds. Though the beasts often preyed on slower wildings in this region, he saw no signs of them stirring dust.

Skyler yawned.

"I know it's not the company. You're tired. It's time to return. We'll jump to Scath from here."

"But we haven't seen the prison area. Outcast Keep."

"You can skip it."

She stifled another yawn. "I think you're right."

Kole tapped his D-chip as Skyler punched her synced handheld jumper. When nothing happened, the muscles in Kole's jaw tightened. "What the fuck? Try again."

Nothing.

"Here. Let me look at your jumper."

She passed it to Kole. He turned it over in his hands. It looked all right. No exterior damage. No moisture. He crammed it into his pocket. "Hold on to me." When she slipped her fingers through the crook of his elbow, he pressed his chip again. Still nothing. He tried several more times, convinced it would work.

"What's wrong?"

"We're fucking stuck. How's that for shit happens?"

****

Chay shifted his body on the sofa. "Stop with the rub-a-dub-dub, Red. I'm hard as a rock."

Margo's feet wiggled in his lap. She swiped a hand across her freckled face. Her lids slid up. Down. Sluggish-like. When they opened again, she eyed him. "You're still here." She was groggy, licking her dry, puffy lips. "Boy, am I thirsty."

Chay's gaze followed her tongue. He lifted her legs to adjust his pants.

Margo raised onto her elbows. With her spine arched, her breasts strained against her shirt.

While Chay's eyes popped each button, he envisioned his hands sliding across her creamy exposed skin.

"What? You're staring."

The healer must have cast one helluva spell. You wouldn't think such a little human would need such a big dose of knock-out.

She's awake now. I should boogie, but I don't want to go.

Margo shifted to an upright position. "Say. I told you guys to leave." She flung herself against the pillows. "Ooh. My head didn't appreciate the sudden motion. What did you do to me?"

"We sedated you so we could take your blood. Just wait. You'll be fine in a few minutes."

"Where are the two women?"

"They left."

"What are you going to do? Rape me?"

"What? Hell no!" He stroked Margo's legs beneath her full skirt.

"Kill me?"

"Fuck no. Not that either. I parked my ass here to make sure you were okay."

"Let's be straight." Margo slid her feet off Chay's lap, setting them on the floor. She straightened more slowly this time, pressing her hands to her temples. "Who are you guys? You're no lab techs. Don't bullshit a bullshitter. I heard you talk about spells, witches, and Amazons. What kind of crazy shit are you into? And you're sporting a bird tattoo. So was the tall, leggy black-haired woman. What gives?"

"You nailed it, Red. Galena and I are not lab techs. The healer could count as one."

"Healer? What the hell is a healer? A doctor? A nurse? Who are you?"

He settled into the couch, getting comfortable, stretching his long legs out straight. "Chay. Remember? My un-friends call me Chayton."

"Strange name." Margo eyed the tat sticking below his shirt sleeve.

Unable to help a little show, he flexed his bicep, making the feathers quiver.

Margo scooted beside him and grabbed his shirt hem, pulling it over his head in a smooth, quick movement.

Chay assisted by raising his arms in the air. If the female wanted him naked, he was down with it.

Margo's fingers traced the brand, her touch causing his muscles to twitch. "It's beautiful. What's it for?"

"It's a Phoenix."

"Duh. I'm aware. What's it stand for?"

"The Scio … um … my unit."

"Your unit. Are you in the military?

"Sort of."

"Your answers aren't going to cut it with me, handsome. Three people at my door claim to be from the Cleveland Clinic and are making a house call to get more blood. Bull. You tell me you are lab techs. Sure. You and miss beauty-queen, bodybuilder, all-legs girl. You take a knife away from me faster than I can say … hell. Really fast. Then your healer knocks me out with a touch. Bull. Bull. Mucho bull. Stinky and neck high. You're not here to rape me. You're not here to kill me, and I don't have anything of value to steal. So, let's have it."

"I can't tell you." Chay angled his head, taking in her peaches-and-cream complexion, freckles, and green eyes. "I want to, Red." His hand drifted to her thick hair. He rolled strands of it between his fingers. "And I like it when you touch me. I think you kinda like it, too." His mouth moved close enough to feel the heat from her breath.

Margo planted her palms on his chest, pushing. "Okay, now you're just pissing me off. Put it in reverse, buddy. You're not getting a kiss from me."

"I think I am." Chay grinned. Despite what she said, her lips parted in invitation. He swept a lazy tongue across them, tasting, savoring, licking. Chay latched onto her red curls, fisting her hair, arching her neck. He swung a heavy leg over her thighs.

Before he could go hard and fast for the kiss, he snapped his gaze toward the door. A loud crash sounded as four large males slammed into the living room.

Chay jumped off the couch and leaped over the back. He beelined for a drawer in the kitchen. With a couple of the biggest knives in his hand, he sprinted to a now-standing Margo, shoving her behind him, shielding her with his body. He sidestepped them away from the attackers.

"Stay with me, hold on. Go in reverse when I do." All business now, Chay cussed under his breath, wondering what he and Galena were thinking when they had decided to leave their weapons on Scath so as to keep the human comfortable.

Barking dumb idea.

Chay faced the Aeternals. A pride demon broke from the group to come forward while the other three spread out. Chay kept stepping away with Margo, her fists clasped tight to the waistband of his jeans.

The four invaders advanced, but Chay paid

particular attention to the approaching demon. "Stop right there. I'm Scion Firebrand Chay. You are in violation of the Temple of Justice. Any attack will result in your deaths."

"Fuck the Temple and fuck you," said the demon.

Chay dodged left when the male lashed out with a blinding laser-like light intended to cut him in half. In avoiding the assault, Chay forced Margo to keep step with him. With unerring ylve aim, he threw the butcher knife at an angle. The force of it severed the male's head.

As a second demon and the incubus came at Chay, the fourth member of the happy group, a warlock, cast a spell. With it, he pried Margo away.

Chay took his eyes off the two attackers in front of him to fling the last blade into the warlock's heart before the male could flick his wrist a second time.

With the ylve Firebrand's attention momentarily diverted, the sloth demon did what those assholes do best. The guy clawed him. Chay's legs collapsed. His knees hit the rug. He struggled against the lethargy. But each time he staggered to his feet, the guy sliced him again, giving him another dose of the sleepies. Finally, he crumbled, unable to rise, paralyzed.

With his pupils, Chay tracked the incubus who grabbed Margo. He tore open her shirt, his palm hovering over her heart. "I can kill her, Firebrand. You know I can take this female's lifeforce if I press my hand to her bare skin."

While his body regained strength, Chay looked around the room, spying at least four ways to escape. If it had been just him, he could flee. But he refused to desert a defenseless Margo. He turned cold, gray eyes on the incubus.

Options. They didn't seem inspired to kill her outright. They wanted her alive. So, he had to stay alive to protect her.

Chay forced himself onto his knees, still weak, nearly upchucking. "She's ylve-struck. Obsessed. If I leave her side, she'll die. She needs me." His eyes pinched together as he stared at Margo. He hoped his look said it all.

Please figure out what the fuck ylve-struck means. Then act accordingly.

Margo wrinkled her forehead, hesitating, shaking her head negligibly. She glanced at the remaining attackers before returning her gaze to Chay. Her brows arched. "Chay." She reached out a hand, straining to break the incubus's hold, whimpering. "I love him. Let me go to him, please."

Damn. Quick study. Sexy and savvy.

"See what I mean. I was about to use her condition to my advantage, but you came along and ruined a good time." Chay grinned. "Nothing better than imbibing in horizontal refreshments with an ylve-struck female. So sweet." His knees wobbled as he pushed to his feet. He pumped his hips forward. "They can handle a pounding and keep on purring. What can I say? ylves are ylves, and an ylve-struck human is a sure bet."

The incubus paused, studying Margo, who continued to sniffle as she strained toward Chay. "Take him along. We can't risk it. Humans who are ylve-struck die if they are separated from their obsession. But keep him weak until we get to the compound."

"What'll we do about them." The sloth demon pointed to the two bodies on the floor.

"They're worthless. Leave 'em. The mage will probably live, but the demon is done for."

When the incubus released Margo, she sprinted to Chay. "You've hurt my ylve, bastards."

"Not yet. If you must have this male, help him

walk."

Chay looped his arm over her shoulders, struggling to stay upright. He whispered, "Touch me often. Get hysterical if I am parted from you."

Margo's eyes widened, but she nodded.

Chay hoped his smile reassured her. He would save her even if it meant his life for hers. It was the honorable thing to do. Besides, he had a fondness for the spirited, brave, smart redhead.

****

Rein waited in his father's office, twisting his neck from side to side, trying to relieve the strain. "Galena and Chay tagged along with your healer to Cleveland. The Amazon said they got the follow-up specimen from Margo Hunter, but she was difficult. Chay apparently stayed behind to monitor her since the healer used a triple whammy. Problem is, he hasn't reported in yet."

"Her blood sample is being examined now. As for the young ylve, is it unusual for him to be late?" Rein's father shuffled papers on his desk while watching Indigo dance barefoot around his office. "Perhaps he succumbed to the human's charms and stayed the night."

Rein grinned at his aunt. Her braid bounced rhythmically, probably keeping time with the music coming through her earbuds. Her hands punched into the air as her long skirt tumbled around her ankles.

He returned his focus to Alarik. "Though it would be like him to charm a human into a sleepover, he would contact us. What's worse is we can't get a definite trace on him. His D-chip behavior is erratic. Whenever we're near a fix, it fizzles out. Any reported problems with our devices?"

"None. They are highly reliable. Your own Logan oversees production. They cannot be turned off. We are aware of only one way to block the signal, but we will never reveal the secret. Of course, if the chip were dug out of your wrist, it would not function."

D-chips, or Digital Implant Communication Chronometers, were prime tech. Healers embedded them in a Firebrand's arm, wiring them to the brain so the warriors could talk to each other without moving their lips. They had other uses. Portal jumper. GPS. Restraint. Shadowflasher. Hell. They told the time, gave the weather, took selfies, played music.

Rein glanced at his technological marvel. "There's more. Kole should have reported in from Darque by now. Can't reach him either."

"What's he doing there?"

"He's playing tour guide for the Alliance's chief legal officer."

Indigo interrupted with a Willie Nelson song. "On the road again. Just can't wait to get on the road again." She removed an ear bud. "Anyone want to join the sing-along?"

Both males shook their heads.

"Why would he take her to Darque?" Alarik resumed the convo when Indigo shrugged and replaced the listening device, continuing with her dance.

"When she demanded to go, Cadmon backed her."

"Any possibility Kole is giving her a special tour? He is a demon with a strong need to feed."

Rein growled. "With the commander, it's duty first. If he decided to fuck her, he'd wait until the assignment was over. Besides, his chip isn't sending a signal either. We're also pinging her portal jumper, but no response there."

Indigo stopped dancing, pulling out both ear pods. "You two need to worry less and dance more."

"Do you know something, Auntie?" Rein crossed his arms over his chest.

"I think so. I'm a little foggy on quantum physics, and calculus always stumps me, but beyond those I think I know something."

"Auntie, that's not what I mean."

"Boyo, you've lost your zip. Okay. One stream upriver had you losing your commander along with his arm charm. The chick from the party. I told her to rethink her choices. Nobody ever listens to me. I'm just some gorgeous witch bitch with no noggin for serious biz." Indigo paused. "What? Not bothering to correct me? Oh, well. In one future you locate them. In another, he dies. Afterward she gets it on with a new handsome demon."

She tapped her chin with a finger. "Few of those beasts, however, are better looking than the hunky, muscle-bound, fire-eyed commander. Yum-yum. Sizzle." She twirled a strand of hair in her fingers. "Or not. Those futures flowed into each other. Then the view got whirlpooled. No wait, I saw another. Kole and the sexy platinum-blonde bobble were doin' the demon nasty. Say, is it time for a drink yet?"

"No, dear. Listen to your music." Alarik fixed his gaze on his son. "Too many coincidences. What are the Scion Firebrands doing?"

"We've divided our unit. Some are searching for Chay. Some are… Hold on."

Rein tapped his wrist as he moved to the side. When he returned, he stretched his neck from side to side again. "There's a mess at the human's place in Cleveland—broken door, dead Aeternal, recent scent of a sloth demon, mage, and incubus. Residents have seen too much. I gave the order to clean the area. The crew will dispose of the body, fix the damage, and wipe the neighbors' memories. I'll reach out to the Alliance, enlist them in the search for Chay and Margo Hunter Earthside while we do our shit here. Anyway, the rest of my unit is scouring Darque for Kole and Chief Maxwell. Something's wrong. It's knotting my muscles."

"I'll put my scryers on both cases, but they are already busy searching for Blood Coven descendants, sex slaves, and Cerberus."

"Meanwhile, we're prepping the stronghold for guests. We'll be housing any descendants found. The shit is hitting the fan, and we could use Kole. I could use him."

Indigo gave a small bow, popping out her buds. "I could use better music."

Chapter Fifteen

Kole punched his D-chip along with Skyler's jumper again. The fact neither of them worked concerned him. He didn't buy coincidence. He touched his sparking fingers together, containing his surging temper.

"You know the definition of insanity is doing the same thing over and over and expecting different results. Albert Einstein." Skyler sat on a rock, bent forward, tracing a circle in the dirt with a twig.

"Hmph." He tapped his chip again. "Though I may fail a hundred times, may I be judged by the time I succeed. The Cambion of Wales."

From the small rise where they were stranded, Skyler's gaze swept across Narobi Flats. "Can we wait somewhere less exposed until we jump? Someplace warmer?" She pulled her coat tighter around her body. "Besides, can't we just punch a location code into any portal?"

Kole scanned the area, considering their options. Since night would soon be upon them, he didn't relish being here either. She was right. They were too exposed. "Darque isn't like Scath. Travelers can't just punch in location codes. A device is needed. We'll head for Spriggan Enclave a little north. The villagers don't possess jumpers, but it's somewhere to rest, to get more supplies while I figure out what went wrong. If nothing changes, I know a place we can go." He held out a hand for Skyler.

She dropped the stick, placing her palm in his. "Why would both transportation devices be defective? Is it sunspots or some other interference?"

"Doubtful. Never had this happen before. Since a belief in coincidence is for idiots, I think somebody hopes one of us meets with an accident. I have plenty of enemies, but I don't see them coming at me this way. Have you left any bleeding hearts in your past who might want to whack you? How about a pissed off client?"

"None. I'm surprisingly enemy free."

Skyler blinked, as if reconsidering her statement, but she didn't say anything. He didn't press.

"How much food or water do we have?"

Kole checked his knapsack. They had ample water if they were careful until they reached the enclave. They had a week's worth of tablets to purify creek or river water if necessary. As for the rest, they had two protein bars and four dried food packets. "By midday tomorrow, we'll make it to Spriggan Enclave. We'll survive easily with what's here. We sleep outdoors tonight."

She smiled, but her eyes were a worried blue.

Kole slung his pack over a shoulder. "You'll be safe with me. I haven't lost a human CLO yet."

Skyler's laugh was soft, a bubbling fountain. He liked it. "How many regular humans have you lost? If you don't mind my asking."

"I don't mind. None. I have an excellent record." Kole wrapped an arm around her, sharing his body heat.

"I'm sorry."

Her up-turned face and slightly parted lips made Kole want to kiss her. He restrained himself. "Nothing to be sorry about, Frisca. Like I said before, 'Shit happens.'"

He pointed across the prairie. A grassy expanse, it was sprinkled with patches of shoulder-high thorny bushes. In the distance were low trees, thick shrubs, mounds of giant boulders. Behind those, mountains. "I'd like to reach the small outcropping of rocks while we still have light. The Sardasian Stones. We'll pitch camp there, build a fire, eat. In the morning, we'll stick to the base of the foothills for cover."

"Sounds good. I'm starved. You know how hungry I get when I'm nervous. Not that I'm worried." Skyler tripped on a large bone.

Kole examined it. "Questing beast. Femur. We're at the edge of the plains where they roam. Probably taken down by a harpy."

"It's big."

"You've seen them. Better the bone of a dead questing beast than running into a live one." Kole set his gaze on the sun sinking lower in the sky.

"How long do you think it will take us?" Skyler shielded her eyes.

"Depends on what we run into."

She stuck her chin out, a trait he was beginning to like, and said with a wicked grin, "What could possibly happen?"

Kole laughed. "Yeah. What could possibly happen? We're going to walk faster now. Jogging when we can. The area is pretty wide open, making us wilding bait."

"Okay. Let's go."

They began at a slow jog. After a while, Kole turned around. Skyler lagged behind, having trouble with the uneven terrain. When he paused, she stopped, bent, and put her hands on her knees, breathing heavily. "Keep going. I'll make it."

"Hell you will. I could carry you for a while."

"Are you kidding? No. We can't afford to have you get tired. I'll make it. I promise I won't let you down."

"Frisca." Kole cupped her chin, staring into her

blue eyes. "I never thought you would."

She backed away, propping her hands to her hips. "Really? I almost got literally fucked at the Genesis Rite. I got smashed at a dinner in my honor. Of course we're on this abominable realm because I insisted on it. I nearly got a husband at the Yeti camp. Just what about me warrants your confidence? Admittedly, I can draw up one hell of a trade agreement, run a legal office, set other lawyers quivering in their Gucci shoes, and bark orders at my employees. Let's face it, though. Other than that, I'm pretty dismal. I'm surprised you haven't ditched me."

"I'll never ditch you, Frisca. What are a few mistakes anyway? Nobody's perfect. I think your successes speak for themselves."

She cleared her throat, her eyes moist. "Thank you. What's a Frisca, by the way?"

"It's demonish for … um … little one."

"I'm not very little."

He liked her height. She could snuggle in right under his chin. "To me you are. Come on, let's move."

"Okay. Onward. Upward. I'm through feeling sorry for myself … for us. Try to keep up with me, Commander." Skyler took off, jogging ahead, taking the lead, her backpack bouncing.

When they were nearly three quarters of the way to the Sardasian Stones, a *thwump, thwump, thwump* sound carried to Kole's ears.

He yelled, "Get down." Pushing Skyler flat against the grass, he threw his body on top of her. A squadron of gigantic, black birds with human-like female heads flew into view. In V formation, they soared overhead, the light fading when they blocked the sun.

Sharp, crooked, taloned feet hung below the low-flying creatures with faces of ugly hags. The flapping of their wings sent a fierce wind across the plains, ruffling the grasses, spreading the wildings' distinctive odor. Rotting flesh. Just as they had nearly passed, the last two-winged monsters turned their heads and sniffed the air.

"Fuck," said Kole. "I think they got a whiff of us."

"What are they?"

"Harpies." He searched the terrain for a plan. He spotted one. "Quick now. Crawl over to those bushes. We'll hide in them until they leave. Be careful of the leaves on the kas nettle. They can sting. But a little pain is better than the feathered hags' teeth or claws."

Kole rolled off Skyler, giving her space to hand-and-knee it toward the shrubs. He followed her as she wriggled between two close plants. The fine hairs on the leaves were already stinging his bare skin.

But the harpies would never catch their scent as long as they stayed here. Kas nettle camouflaged their odor, and the flying predators relied on their sense of smell. It was better than their eyesight.

Skyler groaned, but Kole clasped a hand over her mouth. Catching her eye, he shook his head. They couldn't risk a noise reaching the harpies now that they were close. Their sense of hearing was only slightly less acute than their ability to smell.

Kole listened to the *thwump, thwump, thwump* of their wings, accompanied by their shrew-like screeches as they searched the grasslands for prey. They circled and circled, a single scout flying low, her shrieks so close by Kole was sure she'd sighted them. Before the sun sank lower in the sky, the female wildings moved on, the wind created by the flapping wings decreasing while their distance increased. When their harsh cries died out, Kole scooted from the bushes. He pulled Skyler out by her feet.

Demon sparks shot from his fingers. Skyler's hands and neck were covered with fine stingers from the kas nettle. A few had burrowed into her cheek. Where they contacted skin, she developed a bright red rash.

Her lashes rolled up. She stared at Kole. "I was quiet."

"You were, Frisca." Kole contained his fire. Extracting the hairy stickers was his priority. But his fingers were so large. Nonetheless, he removed each from her face, then neck, and finally her hands.

She drew shallow puffs of air, her fist to her mouth, while she struggled with the pain. The rash on her skin spread, seeming to eat away at her flesh.

Kole lifted her, cradling her, racing in a straight line toward the Sardasian Stones. When he stumbled, he righted himself without falling. When a bush was in his way or when a large pothole dipped down in front of him, he jumped over them. When his legs and arms grew tired, he shook off the fatigue. He was possessed. His single obsession was to get Skyler to safety before nightfall and make her as comfortable as possible.

Once he reached the boulders, he found an area where a massive stone had fallen across others, creating a cave-like protected shelter. He leaned Skyler against a rock to remove his backpack. As the sun set, he gathered small twigs and grasses, making thick piles, laying a blanket on top. He moved Skyler to the more comfortable spot.

Next, he collected wood. Shooting a stream of fire from his hand, he lighted the sprigs and bigger branches. Since they were inside a covered area, it would not attract much attention.

Curled, her knees tucked tight on her makeshift mattress, Skyler watched. "Nice trick." Her voice was weak.

"It's handy." He put water into a collapsible pan and set it on the fire. When it was hot, he poured it into a dried dinner pouch. Sitting behind Skyler, he pulled her upright against his chest.

"Smells good. What is it?" Kole caught a shudder of pain when she winced.

He didn't understand her response to kas nettle. Stinging hairs had penetrated his exposed skin, but he had nothing to show. Skyler was having a serious reaction. Maybe demons had immunity from the bush's chemicals. Or humans were allergic to it.

He looked at the label. "Yak stew. Butchered and dried on Scath."

Skyler scooped a bite out of the bag. "Hmm. Good. Your turn." She held a spoonful out for Kole.

"Just what I had in mind for dinner." After he snatched a morsel, he handed the utensil back to her.

Skyler waved the spoon at Kole after taking another mouthful herself. "I had a dream while you were carrying me. Strangest. Chay, the Firebrand ylve I met at the ball … I believe his name was Chay … was in a prison with a beautiful redheaded woman. Why would I dream about him?"

She offered a spoon of yak stew to Kole again. The simple gesture while she was in pain made his blood boil, his heart clang against his ribs like a cymbal. He reached for water, giving another bottle to Skyler, who gulped it down.

Kole felt her forehead. "Hot. You have a fever. I think your wounds are infected." He touched a few of the more serious ones.

"Ouch." When he opened her shirt wider at the neck, she slapped his hand. "Keep away from the private parts."

Kole raised his arms in surrender. "I'm certain infection is setting in. The rash has spread. The Healing Pond is this side of Spriggan Enclave. A slight detour but necessary. When we get there, you can bathe in the pond to disinfect the wounds. Once that's done, I'll cauterize them. They'll heal rapidly afterward."

"It sounds painful."

"Not as painful as death."

Skyler shivered, running her hands along her arms. "I'm cold. Cold and tired. I'll just close my eyes for a while."

Kole slipped away, covered her with another blanket and two jackets. Still, she trembled. After dousing the fire, he stretched out beside her, wrapping her tight against him, rolling a little heat through his body. The nettles were acting like poison. She could die.

Groaning but snuggling into Kole's warmth, Skyler flipped around to face him. "I can't sleep. I hurt. A thousand sharp knives are cutting me at once."

"I wish I could help, Frisca. Will talking take your mind off the pain?"

"Maybe. What about?"

"You told the healer you knew of your Aeternal ancestor."

She winced. "Family history. That's substituting one pain for another. Our ugly story comes in bits and pieces. Some was written in journals. Some was told in second-hand accounts. None of it is pretty."

He stroked the back of his fingers along her feverish cheek, wishing he could take away her discomfort. "What else do we have to do?"

****

Jace rested the worn book on her chest. *The Path* fluttered closed when she shut her eyes. She and Celene lay in bed, dressed only in lightweight pajamas, not having eaten since they began the hunger strike several days ago. She sighed, brushing aside thoughts of food, opening the volume again.

"I was thumbing through our favorite book last night when I found some great parables. This Ohngel guy is a hunky winged warrior and a thinker. Do you want me to read a few?"

"No. Not feeling it." Celene rolled to her side, propping herself on an elbow.

Before Jace closed the work, boots thudded across the kitchen floor. When the bedroom door flew open, an unknown man leaned against the jamb. He was taller than six feet, topped with straight dishwater-blond hair falling to his shoulders, and made super scary by brown eyes ringed with crimson. When his lips curled, he revealed sharp fangs.

Jace, her heart pounding against her ribs, hugged her companion. She flashed on her captor, Silas, who had attacked her and sunk teeth into her neck. This man could be a stunt double. He was a vampire, too.

Celene patted Jace's hand while she glared at the intruder.

"You wanted me. I'm here. Get your asses out of bed and eat." His voice scraped across Jace's skin like sandpaper.

Gathering her courage, she spoke first. "You have to give us some information before we do anything."

"We have demands." Celene scooted against the headboard, sitting straighter, crossing her arms over her chest.

"Demands?" He materialized next to Celene, grabbed her arm, and yanked her out of the bed, slapping her across the face. Once. Twice. Her legs gave out. She hung dishrag-limp in his grip. "Now get the fuck to the kitchen. Eat."

Jace winced at his treatment of her friend but threw her shoulders ramrod straight and continued. "No. First you tell us what we want to know. Second, meet our demands." She lowered her eyes. "We're prepared to die."

He tossed Celene onto the bed. Jace pulled her tight, smoothing a hand down her back. Her roommate's cheek was red, already beginning to swell.

"You want answers? Follow me." He stalked out the door.

"Are you all right, honey? Can you make it out there?" Jace asked.

"I'll make it. Asshat won't break me." Celene wiggled her jaw but pushed up, grabbed her robe, tying it around her, and padded toward the outer room.

Jace rose, slipped baggy sweatpants on over her pajama bottoms, and followed.

The women sat beside each other on the couch while the non-human slouched in the large side chair.

He waved his hand at them. "Well. What do you want to know?"

Celene clasped Jace's palm. "For starters, what is your name? What are you?"

"I'm the vampire Lort."

Jace took a deep breath. "Why are we here? Where are we?"

"You are here because my boss thinks you are special females. Don't ask to meet him. You'll starve to death before that shit happens. You are on Scath. Not Earth. It's a different realm."

Celene squinted her eyes. "What's special about us? How long does he plan to keep us? What does he propose to do with us?"

"My answer to all three questions is 'I dunno.' It's the old pay grade issue."

Jace squeezed Celene's hand. None of this information made her feel warm, fuzzy. In fact, she was cold, scared. "Our guards aren't human. What are they?"

"Mostly demons of one tribe or another. Does it matter?"

Releasing Jace's grip, Celene shook her head. "We have demands. We can't survive penned in like this. We need activities. We need fresh air."

"What do you suggest?"

"Movies, games, outdoor exercise, an indoor gym. Shit to occupy our time. We want to meet with you whenever we have concerns."

The vampire unfolded from his chair, his movement liquid, his lips curled into a sneer. "I will see about your *demands*." He emphasized this last word. Lort flashed to Jace, pulling her off the couch, walking her backward until she slammed against the wall. He yanked her sweats down and cupped her sex through her thin pajamas. "If you stop eating again or threaten me or my males, you'll regret it. You will not die because my boss forbids it. Trust me, though, there are worse things than death. Now get out in the kitchen and eat."

He stormed from their quarters, promising to return with solutions if they did as directed. Her eyes tearing, Jace glanced at Celene. She swiped at the leaking moisture. He had answered their basic questions, holding out hope their demands would be met. But their circumstances sounded hopeless. Monsters held them captive for an unknown reason, for an unknown length of time, in an unknown place. The end game of their jailer was a mystery. She would have said life couldn't get any worse, but she was afraid it had.

Celene sprang off the couch, stomping toward the kitchen, opening a can of chicken noodle soup, heating it in a pan.

Jace joined her. Between sobs, she slurped liquid and munched crackers with a water chaser.

Sniffling, Jace let the information settle along with dinner. "Hey. This doesn't mean we stop trying to escape. We will find a way out. This just means we might be a little more comfortable until we do."

Celene charged into the bedroom, returning with *The Path*. "Damn straight." She started reading aloud.

Parable 9: A great mystic sat by a lake…

Chapter Sixteen

Chaumont, NY, 1836

The Arneson Traveling Show came to Chaumont, NY, in 1836, bringing with it colorful wagons and a menagerie of exotic beasts the residents had never seen. A thinly clad woman rode through the village on an elephant, followed by caged wild cats, a polar bear, camel, zebra, and buffalo.

Abrahm Maxwell perched on a wagon seat, a self-dubbed lion tamer. One knee was casually bent with his foot resting on the toe board. His pants were worn, dirty. His flannel shirtsleeves were rolled up, revealing thick forearms. His expression was bored, but his alert eyes searched the crowds of villagers for a pretty female of childbearing age. Ramrod straight, suddenly interested, he spotted the perfect choice. Catching her attention, he displayed a seductive smile and a wink, both intended to make her take notice.

He was successful because later the same day while tents were being set up and the animals fed, she walked arm-in-arm with another female, enjoying the buzz of activity accompanying the preparation for the show. The lion tamer sidled over to her, grazing her shoulder. When she turned around, he knew he had chosen wisely. This was the human he would wed and allow to birth his offspring.

Three days later Abrahm Maxwell married sixteen-year-old Emily Caldwell in a quiet ceremony against her parents' wishes. The judge, a longtime family friend, performed the ceremony with scowling eyes, but since the traveling show con man had already bedded

Emily, he had no choice.

On her wedding night, Emily, despite the inexperience of youth, began to suspect life married to this man would not be what she imagined in her dreams. His lovemaking changed from romantic gentleness to violent self-gratification when he forced himself on her over her objections. Despite her tears. For four days he kept a naked Emily in bed to feed his varied sexual appetites. Then he left to rejoin the traveling show, depositing a negligible amount of money on the dresser for her to use until his return.

Abrahm came back to Chaumont in another month, showing up at her doorstep. In his hand he clutched a small bouquet of flowers gathered from a neighbor's yard, a box of candy from the local five and dime, and a bottle of cheap champagne. Presenting these gifts as if he deserved a great welcome home, he grabbed her into his arms, carrying her into the bedroom where he ripped off her clothes. He took her again and again. When he left, Emily was exhausted, barely aware he had stopped violating her body.

When her parents tried to visit, she hid behind the door, battered, bruised, embarrassed, refusing to let them enter. On trips into town to get food, she donned baggy dresses. With a scarf covering her head, she kept her chin tucked in, her eyes cast to the dirt. Gone was the happy, carefree girl who laughed as she strolled through the carnival ages ago.

Returning to Emily many months later, Abrahm was overjoyed to see she was with child. While he was present, he demanded she cook, clean, wait on him. He berated her continually for her slovenly looks, unclean body, unkept hair, and sullen expression. She shuffled through the house doing what he bid or cowering in the corner until he again called for her.

Abrahm required daily sexual release, but because he feared the unborn child could be harmed, he resorted to activities Emily had never heard of, seen, or dreamed of. When he found her on the bathroom floor trying to slit her wrists with a kitchen knife, he beat her, avoiding any injury to the babe. She vowed she would never bring his baby into this world. To make sure she did, Abrahm tied her to the bed for the remaining month of her pregnancy. Daily she fought him while he fed her, gave her drink, or made her touch him until he could ejaculate.

When the pains of childbirth began, he fetched a midwife from the village. Stepping through the bedroom door, the woman held her arm to her nose. The stench! Emily lay in her own filth with her wrists bloodied by the constant friction of the ropes restraining her to the bed, strings against which she struggled constantly. The villager had no time to do anything but recognize the deplorable conditions. The babe was coming.

Emily screamed, rambling incoherently in her pain, but when the infant breathed its first breath, she lost all hope. She expired, saying to the midwife, "He's not human, you know."

Without a glance or concern for his wife, Abrahm snatched his son from the midwife's arms. The child was strong, healthy, nothing like the lad's mother.

Chuckling, he returned the babe to the female, told her to take him to the Caldwell's house, walked out the door, and rejoined the traveling show. Even if the persistent Scion Firebrand demon successfully avenged the death of his parents, Abrahm's line would continue.

****

Bile rose in Kole's throat. He had stopped listening to Skyler's story after she spoke the name Abrahm.

No. It can't be. The carnal demon who murdered my parents sired a child? The descendant of the monster who orphaned me is the female I'm protecting on Darque? Perhaps that's why we've clashed from the start.

When she stopped talking, Kole bent forward to stare. Skyler had fallen into a fitful sleep, twitching with what he imagined was unbearable pain. He removed his arm from under her head when sparks began to ignite on the tips of his fingers. Rising before the first hint of daylight, he walked from the safety of the boulders, anywhere away from the descendant of Abrahm. He gasped for air, his chest expanding. Contracting. He couldn't get enough of it.

At age ten, Kole had found the bodies. Abrahm and a band of renegades fighting in the Demon Insurrection had killed his parents in their own home. A Firebrand investigation revealed Hestia had died first, her head severed from her body. Likely, Aedon, distracted and trying to save her, lost his own life to the same blade.

Logic told him Skyler was not to blame for Abrahm's actions. Still, his enemy's blood ran through her veins. He had spawned her line. Kole jerked around when she moaned.

Skyler shifted under the blankets and coats. "Kole?" Her weak voice was barely above a whisper.

Ignore her.

She'll give up, go back to sleep.

He couldn't be anywhere near the descendant of his parents' killer. He released a stream of fire at a nearby boulder.

"Kole, are you out there? Are you okay?"

He heard the soft shuffling of the blanket and jackets. She was getting off the pallet.

Fuck.

"I'm right here. Stay put. Damn it." He inhaled, blasting the boulder once again before he returned to her.

****

Though Kole lay beside her again, she was unable to sleep. So, Skyler finished her story, despite his apparent mood change.

Abrahm's son, Raymond, grew up in the Caldwell house hearing only how his father was a beast. For all the Caldwells knew, Raymond could be the same. Never able to move out of this evil shadow, at age thirteen he tied a tablecloth around what few clothes he owned, walked out the door, and hopped a train.

He traveled the rails for years looking for a small carnival with a lion tamer. When he found the Arneson Traveling Show, they directed him to one of the wagons where he located his father.

Raymond suspected the Caldwells exaggerated his father's cruelty, but they hadn't.

After Abrahm studied his son, he declared him to be short and scrawny. "Turn around," he commanded. "Let's see what you've got. Do you eat enough, boy?"

Raymond shrugged. "Enough. What I can git."

Abrahm, wanting some sign his genes had been passed on to his son, decided to conduct a test. "How often do you bed females?"

"I haven't. That don't come up on the rails."

"Hmm. Follow me." The lion tamer took his offspring into a run-down part of the city where life was cheap. "Look into my eyes, Raymond."

Raymond looked. His father's irises glowed with an inner power. When Abrahm saw a female on the street, he lured her into an alley with his smile. "Let me see you take her, boy."

"What do you m-mean?" Raymond glanced at the puzzled woman.

"I ain't doin' no kid. I came here for a man." She turned to leave, but Abrahm pinned her with a glowing light shooting from his eyes.

"What do I mean? Fuck her, lad. Use your power from me to take her. You do have the power to draw others to you, don't you? Your mother was the easiest female I ever had. I barely had to use my gift. She was so compliant."

"I don't even k-know this woman."

Abrahm stormed toward the boy, slammed him against the brick building, and screamed into his ear. "I don't give a fuck if you know her or not. Lure her. Use your eyes. Lift her skirts. Make her beg you. Now!"

Raymond, scared of this man, tried. He approached the woman. "I want to h-have s-sex with you. How about it?"

She sidled along the wall, trying to escape. Terror replaced the confusion in her gaze.

"Let's just do this." Raymond glanced over his shoulder at a frowning Abrahm as he whispered, "Then, he'll l-let us go."

Tears rolled down her cheeks.

"You are not your father's son." Abrahm stomped to the woman, his glowing irises casting a beacon of light. The slack-jawed female stumbled to the boy. She undid his pants, pulling out his cock. She lifted her skirts and dropped her drawers, guiding the boy's rigid penis into her cunt. Once buried inside her, Raymond understood. He grasped her ass, pumping in and out of her. He didn't last long, wailing as he came.

Abrahm pushed his son away. "You aren't through yet, honey."

When Abrahm finished with the sobbing woman, he shoved her to the ground. Draping an arm over his son's shoulder, he led him out of the alley. He told

Raymond he had escaped Scath and was a pride demon. He explained since his mother was human, obviously Raymond had inherited none of his abilities.

About ten years later, Raymond heard his father had been killed. He felt nothing. Yet, strangely, he spent his entire life feeling somehow "deficient."

Raymond married a "deficient" woman at the start of the Civil War. Having been drafted, he was incarcerated from 1864 till the end of the war in the infamous Andersonville Prison. Though he didn't die there, the disease, poor sanitation, malnutrition, and exposure took a toll on his life.

He returned to a failing farm at the end of the war, more broken, sickly. When he died, he left his wife two things—a son, Samuel, born in 1867, and a journal documenting his father's cruelties and demon heritage.

The child, Samuel Maxwell, grew up in post-war Illinois on a farm that was mortgaged to the hilt. The land was incapable of raising crops despite neighbors who did quite well. But he was strong. He was determined. Determined to make money, determined to have a good life, determined to make something of himself, determined to marry well, determined to find others who claimed to have Aeternals in their family history. He did those things, becoming an early founder of the Earth-Scath Alliance. Over the years, the name changed to the Alliance Security Agency. Modeling itself after the famous Pinkerton National Detective Agency, it became a private protection operation with investigators and a paramilitary. Behind the scenes, it cooperated with new-found ancestors on Scath.

Samuel's son, born at the turn of the century, rose higher than his father. Jedson Maxwell was the first in the family to attend law school, graduate, and pass the bar. He labored at private firms for years until the

Alliance opened a legal office to handle their growing businesses.

Jedson's son, Skyler's father, Alden Maxwell, followed in his father's footsteps by attending law school. Working for the Alliance, he eventually rose in the organization to become chief legal officer.

Skyler winced as she shifted onto her hip. Propping her head on a palm, she sighed. "There's the whole ugly story. I attended Harvard, graduated at the top of my class, passed the bar, and at the age of thirty-two became the Alliance's youngest CLO."

Kole brushed a tear from her cheek. "Pain?"

"Yes. From the kas nettle as well as the memories of my father. Truth be told, I disappointed him from birth. I wasn't a man. I'd never measured up to the Maxwell standard. If you can believe it, I'm not cutthroat enough despite my father's best efforts. He berated me for any perceived weakness, lapse, error, or fault. He called it building character. When my mother died in childbirth, he deposited me with a succession of nannies. I … I…"

Skyler's voice trailed off and her head bobbed. After a few moments, she awoke with a jerk. "I have none of the pleasant childhood memories others talk about. No family picnics, no movies and popcorn, no birthday parties, hugs, smiles, chats over dinner, or friends. It was work, work, work. Work harder. Even Christmas sucked."

Skyler tried but failed to find a more comfortable position. "When I was quite young, my nanny took me to the mall where Santa sat on a big chair. At least, it seemed big to me. I crawled onto his lap. He asked what I wanted. I was stumped for an answer. He told me to think about it, to write my wish in a letter, address it to the North Pole, and give it to my mommy. I said I didn't have a mother. He said it would work if I gave my daddy the letter. My wish would be under the tree Christmas morning. I wandered through the toy section where I saw her. She had blonde hair like mine, blue eyes, a pink tutu, leg warmers, and ballet shoes. When I held her hand, she danced on toe, spinning around. She was everything I wished to be. I spent so much time getting my sentences just right for Santa. I handed it to my father, interrupting him during a phone conference. He was furious. But I gave it to him anyway, quite excited…"

Skyler's eyelids fluttered as she struggled to form words. Her head slipped from her palm, and she slept again as the sun crept above the horizon.

****

Chay's eyelids were heavy, his muscles weak. The sloth demon had kept him drugged through the night. Hell. He didn't even know the hour. Early, he guessed.

Hampered by his manacled leg along with the demon's whammies, he halted near the cell door where he wrapped a hand around a rusty bar. He shook it, gently. Harder. When it didn't budge, he blasted himself for not killing the four assailants and protecting Margo.

He yanked on the chain hooked to an iron ring embedded in concrete. No give. Though still light-headed, he was responding less and less to the sleep inducement. Soon he would be at full strength even when the demon zapped him. He just had to be patient while his ylven body began to protect itself from the asshole's power.

Why hadn't his *frerons* found him? The Firebrands should have started looking for him when he didn't return from Margo's. A search party could follow his D-chip signal.

Margo was on the cot with her elbows on her

knees, palms propping her chin. She raised her eyes. "Tell me again what's going on."

"Sure." A song on the radio distracted Chay. "I hate country western."

"What?" Margo's nose wrinkled.

"Country western music. I hate it. The fuckers have been playing it all night." Chay motioned toward the radio. "Being caged isn't torture enough? They put on some shit-kicking crap to maximize the pain?"

While Tammy Wynette sang "Stand by Your Man," Margo smacked her forehead. "Stop changing the subject. You were telling me some fairytale. Continue."

He flung himself onto the bed, his head in Margo's lap, her soothing fingers brushing through his hair, feathering across his temples. "It's not a fairyyarn, Red. Promise. The dudes who broke into your apartment are renegade Aeternals. I exed a demon. I decommissioned the warlock. The two left standing brought us here. The sloth freak keeps dropping me with a sleep inducement. The incubus probably smells good to you."

Her eyes flipped side to side. "Like a woodsy aftershave. Okay. You're an ylve. Vampires, nymphs, witches, berserkers, and other magical things live in this Scath place?"

"Yoopadooka. Though I wince at being called a magical thing."

Red tucked her feet under her cute tush, leaning to the side on a stretched-out arm, still stroking him with her free hand. "Shouldn't you be a lot shorter with pointed ears?"

Chay snorted. "Good one."

"So, you, along with the too-tall Amazon, escorted a healer to come take my blood?"

"Right again. You have a witch or warlock in

your family tree. It's a gamble, but you might have a Blood Coven ancestor. We were gonna check it out when this mishmash broke into your apartment to snatch us."

"Why?"

"Like I said a few secs ago, bad guy Cerberus, Blood Coven descendants, poofing portals, world domination. His crew was likely after you." Chay scratched his not-pointy ear. "Time was, we thought his guys were running a human sex slave op on Scath. They were, but it was a side gig. Now we think they're hunting for offspring of the witches and warlocks who created the realms."

Margo's fingers tangled in his hair. "And you're saying I could be a descendant?"

"Out and out."

She stopped petting him. "What if I don't drink your Kool-Aid?"

Chay held her palm to his cheek. "Don't stop. I love it when you pet me. What do you mean?"

"What if I don't believe you?"

"Why would I sham you? You explain what happened."

"I can't. The one guy does keep making you fall asleep while the slick guy smells so good I tingle everywhere."

Chay flipped her a disappointed look. She added, "Of course, you make me tingle more."

"Damn straight, Red." He cupped the back of her head, pulling her down for a kiss.

She swallowed hard when Chay released her. "Um … then we were both whisked away in a puff of magic to this prison." Margo took a deep breath. She exhaled, her ample breasts inflating, deflating right beside his nose.

He couldn't help it. He molded his hand to a

tempting mound.

Nice.

Instead of smacking him, she smiled.

"I'm being straight with you, Red. Who would fantastasize a crazy story like this?" He let his arms fall to his sides. No use getting aroused here because, no doubt about it, Margo had the crotch of his pants ready to party.

"It's a lot to swallow." Her fingers trailed over his Phoenix brand. "There is something so soothing, so right about touching you. It goes beyond my tactile desires as a sculptor."

Chay nodded. He liked her hot little palms on him, too. But if she kept at it, he was passing sweet and racing to swollen dick. The radio grabbed his attention again. "What is worse than country western? Static. It's messin' with my mind."

"Yeah. The station keeps losing a signal. Ignore it. Continue, ylve man."

He held a finger to her lips, shushing Margo. "Here they come."

The music stuttered when the incubus strode through the door. "Get to the rear of the cell, ylve."

Chay Jack-in-the-boxed to his feet. "Make me."

"I would love to send you to your grave, but the moment is not right. It will happen."

"So, you don't pull your own strings. Who owns your balls?"

The incubus's mouth twisted into a sneer. "When it comes time to put you down, I will have the pleasure myself."

"Yeah? I don't picture myself being killed by a sweet-smelling, mother-humping puppet. Not in my future, incubutt."

The sloth demon stepped from behind the incubus

and stalked into the cell. Chay rushed to the edge of his chain trying to get at the guy. When he flicked out a clawed hand, Chay's dodge to the left was too slow. A nail caught him, its poison sending him to the cement floor in a puddle, his legs and arms paralyzed. When it was safe, the other Aeternal entered, delivering two swift but Nancy kicks to his ribs.

"Baby ylves kick stronger than you do," slurred Chay.

Before the guy could do more damage, the demon prevented him from attacking, a firm grip on his shoulder. "We have a job to do. You can have the ylve later."

A vein pulsed on the side of the asshole's neck. He clenched his fist, though, beating a retreat.

Both males grabbed onto Margo, who flailed her arms, kicking hard, screaming like an angry banshee.

A helpless Chay watched from the floor while they dragged Red from the cell and into the other room. She was really getting into the ylve-struck role. Chay moaned when the radio played Johnnie Cash's "Fulsome Prison."

Perfect.

Chapter Seventeen

Kole tucked the blanket around Skyler's neck, drawing her closer, alone with his own memories. Since she seemed more peaceful now, he would let her sleep for a few more minutes.

Unlike Skyler's father, his parents had cherished him. He was a prince. While spoiling him with love, they taught him values. Honor. Duty. Family. Despite both being famed warriors who were busy keeping the peace on two realms, they made time for him and themselves. They played. Laughed. Argued history, science, magic. Hugged. Treated each other with respect. Even before he reached the age for his Awakening, he learned basic control and use of fire.

Then, when he was ten, they were gone. His memories were tied to visions of blood. Everywhere. Their murderer had mutilated their bodies, raped his mother.

Afterward, Kole's own relatives rejected him, his parents on the side of the Firebrands during the Demon Insurrection. Ranca, a trusted family friend as well as a fellow warrior, took him in. She was a good person whose generous hugs and kisses could not replace the only ones he missed. Having no children of her own, she was ill-equipped to handle a ten-year-old resentful, angry animus demon bent on self-destruction. He wanted the ruination of anything or anyone in his path.

Once he turned sixteen, he searched for his parents' killers, ways to assuage his pain, and females willing to teach him about the pleasure of feeding. Ranca, though she loved him, was at her wits' end, spending most of her days yelling at him after extracting him from one scrape after another.

At an early age for his breed, he went through his Awakening ceremony. His anger simmered, manifesting itself in dangerous ways. His only release was fire. His single goal was to use it to kill Abrahm and his renegade companions. He thought of little else.

At age thirty-five pain took him to his knees. A Phoenix burned into his flesh, the fierce symbol of a Firebrand warrior. At first, Kole resisted the call because to serve would be a distraction. But he understood honor. He understood duty. His parents had taught him well. So he reported, trained, hunted, and killed for the good of Scath. Along the way, he found an outlet, a place where he belonged, a place among his *frerons* in arms.

In secret, he continued his search, visiting justice on all except Abrahm, who had fled to Earth. Some two hundred years after the death of his parents, Kole received a reliable tip. He tracked Abrahm, cornered him, electrocuted him with massive volts of electricity, burned his body minus a single part, and returned to Scath, avenged.

Before reporting for an assignment, he made a stopover.

The color of the setting sun blended into the red hues of the Blud Dunes where Kole stood. In this spot in Knife's Edge, he had scattered his parents' ashes many years before. Despite the scarcity of water and vegetation, the area had been a favorite family stopping-off point to watch migratory herds of Scath elk and pronghorns who roamed through the region. He knelt to dig a hole. Removing a brown pouch tied to his belt, he opened the drawstring and reached inside to extract Abrahm's bloody heart, the heart of a traitor, a murderer. Cradling it in both hands, he placed it in the hole, brushing sand over it, burying it forever near the ashes of the same Firebrands this demon had killed. It was an offering to his parents. They could punish their killer until eternal darkness ruled the realms. He rose, clasping his powerful hands together, staring out over his beautiful desert valley to the mountains beyond. When the sun set, the wind picked up, the sand spun and twisted at his feet, ever widening, moving outward until it spread across the valley floor. He nodded, knowing his parents accepted the offering.

Now four hearts were buried here—his mother's, his father's, their killer's, and a ten-year-old boy's. His was the broken but still beating one.

The memories too painful, Kole got up to sponge cool water on Skyler. A belief in ancestral sin was fused into his soul. Demon justice held that the sins of the fathers are visited upon his offspring. The human bible said something about unto the third and fourth generations. He would have believed his breed had crafted the passage, but no. They would have gone long past the fourth generation. So, carrying a grudge was a biological imperative for him.

As he watched Skyler's restless sleep, heat formed beneath his skin, the old familiar rage of his parents' death revisiting him. But when Skyler turned her face toward him, he gently brushed a stray lock of damp, blonde hair off her cheek.

No child should grow up unloved, especially a female. Sure. His belief was sexist, but it was what it was. She had survived her father by encasing herself in ice. He had glimpsed beneath the frost, liking what he saw.

With the sun fully above the horizon, he rose, packed his knapsack, lifted the feverish Skyler into his arms, and ran at full speed for the Healing Pond.

****

In a dingy, Spartan room off the cells, the incubus bound a still kicking, screaming Margo to a straight-back chair. While continuing to behave like a hysterical female separated from her obsession, she scanned for a weapon, anything to use or sneak to Chay.

Nothing.

A cellphone played "Devil's Child" by Judas Priest. The demon took it out of his front pocket. "Hello? Hello?" He looked at his partner. "Dropped."

Then the other guy's phone buzzed. He answered, shrugged, tossed it onto a table. "Nobody. Let's hurry. I wanna get this over with."

With a syringe in his grasp, the incubus swung his gaze from his cellphone to the television. "The thing's on the blink. It's all snowy. This place is crappy, and we have to stay until told different. I'm gonna go fucking nuts with nothing to do except listen to her scream. Shut her up."

"Devil's Child" rang out again. "What's going on? Hello. Fuck." The demon rammed his cell into his pocket.

Despite Margo's wiggling, the incubus jabbed the syringe into her arm. "Let's hope this shit calms her. I need to draw some blood. Damn, she's struck bad."

While Margo's head rolled around a bit and her chin bounced to her chest, he grabbed a second syringe. Her lids drooped. Slid open. She had to stay awake.

The television sprang to life again as the demon's phone rang out once more. He took the call, shouting, "What do you want? … Oh, sorry, sir. … Yes, we're working on her now. … Will do."

When the demon disconnected, the incubus raised his brows. "Lort, the new boss. He's got a rod stuck in his ass. At least he's not as far around the bend as Silas was."

The incubus held Margo's limp arm steady while he stabbed the needle into her. It took him three times to find a vein. Once he did, he filled four vials with blood. She thought it was four. Things were a little blurry. "After we return her to the cell, you can run this sample to Lort. The sooner it's tested, the sooner we can leave this pit."

****

Alarik swept his long, sable-brown hair out of the way. Standing, he pushed back his chair. "Thank you for coming. No Scion Firebrands are present because they're spread thin. Our head scryer has information to share with the group. Cleatra?"

A tawny-skinned witch with dreamy, lavender-gray eyes, Cleatra used big hand gestures. She stood to give herself the space while she explained what she had found. "I use smoke to locate people." Her hands billowed out as if she were painting a puffy cloud. "I'm closing in on the exact location of two human sex slaves. In Bludhaven and in Amori. I'll get closer. If the past is an indication, they will have trace DNA of ancient witch or warlock. No Blood Coven ancestry. Am I correct, Braelyn?"

"Yes. Silas would have re-tested their blood in one of his hell holes. When it didn't show they were descendants of the famous mages, he would have sold them, possibly after they were passed around for the guards' pleasures."

Cleatra's pensive gray eyes turned black with anger. "The minute I find them, I shall notify Jarek."

"Thank you, Cleatra." Alarik struggled with the effort to smile. He was weary, his ministry juggling too many balls. "Healers are testing all Alliance employees. They identified an agent in Chicago as a Blood Coven descendant. Rein is sending warriors to bring him to safety. On another note, with Logan's help, we found a Margo Hunter who has mage ancestry. We sent a team to her place in Cleveland. Though they were able to get a blood sample, an unfortunate situation arose. She's been kidnapped along with the Firebrand Chay. The stronghold is searching for them now. It's imperative we find her. Her test shows she is indeed Blood Coven."

Of course, Alarik was aware of another descendant sitting right at this table. He avoided glancing her way. Nobody except family knew Braelyn's ancestry. "Braelyn's trap may have proved successful. A human who claims Masoud as his ancestor phoned her call center. She must still verify his story. Any word from him?"

"None. No call back yet." Braelyn tapped a pen on the table.

Cleatra raised her hand. "Shouldn't he be brought to safety?"

Braelyn pressed her lips into a frown. "The English guy is real paranoid. Someone already tried to kidnap him. He eluded them. Though Firebrand techie Logan is searching for him, so far no luck. The Brit's in deep hiding. No credit charges. No driver's license. No electronic or paper trail. The guy's a ghost. He wants the contest money to keep running. Apparently, he's worried about giving his location away if he taps his own accounts. It's likely he'll call again. When he does, I'll persuade him to meet."

"Keep us posted. Promising news. Eliphias, have my scientists found a faster way to detect those with mage DNA markers? Our current method, computer searches of medical records, is slow, unpredictable."

Eliphias shook his head. "No, Director. Sorry to say we have not. We are still pursuing solutions, however."

Alarik steepled his fingers, resting his chin on them. "Echo, any success tracing descendants through historical documents?"

"I thank Eliphias for his recommendation of Sauro, who has been removing spells from ancient tomes to prevent them from self-destructing. We've been poring through these accounts. Many families consented to give us access to their written histories. My people already visited several homes. We are creating a giant tree and filling in the blanks. I plan a trip to Salt Lake City. I want to wait, though, until we have more to go on at this end. Also, and I almost hate to mention this for fear I will jinx it, Allias, a historical researcher who is a veritable bloodhound, says he has uncovered an obscure document of interest. Within it is a tiny reference which could have monumental consequences for our hunt. Though he is tracking it down, he refuses to tell me his suspicions yet. Says the possibility is too far-fetched at this point. Anyway, I hesitated to mention it. I thought, however, we could use some hope even if it bears no fruit."

Ever since Braelyn had spoken, Indigo's hand kept flying up in the air as if she were an eager student sitting in her desk, her teacher having posed a question.

When Alarik called on his sister, she sprang to her feet. "Miller Nash. We must find him now. He's in grave danger. In the River Am, I saw some very bad Aeternals hound dog him. Three of them. A nasty coyote shifter. A demon. And a vamp. We can't let him get his fangs into the guy. Blood is like GPS to those suckers."

Her eyeballs flipped high and to the left. "Alarik, remember the lean, mean young coyote shifter who used to sneak onto our property? Blond, bushy-tailed devil?"

"Is he the male after this Miller Nash?"

"What? Why would you think that? No. He's the hotty-totty who popped my cherry. Back to the river. In another stream, Miller was with a brunette chick who wore these ankle-strap heels I'd kill to own. She had these big bazoombas which were about to meet with a serious clothes malfunction. Whichever stream you believe, things won't go well for Miller Nash. Bad if the evil trio snag him. Embarrassing if he goes on the hot date with the brunette."

"Indigo, Miller Nash is my Englishman on the run," said Braelyn, her eyes wide.

Indigo tapped her chin with a finger. "How very ungood."

****

Chay sat on the cold cement floor, leaned back against the wall, and yanked on the chain attached to his ankle. It was solid. When the door opened, the demon motioned for him to stay put. Chay nodded.

His buddy, the incubus, opened the cell to shove a pale Margo inside. When her legs wobbled, she crumpled to the floor.

She was beyond Chay's reach. "Red, scoot closer. Once she did, he carried her to the bed, where he cradled her head in his lap. His chest pumped like a bouncing ball.

What had they done to her?

"How was I?" She blinked. "Could you hear me? Was I ylve-struck enough?"

"You were perfect." Chay caressed her cheek, brushed her hair aside, and kissed her forehead. "I believe you might actually be ylve-struck."

"You wish." Her head rolled to the side. Her eyes drifted closed, and she was silent.

"Red, talk to me." He patted her face a few times until she swatted his hand away. "What happened in there? Are you okay? Did they hurt you?"

"No. Thing One and Thing Two gave me a sedative after they strapped me to a chair. Then they took my blood. Everyone wants blood. S' my blood." Her lids slid down again. She slurred her words. "S'mine."

"They wanna see if you have a Blood Coven ancestor. If you don't, they'll have no use for us. If you do, our futures could get worse."

"Worse than death?" Her eyes sprang open.

"Possibly."

She swiped a hand across her face. "Need to sleep 'fore chatting." Her lips sagged while every so often she wrinkled her nose or snuffled.

About a half hour later, Margo awoke more lucid.

Chay jumped right in with questions. "They took your blood? You're sure?"

She nodded.

"Fuck. We need to fly this coop. My *frerons* should've found us. It makes no sense."

"Yeah. Something's strange." She paused to think about her statement. "Hah! I mean, something's stranger. Vampires, ylves, witches, another realm aren't weird enough." She waved a dismissive hand through the air. "Anyway. Cellphones are dropping calls, televisions are on the blink, and radios are staticky."

After the door flew open, the demon strutted into the outer room. Margo slapped her hands to her ears when "Devil's Child" played. "Not again."

"Hello?" The demon held his phone at arm's length, shaking it. "Damn interference." He rotated toward the radio. Static. "Maybe sunspots are messing with shit." He left, muttering.

Chay rubbed his chin. "Give me the play by play again, Red."

Both Margo and the incudick thought something

was strange. He was beginning to agree.

"The radio's wonky. Their cellphones are screwy. The TV in the syringe room is snowy."

Chay eyed the radio on the desk outside their cell. It was playing okay now. Still country-western shit. "You're sure you didn't dream this?"

She tried to pinch his thigh. "Yes, I'm sure."

"Was a warlock or witch with them?"

"Only the two guys who kidnapped us. I'm positive."

Chay paced to the end of his chain, scratching his head.

It makes no sense unless ... unless. Impossible. No, not impossible, just improbable. Still, who else could it be?

He turned to stare at Margo. When he tapped his wrist where his D-chip was embedded, the signal went dead-live-dead-live. "Red, we're gonna try a science experiment. Come here." Chay clutched her shoulders, pointing her toward the desk outside their cell. "This will sound crazy, but ... concentrate. Try to whammy the radio."

Margo giggled. "You've lost it, ylve man. You want me to whammy..."

Chay nodded.

"...the radio."

"Yes. I want you to make it go wonky. I think you can, and I understand these things better than you do."

"This is lame." She faced the radio, straightening her arm, using her index finger like a magic wand. "Abracadabra." Garth Brooks continued singing his tune. "Surprise, no whammy."

Chay cradled her face in his large hands. He angled his head, touching his lips to hers, his tongue tracing the full softness of her mouth. When she let him in, he tasted her sweet, sassy flavor. With reluctance, he released Margo and stepped back.

"You've got no reason to trust me, Red, but I wish you would. If we don't get out of here, they're probably going to kill me. I'm okay with that. I signed on to be a warrior. If they ex me, though, I won't be here to protect you. I'm not okay with that. So give it a shot. We've got nothing to lose."

When she tried again, eyes closed, lips squeezed together, Garth's voice quivered but never went silent.

Again. Again. Once more. No change.

Margo flopped her cute ass onto the bed, her hands rubbing her temples. "I told you so." She brushed away tears. "I don't want you to die."

Chay nudged her over, tossing an arm across her shoulders. He pulled her close. "Please, once more." His heart banged in his chest. "Try for me, Red."

She sniffled, pushed to her feet, stared at the radio for a few moments. She wiggled her fingers. "Stop."

Garth paused ... sang a few beats ... paused again.

A wide grin spread across Chay's face.

Margo's mouth flopped open. "Am I doing that?"

"You are. Now, here's a question, Red. Do your eyes ever look violet?"

She wrinkled her nose. "No. They're green. Always."

"Not anymore. You stirred up your inner mage, Red."

He hugged her until she gasped, pounding on his shoulders. "Too tight."

****

Cerberus settled into the armchair, rolling amber fluid around in his glass. The smooth taste, the spicy notes of ginger, dried fruit, and orange zest relaxed him. "Your hacker's recent information paid off, Dante. We have captured Margo Hunter. Her blood sample is being tested."

"How were you able to get her to Scath?"

"Since we can no longer clone portal jumpers, I developed a source in the Ministry of Compliance. They issue us real ones which they fail to log into their records."

Dante crossed his legs, picking at a speck of lint on his sharply creased trousers.

"A slight glitch, though. A Scion Firebrand was at her apartment. He could represent a wrinkle, a signal the Temple is on to us. My people tell me she is ylve-struck. If so, his presence could be happenstance. Nonetheless, we have them both. If the results from her test disclose she is descended from the legendary line of mages, we will keep her with the other two we hold captive. If she is not ... there is always the slave market. It was a clever, lucrative ruse once. It can be again."

Dante set his tumbler of scotch on the table. "I jolly well don't give a damn what you do with the rejects. If you want to run another slave ring, do it. Leave me out of that part. What I don't like is hearing a Firebrand was with her. What if they are on to us? It could ruin our plans."

"You worry too much, old friend. Even if they are, they cannot stop the hunt. This race goes to the swiftest, the most powerful. The warriors and the Temple of Justice have grown sloppy over the years. They can impede neither me nor the prophecy. As it is written, the world will be one realm where all species walk together. And of course ... you and I shall benefit from any economic gains."

Cerberus stopped himself. Because of his hubris,

he had almost exposed his true goal. With no barriers between realms, the inferior humans would become an unlimited supply of food for Aeternals, the sweetest fodder for his species.

For now, he needed the Englishman. Though Cerberus had amassed huge sums of money over the centuries, Dante's wealth was an added blessing. Raising an army on Scath, housing it, feeding it, and supplying it was an enormous drain on resources. To say nothing of the cost to curry the support of Aeternals by greasing their palms, planting the seeds of rebellion. Yes, for now, he needed the extra funding. The human's capital. His connections. His labor on Earth.

With a warm smile, Dante tilted his glass toward his lips. "Have you taken care of the Skyler Maxwell situation yet?"

"No, but I am close. She made an unexpected trip to Darque, where we have trapped her."

Dante sipped his Macallan. "I leave the matter in your capable hands."

Cerberus finished off his drink and unfolded from the chair with the grace of his breed.

Chapter Eighteen

Miller Nash forced the burner phone tight to his ear. "Bollocks. You need to prepare better than I did. Acquire multiple dwellings now. Establish new identities. New lives. Pack a bug-out bag. Have a stash of money. Cash. That's where I made my mistake. We've run the drill. You'll do fine if the need arises. After all these years, I'm on the lam. Everything is arse over elbow, but I'm going to find out why. Keep your pecker up, mate. ... Me? I'm heading off to the nearest pub to get bladdered."

Miller had called to check Braelyn James's claim. Tossing the phone in the trash bin and the chip into a different can, Miller did as he stated. He opened the door to a noisy, crowded bar, a Patriot's cap pulled low over his eyes, slipping onto a stool in the dimmest section. The bar top was well-worn, chipped, marred, slashed. It had character. It looked, smelled, and sounded just like an Irish pub in Boston should.

A cheerful barkeep nodded at Miller, wiping the counter with a damp rag which had possibly never been washed, the rancid odor eye-watering. "How are ya keepin'?"

"Feelin' a bit knackered. A Kilbeggan will help. Bring a glass along with the bottle, mate."

The bartender disappeared, returning with a tumbler and half-empty bottle of Kilbeggan Irish Whiskey. "*Slainte mhaith*, pal."

"Thanks." Miller threw back the first shot, poured a second, and downed it. He punched numbers into another cellphone. His call was answered quickly.

"Before I get too squiffy, I thought I should touch bases. I'm ready to meet... No. I'll decide on the place. ...I'll reach out in a few days with the city, an exact location. ... Yeah, well, I must shake these blokes off my six. ... Come alone. I've seen your picture. ... Okay. Bring the hubby. What's he look like?" Miller laughed. "Big doesn't scare me. Don't forget the money from Daddy's paper. I'll be collecting, luv."

Braelyn was legit. Still, he trusted few people completely.

****

Chay spun to face Margo. "I gotta think." He rubbed his unshaven chin while he paced. Grabbing his chain in both hands, he stopped to tug on it, somehow sure it would snap free this time. When it didn't, he rattled it to the ground in frustration. "The lock on the cell. Check it out."

Margo, who wasn't restricted by a shit-ton of metal, clutched a bar and poked the side of her face through the opening as far as possible. "It looks like a big ol' box. No key."

"Yeah. They've been using a remote device to open it. They locked my chain the same way. That's good, I think." Chay studied the manacle attached to his leg. "Red, it's our lucky day. I am so zipped."

"What you are is crazy."

"Come here."

"Why?" Margo lifted an eyebrow, questioning Chay's sanity.

"You're going to unchain me with your new voodoo powers."

"Sure I am. Me along with a really big chainsaw. Got one up your sleeve?"

"I got something better. Hold on to your bloomers. Some witches can manipulate radio waves.

You might be a member of their club. Hence, stuff goes wonky around you."

"I'm not a witch."

"If it walks like a duck, quacks like a duck, and farts eggs. Isn't that what you humans say?"

"Kinda. Not about witches, though."

"We're in my realm now, gorgeous, and I say you've got some mage goin' on."

"Uh-huh. Still not a witch."

"Let's blah-blah-blah this whole I-am-not-a-witch thing once we're out of here. Now, cast a spell. Unlock me."

"Chay, seriously, the only waves I know about are in the ocean."

"I bet you rock a bikini with only a piece of dental floss going up your ass. But right now, as much as I would like to see you in one, we need our focus elsewhere." Chay's eyes betrayed his words when they raked over Margo's breasts and hips. He imagined her beside him on a Covenkirk beach, sunbathing in a skimpy suit. A smack on the forehead helped erase the image. "Okay, about unlocking me, Red. Let the waves roll."

"I'm blank, Chay. How do I begin."

"No idea. I'm an ylve not a frickin' warlock. Cogitate on it or do something witchy. Do what you did to the radio before."

Casting a frown at Chay, Margo sat cross-legged in front of the latch. She stared at it.

Nothing.

"You're going to have to give me a little info. What do witches do when they cast spells? Other than old reruns of *Bewitched* on TV, I've never seen magic performed. I can't even wiggle my nose."

Chay scrunched his brows. "Good one. Mages

have to feed like any other Aeternal. That's how they gather the energy to cast a spell. They channel power. Tap me, Red."

When she rested a hand on his arm, Chay felt heat flow from him to Margo. It gave him an instant hard-on when she fed.

She owl-eyed him. "Okay. Weird feeling. What's next?"

"Let's see. Mages use potions, written spells, objects, wave their hands in the air, rack their brains. I'm in the dark, Red. I never saw the need to peek over their shoulders while they did their jobs. Whodda thunk I'd be teaching a crash course in basic witchcraft?"

"Bet you're sorry you didn't pay more attention."

"Say, Tyr, a *freron*, told me he visualizes spells. A few weeks after his Awakening, his cousin beat the crap out of him. After he got himself together, he closed his eyes and pictured the twerp as a Terranian cockroach." Chay let out a short, snorting laugh. "I guess the guy's parents had to raise holy Angor to talk Tyr into changing the little insect back. Maybe his technique could work for you. Use what you pulled out of me to power your spell. Then envision the lock."

"Visualize. Of course. I'm a sculptor. Easy. Peasy." Margo closed her eyes for some time. Chay took her hand in his. A smile tugged at her lips while various expressions played across her freckled face. Still no change.

Since she was silent for so long, Chay was sure the experiment had failed. Until ... the air cooled. Power race from him, met where they held hands, and sped to her. When it did, the lock sprang open. He was free. Of course, feeding Margo via the channeling stuff gave him the hard-on from hell.

He had barely removed the manacle when Margo

shot off the floor. She jumped into his arms. "Wow! What a blast! I pictured waves, thousands, no millions, of them coming from your body. They rolled over me. All different widths and heights. I collected them, molded them in my hands like clay, and sent them to the lock. Can you imagine?"

Margo's words drifted into a distant echo. When Chay focused on her sweet mouth, he couldn't stop himself. With her ankles around his waist, he leaned down to steal a kiss. Her lips were soft, luscious. Tempting. Distracting.

She didn't pull away. Rather, she pressed into him, surrendering, combing her fingers through his hair.

Ever so slowly, Chay's Firebrand senses took hold. With deep breaths, along with enormous willpower, he withdrew his mouth. "I can imagine, Red. You're spectacular. Now, unlock the cell door."

After it swung open, Chay rifled through the desk for makeshift weapons, anything to throw. "Bonanza! They left a knife here. A letter opener, too. Sweet." Chay clasped a pointy object in each hand, tossing them to judge their heft. "Stay behind the desk." He opened the door to the other room, his movements silent. Gone was the flirt from moments ago. He was replaced by a lethal, skilled warrior who excelled at his craft.

****

Heat radiated from Skyler's feverish cheek, through Kole's shirt, to his skin. She was burning hot.

Skyler passed in and out of consciousness while he raced toward the Healing Pond with her clutched tight against him. In one of her lucid moments, she lifted her head from his chest. "You blame me."

"That would be stupid." Kole jostled her when he jumped over a low bush.

"Yes, it would be stupid."

Kole paused his forward movement, peering into Skyler's innocent eyes, a beautiful shade of blue with lilac streaks. "You did nothing wrong, Frisca. Sleep until we get to the pond."

Yet he thought of Abrahm, who had slaughtered his family, while he was speeding with the demon's descendant in his arms, trying to save her life. Destiny sure decided to fuck with him when it sent him to Skyler Maxwell's office. Screw destiny. No such beast.

"I'm telling you, you're different. You blame me for my ancestor's unforgivable actions."

"I don't. Now shut up." He never should have told Skyler his story, but she had awakened, begging him to distract her. So he had. Through gritted teeth and seething rage, he exposed her ancestor.

"See. You never tell me to shut up. You say a million other rude, even crass, things. Never that."

"Damn, give it a rest, Frisca. Isn't it enough for me to lug you to the pond where I'll heal you? Do I have to listen to you bitch the whole way, too."

"No. Set me on my feet. I want to walk." Skyler smacked his shoulder with the palm of her hand.

"Hey. Stop or I'll drop you here and leave." Distracted, Kole stumbled on a rock, nearly taking them both to the ground.

"You said you weren't going to ditch me. You're a man of your word. I trust you. Even though you blame me for something I had no control over, you would never abandon me." She smacked him again.

"So help me, Frisca, if you don't stop…"

Before she could strike him once more, Skyler's head rolled back. "I don't feel so…"

He stopped running to set her on the ground, gently grasping her chin between a thumb and forefinger. "Skyler."

She was ghostly white.

You cannot die on me. I won't lose you.

"Frisca. Are you okay?" He patted her cheek. No response. He tapped her again. Again. Harder each time. "Do not die. Are you listening to me? I'll paddle your ass until you can't sit the fuck down."

Her eyelids fluttered open, her lips spreading into a small, weak smile. "You're you again."

He sighed. "Yeah. I am." He lifted her into his arms, resuming his sprint toward the pond, all thoughts of her ancestry erased from his mind. While he ran with Skyler cradled against him, fighting the infection from the kas nettle, Kole's soul accepted she was blameless for the death of his parents. An innocent should never be held accountable for the actions of those who came before. Wasn't that the very reason his uncle Horach hadn't taken him in when his mother and father were killed?

****

- Chay crept into the room, dropping into a crouch. He was out of sight and silent.

- A loud gun battle blasted away on the TV while the sloth demon lazed on the sofa, his back to Chay, his feet propped on the table. "Hey! Is my sandwich done?"

- A refrigerator slammed shut in the kitchen. From where he was crouched, Chay saw the incubus prepping lunch. "Give it a rest, slug. It'll be ready when I tell ya it is."

- Chay inched along the wall. Unaware of the visitor, the incudick busied himself slapping mayo onto slices of bread. Next came slabs of meat. Some tomatoes. Chay braced himself against the doorjamb. "Psst."

- The guy hung a one-eighty.
- Chay brought a finger to his lips, motioning for the male to be silent. With a wide grin, lightning speed, and unerring accuracy, he threw the knife, burying it in his surprised captor's throat. Catching the body before it fell, he sliced off the head. A major feat considering the dull blade. On a macabre whim, Chay set the noggin on the counter, posing it as if it was about to take a bite out of a sandwich. Satisfied with the prop, he edged toward the living room.
- The demon was still enjoying his police shoot-em-up even though every so often it went on the blink. He scratched his balls, letting out a loud cheer when some character face-planted with a bullet to the heart.
- Chay might check out the show later. He loved action-packed entertainment. But right now, he had pressing business. "Hey, couch potato."
- When the demon shot to his feet, Chay threw the letter opener with such force and speed it penetrated his chest before he could straighten his knees.
- Dragging the guy out into the kitchen, Chay dropped him beside his headless friend, giving him the same bisection treatment.
- Chay did a quick sweep of the other rooms. Satisfied he'd iced their only guards, he tapped his D-chip. Still no reliable signal.
- He returned to find Margo hiding behind the desk with her eyes closed, muttering, "Please, don't let him be hurt. Please." She jumped when he clutched a hand to her shoulder.
- "I'm A-okay, Red. Not a scratch." Chay pivoted so she could see he was unharmed.
- Margo shot from the floor, flinging both

arms around his waist, planting kisses from his neck to his chin. "I was afraid they'd hurt you. I must be ylve-struck."

• "I wish you were, but it's only natural you're worried. If they'd smoked me, you'd be all alone here."

• Margo grabbed his strong, angular face in her hands, his long, black hair draping over the backs of her fingers. "No. I'm awfully fond of you, as well as your tight buns." She playfully patted his backside, her touch lingering. "I want to explore your body. Speaking as a sculptor, of course."

• Chay swallowed hard. "Unfortunately, we have to cowboy out of Dodge. If you want to explore me later, as a sculptor of course, I'm your guy."

• Margo cleared her throat. "Does your communication device work yet?"

• "On and off. You need to relax your witch. Got me?"

• "How am I supposed to do that with you here?"

• Chay hugged Margo, her back to his chest, rubbing her arms. "Let's calm you down."

• "Bad news, ylve baby. You're making me horny." Margo ground her delectable rear against Chay's growing erection. "I can feel your hard-on."

• "You can? Cool." Chay slipped under her shirt, cupping her breast. "Nice," he moaned. Then he released her. "Okay. Not cool. Not right now."

• Margo pulled away, straightening her shirt. "Right. Business. Let's get out of here. What can I do?"

• "Stand way over there in the corner."

Once she was in place, Chay tapped his wrist. "Still no service."

- "Can we walk outta here?"

- "Doubtful, but in case I'm your problem, I've got an idea. Wait for me. I'm gonna go just far enough away to use my D-chip. I'll call Galena. When she rolls in, I'll pop to the stronghold. Since she won't make you horny, you won't block her signal. She can transport both of you to headquarters." He narrowed his eyes, looking askance at Margo. "At least, I hope she doesn't make you horny. Can we do this, Red? You won't be scared if I leave for a minute?"

- "We can do this, Chay. Remember, though, hormones might not be my only trigger. Fear might make me a little crazy, too. Tell her to be extra nice."

- Kudos to Margo. She steeled her spine. Chay was learning redheaded sculptors were fearless.

- ****

Portaling inside the Chicago Alliance headquarters with a soft pop and a flash of light, Sabine shook her head. "I hate traveling between realms. Messes with my stomach. Probably screws with my neurons."

"Yeah. Well, I worry it'll make my dick limp."

"Fewer horny warlocks are a good thing, Tyr."

"Tell that to my unknown future mate." Tyr looked both ways after opening the door. He signaled the all-clear for Sabine.

Beaucoup eyes were on them when they strode into the Alliance Security Division fully armed, blades in chest sheaths, guns strapped down. Hand on hip and her foot jutted out, Sabine paused in front of the first occupied desk. "Point out Agent Nico Abello. He's expecting us." Despite her long blonde hair pulled into two braids which swished when she walked, her sultry eyes, and angelic face, nobody would doubt she was a tough warrior.

"Lucky him." The redheaded agent shook his thumb toward an office in the back. "Thatta way."

"Thanks." Feeling the Alliance guy stare at her ass as she walked away, Sabine gave her hips an extra swish to make his day. "Males." She smirked at her Goth-like, pierced and tattooed companion.

"It's in our genes."

"Yeah. If only you could keep it there." Sabine knocked on the office door. Rather than wait for an answer, she opened it and marched in.

A male leaned back in a chair, his large, well-worn boots propped on the desk, nose in a book. Black hair, just long enough to curl at the ends where it met his neck and looking as if he combed it with his fingers, fell lazily across his forehead. With broad, muscled shoulders, the agent was not what Sabine expected for a human male. He obviously worked out enough to give him some seriously spectacular biceps. His thighs, even relaxed, stretched the fabric of his pants. *Yeah.* She'd like to handle all those hard muscles. Her nymph hormones darted around, slamming into each other.

"Whaddaya want? I told you not to bother me." The guy didn't look up as he spoke.

Sabine cleared her throat, wishing she could clear her mind as easily. "Kole's office called ahead. You're expecting us. From Scath."

"Oh, right." He slammed the book onto the desk and jacked his chair upright. When his chin tilted up, a wide smile revealed dimples and bright, laughing eyes outlined with long lashes. He stroked a day-old shadow on his jaw, his gaze locked onto Sabine. "Hello, sweetness. And you, too." He hardly glanced at Tyr.

"Where are my manners? Have a seat. I'm Nico. To what do I owe this visit?"

Her warlock partner slid into a chair, his open smile hiding his lethal powers. "I'm Tyr, and sweetness here is Sabine. What we have to say is confidential. So confidential you're invited to Scath, where we'll drop the news on you."

"I'm not a very trusting man. While I'd follow you almost anywhere, sweetness, I think I'll draw the line at shadowing your ass to another realm. Unless, of course, you want to give me a few hints or a really big reward when I get there. And I'm not talking cash. Besides, I'm leading an investigation here."

Sabine shifted in her seat next to Tyr. Though the human male was alluring, he was full of himself. Worse yet, she truly hated terms of endearment. "Cut the *sweetness* crap. I can take you any day of the week. You'll come quietly or else." Her temperature rose as she thought of putting her hands on the male, and all those nymph hormones played dodgeball again.

A slow grin played across Nico's face. "I love how you want to get rough with me. That's normally a big turn-on … sweetness. But here's the thing, I'm pretty sure the warlock could take me in a fair fight. I don't fight fair, though. Of course, you're not as strong as he is. I'm guessing you're a nymph. A truly healthy, fit nymph who obviously works out." He hesitated while his hungry, honeyed gaze dripped down her body, making her instantly sticky. "But it's likely I can take you fair and square. And again, I don't fight fair. So, unless the two of you intend to smack me around in front of an entire office of Alliance agents, you better pay me a little respect and tell me what the hell is going on."

The human's muscles were coiled to attack even though he looked relaxed. Like a rattlesnake.

Tyr frowned at Sabine. "I think we got off to a bad start."

She rose to perch on the edge of Nico's desk. Her legs brushed his knees. "Tyr's right, cuddles. We didn't get off to a good start. Let's begin again. We have some seriously confidential information to share with you. For your own welfare, it's best if you go with us to Scath and talk to Minister Alarik or Acting Commander Rein."

"So, because you have a nice, tight ass and, from what I can see, spectacular tits, I'm supposed to follow you?"

Grrr.

Sabine growled like a wolf shifter rather than a nymph. This guy pushed her buttons. "No, you're supposed to follow me because I'm a Firebrand, you're an Alliance agent, and I'm here to save your life."

"No." He leaned back in his chair, his delectable, muscled arms folded behind his head.

"No, what?" Sabine narrowed her eyes in disbelief.

"No, I'm not following you. My office is secure. Tell me now or get the hell out. By the way, slide your tight ass off my desk, sweetness."

"I tried the nice way. Screw you." Sabine rose.

"Now there's an offer I might…"

The Alliance agent didn't have time to finish because Sabine signaled Tyr, who flicked a wrist in Nico's direction.

The agent's eyes blazed with fury for one second. Then a chill spread through the room. "Hey! What was…" His lids half-shuttered his eyes, his coiled muscles unbunched, and his shoulders relaxed.

"It was a spell to make you my bitch, cuddles. Now smile while you stroll out of here with Tyr and me. You're gonna tell everyone you are assigned to Scath for a few weeks. Afterward, we're off to your place to pack for the vacation."

Chapter Nineteen

On her feet but swaying, Skyler stared into the depths of the gray, murky, bubbling Healing Pond. Clumps of sludge erupted from beneath its surface. She pulled on her jacket collar until it covered her nose. "Are you sure this is necessary?"

Kole steadied her while he tugged a sleeve down her arm. Coat removed, he dropped it to the ground. He started in on her shirt buttons. "You need to soak to sterilize your wounds. Afterward, I'll cauterize them."

Skyler half-heartedly slapped at his hands. "What do you think you're doing?"

"You can't wear clothes into the pond."

Skyler pushed away from Kole's grasp, wobbling but righting herself. Her chin popped up. "Let me. Turn around." She dropped her shirt on the ground.

"Don't be childish. I've already seen what you've got. Besides, you can hardly stand, let alone undress yourself."

"Close your eyes."

"No."

Skyler's vision blurred. When she tumbled sideways, Kole swept her into his arms.

He rested her against a boulder, removing her boots and socks. "Everything, Frisca."

When Skyler fumbled with the snap on her pants, Kole finished the job, sliding them and her panties down her legs. "Lean forward a bit." He reached behind her, unclasping her bra, slipping it off her shoulders.

Snagging onto the shirt, she covered her breasts and sex. "Turn around while I get in."

"Not happening."

Damn him.

While Kole removed his chest harness loaded with weapons, his axe, his long blade, laying them on a rock within reach of the pond, Skyler struggled to get up off the ground. She failed.

After he pulled his tee over his head, his fingers went for his pants. "Stop! What are you doing? You can't get in there naked with me."

"Frisca, I have to keep you from drowning in this muck while I check out your wounds. Make sure the mud's doing its job. The clothes are coming off."

She groaned.

Kole unzipped his pants. "Besides, you've already ogled my ass and other parts."

"Don't keep bringing that up. I told you it was an accident. You have nothing I want to see again. Nothing."

Lie. He has everything I want to see.

To prove it, she gawked, lips parted, as Kole stepped out of his pants.

His head angled down, he stared at his sizable erection, an annoying satisfaction brightening his eyes. "Well, not nothing as you can clearly see." He spread his legs further apart. "I guess my dick likes you better than I do."

Skyler's mouth fell open. She swallowed hard at the sight of Kole with an erection. He was long. Thick. And so aroused.

"Close your mouth. You can't have it."

"You're a vulgar, dirty, brutish animal."

"Me? Vulgar? I wasn't the one with my mouth guppied and my eyes glued to my cock. Here. Grab me around the neck." He winked when he reached down to lift her.

"Do. Not. Touch. Me." Skyler knocked his hands aside.

He bent, scooping her into his arms. "Even with a fever and infection, you are stubborn, female." Kole climbed into the Healing Pond with Skyler hanging on so tight her nails bit into his skin.

Once he settled on a flat boulder beneath the surface, he positioned her on his lap. She felt the nudge of his large, very firm penis. "Put me down. I insist."

"Hell. Go on. Drown." Grabbing her under the arms, he plopped her beside him. "Slide deeper into the water. Cover as much of your body as possible in the muck."

Skyler sank into the pond up to her chin, the odor of rotten eggs strong. But she had to admit, the warm, muddy water soothed her burning rash and open sores. She sighed, instant relief easing her tense muscles.

Kole poked a finger into a sore. When she flinched from the pain, he drew back and submerged. She felt him probe a spot on the inside of her thigh. The rash must have traveled to her legs.

"Ouch. That hurts."

He moved his examination to her hips. Then on to her abdomen. Skyler clasped his head between her hands and pulled it out of the water. "What do you think you're doing?"

Gray mud dripped from his chin and nose. He swiped a hand across his eyes, flicking goop off his fingers.

Skyler couldn't help herself. She laughed.

When she finally took a breath, Kole's lips spread into a wide grin. "You think I'm funny." He cupped his hands to scoop up muddy water, dumping it on Skyler's head. "Hold your nose." He dunked her underneath.

She surfaced, sputtering, gurgling. "Are you

finished?"

"Almost. Turn over."

"What?"

"You heard me. Turn over." When she argued with him, he simply flipped her. To keep her nostrils above the surface, she clutched a stone on the side of the pond.

Kole straddled her while he traced fingers over the back of her head and neck. Despite a sharp, occasional bite, all she could think about was his thick, rigid erection poking her butt. She was hot, and it wasn't the fever or the Healing Pond. He was too much. Skyler managed to spin around. But the position was worse. Now his arousal brushed the top of her thigh.

"I'm checking your wounds. This isn't easy for me either."

"Don't be insane. It's just because you're hurting me."

"Sure. I can smell lust. Demons are sensitive to pheromones. But I refuse to let you have your wicked way with me."

"What? I do not smell like lust."

"Yes, you do." He moved to sit beside her again. "Now soak for a while and stop trying to fuck with me."

"I ... I" She was at a loss for words. After some time, the silence got the better of Skyler. Since a naked Kole definitely aroused her, she needed a distraction. Talk would provide it. "You have a beast inside you?"

"Yes."

"What's yours look like?"

He flashed his irritating, sexy lopsided grin. "You're getting quite personal, Chief Maxwell. I don't think we're that close yet."

"Oh, blather. Do you ever lose control of it? Like some of the demons at the Genesis Rite."

"Not since I came through puberty."

Skyler hesitated, recalling the blog and what Kole had said about demons needing orgasms to sustain themselves. "How have you been feeding?"

Laughter erupted from deep in Kole's chest. When it finally stopped, he cleared his throat. "Are you offering your services, Frisca?"

She was certain she blushed, but with all the mud on her face, surely Kole couldn't see it. "Don't be ridiculous. I … I … was merely curious?"

"I'm a warrior, not a prepubescent demon who can't keep his junk in his pants. I've learned to overcome my needs when required. Besides, I take care of myself. After a while, though, I get a trifle crabby. Then I need an assist."

"Hence your moods." She smirked. "Why don't you have as many tattoos as your uncle or others of your breed?"

Kole frowned. "Those tats are ancestral runes. To me, my family began with my parents. My relatives were traitors. I burned off the lineage."

She cast her gaze toward the muddy water, wondering why she was so curious about Kole. "Do animus demons release electrical impulses as well as fire?"

"Are we talking about sex again, Chief. Are you planning to fuck a demon?"

"Absolutely not. As you have learned, I know little about Aeternals. I'm adding to my knowledge."

"Enough questions. Come on, it's time to get out." He grabbed her up in his arms, both of them dripping gray goop. Setting her on a flat red rock which jutted out from the pond, he ordered, "Lie on you back first."

"What are you going to do?"

"Not what you want me to do."

"Stop that. I'm through letting you push my buttons for your entertainment."

"Caught. Rest here in the sun. While the mud dries, it will pull out the infection. You already look better. After I cauterize a few of the more serious wounds, they'll heal immediately."

"I am tired. A short nap sounds good."

Kole pointed to a clearwater pond nearby. "I'll be over there getting this shit off."

Skyler watched Kole's spectacular ass until she could no longer see him, her lids drifting closed. When she awoke, he was standing over her. Still naked. Still erect. She vaulted upright. "Pervert."

"You wish." He scooped her into his arms and settled her with a slight toss.

"My clothes."

"Aren't we beyond this foolishness? I refuse to have sex with you no matter how much you beg." Kole gave her his boyishly handsome smile. "Besides, you're all muddy. I like clean females."

"I don't see you as very particular."

"Now who's rude?"

She tightened her arms around his neck. Kole stepped into the clear, cool pond, brushing hands over her skin to wash off the mud.

No. I think not.

When Skyler shot him a warning squint, he backed off, leaving her to cleanse herself.

"I may not always be particular, but I'll have you know I'm considered quite a catch." Kole rested his elbows on the rocks behind him, his broad chest proudly on display.

"Has anyone ever told you you're conceited?"

"It's not conceit if it's true."

Skyler laughed, ducking under the water, washing the healing mud from her face and hair.

****

Margo gulped when the front door creaked open. She hoped it was Galena. Chay had walked out minutes before, saying he was sending the Amazon.

Boots clunked across the room, stopping where she crouched on the floor. "Let's go, human. This is a real screw-up." A smirking Galena extended a hand to Margo, pulling her to her feet. "I leave you alone with the ylven stud for an hour, and the two of you get nabbed by a couple of lame-o renegade Aeternals."

The six-foot-tall, fit Amazon was clad in low-slung jeans, a crop top, and an unbuttoned jacket. Standard wear for her. In addition to the knives in a belt holster, she clutched a short spear.

Margo shook off the hand, rising on her own. "To be fair, it wasn't his fault. They broke into my apartment. Unexpectedly. And they were big. Really strong. He killed one and stopped a warlock before a sloth demon whammied him. You need to give Chay more credit. Besides, he figured out how we could escape."

Galena held up a hand in surrender. "Okay. He's a big hero. What were the two of you doing at your place so Chay didn't hear four males tiptoeing to the door? Playing suck face. No. Don't tell me. I don't want to know."

"I don't intend to tell you. Where are we going?" asked Margo.

"Outta here."

Margo's lips bowed into a frown.

"To the commander. I mean, Rein. Let's go outside so I can throw a portal. We can't risk hoofing it to the gateway. It's a distance from here."

Once they were in the fresh air, Galena wrapped a

hand around Margo's wrist. "You better not mess with my D-chip."

"Then don't threaten me. It makes me more … I don't know. Contagious."

One minute Margo was in a rundown yard. The next, she wasn't. They walked through a hallway where a drop-dead gorgeous blonde held a door open for them.

The woman's mini-skirt fluttered as she tapped an ankle-strapped shoe on the floor. *Tap. Tap. Tap.* "Hurry. I'd love to finish my manicure." She waved a hand in front of the black-haired Firebrand. "This is Orgasm Red." She flipped out the other. "This is Pink Taboo. What's your choice?"

"I'd go with the red. Looks great on you," blurted Margo.

The woman dropped her gaze to that hand. "I think you're right. Thanks."

Galena answered Margo's questioning arched brows. "Bounty's a vamp. Kole's executive assistant."

The impatient Bounty escorted them through her office to another. Margo sucked in a breath. Waiting was an exceptionally large, armed man with a fierce guy sitting behind the desk, a scar through his brow and a snarl on his lips. When Chay stepped into view, his arms open, Margo rushed to him, snuggling into his chest while he whispered soft words in her ear.

Galena propped a fist on her hip. "Thanks, Amazon. Thanks for going to get the human."

Chay peeked up. "Yeah. Thanks, Galena. Precious cargo here."

"That's so sweet, Chay."

"I'm a sweet guy, Red."

****

Skyler was once again on her back atop the red rock, stretched out and naked with the demon crouched next to her. No pants. No shirt. Lots of skin and a still-huge penis. Any pretense at modesty was gone.

"I should warn you, there may be side effects to my fire which I haven't mentioned."

"Just zap me. Stop talking about it. Can't you put your clothes on? At least your pants."

"You want me to cover my best asset?"

Skyler released a sigh.

"If you insist."

He powered off the rock, yanked on cargoes, and returned to kneel at her feet, walking her through the procedure. "I'll apply as little fire as possible to each wound. Prep yourself, though. It's going to hurt, Frisca."

With no more warning, a flame streaked from his index finger. Each time he touched her, she flinched. Squeezing her lips tight, she tried not to whimper. Kole whispered soothing words she couldn't understand. "What are you saying?"

"Nothing important. The old language. Demonish."

"It's lovely." She bit her lower lip, swallowing any sound that might make him feel guilty.

"Flip."

On her stomach, she rested a cheek on her folded arms. More sharp bites of pain, but Skyler breathed through it all.

When Kole sat butt to heels, she rolled to the side, pulling her knees into her chest for comfort, softly moaning. Skyler closed her eyes, willing the pangs to subside.

The last thing she remembered was Kole saying, "I'm sorry, Frisca."

Darkness.

She shot upright. The sudden light was bright. She gasped, taking short, rapid breaths to relieve the sensation flooding her body. She glanced down. No wounds. Not even a scar. She twisted toward Kole. He was lying on his back on a flat-top rock near the clear pond, his lids closed, his head resting on his muscled arms.

Skyler padded on bare feet to the delicious commander, heaving herself onto the stone. Beside him, she ran a hand over his high, wide cheekbone. She swiped a finger across his full, sensuous lips and trailed feathery touches down his thick, corded neck. She stroked a wing on his Phoenix brand. Wanting more, she brushed a palm along his chest, traveling to the dips of his solid abs. Locking her gaze on the spot where his pants rode low on his hips, she flicked open the button and pulled on the zipper. She slid inside, where she grasped his stiff cock.

Smooth. Firm. Huge.

His deep voice interrupted her exploration. "You might be exhibiting the side effect I warned you about, Frisca. Demon healing can be arousing." Kole's fire-gold eyes were checking out where her hand tucked into his pants.

Skyler was aching. She wanted Kole more than she had ever wanted any man.

No. Not wanted. Needed.

She swung a leg across his thighs, still clutching his shaft, which she planned to have buried deep inside her, thrusting into her drenched sheath.

But he flipped their positions, capturing her hands above her head. "Let's control ourselves for a minute while I put the toy back in the box." Kole grimaced, struggling to return his penis to his pants and zip up.

Skyler bucked her hips, but there was no moving Kole. "Fuck me."

"You don't want that."

"I know what I want. I want you inside me."

"You do now. Later, I wouldn't hear the end of it." He leaned in close to whisper in her ear, his hot breath only arousing her more. "But mark my words, Frisca, someday you won't be drunk, and you won't be under the influence of my healing. You'll want me to fuck you. And I will."

"Oh, just stop talking. Please." Skyler's hips rolled up. She needed him to fill her, to take away the ache. Everything hurt. Her breasts were heavy. Her sex quivered. Her skin was on fire. "You've got to make this stop."

She had never seen anything more beautiful than the sparks shooting from Kole's eyes. His breathing ragged, he bent closer and licked around her nipple.

"Yes. More." She arched into him, begging.

He took the peaked bud between his teeth, nipping it. His gaze flipped up to fix on her irises. Only then did he take more of her breast into his mouth, suckling hard. Skyler moaned, grinding against him. He lavished his attention on the other breast.

It wasn't enough. She wanted more and more. "Kole."

He abandoned her breasts to press his full lips to hers, gentle at first. But when he plunged inside her mouth, he devoured her. His tongue tangled with hers as if they battled for dominance. Too soon, he stopped, releasing her.

"Please, Kole. I need you." Skyler heard her own pathetic, needy pleas.

He slid down her body, unclasping her hands, pausing to lay kisses on her stomach. "Push your knees up, Frisca."

When she did, he spread her thighs wide, settling between them. The cool air on her sex gave her momentary relief.

"Is this what you want?" Kole's voice was raspy, hoarse.

"Yes. Hell, yes."

He cupped her ass, lowering his head to lick slowly between her folds. Testing. Teasing. Torturing.

Too gentle. Her hips bucked upward. "Kole."

His hands stroked her thighs while he continued. Back. Forth. He stopped.

"No." She clawed his skin, frantic.

But then he drew her clit into his mouth, flicking his tongue around the swollen nub, nipping, sucking.

"Oh, God. Yes." Skyler couldn't contain the wild need flowing through her. She begged the demon for more.

He responded, plunging a rough finger inside her. In. Out. Again.

"So good." When she lifted her hips to encourage him, he thrust in two fingers, his pace faster.

"Don't stop." She closed her lids to savor each stroke. "Harder."

His finger pounded into Skyler, hitting all the sensitive spots. As she neared release, an electrical impulse surged through her. Her eyes slid open to find him peeking up at her, his gaze burning into her soul.

He was hungry, but instead of fulfilling his own needs, he returned to satisfy her with his fingers while he sucked on her clitoris.

"Yes. Yes."

When his tongue speared into her, Skyler spiraled out of control. Her hips rocked against his mouth, the pleasure building. She trembled, gripped his temples in her hands, and screamed his name as another pulse of electricity shot through her, followed by an all-consuming orgasm.

Still Kole licked, bit, sucked until she collapsed, exhausted though sated. When she straightened her legs, she let her arms fall limp to her sides, and he rolled onto his back.

Skyler drew slow, deep breaths. "You were spectacular." Then, sanity nudged her, urging her to sit upright. She dragged open her lids, heavy with sexual satisfaction. "Oh my lord. What did we do?"

"I would think you might know." Kole swiped his arm along his mouth, coming away with a big grin.

"Shut up." Heat flowed from Skyler's toes to her cheeks until she was sure they were as red as the boulder.

"Is your fiancé spectacular?" asked Kole.

Skyler blinked. *Her fiancé?* "No, he wasn't … isn't," she whispered.

Kole swallowed hard, his throat bobbing. He slid off the rock and tossed clothes at her. "Get dressed. You're healed. No need to thank me."

"Thank you? Thank you? I should report you to … to … somebody!"

"For what? You snagged my dick. I thought I was quite the gentleman. Should I have used words instead of my tongue on you? Is that how your fiancé does it? With a good chat?"

"Leave my fiancé out of it. You made me … uh…"

"Horny?"

"Yes. You knew this would happen." Skyler buttoned her shirt. She wiggled pants up her legs.

"Some get it worse than others. Some not at all. You had it bad, Frisca. Says something about the passion you keep bottled. As side effects go, you gotta admit, wanting to screw is a good one. Of course, I could have let you die from the infection. Having me go down on you was better, don't you think? Besides, I had a fine time."

"Uh … uh … I'm at a loss for words."

"Terrific. You'll be less irritating." Kole turned around to retrieve his shirt and weapons.

Despite everything, Skyler ogled him while he dressed, his biceps flexing as he strapped on the harness, loading it with knives. He shoved an axe into a holster on his belt. She shook her head. No good. She wanted Kole's mouth on her again. And more. But she feared it had nothing to do with the side effects of his healing power. Kole simply set her on fire.

After securing his last weapon, he pivoted around, a deep furrow between his brows. "I have enormous control over my demon urges, but even I have limits. I've reached mine, Frisca. If you keep looking at me like that, I will fuck you."

"Do you have to ruin everything by being vulgar?"

"Nothing vulgar about fucking if it's done right."

Skyler found herself nodding in silent agreement as she let out a loud sigh.

She pulled up her socks, jammed her feet in her boots, donned her jacket, and slipped her backpack on. By the time they left for Spriggan Enclave, she was clear-headed and physically healed. She wasn't so sure her emotions would ever be the same.

Chapter Twenty

"She's precious. You're sweet. And I'm gagging over here." Rein leaned back in Kole's chair, his arms folded across his chest. "Make the intros, Chay. Let's get on with it."

The ylve tucked Margo into his side as if Rein might attack her. "The big guy at the desk is my mentor and acting commander. His scowl is fierce, but he's a good male to have at your six. The brute with all the blades and spiffy hair is the satyr Ramirez. While I trust him with my life, I wouldn't trust him with you."

Ram touched his heart. "Ylve man, you hurt me." He winked at Margo.

"Galena you've met," said Chay.

Margo's gaze took in the room and its inhabitants. "Boy, I could do a lot with your bodies."

Galena chuckled, but Rein scowled and Ram's brows shot up. "The human's a sculptor. She's into bodies."

Rein pushed out of his chair. "You guys get the hell out of here while I talk to Margo. I've got something to explain to her."

Chay stood his ground. "I'll stick around and listen."

"I don't think I invited you."

"I don't think I care." Chay dropped his arm from Margo's shoulders to advance on Rein.

Rein strode toward the ylve, nose to nose, eyeing the clenched fists. He wasn't looking forward to outing the ylve's lights. *Damn.* Was this the kind of shit Kole put up with all the time?

Likely. A bunch of aggressive hotheads with short fuses. Still, this isn't Chay's style.

Margo slid between them before they could come to blows.

Chay grabbed her arms, gentling her to the side. "Red, sweetie, don't ever step between two Firebrands about to go blow-to-blow." With a hand on Margo's back, the ylve guided her toward the door. "Leave us alone a minute. Stay right outside, though. Close by."

"Sure, ylve baby." She complied after giving each of them the once-over. Once she was gone, Chay tensed again as he spread his legs.

Rein fixed on the ylve's challenging stance. "If you keep this up, they'll be sweeping your body parts off the floor."

"I'm not leaving my female alone in here. Deal."

Rein squinted at the ylve. "Your female?"

"Yeah. Mine."

"Do you hear yourself?"

At Rein's question, Chay's expression changed from pissed to what-the-hell. His shoulders slumped. He unclenched his fists. "Aw, man, I need advice. You recently mated a human."

Rein tapped his wrist. "We're on a tight schedule, Chay. We've got to find Kole, and a whole bunch of other shit is going down. No time for drama."

"I agree, man. I need my head screwed on straight for all the action. To do so, I require wisdom from my mentor."

Rein swiped a hand across his hair. "Make it quick." He sank into the chair, propping his boots on Kole's worn desk.

"I'm obsessed with Margo. You saw me. I was ready to go fist-to-fist. That's not me, man. You know it's not. When I transported here, I thought I'd chuck her and go through with mating Anjeli. But one look at the gorgeous redhead, and I can't bring myself to do it. Another thing. Bounty was at her desk when I came in. I didn't give her a glance. And you know what? I suddenly knew she'd never catch my eye again. Me! Can you imagine? I have wet dreams about her vamp pussy. Of course, I'd never share that with her. She'd probably snap my neck."

Rein smirked, lacing his fingers behind his head. "Yeah. I can imagine. Frustrating, isn't it?"

"You do understand, man. What's wrong with me?"

"Figure it out yourself, Chay. I'm not a fucking relationship counselor."

"I want to introduce her to my family. What's going to happen when she meets my mother?"

"You care what your mother thinks?"

"Hell, no. That's the crazy part. I care what Margo will think about my parental units. What if she doesn't like them? What if she wants to dump me? You've met my mom and dad. They're kind of stiff."

"Chay, it seems to me she's more likely to accept your people but dump your ass because you're such a screw-up."

"Right, man. I'm so fucked."

"Okay then. Back to business. Call her in."

Chay didn't move. "But what am I going to do?"

"Does this look say I care? We've got serious stuff on our plates."

"But I need help." Chay tapped his temple as a reminder. "Head. Straight."

Rein sighed, nodded, and flashed on how Braelyn had messed with his legendary control. His freckled, smartass human had him by the short hairs leading him into the twilight zone. "I'm only going to say this once, so listen close. If she's your fated mate, you're screwed. Females scramble your brains. You may never figure out why she drives you crazy, but she will. Here's the sick part. She may aggravate the hell out of you, but you'll keep coming back for more. She'll push every button you've got, but you can't wait until you see her smile. You can't breathe if she's out of your sight for too long. You want to kill anyone who even hurts her feelings. She will trust you with her life, and you won't let her down. If her feet are sore, you'll rub them. In short, you'll wonder who in the hell you are. She'll become your best friend, eternal love, light in the darkness, greatest strength. So, wave the fucking white flag. You're already a goner. Ask her to be your mate. Now, get Margo in here."

Chay slapped Rein on the shoulder. "Thanks, man. Best advice you've ever given me." He opened the door. "Red."

Rein scrubbed a fist across his head, ready to pray to Gahya if it would bring the commander home.

I don't want to deal with this crap. No wonder he sets walls on fire.

Margo returned to the office, arms crossed over her chest.

Rein's cobalt blues studied her. "He can stay. I'm beaten. Does she know what she's getting?"

"Red's ylve-struck," answered Chay with a shrug.

Margo jammed a springy curl behind her ear. "I am not. You're human-struck."

Rein expelled a sigh. "You deserve each other. Anyway, sit down. Chay says he told you about our search for Blood Coven descendants, which took us to you in Cleveland. The short of it is, you are one."

Chay squeezed Margo's hand. "We guessed as much. Now what?"

"Margo, you have a big bullseye on your chest. The biggest. Cerberus already kidnapped you once. Our job is to protect you from the asshole."

Rein clasped his hands behind his neck. His lip curled into a snarl, revealing sharp fangs. "That's why you'll live here."

Margo looked a little bleary-eyed. "Okay. Maybe I am a witch. Blood Coven descendant. Fodder for this Cerberus character."

Tears gathered in her eyes.

Shit. Chay's female is getting weepy.

"How long are we talking? My life's on Earth. My career is only now taking off. Some of the bigger galleries are starting to exhibit my pieces. I didn't ask for any of this. I spent my life wanting to create my art, finding the perfect studio, developing my own style, becoming known in the industry…"

Rein interrupted. "Make no mistake, Margo, if you're on your own, you will be snatched again. We can keep you safe. Kole, our real commander, talked about housing descendants here at the stronghold. But I don't know how long you'll have to be here."

Chay sent her a grin. "Red, you can set up a studio right here on Scath. And we have a huge art community. I'm not part of it, but I'll make damn sure you are. You can keep in touch with the galleries on Earth. Visit whenever you want. Nothing you have gained will be lost. I promise." Chay brushed a tear from her cheek. "Of course, I'll be the gum stuck to your shoe wherever you go."

Margo's lips tilted into a smile. "At least, there are perks."

"You bet. Perks in the morning, perks at night, perks pretty much anytime I'm not on duty."

"Find an apartment on the second floor. They're

big. Some bigger than others." Rein swiveled his chair toward Chay. "Show her around. Take her on a tour of the art district in Bludhaven. And, Margo, make the place your own. Whatever you need is yours. Chay, you're in charge of finding her two trainers. One for weapons. Another for skills."

"I went to school to become a sculptor. It only stands to reason witches need training also. Anyway, controlling this radio wave thing is difficult?"

Chay gripped both of her upper arms. "Hot damn, Red. We'll pick out an apartment here for us. You can jazz it up however you like. A two-bedroom so you can have your studio." He stopped abruptly. "Hey. Brakes on. Maybe I'm getting ahead of myself. Maybe you'd rather have a place by yourself. If that's what you want, then I'll plant myself in the one next door to make sure nobody bothers you. Not even me, if that's what you want."

She hesitated for only a sec. "Don't be silly, ylve baby. I want you with me. Just try to escape."

"Sabine and Tyr brought in an Alliance agent, another Blood Coven descendant. You'll have company. Nico Abello. A real charmer." Rein didn't mention he was the guy who had kissed Braelyn right before Silas knocked him on his ass. "He's cooling his jets in an upstairs apartment. The hothead can use some chill time."

Rein glanced at a pile of paperwork on the desk. "Okay. Another job well done. Off you go while I throw myself into all this administrative bullshit."

****

Skyler paused, tilted her head to the side, and scowled at the endless, serpentine steps leading up a windswept rocky cliff. At the top of the plateau, barely visible in a cloud, perched Spriggan Enclave, a gigantic circular stone wall topped off with a thatched roof.

"It's quite a climb." She whistled.

"Are you game?"

"I didn't imply I couldn't make it."

"Of course you didn't. You can do anything."

Skyler tossed a frosty smile at Kole before starting the uphill journey. About a third of the way there, she collapsed onto a step, gasping ragged breaths.

Kole halted. "Is this you making it?"

"I'm resting. Leave me alone." Her chest bounced up. Down.

Kole's attention darted to the enclave.

Weary of his impatience, she stood, brushing dust off her pants. "For heaven's sakes. Can't a girl take a break? Let's go." She made it over halfway before exhaustion and altitude had her flinging herself down again. She dropped her head between her legs to fight for air.

"I could carry you."

She hurtled upright, her gaze flipping over her shoulder at a taunting Kole who showed no signs of exertion. She chuffed, turning her back on him, massaging a cramped leg furiously.

Retracing his steps until he was below her, Kole crossed bulging arms over his chest. "Here. Let me." Before she could object, he grabbed her calf, kneading her muscle while she leaned onto her elbows.

The heat from Kole's hands penetrated her pants, sending erotic shivers through Skyler. She didn't want to react to him, but there was no denying his effect. Surely, it was a residual response to his healing fire. As her eyelids fluttered, she visualized his palms sliding along her body. In her mind, they moved from her calf to her knee to her thigh, his rough massage shifting to a caress. A warm sensation rose until she squirmed, an ache in the wrong place. She swatted at his hands. "It's fine now. Stop." Pushing off the step, Skyler resumed climbing.

Kole followed, his boots thudding on the steps below her. "I could just grab your nicely rounded ass and nudge you up the hill."

She whirled around, eyes narrowing.

"You know, you give me the Skyler glare so often I'm starting to find it sexy."

"Trust me. It's not meant that way."

"Are you sure?"

Kole paused when Skyler stopped again. Before she could berate him, his eyes sparked while the edge of his mouth curled into a grin. He bent, put his fingers to the ground, and sprinted forward. For a big man, he moved fast.

Skyler's mouth fell open when she realized his intent. "Oh, no you don't." She lunged for the steps but not before Kole caught her and swept her into his arms. Wiggling to be released, she accomplished nothing. "You're acting like a kid. Put me down. I can make it."

"I want to get there before nightfall. Besides, I've developed a fondness for carrying you, Frisca."

"Have it your way. You always do." She gave in too easily, but Kole's embrace was familiar, comforting. She wasn't feverish or delirious this time. Cradled against his body, she rubbed her cheek against his chest, absorbing his masculine scent as he bounded up the stairs. She nestled closer to enjoy the ride. Maybe something in the air on Darque made her less able to make rational decisions.

When they reached the entrance to Spriggan Enclave, Kole set Skyler on her feet, breaking the spell. "I don't have to tell you to let me do the talking, do I?"

"No, but thanks for being a jerk and reminding me of my mistakes."

"That's what I'm here for, Frisca."

Two guards posted outside the enclave stepped forward. Similar in appearance, they had wide lips, long noses, and beady eyes. Branches sprang from their heads like deer antlers. Their skin was the color and texture of brown bark. *Interesting.* Shorter than Skyler, both were dwarfed by Kole.

With wooden spears tucked close to their sides, they squinted at their visitors. The taller, grim-faced guard lifted his weapon, pounding it handle down into the dirt before he spoke. "Commander Kole. What brings you here?"

"We need a place to rest tonight. Food, too."

"Who's she?" A corner of the guard's mouth twitched with a snarl as he nodded toward Skyler.

"My guest." Kole growled, palming the hilt of his knife. "Tell Sparse I'm seeking sanctuary. Now!" He assumed a wide stance, his threat obvious.

The silent man pivoted around to enter the enclave. He returned with a male who resembled the two guards. Only his clothing distinguished him. He wore breeches of soft leather, fine boots, and a bright red shirt. His rigid posture along with the bitter line of his mouth showed hostility toward Kole. "You ask for sanctuary?"

"I do. Also, food and a few supplies."

"I am required to give you one night and what you need to survive. Come." Sparse extended his cold back, reentering the enclave, motioning for them to follow.

Kole grabbed Skyler's hand, a possessive hold, protective. Inside, noise assaulted her ears. Merchants were hawking goods in front of tents which lined a maze of crowded paths. The traders bartered for woven rugs, jewelry, carved art, trinkets, strange fowl hanging by bound feet, large cuts of red meat, pottery, cloths. A merchant waved red silk fabric in her face, causing the commander to let out a feral snarl before he shoved the guy aside.

They journeyed through the market, the many turns playing with Skyler's sense of direction. As the stalls fell behind them, the scenery changed. They were in a residential area with intricately tiled high walls, accented by brightly colored entry doors. Their guide, Sparse, led them to one such door painted cobalt blue. "In here. Food, drink, and supplies will be brought. Be out by first light." Before he left, his eyes narrowed on Kole, a grumble burbling from his throat.

Kole swept Skyler behind him to meet Sparse's challenge head on. "Do you violate sanctuary, Sparse?"

"No. I can wait until morning, Firebrand." When the Spriggan closed the door, the tension evaporated.

Skyler had expected an exotic room. Instead of the beauty promised from the outside, the quarters were cold, empty. "This is lovely, and he's certainly friendly. I don't think he likes you. I'm surprised with you being so likable."

"He hates me. I killed his brother, but a Spriggan cannot refuse a request for sanctuary."

"You killed his brother, but you had the nerve to ask him for shelter?"

Kole snapped his head in Skyler's direction. His eyes flared. "The asshole deserved to die."

His spoken vehemence against Sparse's brother made Skyler shudder. Perhaps Kole was closer to a barbarian, as she originally thought. "Can we trust the food he'll send?"

"It'll be safe, not particularly appetizing, but safe."

The door opened a crack while hands thrust a tray filled with large steaming bowls of food and drink inside.

Kole set it between them.

"What's this?" Skyler lifted the lid off a bowl. She bent her head to sniff. *Hmm*. Not bad. Familiar.

"Think of it as brown rice."

"This?" The bowl held lumps of yellow, grisly meat floating in a brown sauce.

"Think of it as chicken."

"Not so easy. And the carafe?"

"That's actually red wine." Kole poured it into two goblets and lifted one to his lips, taking a long drink. "Good red wine." He tipped the glass again. "Bottoms up."

Skyler ate little, thinking the dishes in no way tasted like chicken or rice. After Kole gobbled his down, he lumbered over to the wall opposite the door. He removed the blankets from his knapsack, spreading one on the ground. He motioned for Skyler to take the other. He unbuckled his chest harness, putting his three daggers, long blade, and axe within reach.

Skyler marked his actions. "You said we were safe here."

"We are, but we're safer when I can snag my weapons."

If Skyler expected Kole to lay out her blanket, she was disappointed. She shook hers before settling it on the hard floor far away from the commander.

"Take both of the jackets."

Despite the blanket under her, Kole's coat clutched to her chin, and hers over her legs, her teeth chattered from the cold.

"Warm body over here."

"I've had enough heat from you."

"Suit yourself." Kole closed his eyes. His breathing fell into an even rhythm.

Skyler rolled onto her back, listening to him

inhale and exhale. She was not an impulsive person. Her hormones had never been out of control. She reminded herself she was a successful businesswoman. Chief legal officer for the Alliance. A human. She could never be attracted to a barbaric demon. Still, sleep didn't come. After what seemed like hours, she was desperate. "Are you still awake?"

"I am now." Kole groaned.

"Talk to me. I can't sleep."

"Why is it when you're in pain or can't sleep you want to talk? Never mind." Kole lit a torch on the wall with a stream of fire. "So, you decided to keep me awake, too?"

"Yes."

"Give me a minute to think." Kole scrubbed a hand across his close-cropped hair and yawned. "Did you get the doll?"

"What?"

"For Christmas."

Skyler's answer was a long time coming. "I ran down our grand steps early to look under the tree, sure she would be there. Santa had promised. But there was no My Pretty Ballerina. That's what the doll was called. I found my letter in my father's trashcan later. Another disappointment for me."

"I'm sorry." Kole spoke barely above a whisper. She thought he muttered, "Bastard."

"Did you ever want something badly when you were a child?"

"Yes. Parents." Kole rolled over. Eventually, she heard his rhythmic breaths.

Pain stabbed Skyler's heart. She wished she could settle on one version of Kole. Was he a brutish barbarian? A loyal warrior? A killer? A little boy who missed his parents? A man who made her blush with desire? While she concentrated on these possibilities, she fell asleep. In what seemed like seconds, she was being shaken.

Kole loomed above her. "Let's go. It will be dawn soon."

"A few more minutes, please." She rolled over.

"If we overstay our welcome, we'll be hanging from a tree in the noonday sun. Sparse meant what he said. Best we leave before first light."

As they reached the winding path of the marketplace, Skyler hoped Kole remembered the route because she didn't. "We took so many turns. How can you be sure of the way out?"

Kole pointed at a close scattering of black pebbles on the ground. Skyler's mouth fell open. "I didn't see you leaving those."

"If you had, Sparse would have also."

She spied more ahead of them. "How clever."

"I bet you thought I was no more than a pretty face and a big dick."

Chapter Twenty-One

Tap. Tap. Tap.

Nico rolled his head from side to side as his lids scraped up his eyes like sandpaper. He sprang off the couch where he had fallen asleep last night with a bitch of a headache. This morning, he was still feeling the loving from the warlock's spell.

Where am I? Oh, yeah. Paradise.

He pressed on his brow to stop the pain. "Damn. That hurts." Somebody knocked again. "I'm coming. Keep your shit together." He hitched up his jeans and opened the door, bare chested.

Sabine rolled her eyes. "What? No sweetness? Invite me in, cuddles." As she shoved by him, her fingers trailed along his chest. "Nice."

"While flattery will get you into the sack with me, it won't get you anything else. What the hell did you hit me with in my office? I'm still groggy with the effects."

"Don't be such a pussy. Tyr zapped you with a spell so you'd leave with us. No fuss. No muss. Not our fault you're a lightweight."

"When do I meet this Rein?"

"Since he's busy, I've got the okay to answer any questions you might have."

Hmm. She's still gorgeous, even with my throbbing headache, but I'm gonna kill her.

He reached for his gun, remembering he didn't have it.

"Aw, cuddles. We took your weapon away. No guns on Scath."

"Cut the 'cuddles' shit. What was so important you kidnapped an Alliance agent? I thought we were all on the same team."

Sabine sighed. "We are. Sorry about the whole spell routine, but you weren't cooperative. You've already got a rep around here for being a jerk."

"I'm sad. Should I smile more while you guys ream my ass? Why don't you tell me why I'm here so I don't have to guess. I assume it's not because I'm so devastatingly good looking you want me for your personal sex toy. Or is that it?"

She snorted. "You know you got stuck two times by a healer who came to your office, right?"

Nico ran his fingers through his hair, mildly interested in the direction of the conversation but still working with a headache. "Sure. I was there." He plopped back onto the couch.

"You already knew you had some Aeternal running through your veins."

"Obviously. That's why I joined the Alliance and became an agent."

"The bad-news-worse-news is the first blood test showed you are descended from a mage. The second confirmed you are related to a member of the Blood Coven."

"Okay. Big deal."

"Actually, it is. It means you are in deep shit, and Cerberus, the hound of Hades from prophecy, is hunting your kind."

Although Nico heard what Sabine was saying, he stared at her kissable lips. Then his gaze roamed to her pale, translucent eyes like sea glass, a distinguishing mark of a nymph or satyr. He fantasized about taking her sun-streaked blonde hair out of the braids and letting it flow down her back, his fingers rubbing along her baby-soft, cream-colored skin and nicely muscled arms. Maybe she'd wrap those strong, shapely legs around him while he buried himself in her core.

What in the hell was she going on about now?

"...for your protection."

There you go. She just pissed him off. He brushed an unruly strand of hair off his forehead. "Fuck your protection."

****

After a sleepless night in a crowded tent where Kole contained his urges, the craggy rock aerie of the Spriggans was far behind them. As he had been doing since leaving the enclave, he marked their trail with bursts of fire, ashing a shrub or two. "We'll reach my cave before nightfall. Since it's stocked with emergency supplies, we can hide out there until my Firebrands find us."

"They know about your cave?"

"They know I have a hideout. They don't know where it is, but at some point, they'll check with the Spriggans. Once they do, they'll see my marks along this route. In the meantime, we'll wait it out. Don't worry."

Skyler hit him with the frosty-chin-up look. "I'm not worried."

"Of course you're not. You're tough."

At midday, Kole paused. He passed Skyler water along with the Spriggan version of a protein bar while they rested on a grassy slope at the base of a mountain.

She perched on a boulder with her knee bent, her arm clasped around it while she took in the scenery.

Kole thought he might enjoy being stuck in his cave with Skyler. He peeked overhead at the bright sun. It must be affecting his mind. Still, she presented a beautiful picture, her platinum hair hanging loose, her skin glowing, and her face tilted upward with her long, luscious neck begging to be kissed. In the light, her eyes were blue with strong lilac highlights today. The sun was getting to him, possible sunstroke. She spoke, jarring him from a vision of her in his arms, his lips pressed to her very enticing neck.

"Which way are we going?"

Kole rose, pointing. "Up there."

Skyler put a hand above her eyes, shielding them from the glare while she fixed on the area. "I don't see anything."

"If we climb from here, we'll come to a river. We'll follow it as it snakes through a gorge. In some places, we'll be hugging the rocky edge. When we're lucky, we'll be strolling on grassy inclines. The farther up, the more treacherous. Big boulders. Steep cliffs. At the top is a waterfall. Behind it, the entrance to my cave."

Skyler sighed. "Of course it's uphill. Does everything have to be uphill?"

"Excellent vantage point. Defense counts."

"Okay. Up it is."

"You're a good sport, Frisca."

"Do I have a choice?"

Skyler was a classic beauty. A body of elegant curves. Legs, long and shapely. Way out of his league. But her courage surprised him. He had pegged her as a whiner. She wasn't. Her father may have made her cold, but she had made herself strong.

She slid off her perch, zipped her jacket, and started uphill. "Let's go, Commander."

"You lead for a while. I'll enjoy the view."

Over her shoulder, she quipped, "It's only fair. I was enjoying your ass the entire morning."

"You make me blush, Frisca."

She adjusted her pack and kept moving in the right direction. When the terrain became rockier, steeper,

Kole took point. After a while, he froze, snapping his head around. Looking downhill, he sniffed the air. "Gagans. I can smell them from here." He pushed Skyler, growling. "Climb fast. We're no longer out for a stroll, Frisca. Double time it."

When they reached an outcropping of rocks, Kole threw himself behind a boulder where he had a good view to the base of the mountain.

Above him, Skyler halted. "What do you see?"

His vision was far superior to a human's. "They're just starting the climb, but they'll gain ground."

The wildings scrabbled up the grassy knoll at the bottom, the sunlight bestowing a brownish-grey cast to their skin. Four large curling claws on each hand and foot tore into the dirt, propelling them forward. Flesh was drawn tight over their faces while sharp canines poked like daggers beneath their upper lips. Tufts of hair sprang from their heads. Spines protruded down their backs, ending in long knobby tails.

"It's a six-beast hunting crew." Kole clutched Skyler's shoulder. "I've described the cave's location. Run for it now. To the river. Follow it until the waterfall. Up again. The cave is behind the waterfall. If I don't join you, stay put until the Firebrands arrive."

"I won't abandon you. Between the two of us, we can beat them. I'll help."

"How? Frisca, you wouldn't want me drafting a legal contract. I don't want you facing gagans. In fact, if I have to worry about you, I won't be at my best. Don't argue with me. Run."

"No." Skyler's eyes welled up.

Kole wrapped an arm around her waist, cradled her chin in his palm, and lifted it. "Tears for me, Frisca? What's the world coming to? Maybe I'm growing on you."

"Don't be ridiculous. If you die, I'll be alone. Then I'll probably die, too."

"Attagirl." He rubbed a calloused finger along her mouth before gently brushing his lips across hers, kissing her with a tenderness that surprised him. She let him in. He felt her quiver when his tongue stroked hers, sliding, caressing. Taking a sharp breath, he withdrew, wanting to hold onto the memory of the all-too-brief kiss.

He stepped back. "No. I think you're starting to like me."

Her voice wavered. "I am not."

Kole wiped away an escaping tear from her cheek.

"For once, Frisca, obey me." He thrust a dagger into her belt.

"No. You'll need your weapons."

"I've got two more blades, a short sword, and an axe along with my own powers. Plenty. Now go."

"Don't make me leave you, Kole."

"You're going to put one foot in front of the other while you march your pretty ass up the mountain." Kole swung her around, swatting her hard on the butt.

He watched her ascend the hill, slipping but steadily climbing. She did have a fine ass. If it was one of his last views, he was a lucky male. Kole twisted to face the deadly hunting party. He only had to hold them until Skyler reached his hide-away. They would never find her. With luck, he would kill or severely injure them so they couldn't follow her. After his Firebrands found him, they'd track her to the cave. A solid plan. He dropped his pack on the ground.

Trash the hunting crew. Save Skyler.

When the first gagan clutched the rocky ledge, pulling its body over the top, it charged Kole.

With over three-hundred pounds of snarling beast

coming at him, Kole swerved to the side, plunging a dagger into the howling gagan's heart. He twisted the blade.

By this time, a second member of the hunting party catapulted over the edge, landing with a thud. Another joined it. With a gagan at his back and the other facing him, Kole shaped balls of fire while they pawed at the ground, preparing to attack.

There's a bene to being ambidextrous.

Twisting sideways to keep an eye on both beasts, Kole juggled the blazing orbs like a circus performer. He zinged them at both opponents. The first launch hit a bullseye. One down. Its partner, the creature who had hoped to sandwich him between them, was luckier. Ducking Kole's barrage of fire, the beast launched an iron claw. Kole dodged the deadly projectile. He didn't escape the second. It sank into his shoulder. He pulled it out fast, skin and muscle tearing, blood pouring from the wound. But the poison coursed through him.

He prepped more fire, streams of it shooting from his fingertips. This gagan was quick, bulleting iron claws at him. He took one in the chest. The creature launched flying iron again. Kole danced aside. When a blast of his fire ashed the wilding, the beast's ear-shattering shrieks and howls were like music.

The remaining three in the hunting party topped the ledge, crouching, growling. When they eyed their dead comrades, they approached with caution. Though weakened by the iron coursing through his blood from multiple hits, Kole managed another blazing stream.

One more beast down. A point for the good guy. Two to go.

His fire was depleted. He couldn't use his electric power unless he got close enough to touch. A dagger, a short sword, and an axe left. While taint from the claws hurtled through his arteries, he was in a race against time. What was faster? Him? Or gagan poison?

With the acrid odor of burning gagan flesh irritating Kole's nose, the last two wildings stepped back, waiting for him to weaken.

Brilliant strategy.

He shook his head, trying to dispel the dizziness caused by the iron. He looked up the mountain, relieved that Skyler was gone from sight.

Then the bulkier gagan launched a claw at Kole who, struggling against his fog, lurched to the right. Missed. Again, the creature hurled a lethal projectile. Another painful weave to the side. Success. When the smaller opponent propelled its nail, it hit the target, lodging in Kole's thigh. Falling to his knees, he felt the searing agony spark every nerve ending.

He pushed through the pain, shoved to his feet, and rushed the bigger attacker, determined to fight the stronger beast while he still had any energy left. Charging, he drew his axe from his belt. When they crashed chest to chest, the gagan buried its iron teeth in his upper arm. Suppressing convulsions, Kole broke free, swung his weapon around, and planted it between his opponent's neck and shoulder. The wilding released its hold, howling, stumbling backward. He sank to the ground, injured but not dead.

The last hunter standing came in for the kill. Kole sidestepped the creature. Too late. A claw scraped his leg. The pain buckled his knees.

While the wilding was off balance, Kole rose, turned, and launched himself at the beast, clutching around its waist, sending megavolts of electricity into the creature's body. No surviving that.

Kole stumbled, shaky from launching multiple fire attacks, using electric power, and the beasts' poisonous iron. Gathering what strength he could, he motioned at the injured creature he had taken down moments ago, the bloody axe still in its hide. His words were slurred. "Come get me."

The remaining member of the six-beast hunting crew shoved off the ground and heaved a claw. His eyesight failing, Kole swerved. "Missed." Once again, a projectile whistled through the air, sticking in Kole's thigh near the other wound. He fell to a knee, his chin dropping. The gagan charged, but Kole, staggering to his feet, came in low to sink his dagger into the monster. When the creature bellowed, Kole dragged the blade from stomach to chest. Then he thrust a hand inside and ripped out its heart.

Kole crawled in the dirt until he reached a rock to lean against. The bite on his arm hurt like a sonofabitch. He scanned his body, drew out the claws in his thigh, patting around for the remaining nail in his chest.

Found it.

He yanked it out. Unfortunately, he couldn't release the poison without help. Lifting his heavy lids, he gazed toward the river. Skyler was safe. That's all he cared about.

It would have been nice to kiss her a last time, to hold her close, to feel her fingers stroke his jaw, to hear her pleasured sighs.

Kole's eyes slid closed. His head slumped forward. The iron was killing him. His hallucinations took him to the top of the Blud Dunes looking out at the sun setting behind the distant mountains. Dust devils skittered across the red sands while a migratory herd of Scath elk traveled among the drifts. The beauty of his beloved Knife's Edge lay before him. He hoped his ashes would rest there.

He hoped Skyler shed a tear.

****

Cal perched on the edge of Anna's desk, chatting when the buzzer from the lobby sounded.

Skyler's administrative assistant answered the intercom with her usual musical greeting. "Send him up." She arched her eyebrows, frowning. "Dr. Callahan is on his way. He wants answers about Skyler."

"I'll handle it." Cal planted his feet on the floor, tugging on the lapels of his sports jacket, straightening it, preparing to meet Winston, Skyler's fiancé.

The tall, blond emergency room doc blustered through the door, his Italian shoes tapping on the tile as if everyone should jump when he snapped his fingers.

"Winston." Cal put a friendly hand on his shoulder. "Let's go into my office."

He shrugged off Cal's gesture. "I need answers not a buddy. I keep phoning, but all I hear is how Skyler's trip is taking longer than expected. I tried her cell. It immediately went to voice-mail. What's going on?"

Cal closed his door, sinking into his high-backed desk chair, crossing his legs, straightening the crease in his slacks. "Coffee, tea, or water?"

"No. Answers."

"Nothing's wrong, Winston. Skyler reported in this morning. The deal is taking longer than expected. The parties, according to the chief, are near an agreement. I guess she has worked night and day on this, the clients being difficult to please. You know how she is when she's negotiating business agreements. She's like the proverbial tiger with a tail. Is that the saying? Hmm. Not quite. Well, something like that. Anyway, she's terribly busy. We hardly speak to her."

Cal took a much-needed breath while he pushed a button on the intercom. "Anna, can I have two coffees in here? … Thanks."

"I received a message from her secretary saying my dinner date with Skyler had been reset. The next time, she said it was temporarily on hold. That's the last I've heard. Next, I get an Alliance gal in my ER who was shot in a home invasion. I demand answers."

"Of course you do. Skyler should be more considerate and call you herself, but she is chin-deep in negotiations. Cut her a little slack, Winston. When a power couple gets together, problems are bound to arise." Cal hefted his pen. *Tap. Tap. Tap.* Getting an irritated glare from the arrogant doctor, he rested the Mont Blanc on his desk pad. "This is one of those problems. I bet you have days when you don't have a free finger to punch Skyler into your cell. This time, unfortunately, she has a week of no spare digits. Casualty of the job. Besides, I'm betting she's not a great communicator on her best days."

"You're right. This is so like her. Where is she, by the way?"

"New York."

"What hotel?"

Cal did the sorry grimace, hissing between his teeth. "She's been dashing between two. The first client is in the Big Apple. The other's in the capital. Hence, the hotel hopping. I believe this morning she said she would be on the road again today."

"Where is she staying?" Winston glanced at his Patek Philippe watch.

"I'm not sure. Let's ask Anna when she brings in our drinks." Just then, she walked in balancing a tray of two coffees, cream, and sugar.

"Where is Skyler staying in New York and Albany, Anna?" Cal motioned for Skyler's admin assistant to serve Winston first.

Offering the doctor a cup, Anna didn't skip a beat. "The Plaza and the Morgan State House in Albany. Cream? Sugar? Dr. Callahan?"

"No, thanks. Black. Why didn't she tell me this before she left?"

"I made the arrangements last minute." Anna set Cal's coffee, cream, and sugar on his desk. "My bad."

"I'm a busy man. I don't have all day to chase down Skyler. Do you have the numbers for both hotels? I'll see if I can reach her later. As it is, I took time out of an already crowded schedule to come here for information since no one was forthcoming on the phone."

"I'll e-mail the info to you when I return to my desk. You'll have it in a jiffy. When you talk to her, ask her to give me a call, would you?" Anna blinked, curling her lips down in a contrite pout. "I forgot to tell her something this morning."

After Cal led Skyler's fiancé to the elevator, he returned to Anna.

She disconnected from the phone. "I contacted the two hotels to request our contacts there to backdate reservations. They know the game. We pay them handsomely for special arrangements."

"Winston's kind of a horse's patootie." Cal propped a hip onto Anna's desk.

"My impression, too. Of course, Chief Maxwell can keep him in line. I'm sure he doesn't bluster around her."

"Still nothing on Skyler or Commander Kole's whereabouts? I'm worried. What with all that's been happening. Are the bloggers silent today?"

Anna sighed. "So far, yes."

"You spoke too soon," piped Laurie from across the room. "Got a message. It's a doozy."

Anna and Cal hustled over to her computer, both

leaning over Laurie's shoulder.

"Despite your tainted blood and lies to keep the Alliance on the DL, we are willing to stop knocking you off for a small fee. Did we say small? That may have been a fiblet. We want $1,000,000 wired to an account we provide. We know the company is good for it. If we get it by 5 pm two days from now, you can keep your secrets, along with your heads. You might even get your precious Skyler back. We'll be in contact two days hence. Be ready with the money or you ain't seen nothin' yet."

The three exchanged scrunched eyebrows. "They know Skyler's missing." Cal's lips squeezed tight in case his lunch decided on a round trip.

Laurie and Anna shook their heads.

"I'll meet with the board to discuss the one mil, but I doubt they'll capitulate. The big bosses aren't keen on blackmail. Still, if it means keeping our secrets, who knows? Our agents will step up their efforts to find these assholes. Excuse the language, ladies. I'll check with information services to see who's tracing TheBigReveal since Siri's … uh … no longer with us."

Anna gave a dismissive wave with her hand. "You have a lot on your plate, Cal. Thanks for pitching in on Skyler's workload in addition to your own. Farm-to-table Grocers has not been a patient client. She'll appreciate your team spirit when she gets back. You're proving your worth to the Alliance."

Cal's chest puffed out. "No problem, Anna. We're all here for each other."

Chapter Twenty-Two

Tears soaked Skyler's cheeks as she half ran, half clawed her way up the hill, searching for the river. She climbed higher, always moving in the direction Kole had told her to go. Pausing to glance behind her, she no longer saw him or heard the frightening howls which arose from the battle below.

After struggling up a steep bluff, Skyler pulled over the top. While she rested, she spied the river flowing beyond the grassy meadow.

Her breathing steady again, she lurched to her feet, trailing alongside the swirling, roiling whitewater. After a half mile, she caught sight of the waterfall in the distance. Skyler hitched her backpack onto her other shoulder and hastened toward the thunderous falls. The nearer she got, the more slippery the rocks, the more arduous the climb.

Her breathing labored, Skyler plotted her path. Gazing at the steep cliff, she squinted into the sun, hoping to see the cavern entrance behind the cascading water. She still couldn't make it out. Kole had said it was well-hidden.

She slipped both arms into the knapsack's straps, adjusting it on her back. Nothing looked easy. But she had to reach the cave. She had to follow Kole's orders.

If... No. ... When he joins me, he'll be happy I obeyed him. For a change.

Finding a dry foothold and a spot for her hand, she climbed, struggling up the rock face. Pausing to catch her breath on a wide ledge, she mulled over her progress so far. Her strength and stamina amazed her since she had been ascending the mountain for some time but was barely tired.

Strange.

Skyler searched for the entrance. There it was ahead, hidden by a gnarled, sparsely leafed tree which leaned in front of it.

Get off your ass. Keep going. It's what Kole wanted.

She climbed until she was left of the cave opening. To reach it, Skyler had to traverse a narrow, algae-covered ledge by planting her nose to the rock wall, holding on somehow, inching along the path, never slipping.

No problem.

Her fingers latched onto a handhold. She stretched until her foot found the ledge. Swinging out, she set her left one beside it before she grabbed for the next hold.

Another step closer.

Clinging to rocks free of algae, she shuffled along behind the waterfall, her footing tenuous. Finally, the entrance was a bit above and to her right, too high to just step into. She'd have to heave herself up.

The muscle in her arm quivering, Skyler left the relative safety of the ledge to grab for a small crevice above her head.

Here goes.

Pulling up more easily than she thought possible, she lifted her body until she squeezed the toe of her shoe into another spot. Using the few handholds she found above her, she drew level with the opening.

With both toes barely gripping a hold and her fingers jammed into small cracks in the rock, she cussed. Now the scary part. She had to let go of a foot and hand to swing into the opening.

Please let me make it.

Skyler made a literal leap of faith, slamming belly down into the dirt at the entrance. She crawled further into the cave. Exhausted, she huddled against a wall, shaky arms wrapped around her knees.

Not moving from the cavern mouth, Skyler listened for what seemed like hours. But the only sound was the thundering roar of the waterfall. No Kole.

She nodded off, dreaming the commander was slumped onto the ground, injured. She called to him, shouting to get off his demon ass, no matter how bad the pain. He didn't hear her. Her eyes snapped open, and she shook her head to wake up.

Hours passed. The light began to fade. Still, she huddled near the opening, not exploring for the supplies Kole said were here. Her chin bobbed up and down until she awoke with a start.

Skyler crept to the entrance to peek outside where she saw a dark shadow. It was Kole, struggling on the ledge. He was bloodied, barely inching along it.

But she had never been so excited to see anyone. She realized she cared for the brutish savage commander. More than she wanted to.

Skyler leaned out the mouth of the cavern as far as she could while keeping a grip on the inside wall. She extended her hand. "Here," she screamed above the roar of the falls.

"No. Get back."

Ignoring his growly shouted order, Skyler snagged Kole's wrist. With a firm hold, she grasped his arm to steady him. When he was level with the cave entrance, she scooted to the side to give him room to maneuver.

At the opening, Kole lost his footing. Slipping, he dangled from the edge, holding on by only his fingers.

Skyler, in a panic, grabbed for his hand. "Use me."

"Get away. I'll take you down with me."

"Listen to me, you ape. I'm helping you. Now, pull the fuck up."

Kole flexed his biceps as he leveraged himself higher and higher. When she could, Skyler latched onto an elbow to help drag him through the entrance.

On his stomach, he gulped for air. After a few moments, Kole struggled to his feet, which was when she got a good look at him.

"Oh my God. What did they do?" She put his arm over her shoulder, leading him toward a wall.

Leaning him against it, Skyler slipped Kole's shredded tee over his head. On his chest was a gaping hole. In the dim light, she saw his arm had been chewed. Those, along with other wounds, were oozing black gunk, spreading even wider as she studied them. Skyler glanced down at his pants, which were slashed at his thigh and lower leg.

"Iron," he gasped. "Poison."

She looked for a comfortable place to lay Kole.

"Gagans release claws. Like throwing stars. Couldn't dodge them all." Kole pushed away from the wall. "Bedding. Food. Water. Everything we need. Further back."

"You can't make it."

"Yes, I can." He shoved her aside, stumbling toward the dark interior, growling.

"Stubborn man." Skyler grabbed his arm again to steady him. Deeper into the cave, she could no longer see. Kole touched his fingers together, creating fire, illuminating a large chamber where boxes were stacked.

When he collapsed onto the ground, he plunged them into darkness.

Skyler sank beside him. "Kole, I need to see to find stuff."

Fire again streamed from his fingertips while he pointed toward a long cut-out section in the rock.

"There. Ledge." Kole panted, clipping his words.

She rushed for the shelf, grabbing five lanterns, noting they were filled with oil. She took them to Kole to light. With the cave brighter, she eyed a large mattress on the floor near one wall of the chamber.

"Come on." She urged him to his feet, trying to lift him. "Let's get you into the bed."

He shook off her hand. "Can't touch. No bedding. Contaminate. Poison."

"Is there a medicine here? I don't think you can make it to the Healing Pond or Spriggan Enclave. Of course, we'll do it if we must."

"Orgasm."

****

Skyler's unblinking eyes widened. "Orgasm? What do you mean?"

"Only way. I must orgasm to kill the poison." Kole flinched as if hit with a sharp pain.

"Is sex the answer to all demon problems?" When Kole nodded, she caught on. "Oh, you want me to help? No. Use your own hand."

"Can't. Orgasm was the wrong word. Give me a break. I'm hurting. I must ejaculate. My fist won't do it. Gotta have a female. No cum. No cure, Frisca."

Skyler wasn't sure whether he grinned or grimaced.

"You're kidding me."

Kole's coloring was off. She touched his cheek. It was hot, clammy. His lips compressed as spasms wracked his body, the usual red-gold fire gone from his eyes.

With his teeth clenched, Kole gritted out his response. "It's your hand, your mouth, or, crudely put, your cunt. Your choice, Frisca. Now would be better than later, though. This shit's killing me."

I won't let him die.

The thought left a pit in her stomach. Skyler drew a deep breath, scrunched her brows, and leaned over him, her trembling hands unfastening his pants. While she tugged on his zipper, he lifted his hips to help her slide them to his knees.

The Firebrand, the male she once considered a barbarian, was a buffet. Even though he was injured and bloody. The hard planes of his chest, his tight … what would Anna call it? … six-pack, his formidable size. Despite the pain he must have been feeling, he was erect, ready, proud.

Skyler clutched the base of his long, thick shaft, her hand unable to circle its solid width. She began with tentative strokes. Up. Down. He was magnificent. Steel coated in velvet. A warm tingle rushed from her fingers to her womb.

She shouldn't be reacting to the demon this way. What she was doing was for a medical purpose.

Kole moaned, shifting. When Skyler glanced at him, his eyes were closed, his lips parted, his chest expanding with each breath. She threw a leg over his thighs to straddle him, getting a better angle though she was cautious to avoid his wounds. His lids popped open, sparks flickering from his pupils.

"Tighter, Frisca. Rough. Take off your shirt and bra. The view will help me."

She did as he asked. After all, anything to make him come faster. Her goal was worthy. It was to save his life.

With her breasts exposed to Kole's heated stare,

Skyler resumed fisting his length. He throbbed against her palm as she stroked him crown to hilt, growing impossibly bigger, harder.

She tightened her grip. Kole's gaze fixed on her hand, watching her manipulate him. His desire slammed through the cave like waves pounding against a shore in a storm. When his emotion swept over Skyler, she attempted to control her breathing. No luck. It was shallow, rapid, excited.

Kole reached forward, his hands molding to her heavy breasts, squeezing, kneading them. He pinched her nipples until the delightful pain sent a jolt of fire to her sex. She wiggled her bottom against his thighs, trying to lessen the heat flowing between her legs.

Skyler bent her head, pausing for only a moment before she touched her mouth to the tip of his shaft. When she rolled her tongue around the crown, her heart pounded against her ribs. He was delicious. She licked him from top to bottom. Her lips parted to suck on him.

Stopping to fix on Kole's eyes, she asked, "Is this good?"

"Bloody Coven, Frisca. Yes. Take me deeper. Get serious. Stop playing."

Playing? She was about to give Kole the best blow job of his life because … she had to. If she didn't, he would die. This was not a lie. It wasn't the truth either. She wanted to taste him, to pleasure him until he came. But he seemed immune to her. She had offered herself on a platter. Naked. At the Healing Pond. Kole had done no more than relieve her need.

Skyler stopped her teasing licks, opening wider to swallow what she could. He was huge. With a firm grip around his base, she slid up and down his thickness, her mouth working him.

He arched his hips off the ground, thrusting in

time with her rhythm, driving himself to the back of her throat.

She moaned. He tasted so good, the knowledge he was at her mercy carnal, powerful.

With her lips wrapped around Kole, she used her tongue to flick along the underside of his cock as he rocked into her. In. Out. His hips pumped upward, pushing him deeper.

"Damn, Frisca."

Skyler's nipples hardened to the point of pain, pressed against his thighs. Her free hand stroked his balls as she sucked harder, increasing the pace until he was frantic. He tangled his fingers in her hair, sliding himself deeper into her throat.

Suddenly, Kole yanked Skyler off him. "Stop. I'm coming."

Growling, he seized her shoulders, pushing her down until his hard length was between her breasts. Rotating his hips against her, he exploded. Then his body went rigid while his hot, thick semen burst forth in what seemed an endless stream.

After a while, he tucked Skyler against his chest, an arm wrapped around her, his palm molded to a breast. "Frisca," he whispered before he fell asleep, his full lips parted, peaceful.

When she was certain he was out, she pressed a finger to his pulse. It was steady. His skin was cool. Breaking from his clutches, she sat up, fighting to control her own arousal, her chest hammering. She pushed to her hands and knees, rising, deciding a distraction would be good. It was time to go through the supplies.

Though she checked on Kole at regular intervals, Skyler opened boxes, searching for something to wash with.

Found it.

Pouring water onto a towel, she cleaned herself first. Slipping back into her bra and shirt, she kneeled beside Kole. With another cloth, she wiped away blood, dirt, and gooey black residue from his wounds.

Her hand paused on his chest. Nothing about this man was soft. His features were rugged but extraordinarily handsome. His cheek bones were sharp, angular blades. His nose was wide, bent, probably from too many fights. She swiped across his unshaved, hard jaw, his prominent chin, moving down to caress his massive shoulders and smooth pecs with their lineage runes. Her fingers glided across his tight abs and along a thigh as she enjoyed the feel of Kole, his taste lingering in her mouth.

Focus.

They could never be together. They were fire and ice. Oil and water. Apple and Microsoft. Bathtubs and toasters.

Get your head straight. Still...

She studied his injuries. *Good.* They were healing. Rising, she returned to the boxes where she found fresh pants along with a T-shirt for Kole. Skyler placed them beside him on the cave floor and covered him with a blanket.

She pulled out sheets, food, drinks. Making the bed, she thought about lifting Kole into it. *No.* He was too heavy. Besides, she feared opening wounds. Not wanting to wake him, she would wait until morning and hope he was healed enough to crawl into it on his own.

Certain he was comfortable, she grabbed a bottle of water, snatched up a package of chips, and opened a can of tuna from the supplies. She placed them on the bed in front of her. While she ate, she puzzled over her strong attraction to the warrior on the ground.

Winston is educated, professional, someone she

could proudly introduce to family and friends. What family and friends? He is the man my father picked for me. Of course, dear ol' Dad would never have approved of Kole.

Skyler glanced at the demon, his chest rising and falling, unlabored.

But Winston never inspired passion. I've never wanted my mouth on his cock but, then again, he doesn't have one that takes my breath away.

Cutting short her thoughts and having satisfied her hunger, Skyler removed her boots, socks, and pants before she slipped under the covers. Sleep came quickly.

****

Chay had arranged for Margo's furnishings along with her studio to be packed up and moved lock, stock, and barrel of monkeys into the stronghold apartment they had chosen. He helped her set up the stuff in record time. The first night in the new place, he had Firebrand duty. Tonight, he had to bug out on her again. He felt bad about it, but he had some required tasks to do if he wanted a clear conscience.

Margo wasn't upset, saying she'd enjoy being alone with her things for a bit. Chay, still feeling guilty, okayed it with her for Galena to stay while he was gone.

When he called, the Amazon said, "Great. A pajama party. I'll bring the booze."

Chay spent the night with his parents. While there, he told them about Margo. His parental units, as expected, didn't take the news well. Afterward, he phoned Anjeli to clean the slate. His ylve-almost-mate was smooth about the whole break-up thing.

He returned to the stronghold in the morning. Now, he was sitting on a tall stool, buck-naked, his black, straight hair draping down his chest while he sported the hard-on from hell. He rested an elbow on his knee, chin in palm.

Margo giggled, swiping at the clay on her face but only making the damage worse. "I've never had a model whose penis was so big. And so stiff."

"Any male near you would sprout a woody."

"Not true. Just you, baby. Finish your story. You were telling me how ylves feed. Fairly sure I need to know this."

Chay shifted, not knowing how Margo would take the info. "Ylve's snack on soul. But don't worry, I can get my nourishment elsewhere."

"Hey. Stay still." She frowned. "You'll be getting everything you need from me. Try to dine on some little hot number, and I'll stab you with this." She picked up a carving tool, waving it at him.

He grinned. Inside and out. "I have a serious question, Red."

Margo stopped pushing clay. "Ask." She wiped her hands on a damp cloth.

"I know I'm not a great catch. I'm a Firebrand warrior who has commitments to his *frerons* and shit. But you're it for me."

"What are you saying?"

Margo sauntered over to Chay, her hips swaying.

He groaned, his dick needing relief soon. "Be my mate."

She flashed a wicked grin, sliding between his legs, wrapping a fist around his aching dick. "Would this be mine? Mine alone?"

He moaned. With great reluctance, he pried her hand off his eager cock, swept her into his arms, dirty apron and all, and carried her to the bedroom. He set her feet on the floor.

When he backed away, he gripped himself. "This will always be yours. Only yours." He pressed his other palm to his heart. "And this. Now, take off your clothes and climb aboard. You're gonna get what belongs to you."

The mattress sank as Chay bounced onto the bed, flinging himself against the plump pillows, his arms crossed behind his neck as he ogled Margo. "I know this is fast, Red, but that's how it happens to true soulmates. No mistake about it. You're mine."

She shucked her sandals, apron, shirt and wiggled her pants down her legs. She posed before him in a bra and delicate, see-through matching panties. Both showed off her assets, her gaze crawling up his body. "Chay, I was mad about you the moment you walked into my apartment in Cleveland. If being your mate means a lifetime with you, count me in. But don't be disappointed with me. I can be a little crazy. Offbeat. Are you sure I'm what you want?"

He swallowed hard, eying his beautiful redhead, thinking about where he wanted to start on her lusciousness. "Gahya, you're so perfect. You could never disappoint me, Red. I'm glad you're different. And I've never been surer of anything."

She slid alongside him, propping a cheek on her fist, a palm gliding across his chest. "You're flawless. When I touch you, it's like I'm caressing a beautifully created sculpture." Her fingers drifted down his abs, his muscles twitching.

"Come here." Chay unclasped her bra, freeing her breasts, fascinated with her plump nipples, darker than her pale skin. "Wow."

He pushed Margo onto her back, capturing her in a kiss, exploring her with his tongue. Breaking away, he trailed his lips along her neck and downward. He nuzzled her breast, sucking a nipple into his mouth, nipping until it was a hard pebble. He moved on to the other. Eager for more, Chay slid between her legs, spreading them for a feast.

With Margo stroking his shoulders, he licked the inside of her knee and inner thigh. Once he positioned his head, his tongue took one lap through her folds before he peeked up at her. Her lids were heavy, her hands tangled in the sheets as he stroked back and forth, savoring her with long, slow laps.

Chay sampled her with his finger. She was wet for him. Staring into her eyes, he wanted to see what turned her on.

"Yeah, Chay. Right there." She lifted her hips.

He added another digit, a loud groan rewarding the action. By the time he was working three digits in and out of a drenched Margo, she was frantic, tossing around. He stayed her with a free hand on her belly.

When Chay removed his soaked fingers, a wild-eyed Margo lamented, "No."

"Simmer down, Red. You'll like this." He returned to the business of satisfying his female. He opened her wider with his thumb and forefinger, burrowing to lick and suck on her clit. His lips closed around her tender nub, bringing her to the edge until he'd stop and start again.

Margo fisted her hands in his hair, pushing him hard against her. As she rocked into Chay, he thrust his tongue deep inside her, plunging it in and out. Her grip directed him to her sweet spots as she wiggled her hips. His female was not shy.

"Oh, God. Yes. Yes."

When Chay assaulted her clit once again, he felt tremors roll through Margo's body. She bowed off the mattress and forced his mouth tight against her while she shuddered.

Holy schism, he was human-struck, but only for

his wild female with the touch of an artist.

Moments later, she relaxed her hold on Chay's head. Falling back against the pillow, her chest heaving, her lids closed, a sated smile on her face, her arms loose at her sides. "Good lord, what a ride. I thought you might kill me with your clever tongue."

Margo clasped Chay's jaws between her hands. He saw himself reflected in her violet eyes. "I love you, ylve baby. You're not only a handsome guy with a spectacular body. You're much, much more."

For the first time in his life, he took more joy at giving pleasure than receiving it.

Hell, he didn't understand this new male he was becoming. But he knew he had found the only mate he'd ever wanted. And he would do right by her.

Chapter Twenty-Three

Margo slapped at Chay's hands. She shoved him flat on his back with unexpected force. Straddling his waist, she spread her fingers apart on his hard chest, caressing the lean, chiseled hills and valleys of muscle. Angling her head, she tweaked his nipple with her teeth, her breasts smashed against his stomach.

This sexy ylve was a good man. He could have bolted from her apartment to save himself. Yet he had stayed with her. Before, she had known only dead-weight jerks. Her only live-in boyfriend had been a big one. She remembered getting up in the morning to find her bank account wiped out and her car stolen.

Yep. The ylve's a keeper.

Chay moaned, his palms stroking her arms.

"You are human-struck, ylve baby." Leaning upright, she scooted onto his thighs. Her nails trailed a path along the delectable line of hair from his navel to his groin where his fully erect cock greeted her.

"Grab me and start sculpting, Red. Don't be gentle. I like a little rough handling." Though his voice was husky, his eyes glittered with mirth.

That's what she loved about Chay. He was seductive and frolicsome at the same time. Margo closed her hand around him and alternated between feathering the crown of his dick with light, fluttering touches and running a finger up and down his shaft.

"Harder, Red. Always hard."

She clasped him in earnest, her strokes firmer, more rapid. She lowered her head to lick him like an all-day sucker. When he was wet and slick, she pumped up and down.

"I love your touch. And I wouldn't mind if you talked dirty to me."

"Dirty, huh." Still stroking him with a slow, teasing rhythm, she searched for something nasty to say. "I'm gonna take this long, thick, hard dick which belongs to me and put it where I need it." She held him with a firm grip. "I'm gonna lift up and set it between my thighs." She rose onto her knees. "When it's in the right place, I'm gonna sit down while it slides into my wet pussy."

"Oh, fuuuuucccckkkk. Do it." A loud moan rumbled from his chest.

Margo positioned him at her entrance and sank onto him as promised, one agonizing inch at a time. He felt so good. But before she could enjoy the slow glide to heaven, Chay grabbed her waist and pushed her down hard. He popped his hips so he was deep inside her. She had never been so full.

"Oh, Chay." She reached behind her and fondled his balls. "Fuck me."

He gripped the nape of her neck, pulled her down, captured her lips in an explosive kiss, and rolled them over. "Damn, female. I'm gonna erupt too soon."

She dug her fingers into his biceps as he began a steady rhythm. In. Out.

"Faster, Chay."

With a fist on each side of Margo's head, he kept his weight off her while he drove into her, his cock like a jackhammer. His muscles tensed when her nails bit into his back.

She tilted her pelvis, seating him to the hilt. Wet, full, and warm, Margo locked her legs around Chay.

She had asked questions. She had thought about it. Now she decided. Nobody but her would provide for

Chay's needs. "Feed, ylve baby. I want everything with you." Her voice was breathy.

When he touched her mouth with his lips, he inhaled.

Margo gasped, her eyes rolling up in her head as he tasted her soul. She rocked her hips, her muscles gripping his shaft, squeezing it. He thrust twice into the heat of her body. When she screamed his name with her release, his seed flowed into her hard and long.

"Shit." Chay tapped his D-chip, still propped above her. He flopped to the side and clutched Margo close. He kissed the top of her head before he sprang out of bed, grabbed his pants, and shot her a wistful look. "Red, a bunch of Firebrands are about to invade the living room. Get dressed and join us in there."

"Sure, but tell me how I tasted."

"You were the sweetest, most heavenly ambrosia ever. Your soul is pure innocence flavored with a touch of naughty." With a wide grin plastered on his face, he drew his shirt over his head and stormed out.

****

Chay was pulling on his tee when he charged into the living room, earning a few snickers from Ram, Brak, and Tyr. "This better be a life-or-death sitch. What are you assholes laughing at?"

Ram stifled himself and motioned zippering his lips. A smile crept back to his face when he glanced over at Tyr, who was still chortling.

Rein sprawled on the couch in Margo's living room, an ankle crossed over his knee, his signature scowl in place. "Get a grip. Stop acting like hormonal morons."

A disheveled Margo bounced through the bedroom door, stumbling to a halt when she laid eyes on the gigantic males. The idiots started another round of tee-hees. Chay tucked her under his arm while he threw a thumb in Ram's direction. "You've met the satyr and Rein. The spiky-haired dude with the bling is Tyr. The other guy is Brak the himbo."

Tyr was a lean warlock, not much over six foot. He loved shiny jewelry—a dangling key and hoop from one ear, three hoops in the other, a silver collar at his throat, and a gruntload of metal on his wrist. Brak, a carnal demon, was big muscle, lots of height, tight leather pants, and sapphire eyes.

Short on introductions or small talk, Rein got to the point. "Margo, demo your gift. We keep getting communication dead zones in the stronghold. While not a good thing, it did give me an idea."

With his clothes in better order and his mind on straight, Chay said, "She makes electronic things go wonky. TV's, radios, cell phones, shit that uses radio waves. A reason we chose a suite in the far corner."

"I want a show-me." Rein rested a hand on his boot.

Chay brushed a strand of curly red hair off Margo's cheek. "Start with cellphones. Do your thing."

"Should I visualize?"

"Let me trigger a faster response." Chay grabbed her around the waist, pulling her in tight, and pressing his mouth to hers. He released her when all but Rein whooped and hollered.

Margo faced them with her arms akimbo, her lips squeezed into a frown. Brak, who leaned against the wall, stared sheepishly at his feet.

"Instead of being an ass wipe, Ram, try your Dick Chip." Chay nodded to Margo, clasping her palm in his so she could draw energy from him to work her magic.

Ram, who lazed in a chair, threw his leg off the arm and sprang forward, tapping his wrist. "Hey. Not going through, man. Cool."

"Check out the TV," said Chay.

When Brak pressed the remote, all he got was snow.

"Red, go way down the hall. I'll let you know when to come back. We talked about control. Try to lasso your energy."

Chay waited until Margo was out of hearing before he turned to the males. "I asked Margo to be my mate. She agreed. So, the next Firebrand who disrespects her is going to be eating his balls. Bing. Pow. Read me?"

Rein, who already knew the situation, stoic-ed his expression while Brak, Ram, and Tyr exchanged stunned looks followed by "Ouch," "Hey, man," "Sorry," "We didn't know," "She's a great female," and "You don't deserve her."

"Just don't let any rude shit happen again. Okay, hit the remote." The TV was normal, a weather announcer reporting flash flood warnings in Knife's Edge. "Anyway, guess choosing the distant apartment didn't work." He opened the door into the hallway. "Okay, Red, demo over."

When she stepped into the room, Tyr, who leaned against the fireplace mantel, nodded a greeting. "It's rare. Your witch gift. You're special, Margo."

"Uh. Thanks, Tyr."

Rein scrubbed a hand across his jaw. "Your D-chip tracking was all over the place while you guys were locked in a cell. We couldn't get a clear enough signal to trace you. She draws her mojo from you."

"Yep," said Chay, tossing an arm around his mate-to-be's shoulders. "She's super charged, but she doesn't have a lot of control yet."

Brak pointed to an empty chair. "Hey, Margo, you want a seat?"

"Thanks. I'm fine." She snuggled into Chay.

The ylve snapped his fingers. "Are you thinking what I'm thinking, Rein? Another witch or warlock with her same abilities could be blocking Kole?"

"You mean, maybe somebody's knocking out the comm's chip and the CLO's portal jumper?" Ram twisted toward Tyr and Rein. Tyr was full-blooded warlock, and Rein was a triple threat. Vampire, incubus, and warlock. They'd be in the know.

Rein scrubbed a palm across his jaw, looking tired from the weight of subbing for Kole. "The thought crossed my mind. I'll tap Alarik. See if he knows a mage with the gift."

"Don't bother," Tyr interrupted. "I got a prime candidate. There's an old, powerful dude who could do it. Uwrick. He controls radio waves like Margo. He's two cans short of a six pack and shiesty as hell, though. He hires out to bad guys for a shitload of money. Now, when I say powerful, I mean A-lister."

"He can't control shit with his ass on Scath and his target on Darque, though," said Rein. "Not possible."

Tyr nodded. "I agree. If it's him, he's probably holed up somewhere on the wilding realm. How far away do you think he'd need to be, Rein?"

"A mile, maybe. Maybe not that far. He'd have to keep pace with the commander and Chief Maxwell. Move when they do."

Ram scooted forward in his chair. "Got a plan, Rein man?"

"Always. We need to get to Darque, shield our own D-chips, and acquire this Uwrick, or whoever it might be. The guy isn't working alone. Skyler Maxwell could be the target. Somebody attacked the Alliance office and killed an employee. Maybe Kole is just caught in the net somebody's using to wipe out the chief. Big mistake. Don't piss off Firebrands. Take on one of us, you take on all of us."

Bounty's voice followed a knock on the door. "Open up. I had to walk down here in these gorgeous but uncomfortable shoes. Your chips aren't working. I've got news, and I'm late for my feeding unless somebody here wants me to fang him."

Ram, Tyr, and Brak sprouted immediate bulges in their pants. Strolling inside, Bounty rested a manicured nail on her chin, lifted her brows, and studied the three males. Then she pivoted toward Rein. "Jezzi called from Spriggan Enclave. She has word of Kole and Skyler passing through."

"Bounty, you may be busy tonight. Either use the bagged variety or take your pick from willing volunteers for dinner. I need you energized," said Rein.

Bounty smiled at Brak. "I'm hungry for some carnal demon. This way, stud donor."

The warrior's eyes widened as he stumble-footed behind Kole's executive assistant.

Tyr and Ram both muttered, "Lucky motherfucker."

When Margo tugged on Chay's arm, he said, "I'll explain later, Red."

Rein unfolded his large frame from the couch. "Thanks for the demo, Margo. Ram, I want Dax, but he's not answering calls. Jarek needs him for a mission. The commander's shorthanded. Locate the loner Vamp. Take Brak with you once Bounty's had her fill. Tyr, bring me two mages. A shielder who's powerful enough to protect our D-chips from a warlock like Uwrick and a detector who can trace the mage by following his magic. I have a good feeling about this. If we find Uwrick, I think we'll find Kole and Chief Maxwell. Strap up, Firebrands. We're headed to Spriggan Enclave on Darque. We'll mobilize from the stronghold at O Dark Ugly."

When the living room was empty again, Margo worried her lower lip. "Sounds dangerous, Chay."

"It's what I do, Red. Are you okay with it?"

"I love all of you. I don't want you to change."

Chay read the acceptance in her eyes, something he hadn't felt since his grandfather Rahine's death.

****

Ram paced in Bounty's office, waiting.

Finally, Brak came back, zipping up his pants with a smile on his face. Right behind him, Kole's blonde, buxom executive assistant smoothed her dress down and showed more color in her cheeks.

Dinner had obviously been satisfying for the two of them. Ram shook his head, a little jealous of his fellow Firebrand's treat. "Let's go, demon. We need to find Dax. Rein's looking for him."

Bounty snapped her eyes toward Ram. "What's wrong?"

The satyr shrugged. "He's not answering Rein's calls."

"I'll help you look." Bounty straightened her desk as if preparing to leave with them.

Ram and Brak exchanged glances but spoke in unison. "No way! Not a good idea."

"Okay. Find him yourself." She sat down, staring at the computer screen.

"Damn, Bounty. Rein will have our asses," said Ram.

Bounty was a secretary not a fucking Firebrand. She couldn't go on missions, even if it was just to find Dax. Why would she want to? Rein would punish the three of them if he found out. No telling what pain he would inflict. He was a vampire with warlock and incubus powers along with a barely controlled temper to boot. Besides, Dax would be pissed enough with Brak and him looking in all the sordid nooks and crannies of Scath. The last thing he would want was some gorgeous female witnessing him screw up.

"He'll have your asses if you don't find Dax. What'll it be? With me or without me?"

Brak loomed over her desk. "Why would we take you with?"

Bounty flipped a long strand of blonde hair over her shoulder. "Cause I know his hiding spots."

Dax and Bounty? Nah. She wouldn't stoop so low.

Once Ram decided the vamps weren't getting it on, he decided the female was just sneaky. *Hell.* She probably had a list of where all the Firebrands hung out when off duty. "Come on. Tell us. Besides, Rein needs you here."

"He can do without me for a while." She leaned into her chair, blowing on the nails of her right hand. In the other, she might as well have been squeezing their nads.

Ram glanced at Brak. "This is a fucking terrible plan, but tag along. Where do we start?" He knew when the female bloodsucker had bested them.

"Your word first? And you can't ever tell anyone. Not Kole. Not Rein." Bounty glared at both males.

"Word. Now where are we headed?" Ram countered with a fast answer. He snarled, not appreciating the blackmail.

"Both of you." Bounty didn't move until Brak agreed also.

"Word." Brak smiled, fingering his neck, probably remembering Bounty's lips sucking on it. Lucky bastard.

Bounty hesitated before she spoke. "It's called O Den's Valhalla."

Cute.

Ram had never been there or in any O blud den, but he had heard plenty about them. "We're dead."

****

When the door of the lower-level room at O Den's Valhalla busted open, Dax thought he recognized a familiar chuckle. His vampire hearing was sharp even while he was in the haze of pure bliss.

Ram tee-heed. "I'm not into males, but that is one fine ass humping the female, and I think it belongs to our Dax."

Brak was here, too. Dax pegged his deep, thunderous voice. "Dude, dismount and unfang her neck."

The table Dax had bent the succubus over banged against the wall in rhythm with his relentless drive into her pussy.

Brak sighed loudly as Dax pinpointed the telltale sound of a blade leaving its sheath. "I don't look forward to pulling the buck naked, drugged, stone-cold killer off her."

"Like we really could." Dax noted Ram's mutter as his dagger whispered out of its resting place. "I also don't relish poking this dagger into a *freron*. He'll likely kill us in the process. One more try. Hey, Dax. Pull your wanker out. You've had enough. Come along."

Dax withdrew, releasing the female. Putting all two hundred and fifty pounds of menacing muscle behind a snarl, he faced the Firebrands. He knew his eyes were red-rimmed, glassy, and unfocused, his *frerons'* words drifting to him through fog.

"Shit. He's high on O crap, but he's hung like a jacked berserker." Ram looked a little worried.

He should.

Sounding equally impressed, Brak chimed in.

"Yeah. Gotta respect stamina and pure male design."

Dax pulled his own blade off the table, dropping into a crouch, willing to challenge the Firebrands. If only he could see them better. A feral roar arose from deep in his chest as he prepared to attack. The skin on his face was slack from the drugged blood, and his long dark hair hung like a wild stallion's dirty, tangled mane. He'd been on a bender. How many days? *Dunno*. He bared his fangs.

Ram spread his thighs apart, ready to charge. "You go for his left side. I'll take the right. Whatever you do, stay away from his chompers. Our best bet is to take him down, flip him onto his stomach, and D-chip him."

"Ah, fuck. Get out of my way, idiots." A loud shout preceded Bounty as she shoved the two males aside and stormed toward Dax. "Hey, big brother. Are you okay? You need to calm down and not hurt anyone. Sis is here."

Brak and Ram froze. Probably because of Bounty's brother-bomb. She had promised to keep their sibling state of affairs a secret. Now it was out.

Her familiar image floated to Dax from far away.

A small girl in a raggedy short dress which hung loose on her too-skinny body ran down the stairs to him, her arms outstretched as if he were the best brother in the world. Her smile was wide, her hair uncombed, but she was happy to see him. She dug into his pockets. She was looking for the cheap candy treat he always managed to bring her. It wasn't much, but it was all he could manage. He never forgot to drop a surprise into a pocket.

She found the gift, giggled, and shouted, "Tootsie Rolls. My fave. You are the bestest brother ever." Dax still saw her tiny sharp fangs and her adoring eyes as she smiled at him, her chin tilted. He didn't know why she loved him, but he would never forget.

Dax shook his head, his hair whipping around him while he struggled to focus. "Bounty. Beautiful little Bounty. I'm so happy to see you." She drifted to him as a dream.

"I'm glad to see you, too, big bro. Rein needs you. I need you."

"Rein?"

"You're a Scion Firebrand, Dax. Rein is your commander until Kole returns. I'm Kole's executive assistant. Remember?"

"I'm not your brother?"

"Sure. You'll always be the brother I idolize. Now, you need to get dressed and come with us. I can help you walk, but you've got to put on your clothes."

Dax looked down at his body. "Fuck." He grabbed his pants, stepped into them, and yanked them up. Snatching his shirt, he labored into it.

Bounty footed it over to the O blud whore, grabbing a fistful of her straggly hair. With a rough hold on her, she marched her to the door, shoving her into the hallway. "If you ever service my brother again with your opiate-laced blood, I will seek you out and kill you. It's my sacred promise."

Dax slumped into a chair, his socks and boots on the floor in front of him. Bounty sat cross-legged, lifting a foot, brushing the dirt from his sole. She slipped a sock on him but struggled with his boot.

Dax brushed her cheek with the back of his hand. "Hey, beautiful Bounty."

"Hey, Big D."

"Whatcha doin, sis? Get off the floor."

"Can't. I'm helping my brother."

"Your brother's an asshole."

Having finally gotten his one boot on, Bounty

punched Dax's thigh hard. "Nobody talks smack about him. Nobody. Shut up. He's the best brother ever. Loyal, loving, kind, protective." A tear slid down her cheek.

Dax took the other sock from her hand, put his foot in it, and jammed on his other boot.

Bounty turned to Brak. "Get his weapons."

"Whoa, son. Nobody touches my blades." Dax wobbled to his feet, shot Brak a feral warning, and grabbed his harness. Strapping it on, he loaded it with knives.

When he staggered, Bounty threw his arm over her shoulder, smiling up at him.

"Here, let us." His *frerons* set her aside to each grab under an armpit. They dragged Dax out of the O blud den.

As he looked behind him at Bounty, he watched quiet tears slip from her eyes. "I'm so sorry. Where are we headed, sis?"

"To a legit blud bar, bro. I've lined up a few volunteers to feed from you to drain off the drugs. Then you'll fang a clean donor. When you report to Rein, you'll be as good as new."

"Yeah. As good as new." His chin dropped onto his chest, his words soft. "I had to, baby girl. You know that. Right?"

"I don't judge you, Dax. I love you."

He heard her sniffle. He caused grief. Tears. That's what he did.

Dax snarled between his teeth at the two carrying him. "If you ever bring my sweet, innocent sister to a hell hole like this again, I'll cut out your hearts after I drink you dry. Are we clear?"

"Crystal," said Ram.

Dax swallowed hard before he continued. "And, please, don't tell Rein, Kole, or anyone how a sonofabitch like me is her brother. It'll ruin her. Swear it." The drugged Firebrand stumbled as his head bobbed on his chest.

"I swear." Ram adjusted Dax's weight.

"I swear, too, Dax. Never a word." Brak fixed him with a serious gaze.

Chapter Twenty-Four

Nico strode into the office as if he owned the place, snagging a chair, flipping it around, and straddling it, the back to his chest. Sabine took up residence in the seat beside him.

Behind the desk despite the late hour, a huge, mean looker with a scar through his brow, a short military cut, and a look that said he was too cool to shave everyday started the convo. "So, you're Nico Abello?"

"I am. And you are?"

"Rein."

Okay. The guy was every bit the warrior Nico had imagined. He was in control. He was pissed. Nico knew why.

"I'm also Braelyn's mate. You remember her?"

Nico shrugged. "If it's any consolation, I got knocked on my ass right after I kissed her. Ten stitches along with a concussion. Of course, she didn't do the ass knocking. She also didn't respond to the kiss."

Twisting toward Sabine, Nico explained his side of the story. "In my defense, you probably already know what an obnoxious asshole I can be. My team and I, including Braelyn, had just returned from a raid where we got the guy responsible for making knock-off portal jumpers. Unfortunately, he slit his own throat. A bunch of us celebrated at a bar. Natch, I drank too much. I was high on adrenaline. The kiss didn't mean anything." He had no idea why it was important for Sabine to understand the mouth action was meaningless, but it was.

"Why would I care?" Sabine crossed her legs, her boot bouncing, contradicting her words.

A scowl stayed planted on Rein's face despite his conciliatory remark. "Water under the bridge. Besides, she's clearly mine."

Rein's possessiveness didn't stop him from doing his job as he laid out the situation for Nico. "Cerberus is the problem now. He's kidnapping humans with Blood Coven ancestry."

"Yeah. Hence the blood tests," said Nico.

"Yep. And as Sabine's already told you, you won the lottery. We're gonna keep you under wraps here at the stronghold, not knowing what the madman has planned. Course, bet your balls it's big."

"Am I the only one you've found?"

"No. You'll meet Margo," said Sabine. "She's staying on your floor with her mate, Chay."

"Oh, good. Maybe we'll start a sewing circle. What am I supposed to do here? Twiddle my dick? I'm not a patient guy."

"We haven't thought this out yet what with the Alliance's CLO and Kole out of touch," said Rein.

Hmm. That was news.

Braelyn's mate plopped his boots onto the desk. "But I see the point. It would be hard for me to hole up with nothing to do."

"No doubt."

"Despite the boredom, it is what it is."

"How about I join you guys? And gals, sweetness." Nico eyed Sabine, flashing his sexiest grin as he brushed his hair off his forehead.

"Out of the question." Rein's growl left no doubt he thought Nico's idea was a shit one.

"Trust me. I won't stay caged up. I'll be out of here after a few days. Let me go on missions with the Firebrands. At least I'll be under your thumb. It's the only way I'll stick around short of you locking me in a cell, which I don't think you're willing to do. Bad for Alliance-Firebrand relations."

Rein scrubbed a hand across his jaw. A long silence followed while he studied Nico like a bug with its wings pinned. "We'll try it. Sabine, this sonofabitch belongs to you. Keep him safe. When he's not glued at your side, he's at the stronghold. Show him around. Give him his pick of suites if he doesn't care for the one he's in."

Sabine jumped out of her seat. "Hell, no. He's an obnoxious idiot who won't follow orders."

Shadowing Sabine? Things are looking up.

Maybe she could keep him safe in his bed. He pictured her long, athletic legs squeezing his hips, his hands caught in her hair, and his cock buried deep.

I hope I packed condoms. I was in a bit of a haze as I left.

"I'll gladly follow your orders, Captain Sweetness. Consider me all over your tail."

She glowered at Nico, sweeping her hand toward Rein. "See what I mean? Obnoxious idiot extraordinaire."

"I don't recall seeking an opinion, nymph. *Gahya.* Kole better get back soon." Rein eyed Nico. "She outranks you on Scath. Obey her or your ass is mine. Better yet, Sabine, you have permission to beat the shit out of him. Squash his gigantic ego. Just be sure he lives."

Now Nico pictured Sabine on top, holding him fast to the mat in a gym. That worked, too. *I am such a sick fuck.* He shifted in his seat and hoped the bowling ball in his pants didn't show.

****

Skyler awoke with a start. A sliver of moonlight crept along the cave floor. She kicked off her covers, sliding her feet to the ground. After drawing on her socks, she checked on Kole.

He was sleeping peacefully on the hard dirt floor of the cave. Skyler stroked the back of her hand across his whisker-roughened cheek. She peeked under the blanket. The oozing black holes had completely healed, and he was cool to the touch, no longer clammy. His color had returned.

"I need some fresh air." She pulled on her pants and boots. "I'll only be a minute," she whispered to Kole as she tip-toed toward the entrance to the cave. The light from a full moon was bright though filtered by the waterfall. She stretched, feeling invigorated, so much so she decided a climb along the rocks would be refreshing.

Skyler stepped into the opening, bracing to swing onto the ledge. Getting a good hold with her left hand, she stretched her foot out until it met rock. She maneuvered from one crevice to another, hugging the cliff-side the entire time. What had seemed an arduous climb the other day was an easy descent today. No quivering muscles. No tenuous holds. Quick, without hesitancy.

She scurried over boulders, sometimes jumping across to the next, sometimes half crawling and half climbing. When she reached the base of the cliff beside the waterfall, she dusted off her hands and followed the swiftly flowing river which crashed onto rocks while it wound its way to the bottom of the mountain.

Every so often, the terrain leveled into a flat meadow. In such a place, she relaxed on the grass, her head tipped back so she could admire the stars in the pre-dawn sky. Darque was certainly different from her life in Chicago. No skyscrapers here. The power of the river, the magnificence of the waterfall, the splendor of the fields, the solid dependability of the rocks. She was in the midst of nature, separate but one with it. The emotional response surprised her. She was a city girl, born and bred. Where did this communion with the natural elements come from?

Skyler rose, pushing aside her reverie, and proceeded to journey along the river again. A grunt startled her. Hiding behind a shrub, she peered out at a dog-sized animal tearing into a fish. The critter stood on its hind legs, sniffing the air before it trotted away, its partially eaten catch still dangling between its teeth. Skyler left the safety of the bush to continue her exploration. If she kept at the water's edge, she could always find her way back to the cave.

When the terrain shifted once more to steep rocky cliffs, she climbed down the face, her foothold sure, unerring. Reaching a grassy knoll, she stretched out. The sound of wings flapping overhead startled Skyler. But no harpies. Just normal birds.

Crawling out from the shrubbery, she heard the indistinct hum of voices in the distance.

Skyler crept to the edge of the knoll to peer down the mountainside. Far below her a few men sat around a campfire. Surrounding them were at least twenty small tents.

She descended, getting closer, keeping to hidden paths. Once in the encampment, she stayed out of sight, hiding behind the tents. When she drew nearer, she listened to their conversation.

A man who seemed to be in command spoke. "In a few, we'll break camp to go after the female. Easy pickings now."

His voice was familiar, but she couldn't quite place it. Skyler crept closer, peeking around a tent.

Holy shit. What's Dermott, the victor from the Genesis Rite, doing here?

The demon continued speaking to the man on his right. "You're sure Kole is dead?"

"Couldn't help but be with so much iron in his bloodstream. Barely made it. I tracked him as far as I dared."

"Mowart," he said to the male on his left, "roust the squad. It's time to earn our money, finish off the bastard commander if he's alive, and get the bitch. First, I'll take what is my due with her. Nobody insults me without repayment."

Mowart rose, going from tent to tent to wake the men while Dermott kicked dirt onto the fire, smothering it.

As groggy demons stumbled from their quarters, they grumbled about their mission starting before full-on dawn. Skyler scrambled on her hands and knees until she could safely stand. She retraced her path along the cliff.

At the first grassy area, she picked up her pace, sprinting for the river. She climbed the rocks, looking down at how far she had come. Glancing ahead, she still couldn't see the waterfall. "Damn," she muttered.

Skyler arrived at the spot where the dog-like animal fished. She kept going.

Once they pack up camp, they'll begin to scale the mountain. Run faster. I must warn Kole.

At the large meadow, she looked up toward the worst part of the climb near the waterfall. She scuttled up the boulders, across the cliff face, and onto the ledge, screaming a warning. "Kole. Kole!"

****

Before sunrise, Rein gathered with Firebrands and two unknown mages at the stronghold.

"This is Hason." Tyr jerked his head toward one of the warlocks beside him. "He'll shield our D-chips so we don't lose a signal. When he gets close enough to

Uwrick, or whoever, he'll also negate the spell."

Hason, wearing a dark hooded cloak and soft calf-high black boots, extended an aged hand to Rein, who grasped it firmly. Wrinkles creased the male's face, deep smile lines at the corners of his mouth.

"Can you counter Uwrick's spell, ancient one?" Rein used the honorary address for a much older, powerful warlock.

"I can. I have. This won't be my first tussle with the mage."

Rein nodded, turning to the other male with Tyr, a younger guy. "You can detect magic?"

A lanky, red-headed warlock stepped forward. "Yes, s-s-sir. The n-n-name's Knox. If it's close."

When Rein shook his hand, though, the kid held tight despite his stammered speech and youth.

"I'm pretty g-g-good at finding spells, s-s-sir."

"Stop with the sir shit, kid. Just another Firebrand."

Ram spoke up. "What's the plan, Rein?"

Brak, Tyr, Galena, Sabine, Nico, and Chay crowded together near Ram.

"Dax is dealing with the two human slaves found by one of Alarik's healers. Since Jarek was short scouts, he'd asked for an assist. I sent the vamp. He won't be joining us on this outing. Jezzi's waiting at Spriggan Enclave on Darque. We'll jump there, grab her for a ride-along, and see what the kid Knox picks up. If he doesn't get a read on magic, we start hoofing it. The Spriggans mentioned to Jez that Kole and Chief Maxwell set out on foot. Most likely, the commander left a trail for us to follow. We need to find it. This is a real shit soup sandwich."

Ram shifted from side to side. "We know Kole has a safe place on Darque. Secretive bastard never told anyone where it was, though."

Rein nodded. "Tyr, you take care of Hason. The kid's with me. Get your battle rattle on, *frerons*."

Already toting a chest harness with three long-bladed stilettos, Rein strode to the weapons storage to add a short sword which he stuck into a back sheath.

Chay grabbed his self-cocking, repeating, pistol-grip *chu ko nu* from a rack along with a magazine filled with a never-ending supply of bolts. It was an ylve thing to always have ammo. He finished with a war hammer tucked into his belt and a shitload of throwing stars.

Galena wielded her leaf-shaped shield and short spear, the henna battle ink already drawn on her face.

Nico patted Sabine's elbow. "What's with the tats on the chick?"

"On Galena? The markings tell a tale. Her breed goes into a fight with their faces painted. A strong story makes them powerful against their opponents. Hey, Amazon! What's today's yarn?"

"A glorious victory. My great-great grandmother fought two powerful mages. Dropped them to the dirt. Single-handed, no less."

Sabine stuck a dagger into a sheath at her waist, a double-bladed staff across her back.

Looking star struck in the weapons storage area, Nico whistled. "Wow! I love you guys. What to pick? What to pick?" He settled on three Buck combat knives with a chest harness. Then he grabbed a fighting tomahawk which he stuck into his belt. "A Glock would be a bonus. Too bad they are verboten in your realms."

"Not only forbidden, but Scath and Darque are spelled so they don't work." Sabine's gaze crawled up the human's body, pausing on his weapons. "You know how to use an axe, cuddles?"

"Hell, no, but it sure looks fun, sweetness."

The nymph slapped him on the back. "Watch your ass out there."

"I was hoping you'd watch it for me."

Sabine snorted.

When they were all armed, Rein looked them over and dipped his chin. He would trust any of his *frerons* to have his six, just as he would have theirs. "For duty."

Ram fisted the hilt of his Scottish dagger. "For honor."

The Firebrands let loose a loud whoop.

"Let's boogie. Grab my arm, kid." Rein nodded at the young mage.

The Scath warriors and their two warlock hitchhikers burst almost simultaneously from the stronghold's portal to the jump site near Spriggan Enclave.

Jezzi, the big cat shifter, waited for them.

"Need weapons, Jez?" asked Ram.

"Nah!" She blew on her nails. "I think I'll go panther on their asses."

"Are those the same ones you used to tent-pole the shifter at the Blood Shed last week?" A chortling Ram looked at the other Firebrands.

"The very same. When I scraped them lovingly along his body parts, he couldn't help but pop erect. I have that effect on males. But I bring out the big kitty claws for a fight." She jerked her thumb to the north. "They headed that way."

Rein stared down at the young warlock. "Feel anything, kid?"

"N-n-nope. Nobody's using p-p-power near here."

"Okay. Let's move." Rein waved his hand through the air.

Jezzi and Ram took the lead. Since she was a big cat shapeshifter, she was an excellent tracker. Ram, a satyr, was nearly as good.

Jezzi pulled to an abrupt stop. Rein moved alongside her. "What is it?" The panther angled its head toward a scorched bush. "Spread out, *frerons*. Look for some sign Kole was here. Something burned." Rein walked ahead, keeping his attention on the ground, studying it for clues.

"This way." Ram signaled the warriors.

After three more markers, Rein surveyed the horizon. "If we march straight in the direction the scorched bushes indicate, we reach Mount Exile. There's a river, lots of rock, a waterfall, and the possibility of caves. Kole mentioned he had hidey-hole in a mountain. Do you feel anything, Knox?"

"N-n-no."

"Let's jump to the base of Mount Exile. If it's a wash, we'll pop back here. I know creating our own portals uses a lot of D-chip juice, but we need fast."

****

With a gentle touch, Kole tapped Skyler's shoulder. When she didn't wake, he grabbed her and shook hard. "Frisca. You're dreaming."

She shot upright, blinking as if adjusting to the surroundings.

He enveloped her in his arms, disliking her fear, her confusion. "You've been yelling for me, but you're safe. You're in the cave. In bed. I'm with you."

Skyler trembled in his embrace, wiping sleep from her eyes. "I'm so foggy. How did I get here? I was down the mountain. I remember calling your name from the ledge outside the entrance." She sat straighter. "Dermott's leading other demons to us."

"No, Frisca. It was all a dream. You were asleep."

"That's not possible. It was so real." Her nails dug into Kole's forearm. "It was real. A bunch of males were with him, around twenty. They spent the night in a camp."

"It was a dream, Frisca."

"He was talking to a demon named Mowart." Skyler snuggled deeper into Kole's embrace. He listened to the rapid beat of her heart. With her body quivering, he stroked his battle-scarred hand down her spine.

Kole's eyes narrowed. "I know Mowart. You must have heard his name at the Genesis Rite."

"The dream was so vivid, Kole. Wait. Are you okay? You slept through a full day and night."

"I'm fine, but you're still shaking." Kole released her, brushing a wispy strand of hair from her forehead. "Hush. You're safe now." He lifted her onto his lap, letting her feel his arousal, his arms surrounding her in a tight circle.

He kissed the top of her head, her cheek, her lips. While he licked them with his tongue, she relaxed against him, opening to let him slip inside.

Suddenly, he pulled away from Skyler, his head jerking toward the cavern entrance. He sucked in a sharp breath, jumped up, slammed into his pants, and grabbed a blade.

"What's wrong?"

"A demon battle horn." He shoved an oil lamp into her hands. "Go deep into the cave. Extinguish the lantern. Wait for me."

"I..."

Kole put a finger on her lips, shaking his head. "I'll come for you. I promise. Remember, I've never lost a human chief legal officer."

"Right." Skyler white-knuckled the lamp. She surprised him by lifting onto her toes to kiss him, her tongue sweeping inside his mouth. When she released him, she offered a wicked smile. "There's more where that came from." She turned, eyed the ground, and walked toward the dark.

Kole rubbed a palm over his mouth still warm from her delicious lips while he strode to the edge of the opening. He couldn't see anything, but he was certain the demon call to battle had sounded. He'd wait and watch.

Chapter Twenty-Five

Dermott faced Mount Exile, jittery. The female was there. He would get his due before he earned the money for her capture.

Once his crew had packed up, broken camp, and sounded the battle horn, Mowart pointed uphill. "They're that way. I trailed Kole until he disappeared behind a waterfall. I'm guessin' a cave's there. Doubt he's still alive. The gagans did a number on him even though he downed the six of them. With the poison racing through him, it will have been a slow death. If he's still standing, he won't have any fight left. We can snatch the female easily."

Dermott called the demons to his side. "You heard Mowart. We go up the mountain. Kill the bastard Kole if he's still breathing. The female's mine first. After I'm done with her, we turn her in for the pay."

He gestured to Uwrick, who hung back to focus on maintaining his spell. "Follow us about halfway up the mountain to make sure you keep interrupting their signals."

With the sun barely lighting the dawn sky, Dermott's band began their ascent. They reached the river. Eventually, as the terrain grew steeper and rockier, they climbed steadily upward, their toughened hands clutching protruding stone while they secured footholds in the crevices.

His claws erupting from his fingertips in anticipation, Dermott led the pack. Filled with rage since the outcome of the Genesis Rite, he envisioned a blade in Kole's chest and the human female beneath his body as he finally got what he had been denied.

****

Rein peeked over Brak's shoulder while the young carnal demon, propped on one knee, touched the ashes of the fire. "Still warm."

Jez changed to her two-legged form, comfortable with her nudity like all shifters. "Look. Midway up the mountain. I make them to be demons."

Rein tested his D-chip. "Not working now. Double-time it to the small meadow ahead. Obviously, we're close. Ram, give an assist to Hason. Kid, hitch onto me."

"Your commander couldn't have found a hide-out easier to get to?" asked Nico. Everyone glared at him before they charged up the mountain. "What? Cause I'm the new guy and human to boot, I shouldn't have an opinion?"

Sabine punched his arm before she raced off, Nico on her ass.

Rein snarled, wondering if the guy pissed him off because he had kissed Braelyn. *Nah.* He was just a sonofabitch, meaning he should fit in fine with the Firebrands. "Come on, Knox, I'll help you hoof it faster."

When the Firebrands reached the small meadow, they were breathing hard. Hason and Knox were also panting. Kudos to Nico. He was in great shape for a human. "Feel anything yet, kid?" asked Rein.

The young warlock pushed out a palm as if he were tasting the air. His body started to quiver. "Y-Y-Yes. A spell is being used nearby."

"You're on deck, Hason." Finally, something was about to happen. The search and wait were the worst.

No longer winded and without waving a hand, breaking a sweat, or lifting an eyebrow, the ancient Hason raised a proud chin. "Do whatever you must. Your devices will work now. The mage is Uwrick. I negated his magic. And do not worry, I will restrain his abilities until you secure him. He will be unable to break through my forcefield."

"Kid, can you pinpoint the mage's location?" asked Rein.

"Yes. T-T-That way." Knox pointed a shaky finger toward a boulder just ahead.

When Brock and Tyr pounded uphill toward the rock, a male ran out from behind his hidey-hole, waving his hands wildly, trying to draw the attention of the demons. But they were far away and not looking to the rear.

"I've got him," Brak shouted, launching his humongous body into space, tackling Uwrick.

After rubbing the warlock's face into the ground a few times, Brak grabbed the male's neck and hoisted him onto his feet. When the Firebrand touched his chip, he encased Uwrick in a clear shield, his body rigid, his arms pinned to his sides. The mage's powers were as contained as he was in the portable jail cell.

Brak chuckled. "Gotcha, you warlicky asshole. Now don't go anywhere. I'll be back."

The carnal demon Firebrand joined his *frerons*, who were climbing at a fast pace, closing in on the demons ahead of them.

****

Dax leaned against the wall in the Ministry of Well Being's medical facility while the healer tested blood samples from the two humans he had rescued. Commander Jarek had called for an assist, and Rein had sent him for the task. Dax questioned whether he was the best Firebrand for the assignment, but the vamp mix had just glared. Dax shrugged and said, "Your call."

A bludfrenzied vamp had shackled the first

human beneath his home. The slaver tried to stop the Scion Firebrand from entering his house, but Dax grabbed him by the throat, lifting him until his feet dangled off the floor. With his other hand placed to the side of the head, he broke the guy's neck. Feeling no remorse, Dax drew his jungle bolo from a back sheath and decapitated the male. He kicked the body aside.

Problem solved.

Dax sniffed the air, following the blood scent to a cellar with an outside entrance. Thankfully, he had filled his own tank before the start of the mission.

Fight the hunger. You're stronger than some blood-addicted vamp.

Lifting the door, he descended the dark stairs. At the bottom, a human male sat in dirt, chained to a concrete wall. Dax's craving vanished, his stomach flip-flopping. The slave's skeletal hand tugged at the metal restraint around his right ankle. His repeated struggle had torn his sagging, grayish skin at the cuff, opening it to the bone. He was unbathed, his body covered with bite marks and open sores. The human had been fed on and starved by a crazed vamp.

Dax held up a hand in a peaceful gesture, whispering, "I'm here to help you." Dead eyes set in bony sockets stared at him. Dropping to his knees beside the emaciated human, he broke the chain, wrapped the guy in a blanket, and lifted him with ease, the man weighing nothing. Touching the palm of his hand softly to the human's temple, Dax delivered soothing peace to a tortured body and mind, using a mild form of vampire mindwiping.

He delivered the first victim to the healer before he traveled to the home of an incubus in Amori, a respected but low-level Earth trader who hid a secret life. The guy put up no fight as Dax constrained him.

In the center of his living room, a naked woman sat cross-legged in a ten-by-ten cage. She hugged a blanket to her chest, non-responsive, her eyes empty. The incubus had obviously given her food and kept her clean. Her sandy hair shone in the overhead light, and her pale skin was flawless. But her wounds would be deep beneath the surface. Soul deep.

The asshole would have repeatedly raped her, releasing pheromones which made her complicit in her own violation. During sex, he would have fed on her lifeforce until she was at death's doorstep. Once she recovered, he would have repeated the process.

The brutal Aeternal, his eye twitching, couldn't keep his mouth shut. "She likes me. As you can see. She wants my attention." He licked his lips. "She's so sweet. Maybe you want a sip. I'll share. You won't be sorry."

Long, sharp fangs filled Dax's mouth as a growl crawled from his chest. His blood urges wanted to accept the offer, but what little honor he had left refused. He unlocked her cage. When he walked inside, she barely glanced his way.

She clutched the blanket tighter around her neck, not protesting when Dax reached down and cradled her in his arms. "Are you okay?"

She moved her lips close to Dax's ear. "Kill me."

Nearing the slave owner on his way out, Dax shifted the petite human to one arm, dropped the D-chip constraint wrapped around the incubus to hold him in place, and drew his jungle bolo. He plunged it into his black heart. When he severed the head, the woman let a small smile curl her lips, resting her cheek against Dax's chest.

Now two humans lay on gurneys while the healer fussed over them. She had them hooked up to nutrients, and every so often, she'd wave a hand over visible and invisible wounds until they faded.

Dax breathed through his mouth, the air ripe with the blood drawn by the healer. Stubborn asshole he was, he stuck around to prove to himself he was not in the throes of the bludfrenzy. Since nothing could save an afflicted vampire, it was Dax's greatest fear. Of course, it wasn't enough to keep him from glutting on O blud in dens where any craving could be satisfied.

Dax, unmoving against the wall in the lab, had not uttered a word since delivering the woman. His arms crossed his chest, his massive biceps flinching each time his anger surged.

The Ministry of Well Being's healer spun around, dropping the instrument in her hand when she saw Dax still watching. Though he made her nervous, he didn't care. He was what he was. A huge, menacing killer, a block of muscle clad in black and dripping with weapons. A male whose lips were frozen in a permanent scowl.

He didn't bother to hide his most dangerous weapon, his fangs. And when he was angry, which was most of the time, the planes of his face grew sharper and colder. His eyes had lost any sympathy centuries ago. His appearance kept others at a distance, and he had no desire to let anyone get close. Bounty was the only being he genuinely cared for, and he avoided her when possible. He was loyal to his *frerons* and had their backs when needed, but nothing good came from forming attachments.

The healer clasped a hand to her chest, a squeak jumping from her throat before she gathered her wits. "They both have mage ancestry, but they're not Blood Coven descendants. I'll keep them here until they're healthy enough to go home. We'll erase their memories first. Let's hope their minds heal as well. That's the more difficult job."

Dax left the humans in her hands, hoping Jarek's Firebrands found all the slaves quickly.

****

Kole's chip vibrated. *About fucking time.* He tapped his wrist to take an incoming call from Rein. *What took you bastards so long?*

If you want to yell at me, save it until I rescue your ass. Demons are at your front door.

I see them. They're toast.

Save some for us.

Then, move your asses. I see you've all gone to hell since I've been here.

The commander's upper lip twisted into a smile. As he signed off, Dermott swung into the cave. Kole probably could have knocked him off the ledge, but that didn't seem sporting. The renegade demon's eyes showed surprise when he saw Kole alive, upright, and healed.

"Nice to see you, Dermott. Come to make good on your challenge?"

"You can't have survived the gagans' attack."

"Yet here I am. Hale, hearty, and ready to smoke you." Kole wasn't about to explain his secret solution to purging iron poisoning.

Kole forged a ball of fire in his palm, spreading his feet apart. He drew back his arm to launch his personal weapon.

Dermott's body morphed into his beast. He was twice his original size with long sharp claws and extended, razored teeth.

"Oh, you want to go animus-demon-on-envy-demon?" Kole's smile spread cheek to cheek.

How stupid can this guy be? Never bring sharp teeth and nails to a firefight.

Kole tossed the unused ball of fire into the air. As it began its descent, his chest expanded, his arms bulged, and his legs thickened. By the time the flaming ball rejoined his hand, his newly formed body was a red-and-gold bonfire. He breathed deep.

Exquisite.

His roar of release echoed off the cavern walls, shaking the very foundation of the cave. Kole freed his beast.

Dermott crouched, his mouth open to reveal his teeth and his hand curled to accommodate his claws, like any envy demon. He approached, swiping out at Kole, obviously expecting his speed to catch the commander off guard.

Kole stood his ground. When an envy demon stuck claws or teeth into his opponent, the adversary would be overcome with remorse, self-loathing, envy so powerful he would long for death at his own hand. He'd seen victims fall to the ground, curl into a ball, and scratch out their own eyes. But Kole's beast was pure power, vibrant burning energy, nothing of fleshy substance, almost impossible for Dermott to harm.

From the midst of Kole's demon, his words roared out in hot fumes. "You fool. Don't you know what you are dealing with? My Uncle Horach warned you, and yet you chose to fight me in beast form? I will fry your ass with hellfire."

Dermott morphed back into his male form, the earlier hubris erased from his eyes. Kole unwillingly but honorably reined in his beast to assume his physical body. "Wise decision. You stand a better chance, but your odds are still miserable."

"We'll see." Dermott, his deadly claws still extended on one hand, drew a knife from his sheath with the other.

Crouching with his legs spread, Kole tilted his head to the side while waving his blade at the attacking demon. In his other hand, he bounced a ball of fire. "Come get me, asshole."

Dermott hesitated, his jaw clamped tight, his eyes the color of fear. He dodged the fireball and lunged forward, missing contact, stumbling into the cave wall.

When Dermott met the rock, Kole waited. "At least, make this a contest." He stared, letting heat smolder from his eyes, dishonoring his challenger.

Dermott whirled around, charging again. Dodging the assault, Kole snagged onto his challenger's knife hand. The envy demon tried to shake loose, but the Firebrand commander held tight, raised his attacker's arm, and buried his blade in Dermott's heart. Retracting his knife, he swiped it across the neck, decapping him, a sure way to end an Aeternal's life.

Rein swung into the cave at that moment, followed by Brak and Sabine. His hard gaze followed the renegade's head as it tumbled into the dirt.

One by one, Firebrands burst into the cave. Blood spattered their arms, clothes, and faces. Not their own. But they looked unharmed. Each approached, gripped elbow to wrist, saying, "*Freron* or Commander or Comm." He could tell they all needed the contact.

Rein held back until the other Firebrands had all greeted him. With a controlled smile and a slight nod, he said, "Commander Kole, good to see you again. Nice digs."

"Damn, Rein. I don't think I've seen you smile before. Well, except at Braelyn or when you took off that berserker's head." Kole let his gaze wander to a male he didn't recognize. "Who's the human?"

"Nico's the name. Last time I saw you, Kole, we were in a hall outside Chief Maxwell's office lighting it up with smoke grenades."

"Yeah? I recall. Why are you here?"

"I was being held prisoner by your Firebrands until they recruited me." The Alliance agent smirked as Sabine rolled her eyes.

"What?" Kole snarled in Rein's direction.

"The asshole isn't giving you the whole story. I'll explain later."

Kole dropped his bloody blade, turned, and charged into a tunnel leading to the back of the cave, his palms glowing with fire.

He found Skyler huddled against a wall. He swept her into his arms and ravaged her with a hard kiss. Before she could say a word, he dropped her to her feet and pulled her behind him, returning to the main chamber where his Firebrands waited.

Kole dropped Skyler's hand but not quick enough. His warriors exchanged shocked looks and some grins. "She saved my life. When we were attacked by gagans, I ended up with a few iron claws in me. Shut the fuck up before I set your balls on fire. Sabine, Jezzi, Galena, though you lack the nads, you get the drift."

When Nico laughed, Kole zipped a stream of fire to his ear.

The human clasped a hand over it. "Hey. That hurts."

"You know where I'm aiming next?"

"You okay?" Rein asked Kole. "I've never known a demon to survive iron."

He figured he'd share the secret with his Firebrands. "Years ago, I made a deal with a pissed off warlock who owed me. He created a spell so I could fight off iron poisoning. But he had a warped sense of humor. The sonofabitch threw in a zinger. Custom job. Just for me, he said." A grinning Kole glanced at Skyler whose lilac-blue eyes iced over. "His cure is unique but not unpleasant."

****

Alarik glanced away from his computer when the door burst open. An animated Echo, his chief historian, rushed into his office with Zora hot on the heels of her soft-soled witch boots.

"This wand waggler zapped me." His office manager tugged on her already short lavender leather skirt. "I should suck the lifeforce right out of her." Zora stretched out an arm to touch Echo.

The purple-eyed witch spun to face her accuser. "Hold it, succubus. Lay one of those fingers with the Gahya-awful cobalt-blue polish on me and I'll spell you again. You won't like it any better the second time than you did the first. I've got an important lead the director needs to hear about now. And on another note, we do not use wands. Never did. Never will."

Alarik held his hand up to send a calming spell to Zora. "What is it, Echo?"

"It might be the break we've been searching for. I told you Allias was poring over some dusty old volume when he found an obscure reference to an ancient society. This group was tasked with safeguarding important mages of certain ancient bloodlines."

"Go on."

"He found another reference to this society in a private library. You know Allias can be a bloodhound when he has a fact to trace. He created a spell to uncover texts which alluded to this ancient group. He said he had a 'gut feeling about it.' I know to trust his gut."

"I'm still not seeing how this helps us."

"The founding members of this society came together not many years after the Karmic Schism. They were all Blood Coven offspring, diluted of course with human DNA. They formed a society to maintain their genealogy records and to keep an eye on their own kin."

"What! Why didn't we know about this group before?"

"They were a very hush-hush society. Buried deep on Earth. We don't even know if they still exist, but we do know they kept track of each other for centuries."

Alarik rubbed his chin with his thumb and index finger. "This is good news, but how do we find out if they're still active? And where are their records?"

"No idea yet."

"Who are they?"

"Ah. I can tell you who they were. They were called *Custodes Templii*. If we can find them and if they still perform their original tasks, we can unearth the modern-day descendants of the Blood Coven."

"Do you think they are still active?"

"Allias uncovered a reference from the late nineteenth century about a society led by Alistar Wheatley, calling itself *Custodes Templii*. Unfortunately, the group does not seem to be the original one mentioned in various ancient texts."

"Unless," proposed Alarik, "they created a false description of themselves to hide their real purpose. Much as the Alliance does."

"It's possible."

"Any current evidence of the society?"

"None we can find yet. We know for certain the original *Custodes Templii* kept records of Blood Coven lines. Even if they no longer exist, we should search for their ancient documents. Those reports might give us a starting point for locating living descendants."

"Excellent work, Echo. Commend Allias for me. Zora, I think you can let this slight go unavenged, don't you?"

The succubus's eyes narrowed to a squint. "Yes, but listen carefully, witch. Use a spell to bypass me again and I won't be so kind." Zora flipped her hair and turned on a heel, stomping out of the office.

Alarik called Rein, but since his son was on a mission, he left a message with Bounty.

Chapter Twenty-Six

Survive became her mantra. Whenever she thought she would lose it, she heard the word. *Survive.* Whenever he put hands on her, she heard the word. *Survive.* Whenever his dick… *Survive.*

Lizette Lee's gaze followed the hulking male's form as he growled and paced from one wall to another, colorful but frayed, heavy rugs beneath his boots. The hut was built of stone and mud with a thatched roof, a giant open space inside. A kitchen with an old wood-burning stove, a main living area with a ground-to-ceiling rock fireplace, a bedroom, and a storage pantry off to one side.

She sat on the floor of the living area, chained to a post, leaning against it, her legs curled under her.

Lizette wasn't sure how long she had been Spear's captive. She remembered leaving the WMR production studio in New York where she was a call-in radio psychologist. She remembered beings who weren't human kidnapping and imprisoning her in a cold, bare cell where the only comfort was a rickety cot. She remembered other prisoners.

Then this horrifying, savage berserker walked down the corridor. When he chose her, the "boss," the creature she now knew was Aisen, sold her to him. Next, she woke up here, the beast spiking her food or drink to keep her disoriented.

She rubbed fingers across the scarred skin on her neck where he had burned an S into her flesh. Having caught her after an attempted escape, the beast had heated a piece of iron in the fire, telling her she was his slave and his name was Spear. He marked her as his. The memory of the cruel pain honed her survival instincts.

At dusk each day, Spear took her outside. From these trips, Lizette knew the isolated cabin was on a rise with a tree-filtered view of a valley below. Since she didn't see any neighbors, no amount of screaming would attract attention. It was unlikely a friendly neighbor would drop by for coffee, and Spear showed no inclination to let her roam free. Wherever they were, the air was crisp, cool. Perhaps late spring or even summer in the mountains. It had been autumn in New York when the monsters kidnapped her. Of course, she could be in a different hemisphere. She didn't want to think about that.

While outside, he permitted her to walk around like a dog on a tether, exercising, going to the bathroom. If he accompanied her, he held the tether attached to a collar on her neck. If he left her alone, he strung it to a long chain.

During the day, he allowed her out for short breaks only if he felt it was safe.

The berserker stopped pacing and approached Lizette. He kneeled on the floor beside her. When he rubbed his rough hand on her cheek, she avoided the urge to draw away.

Survive.

Flinching would get her beaten.

Spear was gigantic, nearly seven feet tall. Sometimes he dressed only in animal pelts, one wrapped around his waist and another thrown over a massive shoulder. At other times, he donned human clothes—jeans or sweats with a T-shirt. No matter. Either way, he looked savage, feral, his dark hair in multiple thick braids like an ancient Viking. His beard, as dark as his hair, was wild, scraggly.

"I can't keep you. The Firebrands will find out

what I've done." His words were guttural snarls.

Think. Think.

What was Spear talking about? Maybe someone was looking for her. Hope soared.

"Aisen is dead. If they find me with you, they'll kill me, too. Better I get rid of you. Burn your body. Bury the remains."

She swallowed the bile which rose from her stomach.

Survive.

As a radio show host, Lizette took phone calls daily from people who unburdened their problems, sought solutions. An inability to move on after ending a relationship. Loneliness. Abuse. No matter what the caller's situation, she walked them through the same steps. First, clarify the problem. Second, make a plan. Third, carry out the plan. She needed a plan now. A good one.

The problem was simple. Spear was going to kill her. The plan was to stop him. When she found the specifics, she would put it into play.

Scooting closer, she took her captor's hand, clasping it to a breast. "Spear, I wouldn't let anyone hurt you." She had the plan—give him something to look forward to, a reason to keep her alive every day until someone came for her.

He looked at her as if he wanted to believe she cared about him, but he jerked his chin up. "No. No. It's too dangerous for me."

Lizette caressed his hand as it squeezed her breast. "But who would keep you warm at night?"

Survive.

"You would be all alone again." If she stayed alive long enough, she would find a way out of this hellhole or someone would rescue her. She just knew it.

In the meantime, she could bear anything.

Spear rose and resumed pacing the floor.

Lizette sniffed the air. "I smell stew. The one with beef and carrots. It's my favorite. I'm so hungry for dinner."

His shining eyes focused on her. He liked the compliment.

"Yes. It is time to eat." He lumbered to the wood-burning stove, where he ladled the food into a bowl and carried it to her. Spear sat cross-legged in front of her. As if she were a child, he fed her. When he had first brought her here, she had clamped her teeth tight together, refusing to eat from his hand, but squeezing her jaw between his thumb and forefinger, he caused excruciating pain. Now she allowed him the obsession.

Between bites, Lizette spoke. "I want to cook for you sometime. Why don't you let me? I would feed you, Spear."

"You would do that?"

"Of course I would. It's what a lover does, is it not?"

He shoved another spoonful of meat into her mouth. When juices spilled onto her chin, running down her neck, he leaned in to lick her clean. He peered into her eyes. Lizette knew he was gauging her reaction. Instead of cringing, she smiled. A cringe would earn her a slap across the face.

"Get a chicken tomorrow. I make great chicken and dumplings. Have you ever had that?"

Spear shook his head. When the bowl was empty, he pushed off the ground, served himself, and ate, his wild eyes fixed on her. Then he cleaned up the kitchen with water he pumped into the house.

"You'll love my recipe. I could bake an apple pie to go with it. I look forward to cooking for you." Lizette hated cooking, but Spear didn't need to know. At least she knew how to make a few things. Make him want tomorrow with her. That was her plan. Day-by-day survival.

Looking outside at the darkening sky, he smiled. "It is bath time, *kjaer*."

Lizette fought back tears. Bath time came each night before bedtime. The berserker unchained her from the post, attaching the leash to her collar. After stopping to gather a basin filled with supplies, he walked her outside for their nightly ritual.

Near the house was a river. He led her to a spot which was damned to form a pool.

The berserker removed the lead, grasped the hem of her dress, snapped it over her head, and reattached the restraint. Early on, Lizette tried to fight him off, but the blows to her body hurt and her resistance never stopped him. It was easier to let him strip her. Since he did not allow her to wear underclothes, only a thin cotton dress, she stood naked in front of him.

He slipped off his pants and shirt, pulling her into the pooled water with him. Lathering soap onto his hand, he washed her. Every intimate part. He rubbed his soaped palm across her breasts, closing his eyes. Then, spreading her legs apart, his fingers explored and cleaned her sex while he moaned in pleasure.

In the beginning, she gripped her legs tight together, but he drew back his fist, connecting with her jaw. Or he forced her to submit some other way. Eventually, it was easier to let him bathe her. She just had to keep from throwing up. When she had done that, he had knocked her out cold.

Finally, Spear walked her out of the river to dry her off.

"I will bring home a chicken tomorrow. You'll

tell me what you need for a pie." He dressed Lizette, returning them to the hut. He took her to his bed, where the real horror began each night.

Survive.

****

Kole scrubbed a fist across his buzz cut. "You dreamed about Dermott's camp at the base of the mountain. Are you sure you don't have a mage ancestor?"

An exhausted Skyler sat on the couch in Kole's office. "Positive. Family journals, histories, and my father's demented but proud stories are only of the demon Abrahm. I can't explain my dream. Or my increased stamina. But the bigger question is, who wants me or Alliance employees dead?"

"You think Dermott targeted you rather than Kole?" asked Rein.

"It's likely. A few days before I came to Scath, I was pushed from the L platform on my way to work. Afterward, my office received threats from some blogger group who took responsibility. Then Aeternals attacked the Alliance. While I was on the tour, Sarah Jenkins, our head of Information Services, was murdered. I didn't realize getting trapped on Darque had anything to do with these events, but now I think they might have."

Kole unleashed a stream of fire into the far wall as Rein ducked. Rising, he checked his clothes for burns. "Hey! That could have been my head. I've no yen to be toast."

Kole's sneer fixed on the vamp mix but moved to Skyler. "Don't you think the full story might have been important enough to share earlier?"

"No. Obviously I didn't since I didn't realize the incidents were related."

She kept talking despite his fiery gaze, the one

which took warriors to their knees. It had no effect on this icy female whose lips had been wrapped around his cock. Of course, there was no frost in her veins then. Only fire.

Skyler crossed one shapely leg over the other while Kole shook off an image of both wrapped around him as he pounded into her. "You had a front-row seat to the attack on my office. I told you about Sarah's murder, but even you didn't connect the dots. I thought we couldn't use the portals because our equipment malfunctioned. You didn't indicate anything else. Hindsight is brilliant. Yes, in hindsight, I should have said something about the other incidents."

Rein played peacemaker. "I know you're ass-pained by all this, Kole, but the past is past. And how it all relates to Chief Maxwell is puzzling. What's the gain? Uwrich blocks communication signals so you can't leave Darque. Dermott and his band of renegades arrive to finish you off. The gagans had to be a happy coincidence. They don't hire out to anybody."

Kole tented his fingers. What was the gain in killing Skyler or the Alliance techie? The million-dollar bribe from the bloggers to keep zipped made sense, but nothing else added up. "Who wants you dead, Frisca? This blogger group? Why? Bragging rights? My dick's bigger than your dick? Or vagina, in this case?"

Skyler shrugged. "I may not have friends, but I don't have enemies either."

Kole tapped his fingers. He rolled his thick shoulders, relaxing stiff muscles, and flexed his head from side to side. Now that they were back on Scath and not dodging threats on Darque, he'd put his mind on the problem. "If the bloggers arranged for the office invasion and the trap on Darque, they're Aeternals. Dermott would not hire out to humans."

"Regardless of who is responsible, the attempts to kill me make no sense. Sarah's death makes no sense." Skyler paused, a finger running a lazy path along her full, luscious lower lip. "Unless she found out the identity of TheBigReveal. She was tracking them." Skyler drew her mouth into a tight line, her expression business-like, calculating, sexy.

Rein cast a puzzled look at her. "I'm curious. Why the trip to Darque? The realm is dangerous enough without Dermott's attack."

"Anna, my administrative assistant, found a missing page from my father's journal. She arranged it last minute."

Rein propped open the office door with a boot. "You two can search for answers to the big questions. Way above my pay grade. You're back, Kole, I'm demoted to soldier. Perfect. The gaffers are warming up the surviving demons and Uwrick. Maybe we'll squeeze them for the name of who hired them."

Skyler patted her smooth platinum-blonde hair, pulled back in a knot low on her head. She had slipped on her professional mask, having showered and changed in the Firebrand gym. Bounty had provided the duds. Tailored pants. Button-down blouse. Heels. Kole realized he liked her both ways. The frosty, capable businesswoman. The disheveled explorer with a sweat-soaked blouse sticking to her curves.

She rested her hands in her lap. "I'll wait to see if you get anything from the prisoners before I head to Earth." Skyler's cool gaze turned warm, soft when it met Kole's eyes.

"I'll see you home. I want to be sure you're safe. But I'd feel better if you stayed on Scath for the time being. At least, until we find out who's trying to kill you."

Her chest rose and fell with a breathy sigh. "I must get back to my job. I'm so far behind, but I'll wait for you to escort me there. When I get to the office, security will assign agents to guard me."

Kole pictured some of the agents he'd met. Scrawny, poorly trained, and incompetent by his standards. He wasn't being fair, but hell. "Yeah. They're great in a pinch, but... Fuck it. No, they're not. They're wimp-ass weaklings."

Skyler stiffened her spine. "That's neither fair nor true. Besides, Kole, I need some space to think."

"About what?" Now there was a crazy question. Kole wasn't ready to put his feelings for Skyler into words. He needed his own think time.

He had seen the heart beneath Frisca's ice, damaged by an unfit parent but emerging strong and vibrant. His gut and his brain were still battling it out. Though he didn't want her to leave, he wasn't ready to say something stupid. He was tied to a dangerous job. That's how he liked it. He had never considered taking a mate and certainly not a human one with a short life span. Some space was a good idea.

"What I'm doing. Where I am. What you mean to me."

For whatever insane reason, his mouth developed a mind of its own. "Skyler, I want..."

Bounty threw open the door and strutted in on stiletto boots. "I hope I'm interrupting, but the guys down in the Cubes are waiting for their commander. I'll keep the chief here. She'll be safe with me. Maybe I can teach her to make her own coffee. Then she won't insult your executive assistant by asking her to fetch like a mutt."

Kole pried his massive frame out of the chair. Bounty had saved him from being a complete idiot. He'd been about to propose Skyler dump her fiancé and take on a long-distance relationship with him. Swift move.

Thanks for the save, Bounty.

Skyler cast a genuine smile at the vampire. "Go, Kole. I'll be fine here. Like your executive assistant said, she can teach me to make my own coffee and, I bet, a few other things."

Bounty's fist went to her hip, but she looked at Skyler with narrowed eyes. "Hmm. Maybe there's hope."

****

Kole stormed into the Cubes to find Uwrick strapped to the rack. The lines in his face had deepened, terror squeezing his brow. He was stretched out horizontally on a slab with his ankles tied to a roller on one end, his wrists chained at the other. His robe had been removed, leaving him in his boxers.

Chay gripped a handle on the torture device and cranked it enough to make it squeak. "Hey, Com, I was about to explain to our guest how this machine works. This wheel turns. Now when it does, you're gonna start hurtin' a whole lot. You're gonna hear the gears grinding along with a whole bunch of loud popping noises. Cartilage, ligaments, bones. Snap. Snap." Chay rolled his eyes. He shivered. "Ugh. Makes me hurt just talking about it."

Moving closer, Brak hitched up his leathers. "What's really ugly is when you start to break apart. Shoulders, elbows, knees, wrists. Hurts like a sonofabitch. Or so I'm told."

"Uwrick, we can avoid all this if you tell us who hired you." Rein leaned against the concrete wall, cold, his eyes half-lidded with boredom.

Tears streamed from the warlock's eyes. "I told you. Dermott hired me. He said it would be a simple job. Big pay. All I had to do was stay within range of Kole and the female to jam their devices. That's all."

"How did you know where they were?" asked Chay.

"I overheard something about a tracking device. That's all I know."

"Who hired the demon?" asked Kole.

"I don't know. I only worked with Dermott. No one else."

"Didn't you ask about the gig? Why? Who? You know the ushe?" Chay gave the crank another turn, drawing screams from the mage.

"Why would I care? I was in it for the money." Tears streaked the warlock's face, drool leaking from the corner of his mouth.

Chay moved the handle another quarter.

"No. No," Uwrick screamed. "Stop. My ankle."

Kole nodded at Chay.

"Dermott found you outside the Yeti camp, and we stayed with you through every jump. When you were at Narobi Flats..." The warlock gulped so fast he couldn't talk for a few seconds. "...he told me to cut off your signals. I did. When you hid from the harpies, we nearly drew their attention ourselves. Then, we thought the female might die before you got her to the Healing Pond."

"You watched us there?" Kole snarled, not liking what the demons and warlock might have witnessed.

"My ankle needs attention."

"Screw your ankle. Let it roll, ylve." Kole snapped the order.

"Wait! We were close but couldn't see you. We waited below Spriggan Enclave, following you when you left. We stood by when the gagans attacked you. We figured they would kill you, and the female would be an easy target. Mowart watched you climb toward the falls.

Dermott told me to stay hidden while he and his males pursued you. I did. Until you caught me. There! That's all I know. Please, let me go. I'm a businessman, selling my power. You understand."

Brak inhaled, his chest impossibly bigger. "You're an A-hole who'd do anything for a stack of gold. Of course, you wouldn't get your hands dirty with blood. Leave those tasks to some other twonk."

Kole nodded to Chay. "Keep going."

The ylve turned it slowly.

Uwrick's moans morphed into loud screams. "Stop. Stop. I don't know any more than what I said."

Chay paused.

"Keep it up," Kole yelled over the mage's frantic howling until a pop sounded. It was Uwrick's wrist breaking.

"For your sake, I hope you know something else." Kole assessed the injury before he signaled another turn of the handle.

"Wait! I overheard talk around the fire. Dermott said some guy named Cerberus was getting big bucks from a human called Dante. I don't know if that's who hired him. I don't think he cared. He hated you. The female, too. His ego." Uwrick began to weep, his last words caught in his slobbering wails. "That's all I know. Please. My wrist. I think my shoulder's dislocated, too."

"Take him down and return him to his cell." Kole's boots clomped to another cage where a demon slumped, chin in hands, eyes cast to the floor. When the prisoner looked up, Kole released a feral growl. "Bring this one out. Strap him onto the rack."

Two gaffers dragged out the hedon demon, blood dripping from a gash in his abdomen. His feet trailed through small puddles of it as they lugged him to the torture device. He shook his hands, trying to release his claws.

Your powers don't work in here, fucktard," Ram taunted. "You're dead meat." He cuffed one wrist to the top roller while a gaffer on the other side did the same. Then they lashed his ankles to the bottom roller. "You know the routine. We start cranking and you start snapping. I gotta tell ya. This will hurt you a lot more than it will me."

"Start crankin' it, fucking Firebrands. Think you're hot shit. You ain't nobody."

"Oh, my feelings are hurt, demon." Ram put a hand over his heart as he motioned for a gaffer to turn the wheel.

Kole watched, his fiery gold-red eyes cold embers. *Pop. Pop. Bellow. Howl.* Fear struck the demon's crazed eyes like a bolt of lightning. Ear-piercing screams. Moans. More pops. The prisoner's left shoulder separated. Ram motioned for the gaffer to turn the wheel the other way, releasing the pull a bit.

When Ram looked into the demon's pupils, all he saw was pain, horror, and the knowledge of impending death. "Here's the question, man, do you want it slow or quick?"

"Quick." His words were a whisper, his previous bravado gone.

"Tell us who hired Dermott."

"I don't know anything about the gig."

Kole's boots thudded on the concrete as he powered up to the demon. "Let me at him. Have you heard of Arisen Dawn?" The commander studied the prisoner's eyes, looking for awareness. One of the attackers at Skyler's office had let the name pop. Kole hated puzzles.

The demon's gaze turned cold. "Do what you're gonna do. I can't tell you what I don't know."

"Cerberus?" Kole threw out another zinger.

Despite one more crank of the wheel, the demon only glared at Kole. No information would spill from his lips.

Ram strode closer, avoiding the blood on the floor, drew his dagger, and plunged it deep, dragging it from abdomen to chest. He reached in, grabbed the demon's heart, yanked it out, and threw it onto the floor. "He got what he wanted. A quick death."

Kole nodded. "Bring on the next victim. Maybe he knows about this Arisen Dawn or Cerberus or now the mysterious human Dante."

Chapter Twenty-Seven

"Come to Paddy's Diner two days hence at noon. Sit in a booth, both of you on one side, hubby against the wall, all hands on the table." Miller dodged a pedestrian crossing the street and coming toward him. The guy had sneaky eyes, his mouth torquing into a grim snarl. Miller twisted around, tracking the man, prepared to fight. Since the guy was short and his arms looked rail thin, the ex-military man knew taking him would be no challenge. But the guy walked on by.

Bollocks. I've got serious rats in my attic. I think they're gnawing away at brain matter.

As Miller swore under his breath, he reminded himself he would stay alive only if he considered everyone an enemy. Sometimes paranoia could save a life. Though he was tired of running, he didn't think he'd enjoy being some Aeternal's bitch. So, he'd just hang onto his persecution delusions.

Back to the phone and Braelyn. "I know it's been a while, but I have to be careful, luv."

He'd been hopping from hotel to hotel, town to town, returning eventually to Boston. "What? ... How will you recognize me? ... I'll be wearing a strawberry-blonde wig, flowered dress, and red hooker heels. ... No, not really. You won't need to recognize me. I'll know you, luv. Remember. You. His nibs. Nobody else. Now, are you as great looking in person as you are in your picture? ... Ha! I think hubby is the least of my worries. See you soon."

****

Skyler waited for Anna to return with proof of

Alden Maxwell's tour of Darque.

Last night, she had pounded her pillow thinking if she made a comfortable dent in it she'd fall asleep. It didn't work. She flipped onto her stomach, pivoted to her side, curled into a ball. Nothing made any difference. Sleep was impossible. She closed her eyes, drawing a long breath, seeing Kole's muscular arms, deep chest, broad shoulders, and heated gaze. When she imagined him using his devilish charm on other women, her eyes snapped open and life's dilemmas plagued her sleep.

Somewhere around three o'clock in the morning, she had drifted off, still rolling the tour schedule around in her mind. What if Darque had been a set-up from the start? Skyler had told Anna to use her father's journals to recreate his first official visit to Scath. Her assistant had not included Darque in the original itinerary, claiming to have missed it. Had Anna set Skyler up? Anna? No. Not possible. But someone. Someone led Kole and her into a trap.

"Here it is, boss. This is the page which fell out of your father's journal. Read for yourself. That's why I added Darque to your tour. I swear. I only found it after you were already on Scath."

Skyler examined the page, studying the handwriting. "It looks right." It could be her father's. She rubbed the paper between her fingers. "Can you bring in the whole journal?"

Anna's heels clacked across the tiles as she rushed from the office, returning with the diary in hand. It was a brown leather-bound book tied with a black strap. Just one in a series her father had written while he was CLO. It documented issues he had handled, travels, Aeternals and humans he had met, and thoughts about nearly every subject connected with his tenure in the position.

"Here it is. See? Same writing."

"Hmm. It looks the same. Feel the journal paper and then the page you found. Tell me what you think." Skyler handed the book along with the single page to Anna.

The young but efficient assistant closed her eyes, rubbing the stray page between her fingers. She did the same in the journal. "I think this paper is rougher, but I'm not sure." She held up the single sheet documenting the tour of Darque.

"It is definitely coarser." Skyler put both objects on the desk, leaning over them, carefully examining the handwriting. "Look at these closely. What do you see?"

Anna took Skyler's place, bending forward, squinting at the samples. Her mouth open, she twisted her neck to stare at Skyler. "They are not the same. Remarkably similar, but different. Your father's *s*'s were more angular. He crossed his *t*'s differently." Anna let the single page and the journal rest on the desk. Her shoulders slumped forward. "Oh. My. God. Someone set me up, and I almost got you killed. I'm so sorry."

"This is not your fault, Anna. Where did you think this page came from in the journal?"

"I assumed from somewhere in this section." Anna thumbed through the book until she came to the part about Alden Maxwell's tour.

They examined where the pages would have connected to the binding. "I don't see a tear which would indicate something had been ripped out, do you, Anna?"

She shook her head. "No, I don't. I did not go through the journal looking for the spot where the page might have been torn out. My fault. I am so sorry."

"Again. I do not blame you, but how do you suppose this sheet got in among your notes?"

Anna bit her lower lip. "No idea. I often leave

papers on my desk. Anyone who came in could have messed with them. You should fire me, boss." She pulled a tissue from a box on Skyler's desk to dab tears from her eyes.

"Don't be ridiculous. I'm not going to fire you." Skyler looped an arm over Anna's shoulder to comfort her. "I like you. We just need to get to the bottom of the problem. Someone put the false entry among your papers hoping you would find it and add Darque to my itinerary. After you arranged for me to go there, he or she must have hired the demons. Why would those bloggers go to all the trouble? And how does their reach extend into our offices and across the realms?"

With a coffee cup in hand and the unsolved problem on her mind, Skyler picked up the phone to call Winston.

****

Lizette jumped when she heard a fist pounding the door. She struggled against her bindings, but before she screamed, Spear moved swiftly in front of her, his glare menacing.

"It's Golarg. Let me in, *venn*."

Spear motioned as if to cut her throat. "Bringing attention to yourself, *min besettelse*, would be a bad idea. Deadly. *Dodelig*."

The hulking bear-like monster opened the front door, stooping to exit, shutting her in. Lizette picked out voices.

"*Hva,* Golarg? What is so important you disturb my home, my own *tilflukt*."

"You stay longer in your *tilflukt* than you ever have. I never see you at the village roasts or at the bar. *Jeg er mistenkelig*."

"Why do you say you are suspicious?"

"You are a male who loves a good fight. Who

loves to beat *andre hanner blodig.*"

"Perhaps I have lost interest in beating stupid males to a bloody pulp. What do you care? I am not your *underholdning*, your entertainment."

"Will you offer me libation? I could use a strong *traust.*"

"No beer. Go now! *Ga!*"

Boots scraped through gravel as if Spear's unwelcome guest was leaving, but he must have spun around.

"Oh, Firebrands came to the village today asking about a female who might have been bought as a sex slave, a *kjonner*, a human *kjonner*. Of course, no one knew of one. Then I thought of how quiet my friend Spear has been. How he never comes out anymore except when he must work."

A loud growl sounded. Lizette was sure it was Spear. "You think too much. It can be dangerous."

"I said to myself, my friend could not have such a prize because if he did, he would share with his old friend."

Lizette swallowed hard as fear rose in her throat. She was barely hanging on to her sanity with Spear. What if another man used her?

Thud. Umpff. She heard scuffling as if Spear and his guest were rolling on the ground. One of them uttered a feeble plea. *Twack.* Over and over. Then something was dragged off.

After about fifteen minutes, Spear returned with blood on his clothes, face, and hands. His wild eyes darted about the cabin, settling on a wall. He grabbed an axe from the hook and tromped toward the door.

"I'll be back, *min besettelse.*" Then he laughed, heartless, malicious. "Don't go anywhere."

****

Winston held the door, motioning Skyler through. As she stepped into Manfredo's, an image of Kole and her on a date popped into her head.

He doesn't whip open the door for me to enter. No, he storms through ahead of me in full battle mode, expecting trouble. When all is safe, he turns to me, gruffly announcing, "Hurry up. We don't have all day, female."

She grinned.

"What's funny?" asked Winston.

"Nothing." Her heart, however, thumped against her chest when she thought about the Firebrand commander. His smile. His fiery gold eyes. His stubbled, determined jaw. The jolt of electricity to make her orgasm.

Taking Skyler's elbow, Winston led her to the host's desk where Manfredo greeted them. Though they had been coming here for years, the owner's acknowledgment was cool.

At the table, Winston pulled out her chair before he took his own seat. As usual, small talk dominated their conversation.

"How was your trip?" He opened the wine list, his gaze passing between Skyler and his task.

"The trip…" Skyler paused and chose her words carefully, "…had an unexpected turn."

"Such as?" he asked without looking up.

"Nothing of interest to you."

The waiter appeared alongside Winston.

"We would like a bottle of the Domaine Leflaive Puligny-Montrachet Les Folatières."

Skyler smiled at the waiter but held up her hand to stop him. "I'd like a beer."

"No one orders beer here." Winston looked to the man as if expecting support.

The waiter said, "Actually, sir, they do."

The doctor's sharp frown settled on the waiter.

Skyler ignored Winston. "Thanks. I'll have Bud. On tap, if you have it."

"We do. That's one Bud and a bottle of the Puligny-Montrachet." The waiter gave a polite bow, no smile.

Winston nodded a curt dismissal. "What's with the peasant drink? You've never ordered a beer. You're being strange, Skyler. I'm not sure I like it."

Skyler raised an eyebrow as she glanced at the menu. "I don't need your approval. Now, what do I want for dinner?"

They studied the menu in silence for some ten minutes.

"I think we'll order the stuffed sole in a *pâte brisée* for two. A walnut and goat cheese salad and a side of broccoli gratin will go nicely." Winston snapped his menu closed.

"Sounds good, but I feel like red meat. I'm considering the steak Diane."

"You rarely order steak, Skyler."

"Actually, Winston, you usually insist on fish for us. I love steak."

"But I assumed you preferred fish, which is much healthier for you."

"I do like fish, but I like steak, too."

"Well, I think you will like this fish better."

"No. Steak Diane."

"If you insist, but you'll be sorry."

"I can handle that."

Winston scowled when he gave their order to the waiter, who glanced at Skyler. "The steak Diane is wonderful tonight, miss."

Skyler smiled. She was so tired of being at the

mercy of her childhood. Her journey had to start with a single step. She asked, "You've been here for a couple of years, haven't you?"

"Yes. Manfredo is my uncle."

Taking a quick look at the owner, Skyler nodded. "I see the resemblance. Do other family members work here?"

"My sister, Amelia, over there." He pointed toward an attractive brunette.

"She's charming. And what's your name?"

"Anthony."

"Nice to know your name, Anthony. I'm Skyler and my friend is Winston."

Anthony lightly touched Skyler's fingers, raised them to his lips, and kissed them softly. "I am pleased to know the name of such a lovely lady."

Skyler chuckled, and Anthony walked away with their order.

"Really, Skyler, what was all that about? And a kiss on the hand. How phony."

She rubbed her hand as her lips spread into a slow smile. "I think it was very Italian. Quite charming."

"Back to your trip. It gave me some time to think. I know you told me before you left you wanted to end our engagement. I don't think that's wise."

Skyler's eyes widened as he droned on about wedding plans and family expectations.

Winston would have been my future.

A man her father had admired and thrown at her. A lifetime of polite conversation over dinners at expensive restaurants. The golden couple. The respected surgeon and the corporate lawyer.

What could be better? A brutish demon with fire-gold eyes.

"A reception at the Peninsula would be

appropriate, which means we need to set the date and get working on it. My mother will help with the details. Big galas are her specialty. She…"

"Winston, I didn't say I wanted to break off our engagement. I broke it off."

"I don't understand. Why?"

Skyler had tried a gentler approach, but it hadn't worked with Winston. She drew a deep breath. "I don't love you."

"Perhaps you can't do June. But June is the best time to…"

"Did you hear me at all?"

Winston's mouth slammed shut as he stared at her.

"If you're honest with yourself, you don't love me either."

"We are perfect for each other, Skyler. Ask our friends."

"We have no friends. We have business associates who join us for dinner on occasion. In fact, we have no time for friends. We are both so focused on our careers."

"This is about friends? We can acquire friends."

"This is not about friends, Winston. It's about us. You are devoted to your job. I am, too. I know what that type of devotion means. It means there is little room for anything or anyone else in our lives."

"Nonsense. I want you in my life. I'll be devoted to you. I'll give you whatever you want."

"How about a burning romance? Can you give me that?"

Winston's eyes narrowed, his confusion evident.

"I'm honestly not blaming you, Winston. I've changed. I want…" What did she want? She wanted her breath to catch whenever her lover walked into the room.

She wanted fire to dance through her when they made love. She wanted Kole.

"Romance is fleeting, Skyler. You need someone who is steady."

"I thought so, too. Turns out it's not true. Anyway, we are not marrying, but you will always have my respect and my friendship."

"You mean to tell me I've wasted all this time on you? You need me. We are the perfect couple."

"I'm not looking for perfect, Winston."

He reached across the table, grabbing Skyler's hand, squeezing it until she winced. "Your father told me you would be my wife."

"He had no right. Let go of my hand. You're hurting me. I think I should leave."

"You will not leave, and we will marry. Snap out of this mood." He squeezed tighter.

When Skyler yanked her hand from Winston's grasp, his wine glass flew off the table, shattering on the floor.

She stood. "I am sorry. I didn't know you planned to be so insistent tonight. I thought you wanted to hear how I felt. I'm terribly sorry." She walked determinedly toward the door.

"You'll regret this," he shouted, all other conversation in the restaurant coming to a halt.

"No. No, I won't, Winston."

As Skyler started to pass Manfredo, she paused. "I ordered steak Diane. Please give it to the lovely young couple near my table. They ordered with an eye to prices. I think they might enjoy it. Keep it on my friend's bill, though."

The owner gave her a brief nod and grin.

Skyler hailed a cab, riding home with her thoughts.

Now what? Kole's a realm away and seemingly disinclined to return. I'm going to change his mind. After all, I'm known for my cutthroat negotiating skills.

****

Dante rarely met Cerberus outside his English estate, but tonight they had scheduled appointments at the London gentleman's club.

The building dated back to 1720, and it was well-known the Prince of Wales had joined later the same century. Dramatists, statesmen, artists still gathered in grandiose rooms to argue politics, philosophy, and the arts. Unknown to members, Aeternals had been frequenting the posh establishment for centuries.

It was here Dante first met Cerberus not long after his daughter's death. During their meeting, he learned of Scath, the realm of Aeternal breeds. Plans for his revenge began.

They started this evening in a lavishly decorated lounge where they sipped scotch and chose items from a tray of assorted cheeses and sausages. They followed up with a massage. Now, they sweated in the steam room.

Dante scooped water from a bucket, tossing it onto the coals.

Cerberus wrapped a towel tighter around his waist. "Margo Hunter, the female my people captured with the Firebrand ylve, used a spell to escape. The residuals of it were still in the cell when I investigated. It is no surprise her test sample proved she was a Blood Coven descendant."

"Wretched bad luck. But you still have two in captivity. What are their names?"

"Jace and Celene."

"Yes." Dante swiped at moisture beading on his face. "Have they shown an ability to use witchcraft?"

"No. Though wards on the house where they are

kept block magic, we would detect its attempted use."

"To use the descendants to open portals, do you need them to possess magic?"

"Yes. I must learn how this Margo tapped into her gift."

Dante leaned against the wet white tiles, his elbows resting on the ledge above. "What about Skyler Maxwell?"

"The CLO of the Alliance has proven to be a slippery adversary. But, as you have said, I am persistent. Her home will be the best place to reach her now. Though agents guard her door, they will not be a challenge for my males."

"You have Jace and Celene. They have Margo. Since you can trace your heritage back to two mages in the coven, eight of thirteen are still out there."

"I wish it were so simple, friend. It is not a matter of numbers. I will need a witch or warlock from each line to destroy the portals and Whorl. While we locate more descendants, we must also find out how to trace their ancestry. And how to activate their powers. No small tasks."

Dante scooped more water onto the coals, the thick steam obliterating Cerberus. He took his seat again, wrapping the towel tighter around his waist. Though playing a risky game himself, Dante suspected the Aeternal played one of his own. He figured the crafty Cerberus wanted to gather Blood Coven descendants to open the portals so Scath breeds could enslave mankind.

Dante's need was quite different. A slight smile curled his lips as he considered his artfully crafted ruse. He would go along with the hubristic man to fulfill his own goals, hiding his true motives while he provided funds and services to his co-conspirator.

Years ago, when his estate, like others in Britain,

had fallen on bad times, he developed new business contacts. He threw in with London's crime bosses, providing them with legitimacy and access to the elite. His profits exceeded his imagination, allowing him to maintain his family home and invest in other properties around the world. His money grew until it rivaled that of kings.

So far, part of Dante's ill-gained lucre funded Cerberus's hunt for the descendants. But most of it went to finance his own projects, ones which would bring down the pompous Aeternal and his entire realm. His own plan was already in motion. He had almost everything he needed from Cerberus.

Chapter Twenty-Eight

"Yes," shouted Logan, bracing his feet on the desk edge, pushing off to send himself flying across the room in his chair. "I've got you. Bastard." His arms shot up in victory.

Jezzi was catching a few well-deserved winks on a cot shoved against the wall. "What? Who?" Still groggy, she rubbed sleep from her eyes and sat up.

"I got him." He spun like a top in the chair, having pulled an all-nighter there.

Giving herself a lazy panther stretch, Jezzi rose. "Got who?"

"TheBigReveal."

"You clever muscle-bound geek." Jezzi threw her arms around his neck, planting a kiss on his mouth, her sleek, leathered body rubbing against him.

The Firebrand computer genius jumped to his feet. He folded his arms around her waist, swinging her in a circle, all the while keeping his lips locked to her luscious, plump ones.

She disconnected. "Okay, big guy. Come up for air so you can park my feet on terra firma. Let's see what you've got."

Logan grabbed her hand, leading her to his computer. He'd been working around the clock chasing the bloggers across the dark web, searching for an identity.

Logan looked at the screen, a grin creeping over his mouth as he craned his neck to stare at Jez.

"You're a genius."

"Hot damn, female. That's so true. Got a call to

make." He tapped his D-chip.

****

Kole's D-chip vibrated with an incoming call. He tapped his wrist. *Yeah?*

He listened. *Shoot straight to the punch line.*

Without bothering to disconnect from Logan's early morning call, Kole stormed from his office, grabbing a confused Dax, who was chatting with Bounty. "I need a vamp."

He never should have allowed Skyler to return to her job at the Alliance. Of course, how would he have stopped her? By professing his undying love? By mating her? Even had he been ready to do that, and he definitely wasn't, he doubted she would have stayed. She was headstrong. Stubborn. Perfect.

They raced to the stronghold's portal, through the alley to Skyler's condo, and into the lobby. Kole glanced at Dax. "Whammy the security guy so we can get up to the CLO's place."

Dax seized the guy's mind, wiping their visit from it. They rode up in the elevator. Outside her condo, an Alliance agent was out on the floor. Dead.

Kole splintered the door when he burst into the living room, Dax on his six. They halted. A jittery man had a gun pressed to Skyler's temple.

"Don't move. Don't even twitch or I'll shoot her. I promise I will." They guy's eyes were wild, jumpy like the tic in his cheek. "You must be Cal."

He nodded.

"Cal, I'm gonna walk out of here with her." He inched toward Skyler. "How're you doing, Frisca?" Kole was controlled, his fiery gaze fixed on the gunman's eyes. The eyes always indicated what the body was about to do.

"I'm okay." She tilted her chin, her voice calm.

"Can't let you leave here, Cal." Kole's words came out in a low rumble, the rage building inside him. All the while, he glared at the nervous man. Any wrong move could result in a bullet to Skyler's brain. He had to keep his fire at bay. He had to protect his female.

"Why are you doing this?" asked Skyler.

Cal tapped the barrel against her temple. "You know. Of course, I didn't think you'd get company. But it is what it is. Let's just go with the flow."

Kole realized from the human's high pitched, wobbly voice he was teetering on the edge of crazy. Maybe he had already fallen off. "What did Skyler do to you?"

"What did she do?" His voice was almost a squeal. "What didn't she do? I should have been chief legal officer. Since my father's on the board, he let slip the job was practically mine. Though I'd been at the Alliance longer than Skyler, the Maxwells conspired to steal my title. Next you know, she's chief and I'm her errand boy."

"The board offered me the position when my father died. I wasn't about to turn it down, Cal. I worked hard for it, too, but I never took anything away from you. The Alliance values your skills."

"You lie. You stole it from under me." He waved the gun wildly before returning the tip of the barrel to Skyler's temple.

"Easy there, son. We can work this out. Skyler's going with me to Scath. In fact, she doesn't want the job anymore. It's yours." As he spoke, Kole creeped forward, stealthy despite being a big male.

"Like that's possible now. Do you think I'm stupid? She should have died on the L track. She shouldn't have had Sarah look into TheBigReveal. I liked Siri. It was Skyler's fault I had to kill her. I faked your father's trip to Darque. It's such a dangerous place, I thought she might get killed there. At least, the side trip would give me time to come up with another plan." Spittle flew from Cal's mouth as he ranted.

"Nobody at the Alliance needs to know about this, son. Besides, what will you do with her once you get outside?" Kole slid closer.

"I haven't thought that far. Things were not supposed to be this way. I was counting on a fatal accident on Darque, especially when we didn't hear from you for so long." Cal tapped her temple with the barrel.

With each tap, Kole cringed. "What's Arisen Dawn?" he asked, wondering if Cal was working with them. Whoever they were. The captive demons hadn't spilled anything. When he nodded at Dax, the vampire moved into a better position.

"Never heard of it."

Cal's gun hand shook as he waved the weapon around again. "Skyler and I are leaving. I need time to think. If you don't let us pass, I'll shoot her. I will."

Kole signaled Dax with a dip of his chin. The vampire sprang so fast he was a blur. Behind Cal, he grabbed the gun by the barrel. As the weapon swung away from Skyler's head, Cal's finger tightened on the trigger.

But Dax stopped any potential blast from the barrel. He twisted it from Cal's hand and broke the guy's neck with ease. Letting the body slide to the floor, he snarled, kicking it aside.

Kole rushed to Skyler, who stood frozen like a block of ice. He wrapped his arms around her.

She snuggled into his chest, mumbling, "I can't believe it was Cal. At least, it's over."

Kole unraveled the fancy knot low on Skyler's head, his fingers stroking through her loose hair. He was fairly sure she was wrong. Cal had not hired Aeternals to attack Skyler's office or Dermott and his cohorts to take her out on Darque. Her problems were not over.

****

Kole ordered Dax to return to Scath. Once the door closed, he waited until Skyler stopped trembling before he released her. He eyed the great room. Sleek, modern, sophisticated—cool. Boring colors. But he was no decorator. "This place looks like you."

Skyler wiggled out of his embrace. "Cold, you mean?"

His eyes narrowed, fixing on the bright red pillows lining the long beige sofa. "Not completely frosty." He sized her up from head to toes. "How are you doing?"

Before answering, she snagged her cellphone, punched in a number, and connected with the Alliance. Skyler spelled out what had happened before she ordered a clean-up crew. She was about to cancel a new security team when Kole signaled to hold. "What?" Her gaze flipped to Cal's body on the floor. "My would-be killer's dead."

"About that. I'm not so sure." Kole explained his suspicions.

Skyler wasn't rattled. She placed a palm over the phone's speaker, drawing her shoulders straighter, wrapping herself in her usual icy demeanor. So cold, a big gulp of hot coffee wouldn't melt her. "The agent in the hall was new. Seemed like a nice guy. I'll ask for two replacement guards. I'll be fine."

"Yeah, that'll work. The dead guy outside your door did a bang-up job. Didn't the techie from your office have an agent protecting her? Fucking lot of good he did." Kole snarled thinking about anyone but himself safeguarding Skyler.

Skyler fired a glare. "The agent didn't stay with Sarah once she settled in for the night. Also, we didn't suspect Cal. So, obviously, the guard outside my door was taken by surprise. Two agents will work out fine."

Kole waited while Skyler relayed his concerns to the Alliance, ordering another protection detail.

She disconnected. "Ready for coffee?"

"No fancy shit. No espresso caramel frothy thing."

She smiled. "Strong and black. Got it. I've even got a big manly mug."

"Great. Pour me some." He circled the room, looking for the most comfortable piece of furniture. He finally decided on the low beige sofa with the colorful pillows. When he settled on it, his knees stuck up at an awkward angle.

Skyler returned with a tray, two giant cups, and a pot filled with steaming coffee. She paused to stare. "You look like a lion in a small kitty's cage." Setting the load on a glass table, she parked herself beside Kole. "I need to buy a new couch."

"So, I'm invited back?"

"You are."

She poured coffee into one mug, passing it to Kole. After she filled hers, she molded her hands around it as if she were cold.

Cup in hand, Kole leaned against the pillows, straightening his legs as far as the low table in front of the sofa allowed. "I'm uncomfortable with you here and me there." He inhaled the flavor of the brew, pressed his lips to the rim, and swallowed. "Perfect."

"I'm not an idiot, Kole."

He gulped another mouthful of the dark blend. "No. You're not. But you are a trouble magnet. Your guards will not only stay the night, but they'll be on your ass until you're at the office? You'll have them shadow you home again at the end of the day."

He needed to tamp down this over-protectiveness. He didn't like the feeling. He didn't want the feeling. He growled.

"Did you say something?" she asked.

"Nothing."

"What will you do now?" Skyler crossed a shapely leg, her skirt rucking above her knee. "Any more tours in your future?"

Kole snorted. "No. I think I'm off tour duty forever. I'll just be a commander. It's a better fit for my skills anyway. The push is on to find Cerberus along with Blood Coven descendants. We'll keep looking into this Arisen Dawn. See what their story is. What's on your platter?"

"Catching up on my work. There will be added problems managing the office in the wake of Cal's betrayal. Nothing too exciting. I hope."

"You watch yourself." When the conversation lagged, Kole threw back the last of the now-cold coffee before he rose. "I'll be going. Stay safe." He swallowed a keep-in-touch comment. A clean break was best. *Hell.* She had a fiancé and a wedding in her future. He had blood and war.

He opened the door. Snapped it shut. Leaving Skyler was more difficult than he expected. He paused in the hallway.

Kole listened to the deadbolt engage. He jiggled the knob. It didn't budge.

Good girl.

Instead of walking away, he swallowed a gulp of stupid. "Skyler, let me in."

He could tell she was close on the other side. "I think that's a bad idea, Kole."

"Frisca, you better open this door now."

Silence.

"Answer me."

"No."

Two Alliance agents stepped out of the elevator and strode toward Kole. All threatening like. The shorter one asked, "Is there a problem, Commander?"

"Nothing that's any of your business. My advice? Back off while the chief and I solve our own problems."

They looked at each another but seemed to catch the drift of what was going on. Grinning, the female agent said, "Understood."

Kole's attention returned to his crazy mission, which he decided not to overthink. "Frisca, I advise you to move aside or open the door." When there was still no response, Kole stepped a few feet away, preparing to slam his size fifteens into the slab of wood, sending it flying against the wall.

He heard the bolt slide and the door snick open.

Smart female.

"Kole?"

"Skyler?" He sauntered inside. "You haven't had too many Blue Legends. You haven't drowned in erotic oils. You aren't under the influence of my healing."

"All true, Commander." She took small steps backward, but her usual frosty eyes were smoldering hot.

The corner of Kole's lips quirked into a grin. Once he made sure to close the door, his pants got very tight. He prowled forward, sweeping one powerful arm around Skyler's waist and lifting her off the ground. Instead of struggling, she hiked her skirt and wound her legs around him. He knocked over the coffee table in his eagerness to get to the nearest wall.

When he slammed her against it, his mouth crushed hers. He forced his way inside. He moaned when she sucked vigorously on his tongue. Both hands gripped her ass while he moved her rhythmically against his aching cock.

Breaking from the kiss, Skyler tore at the blade harness which prevented her from ripping off his tee.

Kole dropped her feet to the floor. Stepping away, he unstrapped. Flinging his weapons across the room, he knocked over a lamp. When he pressed against Skyler again, she drew his shirt over his head.

Once his flesh was bared, she fumbled with her buttons while Kole returned to ravage her mouth, his swollen erection grinding against her stomach.

Skyler struggled with her blouse.

"Ah, hell." Kole ripped it open. With a sharp inhale at the sight of her, he tore off her bra, exposing her breasts. "There. Better."

Pressing a rough palm onto one flawless mound, he squeezed, pinching her nipple. She gasped when he bent, drawing the hard nub into his mouth. He sucked as Skyler arched into his assault. Wrapping an arm behind her, Kole savored her flavor while she wriggled tighter against him.

Deep, guttural sounds arose from his throat when he filled his hand with her other breast. He proceeded to give it equal attention, nipping and laving it until the nipple was a hard point. Removing his lips, he set his fire-gold stare on Skyler.

He was at war with himself. He wanted to go slow, to draw out the pleasure of touching her, but he also wanted hard and fast. He'd waited so long to bury himself inside her.

As if she understood his agony, Skyler tugged down Kole's zipper until he was free, his pants at his knees. Her hand curled around his swollen, eager cock.

"You keep that up, Frisca, and I'm going to spill

right now. I want to come while I'm deep in your wet, hot cunt."

Her voice was husky. "Then what are you waiting for?"

"Take off the rest of your clothes before I rip them off."

Skyler's hands shook when she unzipped her skirt, letting it pool on the floor. She stood in front of Kole in red thong panties and long, lithe legs.

Kole swallowed hard, his eyes round-tripping her body. "Damn, female. Underneath the wrappings, you're all fire."

"Do you want to take these off me or should I remove them?" Her lips curved into a teasing grin while she tucked her thumbs into the elastic band of her panties.

Kole responded by ripping off the thin strip of material in one swipe of his demon claws.

Drawing her to him, he nudged a finger into her sex. When it was wet, he pulled it out, put it to his lips, and licked it clean. "Hot. Juicy. For me?"

"Uh-huh." She was breathless.

He explored her with two fingers, driving them in and out, each moan from Skyler making him increase the rhythm.

"Kole." She hesitated as if she were choosing her words. "Feed me."

Damned if she didn't say the right ones. She used his favorite demon expression. He lost all reason, withdrawing his fingers. With Skyler pressed against the wall, he lifted her, cradling her ass in his rough hands. He captured her mouth as the tip of his cock prod her wet, hot pussy.

Perfect. More.

He tilted his hips, pushing inside.

Skyler stroked his arms, groaning. "Yes."

He drew back, shoved in, drew out, pushed in.

She gasped, her nails clawing at his biceps.

Her pleasured sounds broke the last bit of his control. With his eyes fixed on hers, Kole drove into her, balls deep. He held still, enjoying the feel of Skyler's greedy, tight sheath gripping his dick.

"Kole," she screamed.

He took possession of her mouth again, his kiss gentle as he withdrew and glided back in, letting her feel every inch of his swollen need.

She moaned softly, rocking against him, forcing him deeper.

His desire to possess a female had never been so strong. She was wet for him. She was his. He punched in and out, harder and faster until they were both frantic, until they were both pumping their hips. All reason lost. No gentleness. The beast wanted to devour Skyler.

His.

Kole pistoned forward. Backward. When he felt on the brink of an orgasm, he reached between their bodies to find her swollen clit. He stroked it with a rough finger. He pinched it. "Come, Frisca. Come hard for me." His balls drew up tight. "Damn, female. You're milking my cock. I'm not going to last."

Skyler shivered, her release building. She bucked against him as if unable to get enough of him, fast enough, or hard enough. He sent a small shock of electric energy coursing into her.

She came, shouting Kole's name as he had imagined. With the sound of her voice, he exploded, his climax a blaze that grew into an inferno. His seed spilled and spilled. Long and seemingly unending.

Inside this human was the home Kole had longed for since he had been ten. She was his. Whether she knew it or not. Whether he accepted it or not.

Remaining still, he held onto Skyler's limp body, his eyes closed, his breathing ragged. When her legs quivered, he slipped out of her warmth, gentling her feet to the floor.

Heavy lids partially masked her lilac-blue gaze. Her lips curled into a sweet smile.

"We're not nearly through, Frisca." He hitched up his pants until they hung from his hips, his still hard dick jutting out.

She whispered, "I ... I..."

"You what?"

"I think I've melted."

"You better show me where your bedroom is, or we'll try out the floor next."

Skyler swallowed. She rasped as she took his large hand, "This way."

Kole followed a wobbly Skyler down the hallway, her nice ass swaying.

Chapter Twenty-Nine

A young, wide-eyed waitress approached Braelyn and Rein's table at the diner as they waited for Miller Nash. She wiggled her peasant blouse further down, exposing more shoulder, flipped her blonde ponytail from side to side, and cast a toothy grin at Rein. "What can I get for you?"

Braelyn answered despite not being the girl's focus of attention. "I'll have a Caesar salad and a bite of his fries and hamburger."

The waitress wrote down the order without so much as a glance in Braelyn's direction. "Uh-huh. And what do you want, honey?" She arched her back enough to pouf out her already sizable boobs.

"I assume I'm having the unhealthy burger and fries. Two waters, please."

The blonde minx twirled a strand of loose hair around her finger while she continued to ogle Rein.

Braelyn snapped her fingers, her eyebrows scrunched. "You can place our order now."

Giving Rein one last ear-to-ear smile, the waitress turned, tossed her ponytail again, and sashayed away. Braelyn pinched his bicep. "Stop making her go weak in the knees."

A wicked grin twisted her mate's lips. "You're the only female I intend to make wobbly in the knees."

Grabbing her hand, he sucked a finger into his mouth, sliding it in and out until Braelyn shivered. "You think I'm so easy, Firebrand?"

"Yes, but I'm willing to put in a little work, too."

"You're arrogant."

"I thought we already agreed on that." Rein moved his palm from where it rested on Braelyn's thigh, sliding it between her legs.

Slapping his hand away, she gasped. "You can't touch my you-know-what in a restaurant."

Chuckling, Rein pressed her hand to his crotch. "You can touch my you-know-what anywhere, anytime."

Braelyn felt the bulge in his pants. She had to admit it was tempting. "You've got a hard-on," she whispered.

"Yeah, you have to help me get rid of it."

"I already got rid of it once this morning. Or was it twice? What would you like me to do now?"

Rein nuzzled into her neck, whispering his desires. Braelyn raised her brows as the waitress brought their food to the table. When she licked her lips, it wasn't because she was hungry for salad.

****

Miller watched from a stool at the counter.

Holy shit. The guy she's with is as big as a two-decker bus. She wasn't kidding.

Miller had scoped out the front of the diner where he spotted another big-ass guy guarding the main entrance. Patrolling in the rear was a long-haired bloke, unsuccessfully trying to hide his menacing presence with a baseball cap pulled low over his eyes.

Leaving money on the counter, Miller grabbed his coffee cup. He sauntered over to Braelyn and Rein, sliding into the booth across from them. "Braelyn. Braelyn. Tsk. Tsk. I told you to bring only your husband."

Rein put his hand on her arm. "My fault. My female goes nowhere without a shitload of muscle. She told you she'd been kidnapped. Not an attempt like with you. They got her. Never happening again."

Miller stared a while. He understood paranoia, being riddled with it himself. "Why did they want you?"

Braelyn leaned across the table so she could speak softly. "A vampire named Silas rounded up human descendants of witches and warlocks. He kept us in cells until he took a blood sample to test for another relationship."

"Yeah. What relationship?"

She looked at Rein, who nodded. "He was testing to see if we were descendants of the Blood Coven. He sold those who weren't. We don't know if he found any. He's dead."

"Why was he looking for Blood Coven offspring?"

Rein tapped his fingers on the table. "We think he was working for a male called Cerberus, but we don't grasp this psycho's real identity. You say your ancestor is Masoud?"

"Yeah. He was one of the thirteen mages of the Blood Coven who created the Schism during which Scath and Darque emerged."

Braelyn and Rein exchanged glances. Miller propped his elbows on the table and rested his chin on his hands, debating how much information to give these two strangers. Could he trust them? Did he believe them? Maybe, but right now, he needed the money. Later he would investigate this couple a little more. "I think I met the criteria for proof. Hand over the $50,000 from the paper."

Braelyn nodded, passing Miller a large envelope. He opened it, examining the contents before he slipped it into an oversized pocket inside his jacket.

"What do you have to do with all this?" he asked Rein.

"In addition to being Braelyn's … uh … husband,

I'm a Scion Firebrand."

"What's that, mate?"

"You can spout off about the Schism, but you're unaware of the Firebrands?"

"Aeternals went to Scath. Wildings to Darque. After the Schism, I'm ignorant of any history in your realms. The coven along with its kin remained on Earth."

"Your family must have kept excellent records if you're on a first-name basis with Masoud. Do you know the others in the famous coven?" asked Rein.

Back to the dilemma. How much intel should he share with these two? The name Cerberus was not a good sign. It was linked to the Prophecy of Karma.

Braelyn leaned across the table. "Miller, for your own safety, come with us to Scath. We can protect you at the Firebrand stronghold. We're gathering the descendants of the Blood Coven there as we find them. We must locate them before Cerberus does. While Cerberus's purpose remains a secret, we know it can't be good. The guys he hires are dangerous."

"How many descendants have you found so far?"

"Three. You make four. Our process is slow."

Miller nodded. "Who are they?"

Braelyn shook her head. "We'll share when you share."

Miller planned to check in with his people. He had been out of touch a bit since his near kidnapping. Which of their charges was missing? How did he contact his blokes and not bring the bad guys down on them? And he had to make sure Braelyn and Rein were the good guys. Of course, he already knew Braelyn was Blood Coven like himself. He had checked. Raymond had verified she was on his list. That didn't necessarily make her a good guy, though. Also, what else did this couple know? He would just drop a hint. "Have you heard of *Custodes Templii*?" Miller watched their mouths pop open as if he had dropped a bombshell.

Rein's eyes narrowed. "They exist?" Bounty had fielded the call from Alarik where he passed on what he had learned of the secret society.

Miller settled his coffee mug on the table. "Too much to drink. I'll be right back." He slid out of the booth to saunter toward the men's restroom.

****

Rein watched Nash leave the table. The bathroom door closed behind him. For a human, the guy radiated pure menace. No wonder he escaped capture. His kidnappers were probably caught off guard, never expecting trained resistance.

"What do you think?" asked Braelyn.

"I think he's more than meets the eye."

"Hmm. I think so, too. His shoulders carry a heavy burden. It's more than his personal predicament. He knows more than he's saying."

Rein tapped his fingers on the table. "Okay, no male takes that long in the john unless he's banging a chick."

"Are you speaking from experience?"

"Uh. No. Chay flapped his lips a lot on stakeouts. Sex was a favorite topic. I'm going after this guy."

Braelyn stood so he could slip out of the booth.

Rein pushed the door so hard it hit the wall and flew back into his hand. Powering inside, he swept his gaze around the small bathroom. He checked under the stalls. He already knew from an earlier surveillance the window was too small for an escape. The only thing left was a locked door marked "Janitor Closet." He clasped the knob, broke it off, and yanked the door open. Standard shit. Mops, buckets, cleaning rags. When he flat-handed the back wall, it gave way.

Stairs.

Rein took the steps two at a time, able to see clearly in the dark thanks to vamp DNA. Three tunnels branched out at the foot of the stairs. "Fuck me."

****

Skyler laughed when Kole grabbed her from behind, sweeping her off her feet. With her in his arms, he strode into the bedroom where he tossed her onto the expensive Frette duvet cover.

She scooted to the top of the bed, propped against the headboard. She got a good view of the buff commander kicking off his boots, yanking off his socks, stripping his pants down hard, muscular thighs. A male more savage than civilized.

Her pulse quickened when he prowled toward her, his bulging muscles in motion. His eyes were ablaze. He paused at the foot of the bed, tempting and beautiful in his fierce masculinity, proudly displaying his arousal. And he was coming for her. A lump caught in Skyler's throat.

When he crawled onto the mattress, it dipped. Straddling her legs, he gripped his cock, pumping it. Once. Twice. "I'm hard for you."

Skyler licked her lips. "Let me." She wrapped her palm around his shaft. Savoring the sensation of his solid length, she stroked him tip to base. To touch Kole. To have him inside her took her breath away.

How will I let him go? I'm falling in love with this man. No. This demon.

Kole gentled Skyler's hand away. Flipping her over, he lifted her onto her hands and knees. He spread her legs wide before he settled between them. Knocking her arms out from beneath her, he shoved her head against the comforter. Pulling her into the curve of his body, he nudged her entrance.

No foreplay. He slammed his hard length into Skyler's core. "I'm still hungry, Frisca. I can't get enough of you."

She bounced forward with his thrust, her muscles stretching to accommodate his thickness. "Yes. Kole. Nice."

"Nice? There is nothing nice about what I'm going to do to you." He tightened his hands on her hips while he pounded into her.

Skyler was trapped, completely at the mercy of this brutish demon. But she couldn't be happier. She trembled against him, his flesh sliding in. Out.

He pulled back only to slam into her so hard, she bumped against the headboard. She returned the favor, driving against him, moaning his name, loving how he filled her.

"Louder, Frisca. I want to hear you scream. Maybe I should stop." As if to prove a point, he slid out until only the tip of his penis was inside, leaving her empty, cold.

Skyler bucked against him. "Kole, don't you dare. Fuck me. Hard."

He obeyed, slamming deep, filling her, his thick length stroking all the right places.

She kept pace with his rhythm, his rough hands tight on her hips. Skyler panted, wanting more. Needing more.

With an arm forced against the headboard, she rammed backward into Kole's groin.

His hand reached around her, his fingers circling and pinching her clit while he drove into her steadily, impossibly deeper.

But she wanted the demon. "More, Kole."

The arrogant male laughed. "Is this what you want, Frisca?" He shot an electrical impulse across her skin, the first jolt making her cry out in ecstasy.

Frantic, Skyler reared into Kole, begging for another shock of energy. "Again. Please."

"Like this?" He gave her what she wanted.

Skyler screamed. "Yes. Oh, yes. Like that. Again."

Kole ground into her, his cock filling her, his fingers working her, rubbing, urging her to come.

The next pulse sent her floating untethered. Out her condo, above the Chicago skyline. She rose beyond the buildings of the city to the prairies. She flew to the mountains, climbing the snow-capped peaks. She saw oceans and islands dotting the waters. She soared among the clouds. Then, she shot back into her body, begging for a release, begging to be free, to be wild. She shuddered when the orgasm started as a tingle. Building, it ripped through her, consuming her, tethering her to this barbarian demon for all her days.

Kole growled. Sparks flew from his fingers while he shot his sperm into her for the second time today. He roared, an arm clutch under her breasts, pulling her tight against him, his pleasure continuing to pour into her.

They held silent for minutes, only their hearts beating, his unsteady breath on her neck. Kole on his knees, Skyler snug against his groin, they enjoyed the aftereffects of mutual pleasure. When he pulled out, Skyler sensed a sudden loss of something special.

She fell forward onto the bed, groaning, stretching while Kole rolled off to the side, looking content but still hard. *Damn.* The demon was still hungry.

Before she recovered from the last bout, he grabbed Skyler and rolled her on top, setting her on his thighs. "Ride me, Frisca. My balls still ache. I can't get enough of you."

Skyler rose onto her knees and guided him into her sweet spot, lowering herself inch by inch. She let out a long, pleasurable sigh until he was buried inside, stretching her.

Kole's hands grasped her hips while he undulated beneath her. His red, fiery beast flickered as he released an electric impulse.

Skyler's eyes widened, a gasp on her lips. "Yes, please."

"You like that, Frisca?"

"Yes, Kole, I like that."

Her palms pressed on his chest. She arched her spine, delighting in his thick shaft pulsing inside her. He shifted her up and down, faster and faster, sending himself deeper, sparking every nerve. Skyler dragged her nails down Kole's abs, drawing blood. Her breasts bounced until his hands cupped them, squeezing, pinching, and tugging on her nipples.

When Kole thrust harder into her, he sent electric impulses surging through her until she couldn't hold out any longer. This time, a gentler, warmer orgasm fluttered from her toes to the top of her head.

The demon roared his release.

Skyler didn't care if the entire building heard him. She had never been so thoroughly possessed. So loved.

Kole rolled her to his side, tucking an arm around her, his boyish lopsided grin making her smile. "I could get used to you, Chief."

Skyler stared at Kole's thick length. He was still aroused. "Is your penis always hard, demon?" Her gaze stayed on him while her tongue flicked across her lips.

"No, Frisca. Only with you."

After a few moments, Skyler sat up. She trailed her fingers softly along the firm planes of Kole's chest, seeing her scratches on his abs. Marks of ownership. Pleased, she rose from bed, sauntering toward the hallway door.

Kole rested on his crooked arm. "Nice ass, female."

Skyler wiggled it, glancing over her shoulder at her demon. "I thought we needed a beer. I need to replenish my weak human stamina."

"Sexy and thoughtful. Great combination. Don't bring me one of those craft brews or anything lite." He flung his head back onto the mattress. "Holy Gahya. You drained me, Frisca."

When she returned, Skyler handed Kole a Bud before she scooted into bed. She set her bottle on the table after taking a sip. As she leaned against the headboard, her possessive fingers traced the hills and valleys of his abs. "Nice." She bit back a delusional thought. *Mine.*

She could swear he muttered the same word, the same mistaken thought. She swallowed a gulp of Bud. Surely not.

****

After two more bouts of lovemaking followed by cold Buds, Kole lay on his back, his arms tucked under his head. His demon had never been so fully sated, calm, or proud.

Skyler faced him, her cheek resting in the palm of her hand, propped up on her elbow. When she brushed her fingers along his bicep, the Phoenix brand twitched, ruffling its feathers.

Skyler drew away. "We can't keep this up, right?"

"I don't know about you, but I can keep this up for days." Kole's lips quirked into a confident smile.

"Don't twist what I say. You've established your

prowess. I mean we aren't a good match. Right?" She held her breath, unsure if she wanted him to agree or disagree.

Now Kole rose onto his elbow, pinning Skyler with a hot gaze. "I can't keep my hands off you, and you love everything about me."

"Everything?"

Kole pointed to his cock, which swelled when Skyler flicked barely a glance at it. "Everything. Some things more than others."

Skyler laughed as seconds stretched into minutes until she spoke again. "I'm not easy."

"I know, Frisca."

"I have a job I love. I work grueling hours."

"Yep. And all demons don't like their females working."

Skyler raised a brow. "What?"

"My breed's an old-fashioned lot. A male dominant society."

"I seriously doubt even your misogynistic demons expect women to be totally subservient anymore."

"Don't doubt it."

"Hmm. That's a problem. Of course, we're different species. You will outlive me by centuries."

The smile evaporated from his face, but before he could respond, he jumped out of bed and tapped his wrist. "I have to take this. Hold those thoughts."

He stepped out of the bedroom to answer the call. When he returned, Skyler was sound asleep, her white-blonde hair splayed across her pillow. He slapped a hand to his stuttering heart.

Kole leaned down, caressing the soft skin of her cheek with a fingertip. She hadn't brought up the fiancé yet. Another problem. Maybe a demon was just a one-time walk on the wild side. Not to be repeated. Of course, she was right about her job. But he had his, too. He put in equally long hours and faced danger to boot. Natch, she had targeted the biggest obstacle. Skyler would die long before he did. Another loved one to leave him, to abandon him to loneliness. Just as he was getting comfortable with it. Besides, she didn't seem too thrilled about being together.

I need to return to Scath before I do something stupid like ask her to move in with me or mate. Neither of us is ready for that. Hell, maybe we'll never be ready. I don't think I can handle being left alone, being left behind again. Better a clean break.

Still … Skyler was the first female Kole had ever imagined himself being tied to. Go figure. The frosty CLO of the Alliance and an animus demon with a hot temper. They made no sense together.

He stared at her sleeping body, her pale skin, her luscious curves and perfect breasts. Getting dressed, he crept out of the bedroom. He hesitated before exiting her apartment forever. He couldn't walk out with no explanation. She deserved better than an asshole move like that.

Spying a notepad with a pen near the phone, he started to write. Four notes later, all crumpled up and thrown into the trash, he left. Words weren't his gig. Besides, how could he say goodbye? Sense or no sense, he was not through with the sizzling hot chief legal officer. And he had an invite back to her condo.

Chapter Thirty

The next morning, Skyler awoke, stretching her arms above her head. She touched her fingers to her warm cheeks, remembering last night's shared passion. The corners of her lips lifted as she recalled Kole's unrelenting desires. She might not have dreamed he was the man for her, but he owned her heart. Somewhere between his walking into her office the first day and her condo yesterday, she had fallen hard for the brutish, hulking Firebrand commander.

Skyler patted Kole's side of the bed. Empty. She listened but didn't hear any sounds from the bathroom. Rising, she slipped into her robe, tying the sash.

"Hmm." Skyler winced, a little sore in certain places. But she was whole, satisfied, appreciated. She padded on bare feet into the great room. Kole wasn't there either. The kitchen was quiet as was the rest of the condo. She checked her cellphone. No voicemail.

The demon had vanished after what she thought had been a spectacular night of lovemaking. She had fallen asleep with so much left unsaid. About Winston. Why had she continued to let Kole believe she was engaged? Maybe because the bigger-than-life demon had overwhelmed her from the start. Her fictitious fiancé had been a shield. She also had planned to tell Kole how, despite all the obstacles, she was falling in love with him.

No goodbye. No message to say he'll call. Not even an empty promise of don't call me. I'll call you.

Crumpled paper in the trashcan caught her eye. She took out four notes and smoothed them flat.

One read, "I don't know how to…" The words

were scratched out.

The next one said, "You're right. We can't keep this up." He had drawn a line through this sentence, too.

The other note consisted of more crossed out words. The last one had only one word, "Goodbye."

Skyler palmed her chest above her heart, drawing a deep breath. Pain. Hurt. Emptiness. She was inexperienced compared with Kole. An animus demon like him thrived on sex. He needed it to survive. Maybe for him, last night was just another roll in the hay, and she was just another…

A meal on two heels. Or what would Anna say? Fuck buddy.

Wrapping her arms around her waist, she willed tears not to fall. This was why a relationship built on common interests, respect, and appreciation of each other's profession was best. This was why passion was not the best emotion to judge the success of a committed relationship. Not buying the hard sell, her heart still ached. And she felt empty not seeing his lopsided, cocky grin and stubborn jaw. Suddenly, she realized a truth.

I don't want safe, boring. I want Kole.

She busied herself pouring water into her Keurig and popping in a coffee pod. Dark roast.

He was uncultured, unrefined, and definitely not a man she would have taken home to introduce to her father. He was totally not her type.

But I survived an unloving father. I studied hard to finish school. I bought this condo with my own money. I got the job I wanted. I'll damn well get the demon I want.

But anger curled its fingers around her heart when she remembered his rejection.

With a cup of coffee in her hand, Skyler picked out a professional suit and heels for the day ahead. The office would be in shock about Cal. She would tend to business today and call Kole tonight. She was determined to make him see how perfect she was for him. Despite the obstacles.

****

Kole had caught up on all the happenings at the stronghold. Margo. Nico. But nothing mattered except Skyler. How many times had he picked up the phone to call her? And now this.

"I knew it," he said. Skyler's eyes. More lilac than blue. It all made sense now. Kole shot up from his desk, going toe-to-toe with Alarik. "How the hell did you miss this?"

Alarik stood his ground, not backing away. "We didn't miss it. My healer assumed her blood test wasn't a priority. Chief Maxwell told him her ancestry wasn't mage. He feels terrible."

"He should. This is a nightmare." Kole's temper surged. Skyler had a bullseye on her back. The attack on her office. Dermott and his demon choir. It all made sense now. The illusive Cerberus was hunting for her.

"I am not one of your warriors. Lower your voice when you speak to me, Commander?"

"Or what?" Kole, his body quivering with an excess of electric energy, bumped his chest against Alarik.

The director chuckled. "I am a seasoned warlock, not some young mage fresh from training."

Kole juggled a fireball from hand to hand, enraged. "Fuck you and fuck your ministry's incompetence." He lobbed the blazing orb at the director.

Alarik flicked his wrist. The fireball disappeared midair. "Kole, we can do this all day. Get ahold of yourself. We need to bring her in, not place blame. It's my fault. Okay? Satisfied?"

Cal hadn't been the only threat to Skyler. The furious Kole took slow, deep breaths, checking his anger. *Hell.* She could already be in Cerberus's hands. Look what had happened to Rein's mate. They'd kidnapped her, almost selling Braelyn as a sex slave. What would they do to a bona fide descendant? Kole had never been the target on Darque. It was Skyler.

Doing an animus demon's version of hyperventilating, Kole's beast flickered, the crimson, blazing manifestation fading as quickly as it formed.

Slow your breathing.

Kole exhaled. Inhaled. Despite the self-talk, fire consumed him again when he pictured Skyler at the mercy of savage Aeternals. He drew back his fist and punched the wall, driving through it elbow-deep.

Alarik approached cautiously. "Relax." The warlock-incubus director lifted a hand.

Kole felt a shiver as a calming spell washed through him. Though less agitated, he yelled out the door to Bounty. "Tell Rein to haul ass up here and get my Firebrands battle ready. Now."

In seconds, Rein pushed through the door, flicked his gaze from Alarik to Kole, and eyed the hole in the wall. "Nice. You want me to sheetrock the place?"

Kole snarled. "You're in charge, smartass. Skyler is Blood Coven. Your father's incompetent ministry back-shelfed her sample. They just analyzed it. Surprise."

"To be fair," defended Alarik, "the Alliance chief legal officer said her heritage was more recent than the Karmic Schism and was not mage. The healer took her at her word. He moved on to more pressing priorities."

"Since when do on-the-ball scientists take someone else's word?" Kole's digits lit up like tiki torches as his voice rose to a thundering pitch. As some sanity returned, he touched his fingertips together, dousing the flames.

"I know you're…"

Kole interrupted. "Alarik, Skyler dreamed about Dermott camped near the cave about to attack." He scrubbed a fist across his buzz-cut hair. "I just remembered. She also dreamed about Chay and Margo." Kole paused to glare at Alarik. "Not a coincidence."

Clearly unintimidated by Kole, Alarik said, "She's a scryer of some kind. Amazing, though. It takes witches and warlocks hundreds of years to develop or manage this craft. What does she use as a medium?"

"What do you mean?" asked Kole.

"Crystal ball, water, mist, mirror, smoke, something else?"

"How would I know? Nothing."

"Hmm. Highly unusual. A witch who can call up visions without a medium is strong indeed. She had to draw power to feed the spell. Did she use you?"

"Don't know. Don't give a shit right now. Feel me?"

Bounty interrupted. "Your Firebrands are assembled in the ready room. They're armed and psyched to go. I filled them in a bit."

Kole loaded blades into his chest harness. "Rein, don't fuck up my office." He poked Alarik on the shoulder with the blunt end of the axe he snagged. "You better hope she's in great shape when we get to the Alliance's headquarters." He jabbed the warlock one more time for emphasis.

Alarik sighed, flicking the weapon off his shoulder.

****

• Kole exited the Alliance's gateway behind Dax and Brak. His jaw set and his eyes hawk-like, he shook off the usual fog which accompanied portaling to Earth. The Whorl did a number on him. His ears buzzed. His stomach flipped. "Let me out of here. Hate to travel that way. Demons aren't meant to have their molecules scattered to the winds."

• The two Firebrands gave the irate commander plenty of space. Dax's long black hair shimmered with static charge, and his dark eyes narrowed as they sized up the arrival room.

• One Firebrand after another exited the Whorl. Ram's head pivoted as he surveyed the arrival space as the vamp had done. He snatched a tactical sword from his back scabbard. Chay withdrew his war hammer.

Brak high-fived the ylve when he appeared. "Wow! What a fucking great ride. Right? Can't ever get enough. I could bounce back and forth all day."

Chay nodded, his grin toothy when it spread across his face.

Kole eyed the young carnal demon, amazed the crazy warrior had survived this long. "You're an anomaly among the breed."

Brak grinned. "Thanks, Comm."

Dax drew his jungle bolo from its sheath, peering into the hallway. He signaled the all-clear.

"Not a compliment." Kole pushed the Firebrand aside to step through the doorway, thundering along the corridor toward Skyler's office. Sabine followed, tapping the hilt of her straight-bladed Arkansas toothpick which hung from her hip. Tyr shook his hands, loosening them, prepared to cast spells if he ran into trouble. Checking her battle axe tucked into her belt, Galena brought up the rear.

The heavily armed warriors exploded through the office door and past the reception area, their boots thudding on the tiles. Anna spun around, eyes wide. The Firebrands fanned out behind their commander instantly, charging the air with danger. The admin assistant's hand flew to her mouth, too late to stifle the scream. When she recognized Kole, her breath came out as a *pfft* while her shoulders relaxed.

Clicking heels brought Laurie on a run from the copy room. "Holy shit." She sized up the kitted-out Scion Firebrands. "Uh-oh. Our agents are about to come through the door. I pushed the panic button. Sorry, guys. Didn't know it was you."

"Got 'em, Comm." Chay rushed back into the corridor to head off the human security force.

Skyler flung open her office door, a gun in one hand, a cellphone to her ear in the other. "What the hell? Wait a minute, Agent Markham." She glared when she saw Kole. "Stand down. It's the demon Firebrand Commander."

She disconnected from the call, sliding the phone into a jacket pocket. "Kole, I mean, Commander, is there a problem?"

"Hell, yes, there's a problem." He barreled toward Skyler. In two long strides, he grabbed her upper arm, roughly pivoted her around, and marched her back into her office.

Bam.

The room shook when he slammed the door.

****

Skyler shook her arm loose from Kole's grip. "What the hell? You storm in here like an invading army. These are my offices. You have no right. What's going on?"

Get mad. He walked out on me. Wham-bam. No thank-you-ma'am. Nonetheless, her betraying heart had pounded against her chest the minute she spotted the fire-gold eyes and hard-muscled frame barreling toward her, looking every bit the barbarian he was.

"You need to sit. Hell, I gotta sit." Kole flopped onto the sofa, legs spread out and head back. "Sit, I said."

Skyler hung over him with her arms crossed. Though he patted the cushion alongside him, she ignored the invitation. Instead, she slipped into her office chair. Propped up by her elbows on the desk, she rested her chin in the palms of her hands. The best move was to stay far away from the demon with his appealing body. "Ready. Now what? Have your say. Afterward, get out of here unless… Never mind."

One corner of his mouth curled higher than the other in his sexier-than-hell grin. "Not happening, Frisca. Your life is about to get more interesting."

"How much more interesting can it get? I've been pushed into the path of an oncoming train, had Aeternals raid my office, almost mated a Yeti, been stuck on Darque with you, survived harpies and Dermott, and held at gunpoint by my trusted legal assistant. Did I leave anything out?"

The cocky, arrogant smile returned to his lips. "Mind-blowing sex with an irresistible demon."

Skyler arched a cold brow. "Hmph. You mean the one who couldn't wait to run from my bed?"

"What? I can explain when we have time, Frisca."

"I have no interest in your excuses." Kole eyed her rising and falling chest with definite interest. His fascination with her breasts made her hot. Heat crawled from the toes which peeked out of her new Gucci shoes to her cheeks. And she never blushed. Never. Except around Kole. Surely, she could ignore thoughts of sex for the moment despite the demon's oxygen-sucking presence.

Kole shook his head as if to clear it before he lifted his eyes to hers. "Your blood test came back."

Skyler stiffened her spine.

"Because you said you knew your lineage, some idiot put your sample on the slow road."

"What are you saying?"

"You are one."

"One what? Descendant?"

Kole nodded.

"Not possible."

"Obviously, it is possible."

"Are you saying Abrahm Maxwell was a demon and a warlock?"

"Unlikely. Could have been your mother's side. Maybe another Aeternal in your father's tree. Small world."

Skyler leaned back, drew a deep breath, and let it hiss out past her lips. "So, not only am I the descendant of the despicable renegade who killed your family but also of a Blood Coven mage."

"Yes."

"Shouldn't I show some signs of witchcraft?"

"Ever since you came onto Scath you've shown signs. Your eyes shifted from blue to lilac. So gradually I thought nothing of it. You had nightmares or dreams which proved true. You were right about Dermott, and Chay was imprisoned with a redhead."

Skyler's gaze drifted around the room as she evaluated Kole's message. "But I don't always have these dreams or hallucinations."

"No scryers do. You need training."

Skyler nodded. "Hmm. Why didn't any of my ancestors exhibit powers?"

"We don't know yet. We're thinking Scath might be the catalyst. Maybe your father wasn't on the realm long enough to power up. But we have two descendants at my stronghold now. Margo, the redhead you saw with Chay and your guy, Nico Abello. Your boy's a pain in the ass, by the way."

"Lead Agent Abello's a descendant? He was part of the rescue team who came to your cave. I heard he was on loan to the Firebrands for a while."

"He worked a deal with Rein. Part of why he's an ass-pain. Anyway, we'll go to your place, pack your stuff, and move you into the stronghold."

"Whoa. Slow down. I'm not going anywhere."

"Yes, you are." He rose to his full intimidating height, fists on his hips. "You want the easy way or the hard way?"

Skyler's eyes narrowed. "We aren't doing this any way. I'm the CLO here. I'll say what I'm doing."

"No problem. As long as you say stronghold." Kole leaned forward over Skyler's desk, his fingers pressing the wood, his arm muscles bunching. "Cerberus has shown how desperate he is by kidnapping humans with a drop of mage blood. What would he do with you? A true offspring."

Skyler tightened her lips. "Are you thinking Cerberus hired Dermott and arranged the attack on my office?" When Kole nodded, she continued, "How did he know about me?"

The demon frowned. "We are the only ones who've tested your blood. Right?"

Skyler cocked her head to the side. "Not exactly. When I was pushed from the L platform, I went to the ER where they took a sample."

"Fuck. Fuck. Fuck. That's why. Get up."

"I told you. I'm not leaving. Alliance agents will protect me."

Kole snorted. "Sure they will. They couldn't even

defend you against Cal the weasel." Before she could blink, Kole was around her desk, swooping her onto his shoulder. "The hard way it is."

He locked an arm around Skyler's knees, her straight skirt held down but one Gucci shoe falling to the floor.

Umpff.

Skyler pounded on his back. "Put me down. This is unacceptable. My shoe, Kole."

"Grab it." He crouched, popping upright again after she snagged her missing heel. He threw open the door and marched through with Skyler squirming in his grasp.

"Anna," she shouted, "call agents. Do not let this ape take me out of here."

The commander twisted his head around to glance over his shoulder. His voice was rough. "Don't do it, Anna. She'll call to let you know what's going on later."

The assistant stood by smiling. "I'll wait for your call, boss. Is there anything else I can get you?"

"Yes. Armed agents. A handgun. A large knife. Preferably with an iron blade. Put me down right now, Kole! Commander! Right now! I demand it. I'm your superior."

"Yeah. Yeah. Now would be a good time to zip those gorgeous lips, Frisca." Kole slapped her on the ass.

"Oh! You're going to be sorry." She pounded more vigorously on his back, using the sharp heel of her retrieved shoe as a weapon.

"I'm already sorry. Chay, get to the stronghold. Arrange quarters for my reluctant piece of baggage. In a second-floor guest suite. The rest of you, with us. We'll head to Skyler's house so she can pack."

"I'm not packing."

He touched a finger to one of her legs.

"Ouch." A mild electric shock fired to every nerve ending.

"You know you're happy to come with me. Now, be a nice female and gather your belongings. You can't stay in this skirt and blouse forever. Of course, maybe you can borrow something from a nymph. Some leather pants. One of those short tops to show your belly. It might be a little on the skimpy side. But…"

"You're despicable."

Kole's shoulder bobbed up and down against Skyler's stomach when he chuckled.

****

The commander paced while the other Firebrands occupied themselves with their usual MO, slinging wisecracks.

"Nice space, huh, Comm," said Brak from Skyler's sofa, his knees almost to his chin with a plate teetering on them. "The chief's got some great lunch meats in her fridge. Grab a bite. Ram made sandwiches." He waved a half-eaten one. "This one's salami. Who'd a thunk Ram could make something good to eat."

"I can hear you, and I'm insulted. What do you think I do for food, demon?" Ram yelled his retort in from the kitchen.

"I think you bang a different female every night so she'll fix you dinner."

"Are you kidding? He doesn't stick around long enough to dine on anything other than her arousal," said Galena.

"I'm insulted by the direction of this conversation. I go out of my way to feed all of you and all I get is a kick in the ass. I can slap a bunch of shit onto two slices of bread. You don't hear Dax biting the hand that feeds him."

"Dax says he's surprised, too," said Galena. When the surly black-haired vampire frowned at her, she shrugged.

"Keep me out of this," he growled.

Kole strolled into the kitchen, eying the sandwiches piled on a plate. They did look good. He was hungry, and Skyler was still packing. The Amazon continued to hassle an insulted Ram, each with a sandwich in hand. Dax leaned against the counter near the fridge, also munching on the satyr's edible creation.

Chapter Thirty-One

"Get out of my way." Skyler rammed a shoulder into Sabine, trying to push her away from the closed bedroom door.

The nymph Firebrand was a lot more immoveable than she looked.

"The commander says you're packing. That's what you're gonna do." Sabine cracked the door, peeking into living room where the males waited. She shut it softly. "You know he's just going to make you. Better to do it yourself. Less embarrassing."

Muttering under her breath, Skyler began slamming drawers. Open. Shut. She tossed items into a suitcase. "He can't get away with this."

"He can."

Skyler sank onto the bed.

Blood Coven. Shit.

She was in danger, but she couldn't go to the stronghold where she might see Kole every day. Not after he'd walked out on her. She was in love with him.

There. I said it. Yes, dammit. I'm in love with a demon brute.

Her pride would not allow her to beg the man who had rejected her. She would have to fall out of love.

Still leaning against the door, Sabine let her arms fall to the side in a more relaxed stance. "We're trying to protect you. You're a smart female. Go with it." The nymph scrunched her brows together.

The Firebrand vacated the door, walking across the room to sit beside Skyler. "What else is going on?"

"I can't stay at the stronghold."

"It's the safest place for you. You'll be with other Blood Coven descendants who share a common interest. Namely, staying alive. Something else is bugging you."

"You're quite perceptive, but it's nothing I will share."

"Okay. The cold shoulder. Now, let's keep packing. Pants, tops, nightwear, something fun in case you go out."

The corners of Skyler's mouth turned up slightly. "Go out? I doubt that."

"You never know. Maybe some buff snack candy will catch your eye and ask you on a date. Bring something fun."

The only buff snack candy I know is a stubborn ass demon who deserted me after amazing sex.

Skyler walked to the closet, sighing. Reaching in, she pulled out a simple black dress, waving it at the female now lounging on her bed.

The nymph shook her head.

Skyler gave the dress the once over, frowning. "It's one of my favorites. Why don't you like it?"

"Too plain. How about that one?" Sabine pointed.

"This one?" Skyler pulled out a candy-apple-red dress with a short, flirty skirt and a deep, plunging neckline. Imagining Kole's reaction if she wore it, she pressed a splayed hand to her chest. "I bought this on a whim. I've never worn it, though. It's so…"

"Sexy. Bring it along. You'll have males panting."

Skyler laughed.

A deep voice came from the doorway. "You should definitely bring the red dress along. You look good in the color." Both women twisted toward the speaker. Kole leaned against the jamb.

When did he see me in… The red panties and bra.

Skyler might have been angry with him, but her heart was stupid. It thumped loudly when she thought back to their numerous bouts of hot sex.

Instead of sighing, she snapped a response. "If I had wanted your advice, I would have sought it." In a huff, she jammed the red dress into the closet, snatched up the black one, and folded it into the suitcase. "That's what I think of your opinion."

Kole shrugged. "Don't forget the black nighty or whatever you call it."

Skyler walked to a drawer to pull out a sleek, silky negligee. "This one?"

Kole straightened from his lean. His fingers sparked while he nearly snorted smoke. "Yep."

Sabine's gaze pinged from one to the other.

Skyler's fingers stroked the smooth, expensive fabric until Kole groaned. "Not a chance." Stuffing the negligee she had worn the night of the Genesis Rite into the drawer, she said, "I prefer pajamas." She took out her favorite plaid cotton ones, cramming them into the suitcase.

The brutish commander snarled, his sexy lips twisting up on one corner. He closed the door a little too hard.

Sabine arched her brows, studying Skyler. "Interesting. I didn't know the commander had such an eye for women's wear. Or is it only for what you wear?"

Skyler's slight squint told Sabine to stifle any conclusions. She stomped to the closet where she snatched the red dress, tore it off the hanger, and packed it into another suitcase. She then opened the top drawer to seize the silky black nightgown, laying it on top of the other item.

Sabine smiled. "Thatta girl. Use the ammunition you've got."

As Skyler grinned back, she grabbed a pillow off the bed and bulleted it at the smartass Firebrand.

After she straightened the duvet on her bed, Skyler tossed a few more clothes, shoes, and toiletries into the second suitcase, closing it. Opening the bedroom door, she eyed the Firebrands in her kitchen and great room. The place had never looked so tiny. "If we're in such a damn hurry, let's go. Somebody get my bags."

Sabine grabbed one. Ram the other.

Kole installed himself beside Skyler. The Firebrands, garbed in black with weapons drawn and grim expressions, joined them.

****

Kole barked orders. "We return the same way we came. Down the elevator. Out. The nearest jump point is in the alley around the corner. Let's not draw more attention than necessary. We already look like an invading army. Maybe the humans will think we're making a movie. Let's make time."

The warriors surrounded Skyler and Kole as he grasped her arm, hustling her along. Nobody would get close to her again. His priority was to protect his female while somehow he persuaded her to be with him. He loved her. Everything else, including a fiancé, be damned.

I will have Skyler.

Grim and silent, they ushered her into the elevator and past the confused condo security guard.

"Dax, handle the human," shouted Kole.

From the front of her building, they hot-footed it into the alley toward the jump point. An alert, jaw-clamped-tight Kole glanced at Skyler to see her shake her head as if to clear it. "Something wrong, Frisca?"

"Just feeling foggy. Occasionally, my thoughts get a little blurry. Ever since our trip to Darque."

Though being pulled along like baggage, she stiffened her shoulders, hurrying to keep up with Kole.

She stroked the hand that gripped her arm, the touch calming him immediately. "You're worried about my safety. No matter what our problems are, I appreciate it."

"We don't have problems, Frisca." He spotted the portal access. They stepped into the fake garage where it hid. At that moment, the air around the gateway shimmered. Armed Aeternals stormed through from the other side. Five, followed by another five.

A long-haired satyr with an ugly-ass scar from his cheekbone to his upper lip yelled commands to the males and females behind him. "Firebrands! They've got our target. Kill them, but don't hurt her. Understood?"

A vampire with sharp fangs scraping his bottom lip, stringy hair flapping in his face, and torn pants charged Brak. The big Firebrand spread his legs, taking the assault head on, not budging. He plunged his blade into the vampire's gut but not before the guy took a bite out of his upper arm.

Kole backed Skyler up until she was sandwiched between him and the wall. Without looking at her over his shoulder, he said, "Shit. I guess we know for sure Cerberus found your lab records."

The satyr leader glanced around before he singled out Kole.

Blocking Skyler from view, the commander recognized the bastard. "Aestes, what are you doing here?" He used to be a gaffer, one of the many policing day-to-day crimes on Scath.

"Making money for a good cause. A shitload of it." The satyr's pale eyes flashed neon green before he shoved out a hand.

Avoiding Aestes's touch, Kole shouted to Galena.

"Stick by Skyler."

The Amazon threw herself in front of the chief, her battle axe drawn.

The satyr's pheromones were thick in the air. Kole reacted, his cock swelling, his eyes stinging. But before Aestes could put skin on him to feed and cloud his mind, Kole shot a stream of fire directly from his fingers, as deadly as a flamethrower. The attacker screamed when his shirt caught the blast. As he tried to pat out the flames, Kole launched a scorcher to his crotch, eliciting another loud wail. No male could stand his nads sizzled.

The injured Aestes again attempted to touch the commander, to affect his mind. In better shape and more agile despite his size, Kole sidestepped the weak attempt.

In another lunge, Aestes's fingers brushed his shoulder. Momentarily dazed, Kole balled his hand into a big-knuckled, steely fist, planting it on his opponent's chin, knocking him off his feet. The satyr sprang up. Having once been a competitive cage fighter for the gaffers, Aestes had a famous, deadly left hook. Kole would have to avoid it.

Having depleted his demon fire, he packed the next punch with massive volts of electricity. Aestes kissed ground. Kole glanced around. His Firebrands had the situation under control.

Sabine, ducking and dancing to stay out of the way, held her own against an Amazon and a pride demon.

Tyr, glimpsing her situation, paused long enough from his own struggle to fling a holding spell around her attacking demon. The warlock Firebrand returned to his own fight with Hedra, a powerful but erratic witch. While Tyr was distracted helping Sabine, she spelled him with an upper cut which landed him squarely on his ass. He jumped up, casting a killing bolt at Hedra's heart. She blocked it. They parried, one launching an attack, the other shielding.

Brak struggled with a second bloodsucker, the first one having taken a chunk out of his arm. In one long stride, Dax pushed his fellow Firebrand aside. "I'll take the toothy bastard. You're hurt. See to the hedon demon over there. This guy's more my speed."

Dax's lips warped into a sneer. "Now these are some real fangs. Sharp. Bright. Hungry to snack on your ass." He brushed his long, black hair over his shoulder. "I love to suck on dirty, blood-raged bangers like you, Laurus."

The vampire stared at Dax through eyes empty of emotion. "Don't look at me like I'm scum not fit to stick on the bottom of your boot. You're just like me, Firebrand. You don't know it yet. You think you can escape this? You can't. I am what you will soon become."

"I couldn't be as ugly as you if I tried. If I go to the bludfrenzy, my *frerons* will put me down so I don't embarrass myself. That's honor." Dax's snarl turned to a roar when he charged his opponent, taking him to the concrete.

Laurus tried to shadowflash. Before he could, Dax pinned his shoulders. "Can't dematerialize, huh? Let me save you the trouble." Dax opened his mouth, his fangs punching from his gums. At the last moment, the Firebrand warrior shook his head, encircled his shamed attacker's neck with his hands, squeezed, and snapped off his head.

Aestus was on his knees at Kole's boots, burned beyond recognition, his body twitching from the electricity which had been pumped into him. Kole withdrew his Boker to jam it into Aestus's heart. With his free hand, he pulled the organ from the satyr's chest, squeezing it until it exploded between his fingers. He let the body slip to the ground, returning to guard Skyler, dismissing Galena.

Hedra was tiring, her arms barely rising to cast another spell. Tyr rested his palm on her head while her wild eyes stared up at him, helpless to block his assault.

Finished with the witch, Tyr removed the holding spell on Sabine's demon. "As much as I love a good fight, I'm tired of this shit." He hauled back his arm to cast a deadly spell, dropping the asshole to his knees. His opponent's face turned red, his eyes bulged, and he clutched his neck, gasping for breath. With his windpipe crushed, he collapsed at Tyr's feet.

Sabine dodged another blow. Her Amazon adversary repeatedly hefted a heavy axe while the nymph bobbed and weaved out of its reach. When the moment was right, she crouched under a swing, brushed aside her opponent's shield, and drove her Arkansas toothpick into the female's heart.

Pumped from her victory, she bounced around, shaking her hands at her side as if to release energy. "Wow? What a workout. That's what I'm talking about."

Kole searched for a victim. But all opponents were dead or in a fight for their lives.

Ram was toying with a female vampire, motioning her forward with the crook of his finger. "Come on, doll. Try me out. I've got this long thing to stick in you." Ram pulled a tactical sword from his back sheath to go with the Scottish dirk already in his hand.

His attacker bared her pointed fangs, saliva dripping down her chin and a growl erupting from her throat.

"You know you've got this very unattractive drool going on, don't you, doll? Clean up your act." When she lunged, Ram stepped aside. Doing a three-sixty, he faced her.

Her hands curled into claws when she charged again. This time she latched onto the satyr, snaking her hands around his neck, trying to snap it. But Ram came in low with his dirk, ripping it from the vamp's stomach to her heart. When she fell to the ground, he used the blade to slice out the organ which meant her true death, her passport to Angor.

Brak stomped a boot on the hedon demon's chest. Applying leverage, he withdrew his sword from the male's chest, wiping it on his dead attacker's jacket. "I'm fucking tired of being injured." Though the wound was already healing, the giant Firebrand gripped his arm where the vamp had snacked on him. "I need a break."

As the battle slowed, Kole spun around to fix on Skyler. He grabbed her waist with one hand and, wrapping an arm around her shoulders, pulled her in close. He willed heat to pass from his body to hers, warming her, empowering her with his strength. "Are you okay?"

Her words were muffled as she spoke into his neck. "Fine, but I must learn to pay attention to my visions. My mind wasn't fuzzy a moment ago. I saw these Aeternals arming themselves at a portal. I thought it was a foggy … something."

"Your power's too new. You'll learn to recognize when your gift kicks in. You'll learn what's real and what's imagined. It's all right." Kole rested his chin against the top of her head, thankful she was safe.

"You might have been killed."

"Look at me." He pulled away, lifted her chin with his thumb. He thumped his chest with a fist, his golden eyes smoldering with fire. "I'm not dead. I'm okay. So are you. We all are."

"Hand me one of your knives."

Kole angled his head. "Do you know how to use a blade?"

"No, but I'm sure in the hell going to learn. Now hand it over."

He shrugged as he passed off a knife. She white-knuckled the hilt, tip pointed forward.

Kole forced his attention from Skyler. A significant amount of dead meat surrounded the Firebrands. Gaping onlookers gathered in the street and on the sidewalk. He bit his lip, growling. "Shit."

"Abso-positively-fucking-lutely," said Tyr.

The Firebrands moved in to form a tight circle around Skyler. Kole tapped his D-chip. First, he called the gaffers. Next, Alarik. "We've got a real cluster fuck here. As we were hot-footing it away from Skyler Maxwell's condo, a bunch of Aeternals came across at our jump point. Their bodies are currently scattered on the street. And we've got gawkers. A lot of them. I have Dax, but he can only scrub one human at a time. You better get a crew down here now. The gaffers will clear the bodies, but your people need to handle the minds."

Tyr moved away from the protective circle. "I'll hold our audience in place."

"You hear that? Hurry." Kole disconnected to comfort Skyler. Not that she needed comforting. He did.

****

Skyler threw open the door to her suite of rooms at the Covenkirk Stronghold. She leaned against the jamb, one ankle casually crossed over the other, her relaxed demeanor false. "Commander."

She had been re-arranging furniture in her new living room when she had a vision. In it, Kole thundered down the hallway toward her on two long, thickly muscled legs.

She opened the door before he knocked. He

halted, fist midair. One corner of Kole's mouth curled into the sexy grin designed to ensnare female hearts. It wasn't going to work on Skyler. She steeled herself against his charm.

"Frisca."

She blocked his way into her apartment. "I'm mad at you."

"Not for long." Kole picked her up, her feet dangling as he carried her into the kitchen to set her on the counter. "Besides, shouldn't I be the one who's pissed?"

She cocked her head. *Is he kidding?* "Why?"

Kole's eyes locked onto hers. "Because you let me fuck you silly even though you have a fiancé. One you won't be marrying, by the way. And despite having taken my cock many times, you recited a list of reasons why we shouldn't be together."

"Hmm. About that, Kole. I don't have a fiancé. I broke it off with him days before I left to tour Scath." She closed her eyes, wincing, waiting for an explosion.

"What?" Kole stepped back, his fingers sparking. "You let me believe…"

Her lids popped open. "Guilty. Self-preservation. I needed a barrier between you and me." She couldn't meet Kole's earnest gaze. "And as far as the billion reasons we shouldn't be together, I fell asleep before I got to the big reason why we should."

Kole pushed into the V of her thighs, her skirt crawling up her legs. "Why should we be together?"

"I love you. Despite all the reasons I shouldn't." She paused, chin up, her gaze unwavering, worried he didn't return her feelings. "Crazy, huh?"

Kole's expression was unreadable.

Obviously, he wasn't going to make this easier on her. "I woke up, expecting to find you beside me.

Instead, I found four notes which showed pretty clearly what you thought."

"Unfinished notes. I tossed them because I couldn't put what I felt into words. You weren't meant to see them."

"You tucked tail and ran."

Skyler waited, but Kole didn't utter the words she wanted to hear. She shoved against his chest to get off the counter.

"Where do you think you're going?" His arms latched around her waist, holding her in place.

Her struggle was useless. "I opened my heart to you. You haven't said anything. I shouldn't even be here. Let me go."

His lips curved into an irritating smile. "You are mine, Skyler Maxwell. I'll never let you go."

She stopped wiggling. "And?" Her voice trailed up at the end.

"And what?" Kole tilted her chin up with two fingers, speaking in a husky whisper. "Oh. I love you, too."

"You do?"

"Yes. I do."

Skyler melted into his arms, her cheek nestled against his warm chest.

Kole broke the silence. "You know you're a distraction. Right?"

"I've never been a distraction." She deserted his chest to lock onto his fire-gold eyes.

"You've been one for me from the first moment I saw you, Frisca."

"Really?" Skyler wrapped her arms around Kole's thick neck. "I have a confession."

"Spill."

"The first time you stormed into my office and

arrogantly threw yourself into that chair to wait, I kept sneaking peeks at you."

"I know." Kole grinned, giving Skyler his sexy, all-knowing, one-sided smile. "What do you think I was doing while you ogled me? In my mind, you were already under me while I was enjoying your wet, sweet…"

Skyler swiped a hand across her damp brow. The room was hot. "Oh, God. I could use a cold drink."

Chapter Thirty-Two

Kole opened the fridge. "Beer?"

"Please."

He grabbed two cold Buds, twisted the caps off, and handed one to Skyler. They clinked bottles.

He leaned against the counter beside her, stalling as he searched for words.

"You have something to say? Don't keep me in suspense." Skyler shifted her skirt back into place.

Taking a deep breath, Kole spit out, "I want you as my mate, Frisca. I want the Settling. It's a demon ceremony."

Skyler cocked her head. "Is there a proposal hidden somewhere in your words?"

"Yes."

"Shouldn't you get down on one knee and ask me?"

"If I'm on my knees at your feet, Frisca, it will be for another reason." Kole hesitated before he sighed, bending a leg.

Skyler halted him with a hand on his elbow. "I don't need that. Just ask."

"Ask?" He quirked a brow.

"Yes. I did not hear a question."

She rested a palm behind her on the counter, took a swig from her bottle, and looked at him with a frosty, no-telltale expression.

"You're tough. Okay. Skyler Maxwell, will you do me the honor of becoming my mate?"

Her shoulders tightened. Then, she uttered words every male hates to hear from his female. "We need to talk first."

And like an idiot, he fell into the trap every male does when he said, "About what?"

"I lived under my father's thumb for years. He convinced me I was unlikable, unworthy, and a mediocre success. Even though I became the CLO of the Alliance after him, I doubted myself. I kept people at arm's length because I thought if they knew me, truly knew me, they would see how incapable I was. I don't believe that anymore. Thanks in part to you."

Kole grinned, proud he had helped Skyler see how wonderful she was.

"I know I made mistakes."

He nodded, still grinning.

"I'll make more. I've accepted we're all a combination of flaws and perfections. But I won't be under a man's thumb again."

"Lucky for you I'm not a man."

"I'm not giving up my job to be a demon's housewife."

Kole shoved away from the counter, tenting his fingers to prevent sparks from flying. "Great Gahya, Skyler. Is that how you see me?"

"You told me your breed was a male dominant society. I assumed…"

"That's not me. I have female warriors who are as qualified as my male Firebrands. Are their skills different? Hell, yes. Doesn't make one better than the other. I don't expect you to give up your job. I'm proud of you. Of what you do."

"You are?"

"I am." He slid between her legs.

"I have a few other faults. I don't cook or clean house. I work long, long hours."

"Again, lucky you. I have a housekeeper who

cooks. And I also work long hours. I only need you. I've been alone too long. Many of my own breed have ostracized me. I've lost *frerons*. I lost my parents. I can't lose you. It makes me crazy how you've got Cerberus's bullseye on your back."

Skyler stroked his arm. "You won't lose me, Kole. Whatever you tell me to do to stay safe, I'll do."

Kole leaned in closer as Skyler curled her fingers around his shoulders. "After the Firebrands eliminate Cerberus, I want us to live in Knife's Edge. You can commute to work from there."

Skyler pictured the red, hot desert of Kole's region, its sagebrush, constant wind, and sparse vegetation. "Okay." She bit her lip as if hesitant. "It sounds as if we're negotiating the terms of our mating. I need to be up front, Kole. I don't think I want children."

"You'd make a great mother, Frisca."

"No, I wouldn't. Look at my role model. He taught me nothing about love or kindness. Is this a deal breaker?"

Kole understood his life expectancy was much longer than Skyler's. After she passed, he would be alone again. No family. But when he saw the reflection of his love in her eyes, he had his answer. If she was his only family, so be it. For however long. After all, he hadn't expected her. She was more than enough. "It's not a deal breaker." He bounced back with a grin. "I want sex. Often."

"So, this is a negotiation?"

"Yes." Sweeping his hand across the counter, sending a bowl onto the floor, Kole gentled Skyler onto her back.

She laughed, rising onto her elbows. "I insist on frequent sex." She frowned. "But…"

"But what?"

"You said demons need an orgasm every day. Maybe more often. How have you been handling things since we got back?"

Kole waved a hand. "With this. It gets me off but no ejaculation. We fully sate ourselves only when we shoot seed. And, as you know, we emit semen only with another being's help. You'll be the only help I seek, Skyler."

"Oh."

He angled over her, trailing kisses along her neck. "Did I hear jealousy in your question? Surely, you don't see my hand as competition." His lips roamed lower while his fingers slipped under her shirt. When he found skin, he traveled until he molded his palms to her breasts.

Skyler shivered. "I'm not jealous. But … I might want to watch sometime."

Kole froze. His head jerked up. "You want to see me masturbate, Frisca?"

She eyed his crotch. "Yes. I touched you when you had iron poisoning, but I want to learn what pleases you."

Kole scooped her into his arms, storming toward the bedroom. "Here's the deal. I'll jack off for you if you take those sweet, long fingers and stroke your pussy."

Skyler's eyes widened.

He set her onto the bed, drew his shirt over his head, and kicked off his boots. "But first, I didn't hear the answer to my question."

"The proposal has been negotiated and signed. It's a lifetime deal, Kole."

"It is. Now if you aren't naked by the time my clothes hit the floor, Frisca, I'll rip everything off you."

She tore at the buttons on her blouse and wiggled her skirt down her hips, tossing both onto the floor. Skyler licked her lips when Kole unzipped his pants and stepped out of them.

"Don't forget the panties and bra." He stood in front of her, his heavy cock jutting out.

Her throat bobbled as she swallowed, unhooked her bra, and slipped off her panties while Kole stared as if he'd never seen a naked female. He thought he might come like a randy youth when she leaned onto both elbows, raised her knees, and spread her thighs. "You first, demon. I expect a show for my money."

He wrapped a hand around his aching, swollen dick. But he didn't move. He tilted his head to the side, his voice raspy. "I'm waiting. Touch yourself."

Skyler's fingers trembled as they trailed down her stomach toward her sex. When they dipped between her folds, she moaned, her lilac eyes fixed on him.

A challenge.

"Spread your legs wider, Frisca. I want to see everything. Now, stroke yourself."

Kole's lids half-masted. He slid his hand from crown to base, at first slowly and then quicker while Skyler's fingers played back and forth through her pinkened, moist flesh. "Faster." She complied with his order. "Take a breast in your other hand, Frisca."

"Like this?" Skyler taunted him, flicking a nipple. Then she alternated between pinching it and circling it.

Damn.

"Nice." Kole's hand stroked faster. His balls were like heavy weights.

Skyler's lids hooded her eyes as she watched Kole. She didn't look so frosty now. She looked as if she might catch fire.

"That's it. Don't you want your fingers deep inside, stretching yourself for me?" Kole moaned, his hand tugging on his dick.

Skyler licked her lips, a soft sigh as she invaded

herself, penetrating her sex with two fingers while she massaged a breast with her other hand. "This feels so good, Kole."

She is hotter than hell, spread out for me. Her breaths fast. Her lips parted. Her skin pink.

She fucked herself harder, faster as Kole pumped his swollen cock until it was about to break.

"Oh, yeah, Frisca." Her hips bounced in time to her hand rhythm. She arched off the bed, her head flinging onto the pillows. "Pinch your clit for me with those wet fingers."

"Kole. I can't last much longer."

"I'm thinking of my cock stroking in and out of your tight pussy." He fisted himself hard. Up. Down, stopping for a moment to massage his aching balls. "Oh yeah." Frantically, Kole's ass rocked in time to Skyler's motions. His hand felt so good as he watched her enjoy herself. He imagined her wet mouth sucking him. Her tongue. His nads tightened. He was close. His cock thickened. "Come with me, Frisca. Damn. You're beautiful."

Skyler shouted his name, an orgasm jolting her off the bed.

"Hell yes." Kole's stomach tightened as he worked himself. He snapped his hips forward when he shattered.

****

Skyler worried over the early afternoon unannounced visit, but Kole dragged her through the front door of a cabin in Knife's Edge, her small suitcase in tow.

"She doesn't mind drop-ins." He set Skyler's luggage on the floor.

A tall, muscled woman with an ear-to-ear smile strolled in from the kitchen, a slice of pizza balanced in her hand. "Kole. I thought I heard your gruff voice." She dropped the unfinished food on a nearby table. "Come, give us a hug."

"Ranca." Kole walked into her open arms, picked her up, and swung her around, her legs flying. Mind you, she was no small woman, at least six feet of solid strength.

Laughing, she pounded on his shoulder until he set her down. "You were always out of control. Nothing has changed. Who's the human?" Ranca bobbed her head in Skyler's direction.

Kole grabbed the female demon's elbow to guide her forward. "This is Skyler Maxwell. She's to be my mate."

"Your mate? Hmm. Kind of scrawny, isn't she?" Ranca sauntered around Skyler with hands on hips, assessing her. "If she wants you, she must be the dull blade in a sheath." The female demon jabbed her in the arm, sharing the joke with a loud guffaw. "Does she know you're an ill-tempered male who never calls or visits his loved ones?"

Skyler cut in before Kole could respond. "Yes. She does know. She's working on his shortcomings."

"What shortcomings, Frisca?" Kole's brows knitted together. "I have none."

Skyler smirked.

"Why are you calling her Frisca?" Ranca asked.

Kole snarled a warning.

Skyler chuckled. "I'm already aware of what it means. No need to get growly."

"You are?" Kole locked wary eyes on Skyler.

"Yes. It means *frigid*. But when you say it, it sounds as if it means *darling*."

With a hand to her stomach, Ranca bent with laughter. "I like her, Kole, maybe better than I do you.

Come, little human, give us a hug."

Skyler hesitated before accepting the warm embrace which nearly cracked her ribs.

Ranca patted Skyler's back before she stepped away. "This calls for demon ale. Sit. Sit." She pointed at the couch as she hurried to the kitchen, her loud voice trailing off. While she carried on a one-sided conversation from the other room, Kole distracted Skyler by nuzzling her neck.

Like guilty teenagers, they flew apart when Ranca returned with a tray of drinks. "Here I am going on and on about what I've been doing. Tell me about yourself, Skyler, or what you see in this lump of a male."

Skyler accepted the tall glass from Ranca while resting her other hand on Kole's knee. "He has his strengths."

Ranca roared. "Strengths, huh? I suppose the boy does. I adore him." She set her ale on a table beside her chair. "What can I do for you two? Other than tell you how happy I am for you."

Skyler regarded Kole before she spoke. "I need a surrogate mother to assist me in preparing for the Settling. I'm here to ask you to fill that role."

Obviously taken by surprise, Ranca blinked away the mist in her eyes. "You want me to prepare you for the Settling?"

Skyler nodded. "If I'm not being too impertinent."

The large woman popped up off her chair to draw them both into an unbreakable embrace. "I never had a daughter. Just this unruly boy for an adopted son. I would love to be your surrogate mother. You pay me a great honor, Skyler."

"Believe me, I'm the one honored. Kole speaks fondly of you."

Though brushed away in haste, tears escaped from Ranca's eyes. "See what you've gone and done, you rascal." She scrubbed a hand across Kole's buzz-cut hair. "You made me weep. I always knew you loved your Ranca, even when you were a trying youth. So like your young Da."

Skyler's lips curled into a smile. "He is?"

"Ah. Aedon. I grew up with Kole's father as my playmate. We got into so much trouble as young demons. Mind you, we were equally guilty as instigators. Lucky for us, we were called to the Firebrands before we ended up imprisoned in Outcast Keep on Darque. That's when we met Hestia, shortly after she became a warrior."

Ranca paused in her story, likely lost in a memory. Then she chuckled.

"Hestia. Now, there was a female. And a handful for Aedon. He never suffered from misogyny, the disease which infects many of our males. Good thing, too, because she would never have stood for it. The first time they met, she challenged him to a sparring match. When she set him on his ass, fire shot from his love-struck eyes. They mated not long after. Since cooking, cleaning, washing, anticipating her mate's wishes were never her thing, I suspect Aedon pitched in around the house. But they kept up appearances. Demons in those days, and especially Horach, their tribe's leader, were tough. Aedon claimed to set the rules. Ordered his mate to fetch and carry when others were around. She did with a sly smile. He told his family he allowed Hestia to be a Firebrand because he could watch over her."

Ranca slapped her knee. "Ha. Good one. The female had a mind of her own though. One Aedon respected. They lived the lie to be accepted. But then the Demon Insurrection came along. They refused to live the falsehood. So Horach shunned them. They never regretted their decision. Proud."

Kole grew silent, but eventually threw an arm across Skyler's shoulders. "See. A strong female is in my blood."

Ranca rubbed a thumb over her lips, lost in thought. "Yes, the Insurrection was a tipping point. Like me, Hestia and Aedon sided with the Firebrands rather than the rebels."

"Horach's still a bastard."

"He is. The male's been grumpier since he was on the losing side. Chapped his demon ass."

"After my parents' death, Ranca welcomed me in when none of my family would." Kole's eyes smoldered.

Skyler leaned her head against his hard, strong shoulder.

"Bastards. Aedon and Hestia were my best friends. Of course I took you under my roof. That's why you're such a fine male. Your relatives never had the chance to turn you into an asshole. Why do you think your female Firebrands are so loyal to you? You are your mother and father's son. You are who they raised you to be. They would be as proud of you as I am. Although … I admit, there were times…"

Kole glanced down at Skyler. "I was an angry boy, acting out often." He twisted toward Ranca. "I don't believe I ever thanked you. Thank you for not tossing my ass to the road."

She brushed aside a tear. "It was my honor to raise you. Even when you set fire to my shed. Okay. Maybe not then. Now, what's the date for this mating ceremony?"

"The Seventh Moon." Kole pulled Skyler closer.

"What! So soon? Boy, though I have missed you, be gone. Skyler and I have much to do." Ranca chugged the rest of her ale, slammed the glass down, and rose.

Pacing, she ticked off plans. "The choosing of the names. We must gather the oils. Prepare for the task she will be required to undertake. Have a gown made. Design the palanquin. Then there are the jewels, crown, and veil. We must select the flesh artist." Ranca sucked in a deep breath.

"I'm sure with your help, we'll make it." Skyler felt her muscles clench, her nerves kicking in.

Ranca halted her anxious back and forth. "She cannot mate with your demon form. It is impossible."

"We'll skip that part." Kole raised his brows, cautioning Ranca to silence.

Skyler spotted the exchanged glances. "What part? We aren't skipping anything, especially something which will keep us from being mated properly."

Ranca jumped in to explain before Kole could open his mouth. "When two demons mate, they consummate the union in human form and demon form. If my boy took you as his beast, he would tear you apart. You can only mate as humans."

"Oh." Skyler's eyelids slumped. "I'm disappointed. I want everything to be perfect, Kole. You deserve no less."

He stroked a hand through the hair she had left loose today. "You're more than I deserve, Frisca. Nothing we do will be less."

"Kole is right. This will not affect the true meaning of the Settling. Boy, be gone." Ranca's eyes focused on Skyler's suitcase. "Good. As is proper, you will live with me until you are mated. And you cannot see her until the ceremony. I will send an emissary with all the plans. Now, get out of our sight."

Kole tilted his head to the side. "Are you sure we can't skip the separation part?"

Ranca drew her lips tightly together. "No. You

can't. Besides, it's only a few days."

"I was afraid you'd say that. Give us a moment alone, Ranca." Once she left the room, Kole's rough, calloused finger gentled Skyler's chin up. "I wish we would have spent more time in bed this morning."

"I'll miss you, too." Skyler grinned. "I'm already jealous of your hand."

Kole snarled. "Your guards are outside. You and Ranca are to go nowhere without them. Brak's in charge."

He bent, pressing his mouth to Skyler's. The kiss blasted from warm to hot. He groaned while his fingers traveled under her shirt, slipped beneath her bra, and molded to her breast.

"Enough." Ranca interrupted their moment, sneaking back into the room. "We have too much to do for you to tap ass on my sofa. Leave now, boy." She pushed Kole out the door.

****

"You will not do this, Brae," yelled Rein. "I forbid it."

"You didn't just throw out the 'f' word, did you?"

Rein could have slapped his forehead the moment the fucking crazy f-bomb escaped his lips. He was in deep shit. "I do not mean 'forbid.' I mean you can't do this. If you admit to others you are Blood Coven, you'll be in more danger." His heart crashed against his chest as he thought about what could happen to his mate.

"Margo, Nico, and Skyler are in danger every day. They need to know they're not alone. Hell, I need to know I'm not alone."

"You're not alone. You have me." He bristled from the insult.

Braelyn stroked his arm. "You know what I mean. We can help each other. Nico does dangerous ride-alongs with the Firebrands. Once Skyler returns to work, she'll be exposed. Margo—well, Margo is with Chay. That's dangerous enough." She chuckled.

"Nico's a special case."

"Why? Because he's male? Think carefully before you respond. Your sex life depends on it."

Rein snorted. "Nico's an ass. I'm not protecting you because you are a female. My female, by the way."

Brae tilted her chin to the side.

"A little."

"Okay, a lot, but also because you've suffered enough. Cerberus kidnapped you. We found you before Silas realized you were Blood Coven. If he had, no telling what would have happened. Now you want to expose yourself again? No."

"We can't hide our heads in the sand."

"You know this would mean we'd have to move into the stronghold. It's the safest place to be. Even with my wards on our condo, talented witches or warlocks could break through for the right price. I will not risk your life."

Braelyn scanned the place they called home, sighing. "If we must, we must. I will be with my peeps, Rein, to support them. Besides, we should all train together as well as individually. I'll keep my personal witchipoo. But nothing says loving like a coven working together. Please say you agree."

"I won't say this is best, but I see your point. There is safety in numbers, and I will feel better with you at the stronghold while I'm on duty."

Braelyn sidled closer, nuzzling his neck.

He snarled, exposing the tips of his fangs. "But I still don't like others knowing you're a descendant."

She threw her arms around his waist, resting her head on his chest. "I know you don't, but you see I'm right, don't you?"

"Don't use your wiles on me. They won't work. Besides, we have a mating ceremony to attend."

"We have time. And don't be silly. Of course, they work. They always do."

She backed a willing Rein into the wall, stood on her toes, lifted her chin, and moved her lips toward his. No sooner had their mouths touched than he grabbed her hips, grinding his arousal against her stomach. As his erection grew hungry, so did his kiss, his tongue finding its rhythm in her wet mouth.

He spun her around against the wall, rucked up her dress, and ripped off her panties, tossing them to the floor. She unzipped his Firebrand uniform dress slacks, pushing them down until she freed him, rocking against him. With his engorged cock in his fist, Rein lifted Braelyn into place and drove into her, his pants around his knees. A real suave look. But this wasn't about smooth. This was about fucking his sexy mate.

A deep, guttural growl slid from Rein as pleasure tore through him with every thrust, his mate's ass pounding against the wall as he took her fast. He withdrew until only his tip was inside Brae. Cocking his hips forward, he slammed back in balls deep.

Damn female. Her wiles do work.

Rein worked himself in and out until Braelyn fell apart in his arms, calling out his name. Then he got down to business and didn't stop until he sank his fangs into her neck and spilled inside her, his lust assuaged for the moment.

Chapter Thirty-Three

On the night of the Seventh Moon a short distance from the demon ceremonial hall, Skyler climbed into a cobalt blue palanquin. Holding her hand, Ranca helped her into the seat which would carry her to the hall where she had watched the gruesome Genesis Rite not long ago.

She leaned against bright-colored, embroidered pillows, her icy white gown trailing to the floor. Her ride was open on three sides, allowing the slight breeze to feather across her skin. Temporary henna tattoos covered her hands, traveling up her arms. Each design, according to Ranca, carried a meaning.

A large crown of shiny platinum beads along with sparkling diamonds adorned her head. Streaming down in front of her face were thin strands of precious metal studded with silver and more jewels, a veil shimmering in the moonlight, obscuring her eyes.

The loving demon who had consented to be her surrogate touched her lips to Skyler's fingers. "You know what to expect, daughter of my heart. I will be in the assemblage of well-wishers. You are the most beautiful mate I have ever seen. Kole is lucky to have found you."

"No. I'm lucky, Ranca. He saved me when I didn't even know I was lost. I have a real family, love, and acceptance. Things I never had before." Behind the veil of beads and gems, Skyler smiled. "I'm a little nervous."

"You are well prepared. Just remember, the boy loves you."

Brak, Ram, Tyr, and Nico hoisted the poles upon which the litter rested. While they strode forward, she could do nothing but relax against the pillows, sigh, and hope all would go as planned.

Once the warriors carried her into the hall, she saw Kole arrive on a similar, though larger, litter carried by six Scion Firebrands. She recognized Rein, Chay, Sabine, and Galena. The others were strangers.

Her mate-to-be was magnificent. He lounged like a pasha, his arm thrown across the cushions, his red robe the color of fire fluttering in a soft breeze, his chest bare. When his fierce, passionate eyes locked onto hers, a burst of power washed over Skyler, its energy almost frightening.

The Firebrands set both litters onto the floor at the same time. Once the bell chimed thirteen, Skyler and Kole stepped from their palanquins.

When Kole stretched out a hand, she grasped it. They strolled through rooms and into the huge chamber. Mosaic tiles of varying shades of white decorated the walls. Like before, the demons in attendance sat on polished stone seats according to their tribes, attired in the color of their kind. Scion Firebrands were easy to spot since they wore formal black uniforms emblazoned with the Phoenix insignia.

Though the chamber was eerie, cold when they approached, Kole's warmth radiated up Skyler's arm, giving her courage. A grim Horach, here to perform the ceremony because he was leader of the Directorate of Seven, loomed ahead of them.

When they stopped before him, hands clasped, Kole's uncle called out words Skyler did not understand. He removed a chalice from a tray held by an attendant wearing a green sash. In turn, he offered it to her about-to-be mate, who drank. Parting Skyler's veil of beads,

Kole gave her a sip of the heady mead. Her head swam.

Kole, also speaking demonish, returned the goblet to Horach. "*Nor bibido.*"

Receiving a tray of food from another attendant, Horach presented it to Kole. After he picked out a piece of what looked like meat, he took a bite. He parted Skyler's veil to feed her from his hand. When she nibbled on the offering, a sexy growl arose from deep in his chest.

"*Nor mandicar.*" Kole's voice was a raspy whisper.

In English, his uncle yelled out loud enough for all to hear, "Tell us your chosen names." His lips drew into a tight slash, his expression somber.

"Ignis," shouted Kole.

"Frisca." Skyler smiled beneath her veil as Kole's mouth arched at the corners.

"Following our custom, the female must prove worthy of her demon. Skyler Maxwell's task of proof is the coals." When the attendees gasped, Horach gestured toward a section of the hall where the ground was ablaze.

Kole's eyes flicked to the hot embers awaiting Skyler. A bed of fire she was to walk across. "Hell no! She is not of our breed. I forbid her to perform this task."

Horach's eyes flamed. "She and her surrogate mother chose this test. It will be so."

Kole broke with ceremony to snarl at Skyler. "Were you and Ranca crazy or soused from too much demon rum? You will not complete this trial." He grabbed her elbow to lead her away. "You are mine and I am yours regardless of this ridiculous challenge."

Skyler yanked her arm from Kole's grip. "No. We will mate today in this ritual. Here, I will prove to you, along with the others present, my worthiness. Trust me, Kole. I hand-picked this test. You must trust I know what I'm doing."

"I will not risk your life. It's sure death."

She linked her eyes with his. "Trust."

He hesitated.

"Trust."

Kole's large body shook, rage simmering like fire on his skin. He glared at Horach. "I will accompany her across the coals. Non-negotiable." When his uncle nodded, Kole grabbed her hand. Together, they walked toward her trial.

Firebrands lined the course, their fists clasped behind their backs, their grim expressions mimicking Kole's.

He spun Skyler toward him, curling his hands on her shoulders before she could lift a foot. "You're more than worthy. You have nothing to prove to me."

"I know. I'm proving it to that bastard Horach and the rest of your family. Now hold my hand and walk with me or sit this one out."

Skyler took the first step into the fire with Kole at her side. She closed her eyes, heeding her witch trainer's instructions.

Kole merged with the inferno. His animus demon body absorbed the flames. The flames absorbed his body. He was in no danger. His fiery arms reached out as if prepared to sweep Skyler into them and carry her away.

But there was no need. The blaze stopped inches from her feet. She floated above it while it danced off her shimmering pale skin.

Skyler imagined the icebergs she had visited on Darque. Their cool purity. Their frigid beauty. Their silent vigil in the Frozen Northlands. The icy terrain was beneath her, solid. In her mind, snow fell around her, the flakes settling on her eyelashes, her arms, her gown. She glided forward, traipsing from ice floe to ice floe.

The moment she exited the bed of coals unscathed, the crowd roared, none louder than the Firebrands who whooped and hollered, their fists punching into the air to honor her.

Kole scooped her into his massive arms. "You did it. How?"

"Witch classes. Long hours with a bossy but patient teacher. Did you think I would let you down?"

"Never. You always amaze me, Frisca. You always will. Forever."

As stunned as the rest of the onlookers, Horach stumbled over the final words of the Settling. "*Iunc esta.* So ends the public ceremony. Go to your chamber. With the last act complete, you will truly be mated."

Kole clasped Skyler's palm to his heart, leading her along the hall into the mating room where a humongous bed dominated the space. Off to the side was a table with two bottles of oil. One red. One blue. Each a different shape.

When Kole removed Skyler's glittery veil of jewels, his breath hitched. He unfastened her frosty white gown, slid it off her shoulders, down her hips, and let it puddle on the floor. His hands traced the silky underclothing from her breasts to her hips. "You are beautiful. And mine."

Skyler slipped off the camisole and panties to stand naked in front of her mate. "You are mine." She spread Kole's robe apart, letting her fingers slide up his thick chest, across his broad shoulders, down his arms, his biceps flinching.

Kole pointed to the bed, his voice raspy. "On your stomach, Frisca." His thick fingers curled around the blue bottle meant for Skyler.

She rested a cheek on her arms, closing her eyes, breathing in the scents of lavender, sandalwood, vanilla, cinnamon, and jasmine. She listened to the faint sound of oil dripping into Kole's palms. His warm hands coasted across her shoulders, pressing into the base of her neck. They glided down her back. Kole massaged her ass, applying pressure, which sent a tingling sensation straight to her core. Then he moved to the backs of her thighs.

Delightful.

"Turn over." Kole molded his oil-soaked hands to her breasts, kneading, pinching, tugging. His eyes smoldered with desire.

When she couldn't take anymore, she shoved off the bed to grab the red bottle. "It's my turn to torture you."

Kole stretched out on his back in the spot vacated by Skyler. He crossed his forearms under his head, his arousal already thick, jutting out.

My demon is spectacular.

"Obviously, you don't need the oil." Skyler was breathless, Kole's massage already working on her, making her burn for his touch. Nonetheless, she treated his flesh to the same pleasure he had given her.

"Have I ever needed help getting a hard-on when you're near?" Skyler had barely started at his shoulders before Kole swung his legs over the edge of the mattress to stand. "No more. My beast is too close to the surface."

A tremor rolled through Skyler when he pulled her close, his arousal prodding her stomach.

Looking as tortured as Ranca said he would be, Kole wrapped a fist in her hair, whipping her head back. His hungry mouth crashed into hers. With his other hand cupping a heavy breast, he kissed his way down her neck, her collarbone, her upper chest. His lips pulled at her nipple where he sucked and nibbled.

Skyler couldn't prevent loud moans from

escaping her throat. She wobbled, her legs weak.

When her knees gave out, he threw her onto the bed, his engorged cock clutched in his hand. "On your knees, Frisca. I want your hot lips wrapped around me while I fuck your mouth."

Skyler smiled at a very aroused Kole. Obliging him as he stood beside the bed, she wet the tip of his swollen flesh with her tongue, licking along his length to moisten it. With a fist around the base of his rock-hard shaft, she stroked what she couldn't get into her mouth.

Kole's hips undulated as he pushed to the back of Skyler's throat, groaning. "That's good. You can handle more, Frisca." His fingers caressed her neck, urging her to take him deeper. She did.

The barbaric male was at her mercy. Though she loved the power she held over him in this moment, she ached for Kole to be buried deep inside her.

Suddenly, he withdrew, shoving Skyler away.

Her eyes flew open.

Kole stared down at his flickering body. "No. Dammit. No." His hands thickened. Claws erupted from his fingertips. His legs grew longer. His chest expanded while he seemed to burst into red, orange, and gold flames. When he squeezed his eyes tight, his body returned to normal. Temporarily.

Holy hell.

His demon was loose, filling the chamber with fire. And he was a gorgeous, spectacular creature. Skyler wanted his beast to possess her.

****

Though it was merely a layer of fire over the male who was Kole, the demon beast was barely sentient. It craved Skyler. In the throes of lust, it had few other emotions.

Domination. Complete possession.

The beast pushed Skyler back onto the bed, lifting her to her hands and knees. Its thick finger slipped inside her sex.

"More, Kole." She begged, obviously not understanding the brutal needs of the demon.

Two fingers thrust into her.

"I want you inside me," she begged.

Gripping its cock, the fiery beast slammed into its mate.

She screamed but rocked her hips backward, forcing him deeper. Suddenly, a chill swept across the room. Frozen crystals coated Skyler's skin. Her hair shimmered with frost. Light bounced off the glistening ice of his cool beauty. Sleet floated in the air, cooling the beast's fire. Snowflakes fell from the ceiling.

The creature hammered its mate, losing control, driving forward while her icy, tight sheath milked its swollen shaft, urging its fertile seed to spill.

Searing fire broke loose from the demon. It danced across Skyler's cold flesh, fingering her frozen skin, licking it with its warm tongue. The temperature of the chamber fluctuated. Freezing cold. Scorching hot.

When the blaze grew too intense, Skyler's ice cooled it. When frost threatened, the beast's fire melted it. A sensuous dance of opposites played out as their elements united, the two forces joining to pleasure each other. The room lit up with flickering shades of fiery color, followed by the hiss of steam where frozen water met the flames. The dance repeated.

Thrusting into Skyler, the beast howled, insane in its need to possess the female, its large cock filling her as she pleaded for more. It hammered in and out of its mate while she matched its fierce desires with her own.

"Yes, Kole. Yes."

It knew when she broke. Skyler threw back her

head, her body convulsing, shouting Kole's name as she orgasmed.

Its mate satisfied, its possession nearly complete, the beast roared. Its hips slammed into her cold flesh, its movements frantic until the explosive eruption. Gripping her waist, it pressed against her until it had nothing more to spill. Still, it hung on, roaring its satisfaction.

Sated, the fiery demon disappeared, leaving only Kole. Exhausted. Complete.

Skyler collapsed onto her stomach, panting, her heartbeat a loud rhythm. Once she calmed, she spoke, her words muffled against the sheets. "That was... That was..."

Kole rose above her on flexed arms. "Fucking impossible. You mated my demon, Frisca."

"But how?"

He rolled them onto their sides, holding her close as he regulated his breathing and heartbeat. "Blood Coven mages are full of surprises," he said. "My witch is particularly surprising."

Skyler's henna tats had faded, but he touched a calloused finger to the skin above her breast. "You have my rune, my name. And here," he tapped his chest, "is yours, now a part of my lineage."

Skyler studied the marks. "They're beautiful."

After a few minutes, Kole pierced the silence. "I'm afraid I'm hard again, mate. I can't get enough of you."

She eyed his erection and smiled. "I'm yours, forever."

****

Each day, guards accompanied Skyler to work at the Alliance. Kole would not budge on the issue. Settled into the stronghold, Skyler sold her desirable Chicago condo, moving a few pieces into their new suite. Not everything. Some of her stuff was boring. She learned she liked color. Not too much, of course.

As the sun streamed through a bedroom window, Skyler stretched, patting a hand on the bed beside her, finding the space empty. She rolled up, tangled platinum hair trailing down her back, the sheet clasped to her breasts.

When the door opened, Kole strode in wearing loose, low-hanging sweats and no shirt. He was barefoot, deliciously handsome, big, virile, every inch her barbarian.

He hid his hands behind his back. "We never got around to the gift part of the Settling. Something kept coming up."

"Often." Skyler laughed. "What are you hiding?"

"Nosy. A gift."

"Let me see it." Having rarely received a present, Skyler stifled an almost childish giggle.

Bringing it forward, Kole offered it to her, his eyes wary.

Skyler smoothed her fingers over a long, rectangular box packaged in colorful foil and tied with a sumptuous red bow. "So pretty. I hate to unwrap it."

"Come on. Hurry."

Skyler slid the bow off, careful to keep it intact. She removed the paper, not tearing it. When she lifted the lid off the box, she gasped. Silent tears streamed down her cheeks. She couldn't stop them.

Kole reached to take the box away. "Damn. I'm not good at this. I thought you'd like it."

Skyler swatted at his hand, sniffling. "Don't you dare. Haven't you ever heard about tears of joy?" She lifted her chin, inch by inch, her cheeks moist. "Like it. I love it, Kole. You remembered."

As her demon grinned ear to ear, she removed the

gift from the box, stroking its slippers, its pale pink tutu. She whispered, "My Pretty Ballerina Doll. She's beautiful."

"You're beautiful, Frisca."

Reluctantly, she lay the doll aside, grabbing his hand. "You gave me a future, Kole. Now, you have given me a childhood." She swallowed hard. "I have a gift for you also."

His eyes lit with fire. "Where is it?"

Skyler pressed a palm to her stomach. "You have to guess."

"Damn it, female. I hate that game."

"Okay, snarly. Here's a clue. If it's a girl, the doll will come in handy. If it's a boy, well, he can have the doll, too."

"No son of mine will… What?"

Skyler opened the bedside drawer. Rummaging through it, she slipped out a piece of paper, handing it to Kole.

He looked at it. At Skyler. At the paper again. "What's this?"

"It's a sonogram." For a moment, Skyler thought Kole swayed. But he caught himself.

"You don't want children, Frisca."

"Funny that. I already love the little fetus." She patted her flat stomach.

The tough warrior who had taken on berserkers, djinn, vampires, gagans, and other demons without blinking swiped a fist across his damp eyes. "You were enough, Frisca. You were more family than I deserve."

"Well, you're going to have to open your heart to a bigger family."

He shook his head, dazed. "Wait. When did this happen? Demons, like other Aeternal breeds, control their seed. I swear I didn't do this on purpose, Frisca."

"I know you didn't. But according to the healer, it seems a demon's beast is sometimes not in control of its sperm."

Kole sat speechless. "I'm sorry."

"I'm not. Ranca's home is a swinging door for demon children. They come in at all hours for cookies, a game, or a chat."

"Nothing has changed there. She was always that way."

"I found out I'm not so bad with them. Our pregnancy may have been an accident, or maybe the beast understands the real me. Anyway, I want us to have children."

"You do? Wait. Children? More than one?"

Her eyes sparkled. "Maybe. I want our place to be filled with laughter. I know Aeternals have few children, but Ranca told me about demon orphans who need homes. We may have more of our own after this little pea decides to join us, or we may share our love with other children. By the way, before you get it into your head I might give up my career, you need to know I'll be a working mother."

When he spoke, his words were halting. "I adore you. And if it had been only us until…" He cleared his throat.

Skyler knew Kole was thinking about how her life would be much shorter than his. But she was okay with that. He would have their child. Maybe more than one to keep him company through the years.

"…Well, I was blessed. But to think you will give me more." He took Skyler into his arms. "After my parents were killed, I gave up hope. I have waited alone for centuries trying not to dream of my own home and family. But here you are, Frisca, and I am complete."

Chapter Thirty-Four

A happy Kole, determined to make Scath a better realm for his mate and child, participated in a catch-up meet with High Commander Cadmon, the other two Firebrand commanders, and Director Alarik.

"My mate, Skyler, had double trouble. Her assistant wanted to toe-tag her with a push from the L. He sent red herring blogger threats and murdered their techie who got too close. On a set-up tour of Darque, he hoped she'd meet her death since he wanted to take her position as chief. When he failed, the psycho got up close and personal with a Glock. He's dead. She's alive. Problem one solved. Fairly sure we can lay the other fiascos at Cerberus's feet. The attack on her office. Trapping us on the wildings' realm. Sending Dermott and crew to kidnap her. The attempt outside her condo."

"So, we've added a Blood Coven descendant to our list." Nace's eyes glowed amber like his beast, the jaguar.

Kole nodded. "But loose ends, too. Braelyn's find—a Miller Nash—is a descendant who has verified the existence of *Custodes Templii*. I don't know where we go from here. Maybe dragging more intel from the reluctant Brit. Unfortunately, he slipped Rein's noose. The name Dante popped up in a recent interrogation. Maybe he's a Cerberus co-conspirator. Also, one of the attackers at Skyler's office mentioned a group. Arisen Dawn. But nobody's talking."

"I can clear up the thread." Jarek's war braids tapped against the sides of his jaws as the djinn commander spoke. "My negotiations with Simonis's

Isolationists are at an end. The group is no longer exclusively ylves whose goal is to separate our species from humankind. Instead, they rant about purity. They rant about domination. Scath nationalism. From what I can tell, they now answer to Cerberus, calling themselves Arisen Dawn. Here's a heads-up. Aeternals in this group are getting access to portal jumpers. How is this happening? We closed the cloning operation."

Cadmon leaned onto his elbows. The imposing ylve leader bristled with authority. "I called Boden at the Ministry of Compliance with that very question. He said, 'I don't know.' Direct quote."

"Fuck-all incompetent director of a fuck-all incompetent ministry. In the meantime, my stronghold's becoming Grand Central Station for descendants. Skyler, Margo, and Nico. Their protection is my primary responsibility now."

Alarik gripped the lapels of his dark, pinstriped suit jacket. "My ministry will continue to search for more humans with witch or warlock DNA. Once found, we will retest them to see if they have Blood Coven ancestors."

Nace squirmed in his seat. Since most shifters had trouble staying in one position for long, the tedium of a meeting in a closed room was taking its toll. "My warriors, along with Alliance agents, are providing security on Earth for those humans with mage ancestry but no Blood Coven DNA. Cerberus could try to snatch them up at any time just to test them."

Alarik nodded. "Though we still have access to medical records thanks to Logan, *Custodes Templii* could prove useful. If we find them or their supposed genealogy records, we might uncover the remaining descendants faster than Cerberus can."

"In the meantime," said Jarek, "we are still

cleaning up Silas's mess. We've found a few human slaves with witch and warlock DNA. Kole, your guy Dax freed two of them when my warriors needed an assist. Because we listen to all rumors, we suspect someone is in the berserker region of the Encampments. And we have feelers out to see if Cerberus has any Blood Coven descendants already in captivity."

"Don't worry about the day-to-day shit," said Nace, his claws popping out. Retracting. Popping. "We're keeping up. Occasionally, I may call on you for help if we get stretched too thin."

****

Spear approached the bed with murder in his eye. Lizette knew he had decided to kill her. She reached out for his pants, unbuttoning them.

His eyes widened in surprise.

She had never taken the initiative before. As she freed his cock, he was instantly hard. Scooting to the edge of the bed, she fisted him, gazing into his savage eyes.

I can do this to survive.

Fighting the urge to vomit, Lizette licked her lips and moved them to the tip of his shaft, where she blew softly. She flicked her tongue along the underside before she kissed the crown. Taking his dick into her mouth, she used saliva to keep him moist. Her hand fisted the base of his shaft and stroked in sync with her mouth movements. She opened wide and took him deeper and then pulled back, creating a rhythm. She remembered to moan and whimper.

Don't gag. Finish him off. You've got to get him to orgasm.

Suddenly, his hands came onto her head, and he pushed hard, ramming his length to the back of her throat. She struggled to keep the hilt of his cock fisted so she didn't choke, but he was powerful. His hips pounded into her relentlessly. She used her one hand to stroke his balls, hoping to make him come faster.

"Don't stop." He paused but grew rigid.

Lizette prepared for him to ejaculate, and he did, in what seemed like a never-ending stream of humiliation.

Survive.

When he pulled out of her mouth, Lizette sat up, smiled, and wiped her hand across her mouth. "I love the taste of you, Spear. Can we do that again sometime. Right now, though, I need to feel you inside me. Please?"

I can do this because someone is coming to get me. I just know.

Spear dropped his pants and pushed Lizette flat onto the bed, scrunching her gown up above her waist. He took his flaccid dick into his hand, working it. When it grew rigid, he drove into her.

If this is the only way I can stay alive, I'll do it. I'm a survivor.

She buried her face in his shoulder, tears streaming down her cheeks.

****

Braelyn chatted with Nico Abello while Rein leaned against the wall, fuming, not only about what she planned to do but probably about the ex-Alliance agent. He'd had it in for Nico ever since she told him about the kiss at her door.

Kole and Skyler strolled into the lounge area of the stronghold, his arm casually thrown across his mate's shoulders. They were a surprising pair. The commander was huge, muscular, square-jawed, a born fighter with a fiery temper. She was aloof, statuesque, sophisticated. Yet everything about them said they were a match.

Chay held Margo in his lap, whispering in her

ear, laughing. "Commander." He slid his redheaded mate onto the sofa and pressed his lips into a thin, serious line.

Skyler smiled at the couple as she chose an empty couch. Kole leaned a shoulder against the wall next to Rein, crossed his arms over his chest, and kept an eye on the doorway.

Nico joined them while Braelyn took a spot on the other spare sofa. She smoothed a hand over the cushion. "Wow! This is such an upgrade. Hey, Rein, remember when you stashed me here to go talk to Kole right after you kidnapped me?"

Three new, large, overstuffed couches in caramel leather formed a horseshoe around a marred oak coffee table. The new seating arrangement was on the first floor outside Kole's office, the locker room, and the gym.

Rein, his blue eyes dark and stormy, nodded.

"Oh, for heaven's sake. Commander Kole, Abello, Rein, take a load off. No one is going to invade the stronghold, and the wall doesn't need re-enforcement." Braelyn figured all testosterone-laden males favored the pose. She chuckled while looking to Skyler and Margo for support. They understood.

The males glanced at one another but pushed off. Rein and Kole strode reluctantly to sit beside their mates. Nico lodged on a sofa arm near Chay.

"There. Not so bad, is it?" Braelyn patted a scowling Rein on the knee. "Who bought the fancy couches?"

Margo tossed a tangle of red hair over her shoulder. "The commander gave me the assignment. Apparently, if you're a sculptor, you are also an interior designer."

Chay looked a little worried, as if he expected Kole to smite Margo with fire.

Instead, the commander shot the redheaded

spitfire a lopsided smirky grin while he propped his boots onto the table. "It worked out great. Just don't start bringing in artsy breakable shit."

Braelyn uncrossed her legs, moving closer to the edge of the couch. She took a deep breath before she glanced around the room. "Let's get to it then. Thanks for coming, everyone. First bit of news, Rein and I will be moving into the stronghold."

Chay threw an arm around Margo's shoulders. "Why? Rein's digs are great."

Braelyn felt her mate's thigh tense under her hand. "That's the next bit of news. I have a confession. I'm a Blood Coven descendant."

Margo gasped while the others exchanged glances. Rein, who had been holding his breath, finally exhaled.

"It's been a secret, but I guess you could say I'm patient zero. Because of me, the Firebrands learned Cerberus was hunting for us. Rein thinks I should stay hidden, but I want you to know the truth."

Kole glanced at Skyler. "The vamp mix is right. I wouldn't let my mate put a big target on her back like you're doing. We had no choice but to come out."

His composed mate arched a regal brow. "You wouldn't have let me? When did you become my master?" She returned her attention to Braelyn. The woman was truly brave for smartassing the demon. "Thank you. I like knowing who we are and how many of us are here."

"You're welcome. I believe sharing my knowledge with you is the right thing to do. Please understand, there are perks to being tagged a Blood Coven mage. I asked Alarik to keep his lips sealed so I could share the news with you. Here's the best. Because of Scath's effect on our DNA, we're likely to live a long time." She ran her hand along Rein's thigh. "So, Commander and Chay, you and your mates will be together for … well, a lot longer. Nico, you'll never need a rocking chair on the porch of an old folks' home."

Kole's eyes slid shut, his chest heaving with deep breaths, his arm tightening around Skyler. She placed a palm to her mate's heart.

Chay swept a tear from his cheek as he hugged Margo closer.

"Also, fellow witches and warlock, your powers will only get stronger. I train at the School of Forging Magic. My personal witchipoo claims my mind creates energy. With it, I guide throwing knives, stars, spikes to their target. Dead-on aim. With practice, I may be able to use my energy to fashion weapons. Supposedly, this advanced skill will take more time, but I'll get there. I can also arrow my thoughts into people's minds. Can't read them. So, whatever's rattling around in your head is safe from me. I don't pretend to understand how to control my gifts, but my trainer thinks I'm capable of a lot more. A scary lot more."

Margo stroked a finger across her lower lip. "I've been going to the School of Manipulation to master radio waves. When I can't control my power, everything around me goes kablooey. I'm getting better. Baby steps."

"Alarik says I'm a scryer." Skyler lifted a confident chin. "He set me up at the School of Investigative Magic. I've attended several sessions. The trainer is amazed I don't need a focus object for my visions. Apparently, my body produces its own. Ice crystals. I also travel to my vision in a spirit-like form."

"Interesting," said Rein. "You're describing Etheric Travel. A big scrying upgrade."

Skyler smiled at Kole. "I learned enough tricks to

survive the demon mating ceremony."

Attention slid to Nico.

He tapped a still dark brown eye. "I haven't got my warlock on yet?"

Braelyn nodded. "You will. We probably each respond to Scath at a different rate. I assume you ladies are getting a workout with a physical trainer, too." She glanced at Nico. "You're already in peak condition."

When Rein growled, Braelyn gave his leg a reassuring pat. "Aren't we beyond that?"

Nico popped off the arm of the couch, his fists clenched at his sides. "I'm not getting any stronger or seeing any weird powers. Are we sure I'm one of you?"

"Blood is blood," said Kole. "You'll get there, son. Maybe you should find a female to take your mind off the problem. I know Skyler scatters my brains all over the place when we…"

The icy blonde scowled, punching her mate's shoulder. "Hush. I can't believe you said that."

"What? You do."

Braelyn rose from the sofa, moving to the center of the area. "Fellow covenists, none of us will be helpless."

She held out a hand for Margo. Palm to palm, they called Skyler. When she joined them, Braelyn knew they would be life-long friends.

The floor beneath her feet trembled. "What the hell! Do you feel what I do?"

Margo and Skyler nodded.

Once the ground settled, Braelyn waved Nico over to the group. "Get your warlock ass over here, Firebrand Abello. You're one of us. Whether you want to be or not."

As he joined the circle, towering over the females, the floor undulated in a steady rhythm. The air shimmered. The walls shook. Kole, Rein, and Chay exchanged cautious, surprised glances.

The Blood Coven descendants, only momentarily taken aback, smiled. They locked arms elbow to elbow, each one breathing deeply to absorb their own energy. A surge of power rode through them, flowing outward as they stood strong in unity, strong in will, made one by an as-yet unknown purpose.

Braelyn was unaware of what they would face, but she knew they would face it together.

****

Kole stood beside Skyler in the early morning dawn on the Blud Dunes of Knife's Edge. In the distance, a coyote loped across the sand, other animals skittering away from the predator. A red-tailed hawk rode an air current above their heads.

He bent forward to finger a small monument. On a rock, he had carved two names. Hestia and Aedon. Mom and Dad. "I made it for them when I was a boy. For some reason I never replaced it with something more elaborate, more deserving."

"They would prefer this memorial. Don't ever change it."

Kole's voice caught in his throat. "Mother. Father. This is Skyler, Blood Coven descendant and chief legal officer of the Alliance. She is the female who holds my heart. You would love her. She is my strength. My fire." He stroked his rough palm up and down her arm. "And she will stand beside me for a long time."

With a smile, Skyler rested a hand on her stomach. "I hope I may call you Mother and Father. Please know your son is the love of my life. I came to meet you, to share happy news." She laced her fingers with Kole's. "You can expect a grandchild soon. More in the years to come."

"If it's a female, she'll have Skyler's lilac eyes, platinum hair, and will to succeed."

"If it's a boy, he'll have your son's wicked spirit, gruff voice, and strength."

Kole bent his head to touch his lips to hers. Gently, he pulled her against his body to deepen the kiss.

When they broke apart, a dust devil kicked up at their feet, swirling the sand while it danced merrily along.

"I think they like the news, Frisca."

****

Dante stepped out of the helicopter once the rotor blades came to a standstill, Mars behind him. They stood on firm ground, a large island in a swamp outside New Orleans.

In front of them was the foundation and nearly completed framework for the fortress where he would house his Humans First army.

"Let me see," said Dante.

Mars unrolled the architectural plans, each man holding a side. "The barracks will go there." Mars pointed. "The offices, indoor training facilities, a mess hall, the labs. The outdoor training area will be behind the fortress."

"It will be completed as scheduled?"

"Yes, sir. The construction workers are paid well for overtime. They're working 24/7."

"And the soldiers to fill it?"

"I've been identifying and gathering them."

After re-scanning the plans he had already memorized, Dante released his side of the blueprints. "I'll want you to meet with my scientists soon. They have some pleasant surprises in store for our army."

Dante turned on his English dress shoe heels and returned to the helicopter, Mars trailing him up the airstairs. The engines engaged, and they lifted from the ground.

Soon, daughter. Soon.

The End

THE DEMON'S FIRE

EVERNIGHT PUBLISHING ®

www.evernightpublishing.com